Blain would find out everything about her.

But right now he wanted to get Rikki out of here. They were too exposed at this location.

She finally nodded. "I need to get my things."

After he escorted her to her room, he put her in his car and turned to stare at her. "Where to, princess?"

She stared at her hands in her lap. "The Bay Road."

Bay Road? Blain whistled. Real estate out there was way over his pay scale. "Okay, then." When they were out past the city, he turned off and followed the dark water. "What's the address?"

She finally looked over at him, a defiance in her voice. "2200 First Bay Lane."

Blain blinked, thinking he hadn't heard right. "Hey, that's—"

"The Alvanetti estate," she finished for him. "Sonia Alvanetti is my mother."

"And…Franco Alvanetti is your father."

"Yes." She nodded and looked out the window.

And suddenly Blain understood so much more about what was going on with Rikki Allen. No wonder she'd been so closemouthed and evasive.

No wonder he couldn't trust her.

With over seventy books published and millions in print, **Lenora Worth** writes award-winning romance and romantic suspense. Three of her books finaled in the ACFW Carol Awards, and her Love Inspired Suspense novel *Body of Evidence* became a *New York Times* bestseller. Her novella in *Mistletoe Kisses* made her a *USA TODAY* bestselling author. Lenora goes on adventures with her retired husband, Don, and enjoys reading, baking and shopping…especially shoe shopping.

Laura Scott is a nurse by day and an author by night. She has always loved romance and read faith-based books by Grace Livingston Hill in her teenage years. She's thrilled to have published over twenty-five books for Love Inspired Suspense. She has two adult children and lives in Milwaukee, Wisconsin, with her husband of over thirty years. Please visit Laura at laurascottbooks.com, as she loves to hear from her readers.

Her Holiday Protector

New York Times Bestselling Author

Lenora Worth

&

Holiday on the Run

USA TODAY Bestselling Author

Laura Scott

LOVE INSPIRED
INSPIRATIONAL ROMANCE

LOVE INSPIRED®

INSPIRATIONAL ROMANCE

Recycling programs
for this product may
not exist in your area.

ISBN-13: 978-1-335-42494-5

Her Holiday Protector and Holiday on the Run

Copyright © 2021 by Harlequin Books S.A.

Her Holiday Protector
First published in 2015. This edition published in 2021.
Copyright © 2015 by Lenora H. Nazworth

Holiday on the Run
First published in 2015. This edition published in 2021.
Copyright © 2015 by Laura Iding

This edition published by arrangement with Harlequin Books S.A.

For questions and comments about the quality of this book, please contact us
at CustomerService@Harlequin.com.

Love Inspired
22 Adelaide St. West, 40th Floor
Toronto, Ontario M5H 4E3, Canada
www.Harlequin.com

Printed in U.S.A.

CONTENTS

HER HOLIDAY PROTECTOR

Lenora Worth

To Winnie Griggs, Beth Cornelison and Renee Ryan

With gratitude for a wonderful retreat during a storm

But let justice roll on like a river,
righteousness like a never-failing stream!
—*Amos 5:24*

ONE

The sickle moon dipped down in the dark sky, reaching toward the gray surface of Millbrook Lake like a slinky hand trying to touch the water. The nip of winter covered the dusk in a crisp, fresh-smelling blanket of evening dew.

Blain Kent inhaled a deep, cleansing breath and hit his stride on the path around the big oval lake, the cadence of his nightly run echoing behind him. All around him, the quaint turn-of-the-century houses shone with pretty white lights and fresh evergreen wreaths tied up with bright red bows.

Christmas had come to Northwest Florida. But tonight, Blain had to work off that big Thanksgiving meal he'd enjoyed at his parents' house two days ago. He also needed to work off his retired law enforcement father's always critical comments. Blain might have followed in his father's footsteps by returning from combat to take a job with the Millbrook Police Department, but that was where the similarities ended.

Serving for over twenty-five years in the sheriff's department and finally becoming the county sheriff, Sam Kent had tried to keep the peace by pandering to the local elite and turning a blind eye on the powerful Alvanetti crime family that tried to run the entire state of Florida. *Alleged* crime family since no one could ever pin anything illegal on Franco Alvanetti.

While Blain tried to do an honest day's work and solve crimes by the book, it irritated him to no end that he couldn't find a single piece of incriminating evidence on the Alvanetti clan. So Blain and his still-influential father had a difference of opinion on which way worked best. Blain didn't pander to anyone.

Blain rounded a corner, his thoughts centered on the harsh words he and his father had slung at each other while Mom was in the kitchen dishing up pumpkin pie.

"Don't be so hard on yourself or anyone else around here," Dad had said in his deep, disapproving voice. "You have to make it work, son. Don't make waves. Just keep the peace."

"I want it to work, Dad. For everyone, not just the rich people who live around the lake and out on the canal."

Blain approached that canal now, out of habit his cop's gaze taking in his surroundings. He wouldn't let that conversation with his father ruin his good mood. Not tonight, with that moon hanging over the lake and the whole world alive with the promise of something true and honest around the bend. Christmas was coming. All would be right with the world.

And then he heard a gunshot followed a few seconds later by a woman's scream.

Blain's radar went into overdrive. He glanced up and down the narrow part of the lake that met up with the Millbrook River. On both sides of the canal, town houses and apartment buildings lined the way. Blain stopped, listening, his gaze sweeping the left side of the river, where the footpath turned into a boardwalk along the row of houses. Footbridges connected both sides, most high enough for large boats to pass underneath.

Where had the gunshot and scream come from?

Maybe a car had backfired but he knew a gunshot when he heard one and the scream had definitely been real. He heard footfalls coming toward him. Blain wasn't carrying his weapon, but he waited, anyway. He knew how to defend himself.

A small figure came running up the boardwalk. As the silhouette came nearer, he grew even more concerned.

A woman. She sprinted toward him, her long dark hair flying out behind her like a lacy shawl. She kept glancing back as if she were running away from someone.

"Ma'am, are you hurt?"

She came to a surprised stop and drew to a halt a few feet away from him, fear radiating off her body.

"I… I need help," she said on a shaky voice, her breathing shallow. "Someone was inside my house when I got home and… I think they shot my friend."

"I'm a police officer," he said to calm her. "Stay there. I'll walk toward you."

She searched behind her and then turned back, her expression full of fear and doubt. "How do I know you're telling the truth?"

Blain tugged his badge out of the inside pocket of his hoodie and held it up so she could see it in the street light's glow. "See? Millbrook Police Department."

When the woman frowned and backed away, he said, "Just relax. I won't hurt you. Have you called 911?"

"No. I just got out of there," she said again, glancing back behind her. "I need…your help. Someone was in my house. I heard them, saw them in my backyard."

"Okay, I'm here." He walked closer, his badge in one hand and the other hand out so she could see it. "What happened to you?"

"It's not me," she said, her dark eyes flashing. "It's my friend Tessa." She pointed, flinging her arm back behind her. "I… I think she's dead. I mean, I know she's dead. I found her there after I heard a gunshot outside my back door. I… I ran out and saw a man running away."

Blain's instincts kicked in. A murder in Millbrook. That was something he rarely had to deal with. "Show me. Can you take me to your place? I can check on your friend and check your house. And we'll call for backup, too."

The woman nodded, pushed at her hair, her dark eyes going black. "Yes. She's…she's at my town house. Up there."

She motioned toward the end of the long canal to a prime spot of real estate on the corner. Nice for sunsets and enjoying the channel that opened up into the lake and river.

Blain clipped his badge on the outside pocket of his hoodie. "Okay, show me where you found the woman and let me check your house."

She waited, her hands fisted against a trim dark jacket. Blain came up beside her. "I'm Detective Blain Kent."

She didn't acknowledge that introduction but she did uncurl her fingers. Blain took the seconds ticking by to notice her hands and her face. No sign of a struggle and no visible wounds or any sign of blood. But she looked shocked and dazed. "What's your name?"

"Rikki."

Okay, Rikki who obviously didn't want to give out too much information right now.

He followed her between the narrow, two-storied houses, each one similar to the next except they were painted in various colors of pastel blues and yellows, mixed in with vivid whites. This new, swank development had the same Victorian flair as the turn-of-the-century homes along the lake. And came with a high price tag to match.

"I live here," she said, hurrying now as they approached a muted yellow townhome. "She's out on the patio."

She went through an open ornate gate decorated with a bright red-and-green wreath, but she stopped and took Blain's hand when he came up behind her.

A charge of awareness rushed up his arm, like a river wake rippling against the shore. Blain held to her, thinking how tiny her hand felt against his. He didn't argue or pull away.

She might bolt if he made a wrong move.

"There," she said with a gulp. "She comes to stay with me sometimes on weekends. I heard the shot when I came in the house and found her when I saw the back door open."

Blain took in the scene. A cedar wooden table overturned, a matching chair flipped over, its striped cushions lying against the brick surface of the spacious patio. He glanced from those items to the woman lying on her stomach against the redbrick, blood pooling all around her. Blain made his way to the woman, careful not to disturb anything. He knelt and checked her neck for a pulse.

None. Dead.

He stood and pulled out his phone.

"Is she…is she dead?"

He nodded to the obvious. "Yes. I have to call it in and I need to check inside."

"I'm going with you," the woman said, averting her gaze from the dead woman. "I… I heard someone and then I heard the gun go off. He shot her."

"Did you see him shoot her?"

"No. I came home and walked through the house. Then I heard the gunshot. He ran away when I screamed."

She was in shock, no doubt about that. "I need you to wait out here, okay? You can sit on the porch."

She nodded and allowed him to guide her to the small covered area where a white wrought-iron bistro set was hidden by a thick jasmine vine.

"I'm calling for backup and then I'll check the scene. Don't move from this spot."

"Okay." She leaned her elbows on the table and hung her head in her hands. "Hurry, please."

Blain went inside, all the while on the phone with dispatch. Nothing downstairs. Just a couple of open drawers and cabinets. He silently made his way upstairs where he found two bedrooms. Pretty much the same. A closet open and ransacked and some jewelry scattered on a dresser in what looked like the master bedroom. A purse dumped in the guest room.

After clearing the place, he came back outside. "I didn't find anyone else inside," he said to the woman.

He studied the scene while he explained things to

the dispatcher. The woman had been shot in the back. Running away? Then he noticed where her right hand lay out from her body. The blood spatter there looked smeared with a pattern that looked like some sort of letter—a *K* with a line next to it. Interesting. He took a picture with his cell phone.

When he heard a soft moan, he turned to find Rikki standing by the porch railing, her gaze caught on the dead woman.

She pivoted, a hand to her mouth. He could see her shoulders moving. He heard soft sobs. While he explained his location and the situation, he also noticed something else about the woman lying there on the cold brick.

She looked a lot like the woman standing there sobbing.

Rikki sat in a chair in the den while several police officers moved all around her. The Millbrook Police Department wasn't that big. Maybe three or four full-time officers and one very good-looking detective. She knew this because her family made it their business to keep up with the locals. But she'd been gone a few years and this new detective was different from the good ole boys she remembered.

He looked too intense and moody to bow down to anyone.

She took another gulp of air and closed her eyes to the scene she'd come home and found an hour ago. The house quiet, her cat gone, and the patio door open. Lights blinking away on the Christmas tree by the fireplace. Tessa? She'd called out, thinking her friend had gone out back, maybe had taken Pebble with her since the big, fluffy cat liked to lie across the patio floor bricks, warm from the setting sun. And then she'd looked up and heard a gun firing.

But when she'd hurried outside, the last rays of the sunset had shown with a bright clarity on Tessa lying there. Still. So still. Rikki had screamed and then she'd hurried to find her phone. But when she'd heard footsteps running away and saw a man in her yard, she'd bolted away. Ran like a coward, to what? Where had she been heading?

Away. She needed to get away. If anyone knew who she really was…

"Rikki?"

She whirled on her chair, her heartbeat drumming against her temples. "Yes?"

Blain Kent knelt in front of her, one hand on the arm of the high-backed floral chair, a notebook and ink pen in his other hand. "Is there anyone you can call? Can you stay someplace else tonight?"

Rikki wanted to laugh but she couldn't muster up the strength. She did straighten in the chair, her gaze grabbing onto his face. If she weren't so numb with fear and shock, she'd flirt with him. But she didn't want to flirt. She wanted to go back and walk in the door and see Tessa standing in the kitchen, waiting for their night out on the town in Pensacola. Dinner and conversation and maybe a little flirting. Just a little.

"Rikki? Miss Allen?"

"I'll be okay here."

"It might not be safe." He rocked back on his heels, his sweatpants stretching to accommodate his solid leg muscles. "Do you know of anyone who might want to harm Tessa Jones or you?"

"No." She closed her eyes and prayed for strength. "I… I left Tallahassee to get away for a while. I just broke up with my boyfriend."

The detective's eyes lit up at that statement. "How bad was the breakup?"

"Bad enough. But he doesn't know where I am."

"Right."

"Did you get a good look at the person?"

She tried to remember. "No. Just from behind. He had on dark clothes, like sweats and a cap. Tall. He was tall. With black running shoes."

"Okay, that's something to go on."

"I left her lying there. I was so scared."

He let that go but Rikki felt sure he'd ask her more on that subject later. Could Chad have done this? Was he that vicious, that cruel?

"Tell me more about Tessa Jones," the detective said.

Rikki swallowed the heaviness in her throat. "Tessa grew up in Georgia but she lives in Tallahassee. We went to college together."

"We'll be investigating her background but if you can think of anything that might help us, tell me now."

His words had gone into what sounded like a firm command. He'd probably investigate Rikki's background, too. "Do you suspect me, Detective?"

His expression was as fluid and unreadable as a midnight ocean. "I'm just trying to put the pieces together." He studied his notes. "It looks like she tried to write something. I can't be sure, but…some of the blood pattern looks like the letter *K* with a line slashed through it."

Rikki's stomach roiled and almost revolted at that

image. "I don't know. She calls me KK sometimes. Her nickname for me."

She lowered her head, hoping to stop the nausea.

"You need anything?"

She glanced up at his face, the five o'clock shadow making him look mysterious. "I'm fine."

"So why was Tessa here alone?"

"We were meeting here for the weekend to catch up. I travel a lot so I don't get up here very often." She glanced around, wondering how she'd ever feel safe here again. "I have clients in the area. Orders coming in for art and furnishings. I was on my way home. She knew where to find the key."

He studied her with an intense inky gaze that left her rattled. "So you're here for work and to get away from Tallahassee and your ex-boyfriend."

"Yes."

"What's his name?"

"Chad Presley."

She looked out toward where the medical examiner was about to take away Tessa's cold body. Should she tell him the truth? Should she admit the things that would cause him to suspect her of all kinds of crimes? Or should she sit here like a lump and pretend her life wasn't falling apart?

"Miss Allen? You said you came here to get away from him?"

Rikki lifted her head, her gaze slamming into his. Did he already have her figured out? "Yes, and to take care of some clients in the area and mostly, for a visit with my mother."

No, she'd covered all of her bases on that a long time ago. No one could figure her out. She should be safe.

But here she was, back in the one town she'd sworn she'd never return to again. For oh, so many reasons.

"Why did you need to get away from your ex?"

She didn't want to talk about Chad. "We've been apart for a while but he's having a hard time letting go. I just wanted some time away, to think about things."

"So you came here. Not that far away."

She bobbed her head. "My mother is sick," she said, sincerity her only hope. "I came to visit her during the holidays. I don't get back here too often."

"And who's your mother? Maybe you could go and stay with her?"

Rikki knew she'd said the wrong thing by the way he analyzed her with that deep blue-eyed stare.

She tried to fix it. "Can I just stay here? I'll lock up."

She didn't really want to stay here but she couldn't let him see how scared she felt right now. He already suspected her and…she couldn't explain anything else to him. The detective would jump to the wrong conclusions.

He gave up and stood. Rikki stood up, too, relieved that he wasn't so close to her anymore and that he seemed willing to let it go. For now.

But he didn't let it go.

"I don't think you should be alone right now, and you can't stay here, anyway. This is a crime scene."

"And I can't stay here because you think I'm in shock or because I'm a suspect or because you think whoever did this will be back?"

"All of the above," he said, not even blinking.

"I see." She moved away from him, her arms in a protective stance across her midsection. If she told him the truth, he would take her in for questioning. That's how things worked in her family. "I... I don't want to upset my mother."

"Then go to a hotel but as I said, this is a crime scene, so you can't get back in here until we've cleared it."

Rikki whirled to stare over at him and tried again. "I can't stay in my own home?"

"Not tonight."

His tone told her not to argue. "Okay, I'll find somewhere else." And she'd have to leave again. Soon. She'd go by to see her mother and then...she'd just go.

"Do you think your boyfriend followed you?"

"No."

She'd found someone in her house and they'd gotten away after killing Tessa. Instincts told her this wasn't Chad's doings, no matter how much he'd threatened her.

"Do you know anyone here besides your mother?"

She did, but no one she could trust. "No. I've been away for a while and as I said, I don't get back much."

He jotted notes. "I could drive you somewhere."

Rikki looked up at him to make sure he wasn't trying to trip her up. Were detectives always this accommodating? "I have my car."

She turned away, her mind on the horrible scene outside the window. And where was Pebble? Where was her cat that traveled with her?

She refused to think about that or the tough-guy detective giving her the third degree. He probably already had her license plate number. Probably had already run it through the system.

He wouldn't find anything incriminating on Rikki Allen. But he could find a whole lot of information on Regina Alvanetti. Then he'd know she was the daughter of the infamous Franco Alvanetti.

"What do you want to do?" he asked, his tone telling her she didn't have much choice in making that decision.

"I want to cooperate with you," she said, resolve settling over her like the night chill. "But honestly, I'm not sure what to do next."

TWO

"I suggest you let me drive you somewhere safe."

Rikki turned to stare at up Blain with dark-chocolate eyes. "And where in this town would that be right now, Detective?"

Surprised, he said, "Well, Millbrook is pretty tame, all things considered. Preferably, with someone you trust. But I guess anywhere you want to go as long as you let me get you there and make sure it looks safe."

"I don't see why that's necessary."

Something was so not right here. Blain hadn't dealt with a murder case since returning to Millbrook after his stint as a marine MP. He'd worked hard serving his country and after doing recon work to track down some of the meanest humans on earth, he'd learned a thing or two about people. They tended to be evasive when they were trying hard to appear normal. Evasive and not so good at faking it.

This beautiful, frightened woman was definitely hiding something but he had to give her credit for staying fairly calm during this whole thing. Had she had a lot of practice?

He watched her pace, saw her glance out to where

her friend had died. She was as nervous as her missing cat probably was right now, but she held it in check with a gritty silence. Natural, since she'd come home to find an intruder and her friend murdered. But why wasn't she opening up to him? Especially about the ex-boyfriend. A case of domestic abuse?

And why didn't this scene make any sense? A robbery? A random act? A revenge killing? What? And what was the victim trying to tell him? He had pictures of the whole scene and he'd study them later. Especially that possible letter *K* written in blood.

He tried a new tactic. "You know, you and the deceased look a lot alike."

She whirled at that, long ribbons of dark hair curling around her face and shoulders. "People told us that all through college. Said we looked like sisters. Tessa is…was…a year younger than me. I never imagined she wouldn't make it past twenty-eight."

So that made Rikki Allen twenty-nine, obviously.

Just a few years younger than him. Blain cleared his head and got back on track. "Look, I'm the only detective in town and since I was first on the scene, this is my case to solve. The more you tell me, the quicker I can make that happen. We need to find the person who did this."

She grabbed at her hair and let it spill back around her face. "I don't know what to tell you. I've been back in Millbrook a couple of days. Tessa drove down today to spend the weekend with me. I was out running errands and checking on some of the homes I'm scheduled to furnish. When I got home, I called out her name and that's when…when he shot her and then he ran."

"What kind of errands? What kind of work?"

She gave him a look that should have been intimidating. It only made Blain more aware of her, in too many ways he shouldn't be aware. "I'm an interior designer. I work all over the Gulf Coast and all through Florida, decorating homes and condos, but lately in Tampa and down in Miami. I have a few clients up here, too."

"So you were with one of those clients?"

"I can provide a play-by-play of my afternoon, if you need me to, yes."

She was well-trained in deflecting questions, Blain decided. "And what about your sick mother?"

"I visited her before I went on my errands."

He wondered about the sick mother part, but Blain would get to the bottom of things, sooner or later. "Okay. So, I've got the timeline pretty much figured out. I'll have to wait to hear from the ME to find out the exact time of death. We've checked all of the upstairs rooms and according to my report, you told my officers that nothing important or valuable had been taken. But it looks like you might have surprised the intruder during a possible robbery."

He read over his notes again.

"But it could be that you returned home before the intruder could take anything valuable, which means we'll continue to comb the entire area around your home and see if we find any signs of someone getting away. We're questioning the neighbors and alerting the media, too. If there's a killer on the loose, everyone needs to be alert."

"I don't want the media hanging around," she blurted. Then she cast her gaze back toward the patio. "I... I need to absorb what just happened. Tessa never hurt anyone, never had an enemy. Everyone loved her."

She whirled back to him. "I don't want the media to harass her family and friends."

Interesting. Or maybe she didn't want the media delving into her personal life?

He stopped and tried again. "We've collected as much evidence as we can find for now so we'll take this up again first thing tomorrow, but there's still the matter of you finding another place to stay tonight."

She glared at him, sniffed back tears she seemed to be trying hard to ignore. "I'll go to a hotel."

"Okay, then," Blain said. "Get an overnight bag together and while you're up there in your bedroom, make sure you double-check everything. Things such as valuable jewelry that might be missing or maybe some cash you left in a purse."

She nodded. "Did you check the guest room? Tessa's room?"

Blain could tell she was slipping fast. She was going to crash soon so he needed to get her out of here. "Yes. Nothing out of the ordinary. Just your friend's purse with the contents dumped on the bed and some clothes scattered around. Everything still intact."

"Tessa is neat," she said, her gaze slamming into his. "She would have put her clothes away. She'd never leave her purse that way."

"Okay." He wrote that down.

"We were going out tonight," she said on a soft whisper. "Just for fun."

Blain remembered fun. "I'm sorry you have to go through this," he said on a low note. "Do you want me to come upstairs with you?"

"No," she said. "I'll only be a few minutes."

"I'll be right here if you need anything."

He watched her up the stairs and then turned to take in the opulent design of the big town house. Did she decorate this one? Probably. A big pot with a healthy palm tree branching out around it sat by the ceiling-to-floor windows. A white leather couch and matching chair graced the spacious den. A modern-looking fireplace decorated in gold-and-white ornaments and shiny green foliage slashed across one wall and a bookshelf heavy with art and design books and a few novels filled the other wall. A vivid tropical-themed painting hung over the fireplace and a tall Christmas tree covered in silver-and-gold ornaments and ribbons stood in the corner by the fireplace.

So she'd been back in town long enough to get this place all gussied up for the holidays. Or maybe she'd hired someone to do it and they'd liked what they saw enough to try and rob the place. Maybe they'd sneaked inside the house, not knowing the other woman was here? Rikki had come home and surprised them? But why shoot the other woman?

Because she'd seen the intruder?

Now he had even more questions.

Rikki dreaded going into her bedroom. Knowing that a killer had gone through her house made her feel violated and ill at ease. She couldn't even look at the guest room where Tessa's things were scattered on the bed so she hurried up the hall to her room. She could see sparkling Christmas lights across the canal on another home's upper balcony. The lights were pretty but a chill rushed across her shoulders, making Rikki shake.

Tessa. Dead.

What a nightmare? Had she been wrong to come

back here? No, she had to see her mother before it was too late. Before she had even more regrets to add to the long list already in her head.

And yes, she'd needed some time away from Chad Presley. Because Chad could never replace the one man she'd loved and lost, and once he'd realized that, he'd turned nasty.

But she wouldn't blame Chad. It wasn't his fault that she couldn't love him. Or that she'd never get over losing Drake.

Drake. Her sweet, young husband, Drake Allen.

We were so naive. So in love.

She missed him every day of her life but missing and wishing wouldn't bring him back. Rikki went about grabbing clothes and gathering the essentials, her mind so numb with shock she could barely walk.

She'd lost Drake years ago. And now she'd lost Tessa. And both had died violently. She'd never get beyond the shadow of her family's questionable legacy.

Staring at her pale reflection in the bathroom mirror, Rikki wondered how she'd ever be able to open her heart to anyone again. It was all too much.

Being back in Millbrook was too much.

And once her family heard about this, her nightmare would continue. Unless she left again. She could do that. Just run away and start over in another place all together.

You should tell Detective Kent the truth.

Maybe she should do that, level with him and get it all over with. But she didn't really know where to start. She didn't think Chad had it in him to follow her here and kill Tessa. In spite of his veiled threats, he was too busy making more money for himself. He didn't even know she'd left Tallahassee, anyway. Did he?

And her clients? While they all demanded discretion, none of them struck her as murderers. That left her powerful family. Could someone close to her actually want her dead?

No. Impossible. She'd been careful to stay out of trouble and to stay out of the limelight. None of this made sense. And like the detective, she wanted answers. Maybe they could work together on this if she leveled with him.

But right now, tonight, she didn't have the energy for a long confession. The handsome detective would find out about her soon enough, anyway. And then, she probably *would* become a suspect.

Blain checked his watch again. And again, he walked around the downstairs rooms of the town house.

The kitchen and dining room were open to the den, all white and bright, with more green plants and vivid artwork. A set of open stairs decorated with garland crawled up the wall by the entryway. Swanky, as his mom would say.

An officer came in while Blain moved around the room once again, anything to help him figure out who'd been through here. They'd already dusted for prints and searched for hair and fabric fibers but Blain doubted they'd find either. The place looked as pristine as one of the ads in his mother's many magazines. A professional job?

His gut burned toward that end but he still needed to pin her down on the ex-boyfriend. "What do you have, Wilson?" he asked the uniformed officer.

"Found some broken branches on the shrubbery near the back gate. The gate has a latch but no lock. Figure they left in a hurry headed that way once Miss Allen ran out screaming." He pointed toward a thicket of woods that followed the far shore of the river. "Anybody could get lost in there, even this time of year. We don't have a lot of bare trees in the winter around here."

"I hear that," Blain replied. A lot of pines and live oaks grew in that thicket. "Footprints? Shoe prints?"

"Yes, sir. Big ones. But only partials. A distinctive pattern, though."

"Get pictures and measurements. Maybe a plaster form."

"Already on it," Wilson replied. "I think we've covered everything for now."

"Okay. I'm waiting on Miss Allen," Blain said. "We're putting her in a hotel room for now. I'll need a cruiser to give us a ride and a guard on her room tonight."

The young officer nodded. "Night, Detective Kent."

Blain nodded and then checked his watch. What was keeping Rikki Allen? He was about to go up and check on her when she came back down with a fancy leather overnight bag on one arm and a smaller shoulder bag on the other shoulder.

"There you are," he said in what he hoped was a casual voice. Taking her overnight bag, he said, "I thought you might have bolted on me."

She almost smiled. "I did consider it for about five minutes." The intense expression on her exotic face showed she'd considered it a lot.

"Why would you want to run away, Miss Allen?"

"Call me Rikki," she replied, not answering that question. "Now, can we get out of here?"

"Sure. I don't have my vehicle here so I'll have a patrol drop us at the hotel and I'll also assign a patrol outside your hotel."

"Did they break into Tessa's car? It should be in the public parking area around the corner."

"No. But we'll go over both your vehicles to see if we find any odd prints or maybe some fiber or hair follicles."

"What about you?" she asked, her head down. "How will you get back to your place?"

"I know my way home," he said, thinking he'd come right back here and do some more checking on his own.

Blain followed her to the front door where an officer was waiting to place crime-scene tape across the entryway and all around the small porch. Some of the neighbors were standing out on the boardwalk, their expressions full of shock and questions.

An officer walked them to a waiting patrol car.

Blain shot a glance toward the woman and remembered the sporty little convertible parked in her garage. Neither the car nor the woman would ever be his in this lifetime. Out of his league. So he needed to focus on work and not the subject at hand, his gut burning for answers.

She got in and glanced back after Blain put her stuff in the trunk and slid in beside her in the backseat. "I don't know what's going on. I don't know why someone would rob me and…kill Tessa."

"Are you sure you don't want to call your mother?" Maybe if he kept pushing, she'd keep talking.

"No. It's late and she's not well."

"I'm sorry to hear that. Who is your mother? I might know her."

"I doubt it."

Again, that nonresponse. "Okay."

Then she sat up on the seat. "What about Pebble?"

"Excuse me?"

"My cat, Pebble. He's missing."

"We'll put out some food for him and alert the neighbors."

The neighbors who were checking out their windows right about now and texting their friends and standing along the boardwalk in clusters of fear. Yeah, they'd definitely check with those neighbors.

He wouldn't push on that matter or the matter of her refusal to give him a straight answer, but he'd certainly do his own research later. So much for a slow holiday season.

He pulled out a business card when they approached the hotel she'd mentioned, one of the few low-budget hotels in town. At least this one was new and located near a busy intersection. No fancy condo-type accommodations around Millbrook. "Listen, if you need me for anything or if you remember anything, call me. No matter the time."

"I will."

Yeah, right.

He came around to help her out of the car but she already had her door open and herself out, tall boots and jean-clad legs first. He got the bag she'd packed out of the trunk. "I'll walk you to the front desk and make sure you're in a secure room."

"Okay."

Twenty minutes later, Blain was on his way to the

station to file his report, his mind humming with the sure knowledge that Rikki Allen knew things she didn't want him to know. He'd head back to her town house once he was done with his work and look for her cat.

But he intended to find out the truth.

And while he did that, he'd try to get the image of those chocolate eyes and that matching hair out of his head. Blain's gut told him there was a lot more to Rikki Allen than she wanted anyone to know.

But he knew enough.

A beautiful, mysterious woman who'd broken up with her boyfriend and who'd obviously lived a life of privilege had interrupted an intruder in her home and had found her best friend dead. A best friend who resembled her. This case shouted hit man.

His job was to find out if someone wanted Rikki Allen dead. But he also wanted to figure out what she was trying so desperately to hide from the world.

THREE

Rikki tried to sleep but being alone in a strange room didn't help her to block out the image of Tessa, beautiful, sweet Tessa, lying there with blood all around her.

Tessa, who knew all of Rikki's secrets. A good friend—her college roommate—who'd taken Rikki under her wing after Drake had died and made her feel as if she wasn't going to lose her mind, after all.

Dear Lord, what happened to her? Help me understand. Help me to accept that she's in heaven with You now.

Blain had told her they'd notify Tessa's next of kin, but Tessa didn't have anyone close here in America since her parents had both passed away over recent years. Her one brother lived somewhere in Europe and Rikki didn't have any way to contact him. Tessa hadn't talked about her older brother a lot.

No one to mourn her. *Except me.*

Rikki had two big brothers, one married and one divorced, depending on which brother and which day, and several nieces and nephews, and a whole slew of aunts and uncles. A network of people who loved her in spite of how she'd abandoned all of them.

Santo and his family lived here and he ran the business now. He'd be all over her about this. Victor was somewhere in Europe. He'd turned his back completely on the family but he didn't mind using the family funds to party all over the world.

Rikki didn't want any of the mighty Alvanetti money.

She'd stayed long enough to appease her father and to reassure her mother, and then she'd left a few weeks after Drake's death. Forever, she'd thought. But she loved her mother and they'd kept in touch over the years. Sonia had always maintained that Drake's wreck was a tragedy. That no one has caused it.

Even so, when she got reports of her mother being taken ill while on a cruise overseas this summer, Rikki had kept in constant touch. But Sonia had not improved, and had had a heart attack as well, so she knew she had to come back. The doctors had verified that the vibrant Sonia Alvanetti had several other health complications and an onset of dementia, but with bed rest and a better diet and several prescriptions, she could improve. Maybe.

In other words, her mother could snap out of this or she could die in a few years. She could be giving up because she missed her one son who had left for good and she missed her daughter who kept promising to come and see her. Rikki's brother Victor didn't care that their mother had taken ill in Europe and he didn't care now. Rikki had come home to help her mother recover.

Rikki had been thinking of coming home since she'd noticed her mother didn't remember things and constantly repeated herself. Sometimes, she'd talk about her husband, the powerful Franco Alvanetti, as if she hated him. Which surprised Rikki. Her parents had always been so in love with each other that they oftentimes managed to shut out the rest of the world. Or ignore it, at least.

The kind of in-love that Rikki had given up on.

Rikki wished now that she'd come back sooner. But then, tonight she wished a lot of things could have been different.

She missed Tessa already. If she'd come home a few minutes earlier, she might have been able to save her friend.

This, with her mother so sick and her ex-boyfriend harassing her. It was just too much. Chad Presley didn't like being dumped. He'd threatened Rikki one time too many and he had powerful friends all over the state. But then, so did her father.

And using that angle had been her saving grace.

"If you don't leave me alone, Chad, I'll have to tell my father and my brothers. You won't like it when they come after you."

The bluff had worked long enough for her to regroup and come home. But maybe Chad wasn't afraid of her family. She should have told the detective the whole story but fear had gripped her, choking her with an intense power. Fear that Chad would make good on his promises and fear that her family would get involved if he did.

A chill moved through her at the thought of Chad finding her here. Would he think to send someone to spy on her? Or had he followed through on one of his threats and found her himself?

Maybe he'd killed Tessa to prove a point. He'd stalked Rikki time and time again but things had never become physical. What if he'd thought he'd found *her* there on the patio? Chad could be the kind to shoot first and run away like a coward.

Please, no.

Rikki called the night nurse at her parents' estate, just to hear someone's voice and to check on her mom. "How's she doing tonight, Peggy?"

"Sleeping, suga'. But you know Miss Sonia. She has the sweetest attitude."

"Yes, that's Mother. Always positive. Even when she's in pain."

"I've got her all tucked in and I'll be right here on the sofa in her bedroom."

"Thank you, Peggy." Rikki swallowed the emotion roiling through her. "What about Papa?"

"He's in his office. He stays in there, most days."

Rikki closed her eyes to that image. Her dad was getting old, too. "I'll try to check on him."

"You gonna come by in the morning, honey?"

"I hope to." Rikki didn't want her mother to hear anything about what had happened, but Peggy kept the television off most of the time, anyway. She liked to read her romance novels while the surround sound played Mother's favorite classical music and show tunes. A paradox of a combination but that was Sonia Alvanetti.

But her father always watched the local news. She'd have to explain this to him so he wouldn't get involved. Of course, one of his bodyguards had probably already informed him of what had happened. His people kept their ears to the ground.

"Give her a kiss for me," Rikki said. "I'll be by bright and early tomorrow morning." And she'd try to explain things to her mother. Of course, once her brothers got wind of this...

Rikki put that scene out of her mind. Her two brothers would hunt down anyone who tried to harm her. Even when they both disapproved of her every move.

"I'll see you before you turn things over to the day nurse," she promised Peggy.

"Okay, sweetie pie." Peggy said good-night and Rikki went back to the dark silence of her room.

Thinking about the horror of seeing her best friend dead, Rikki closed her eyes but opened them wide again, the shadows of the spacious room chasing each other into dark corners. She checked the door. Locked and bolted. She looked at the heavy curtains. Closed tight. She listened for footsteps and remembered a cruiser was supposed to be parked outside her hotel room door. But each shift of the wind caused her to panic and recheck the locked door.

Then because she couldn't sleep, she thought about Detective Blain Kent. Tall, dark and dangerous. But on the good side of the law. Well, that was different at least. The man knew his job, no doubt about that. He'd done his best to get information out of Rikki and she'd given him what he needed and kept the rest to herself.

While her heart hurt for her friend and she'd mourn that loss of the rest of her life, Rikki took comfort in knowing if anyone could figure this out Blain Kent would be the man. He struck her as the honest, determined type.

And what if he figures out who you are?

At this point, she didn't really care if the detective with the midnight-blue eyes and clipped black hair found out she was an Alvanetti. She had been married once, to Drake Allen. A good, simple name and a good simple man. No, a boy, really. A boy who'd loved her in spite of her name. He'd been willing to fight for her and that had been a tragic mistake.

He'd died too young and her heart had not recovered.

He'd died at the hands of her family, something she could never prove. Something they'd denied. But she knew. Drake had been in a horrible accident not too far from the Alvanetti estate. A foggy night, a slick road. And alcohol. But Drake didn't drink.

No one had wanted to hear her shouting that at the top of her lungs. No one cared enough to investigate. And she surely would never recover from that, either.

But once she'd been strong enough to come up with a plan, she'd walked away from her father's rules as soon as she could escape. Walked away and tried to stay away. Except her beautiful, stubborn, scatterbrained mother always called her back. Sonia Alvanetti had a heart so big Rikki wondered how she'd become so frail. Had often wondered how her sweet mother could not see the truth regarding the family "import-export" business. Rikki had always believed her mother would live forever since Sonia loved everyone in such an unconditional way. She couldn't imagine her mother not being there. Rikki had got her strong faith from her mother, thankfully.

That faith would get her through this long night.

Now Rikki had to wonder about what Blain Kent had pointed out to her earlier. She and Tessa did look a lot alike.

Which made Rikki wonder if her worst fears and the detective's not-so-subtle hints were correct. Had that bullet been meant for her?

* * *

Blain's phone buzzed a rude alert. He sat up in bed and watched his phone dancing across the nightstand. Then he jerked it to his ear. "Kent."

"I… I need your help again."

"Rikki?"

"Yes."

She sounded muffled, scared.

Blain shot out of the bed and started grabbing clothes with one hand, the cell phone tucked between his ear and his collar bone. "What is it?"

"Someone came to my room."

Blain's pulse bumped into overdrive. "Are you still in the room?"

"No. I shouted that I was calling 911 and then I started screaming and banging on the walls. Then I called the front desk. The security guard apparently came out and scared away the intruder. I don't know where the patrol officer is."

Blain hopped on one foot trying to get his boots on. "Okay, where are you now?"

"In the lobby bathroom. I didn't know who else to call."

"I'll be there in five minutes. Do not leave the hotel lobby area."

"I won't."

"Stay on the phone with me," Blain said. "I'm leaving right now." He glanced around and saw Pebble the cat staring at him from the end of his bed. He'd found the cat by the back door of her place, meowing and scared. The mostly black-and-white long-haired calico did look like a pile of pebbles.

So now he had custody of a cat. He'd worry about

Pebble later. He hurried out the door of his apartment and hoped Rikki Alvanetti would stay put until he could get to her.

She did as he asked and by the time Blain made it to the hotel, he'd gotten more information out of her. She'd been awake, unable to sleep, when she'd heard someone outside her door. Then the door handle had jiggled. She'd screamed out and threatened to call 911.

But she'd called him instead. Blain radioed in while he kept her on the phone. When he pulled up, two units were parked in the drive-through in front of the bright lobby. But he didn't see the other cruiser or Rikki, either.

"I'm here," he said into his cell. "Come out of the bathroom, Rikki."

"Okay."

He ended the call, furious that someone had tried to get to her in spite of their efforts. But this attack supported his suspicions. Someone was after Rikki Allen.

"Where's our man?" he asked one of the uniformed officers as he slammed out of his unmarked sedan.

"He *was* knocked out in the bushes but on his way to the ER right now," one of the patrolmen said. "He'll be okay."

The man they'd put on Rikki had gotten out of his patrol car to stretch his legs and chat with the pretty front-desk clerk. When he'd returned to his car, he'd been hit on the head and knocked out. Another officer had taken him to the hospital in his patrol car.

Sometimes, small-town police officers did things in a backward kind of way but Blain knew his fellow officers were all hardworking men. He was just glad everyone was okay.

Especially the woman emerging pale and sleep-tousled out of the bathroom. She looked at Blain and walked straight toward him, wearing a dark red zipped jacket and matching pants that his mother would call lounge wear.

He called it nice-looking wear right now but he kept his mind focused on the task and not the way that combo fit Rikki. "Hey, you okay?"

"Yes." She glanced around, not looking so okay. "Did you find anyone out there?"

"Not yet. My men are searching every nook. We'll double-check the area around your door, but I'm guessing whoever found you knew to wear gloves and not leave any clues."

She nodded and pushed at all that tumbling hair. "Now we know, Detective."

"Know what?" He didn't like the gleam of acceptance in her eyes.

"That they were after me."

"Yes, I believe you're right on that," Blain replied. "But they could have been after both of you." At the look of horror on her face, he said, "Listen, you're gonna have to tell me where your mother lives. You can't stay here alone."

"I can't have them in her house, either."

"But you'll be with someone and… I'll make sure no one bothers either of you."

"And what are you, a one-man type of superhero?"

"No, but I think I can patrol a home and keep intruders out."

"He's a former marine, ma'am," a passing officer said in a matter-of-fact tone. "He can take care of you."

She quirked a dark eyebrow and took a calming

breath. "A marine? So that should make me feel safe, I suppose."

"One of the best," the young patrolman said before Blain could reply. "An MP at that. Only, he don't like to brag."

Blain shook his head. "Look, I can watch over you tonight."

She stared at him with a new regard, her dark gaze sweeping over him and making him squirm. "I don't want to go to my mother's house."

Blain took her by the arm and tugged her off to the side where no one could hear him. "Your place isn't safe. This hotel isn't safe even though we had a uniformed patrol on site. I can't take you to my place. Unless you have somewhere you can go that you can assure me is okay, then you'd better tell me the truth, Miss Allen. All of it. Or I'll have to take you to the station and put you in a cell just to make sure you *are* safe until morning."

"I don't know the truth," she said, her voice weakening. "I've told you everything I can." Then she shook her head. "I keep thinking of Chad—my ex. But he couldn't be this stupid. He's threatened me but… I can't believe he'd do this. He has too much at stake."

Blain held his lips tightly together to keep from shouting at her. "And it never occurred to you to give me these details when you mentioned him earlier?"

"I didn't think he'd find me at the town house. I never told him that my family—that I own it."

"Well, maybe he followed you and…tried to kill you." Blain pulled out his notebook. "What's his address?"

She hesitated and then gave him Chad's workplace and home addresses.

"And when did you last see Chad Presley?"

"About a week ago, down in Miami."

Blain got a description of Chad and his vehicle and put out a BOLO over the radio that would go statewide. Be On the Lookout for a possible killer.

"There. We'll see what that turns up. Does this Chad know where your mother lives?"

She thought about last spring when she'd brought him here for a wedding. That hadn't gone over very well.

"He's been here before but only once."

"Okay, then, let's go. Either you tell me where to take you or…you can spend the night in jail."

"You can't do that—force me into jail."

"I can if it's for your own good."

He didn't like playing bad cop with her, but the woman was too stubborn to see that someone was after her. And a nasty ex-boyfriend would be a prime suspect. Surely she wasn't one of those women who kept forgiving over and over until it was too late.

Blain would find out everything about her before this was over, but right now he wanted to get her out of here. They were too exposed at this location now.

She finally nodded. "I need to get my things."

After he escorted her to her room, he put her in his car and turned to stare at her. "Where to, princess?"

She swallowed, dropped her head and stared at her hands in her lap. "The Bay Road."

Bay Road? Blain whistled. Real estate out there was way over his pay-scale. "Okay, then."

Pricey estates out there. A scenic highway surrounding where the big bay met up with Millbrook Lake.

When they were underway and out past the city, he

turned off and followed the dark water. "Which address?"

She finally looked over at him, a solid defiance in her voice. "2200 First Bay Lane."

Blain blinked, thinking he hadn't heard right. "Hey, that's—"

"The Alvanetti estate," she finished for him. "Sonia Alvanetti is my mother."

Blain held tightly to the steering wheel as realization settled around him. "And… Franco Alvanetti is your father."

"Yes." She nodded and looked out the window.

And suddenly, Blain understood so much more about what was going on with Rikki Allen. No wonder she'd been so closemouthed and evasive. No wonder he couldn't trust her.

She was an Alvanetti.

FOUR

Old Florida.

A wrought-iron gate swung open after Rikki gave him a security code to punch in on the big electronic switch pad.

Blain eased the unmarked police sedan along the winding lane and took in his surroundings as the first rays of the sun shone like a spotlight through the trees.

Swaying palm trees and palmetto bushes, massive live oaks dripping with Spanish moss. Scattered orange and lemon trees that would be lush with fruit come next summer. Winter-white camellias blooming on deeply rooted bushes. Wild magnolia trees shooting up through the oaks, their fat, waxy leaves hanging heavy and dark green along the winding garden paths on either side of the private gravel-and-shell-covered drive.

And what looked like a big white barn and stables surrounded by a white board fence off in the distance.

The wild abandonment of this tropical landscape didn't fool Blain. This kind of exotic display spoke of money as old as the camellia bushes. Dirty money.

The sparkling sunrise brought the light of dawn peeking through the heavy foliage like a diamond hidden in the forest. And then, the stark stucco mansion came into view, all creamy planes and angles and glass against rich brown teakwood trim aged with a shimmering patina that shone in the early morning light.

Blain pulled the sedan up to the six-car garage and turned off the engine. Still in shock, he pivoted in his seat toward Rikki. "Why did you lie to me?"

"I didn't lie," she said, her gaze slamming him with an unapologetic attitude. "I… I don't associate with my family very much since I left. I only keep in touch with my mother."

"You could have told me that." He studied the house. "Or at least who your mother really is."

"And you would have immediately jumped to the wrong conclusion."

She was correct there. He would have jumped to the only conclusion and it wasn't a good one. "I want the truth," he snapped. "Now I doubt I'll ever get it from you."

"I gave you the truth," she retorted. "I told you everything I knew, even about my ex-boyfriend. I was so afraid he'd done this I couldn't bring myself to mention him at first. But I should have. If it's him, I have to get out of here." She took a deep, shuddering breath. "I don't know. Could he be the one? I can't let him get away with killing my best friend."

Blain could see the fear and concern in her dark eyes. He understood how abused women could spin a situation to justify why they always returned but he couldn't understand why she hadn't leveled with him to begin with since her best friend *had* been murdered. There was no returning to that.

He'd have to think this one through but right now,

he had to make sure Rikki was safe. Keeping her alive meant he had to deal with the entire situation, whether he liked it or not.

Blain lifted his hand in the air. "He can't hurt anyone inside the gates to this compound. I saw the cameras and I spotted an armed guard with a dog, too."

"Yes," she said, nodding. "If Chad shows up here, they'll probably kill him and then I'll have that death on my hands, too."

Blain grabbed her wrist. "What do you mean, too? Do you think your *family* killed Tessa?"

"No." She gave him an imploring stare. "I was married once when I was around twenty. His last name was Allen. Drake Allen. But he died six months after we eloped."

Blain let that tidbit of information sink in. That explained the last name she used. "How did he die?"

"An accident." Lowering her head, she added, "Up on the road."

"But you think your family took care of him?"

"I didn't say that." She opened the door and got out of the car, her attitude like a solid wall against him. She might have cut all ties to her powerful family, but blood always ran thicker than water. She wouldn't rat anybody out.

Blain got out of the car and came around to meet her, some of his justified anger simmering into a slow boil. She didn't have to say what had happened to her husband. He could see it all over her face. "So you blame yourself?"

"Yes." She whirled and opened the back car door to get her stuff. "But my mother is innocent. She thinks

Drake died in a car crash and he did. I've never been able to prove otherwise."

Shoving one of the bags at him, she said, "So if you insist on going inside with me, you'd better keep quiet about what I just told you. As far as I know, over the last few years, my father has changed. He's not the same man he used to be. He's legitimate now."

"Yeah, because he's turned things over to your brothers."

"I can't speak to that since I don't keep up with them. One is here, running the business and the other one in Europe. I told you I walked away a long time ago. I only came here to get away from Chad for a while and to be with my mother." She stared up at the massive glass doors of the house where two evergreen wreaths hung side by side. "It is Christmas, after all."

Blain couldn't force her to tell him everything. Not yet, anyway. But now that he knew who she really was, things had taken on a whole new meaning. "I'll get you safely inside to see your mother, but I strongly suggest you stay here. Don't go anywhere, understand? I have to do some digging on Chad Presley and I want to go back over the details of your friend's death. That means I might be back to ask you some more questions."

"I'll be right here," she said. "I do have a few clients to meet with this week but I can do video conferences for now and change those appointments to later."

"Much later," Blain retorted. "Like after we find out who killed Tessa."

"Then you'd better get to it." She hurried toward the portico door on the side of the big house near the garage. Turning, she gave him a conflicted stare. "I'm not like them, Blain. I got away and created my own life, on my own terms."

Blain saw the defiant expression behind that sincere statement. Maybe he should cut her some slack. But he wouldn't do her any favors. He refused to look the other way like his dad had done all those years. "I sure hope that's true. I'll have someone bring your car out here once I think it's safe to move it. Remember, don't go anywhere for the next few days."

She nodded, one hand on the brass door handle. "Thank you." Then she glanced around and back into his eyes. "I appreciate all your help."

"Doing my job," he said. Then he took his time scoping the entire place before he got in his car and left.

Rikki entered the side door that opened into the butler's pantry leading to the massive gourmet kitchen where her mother used to cook and entertain on a weekly basis. Those days were few and far between now that her mother had gotten sick. Her parents were probably lonely, but no one wanted to acknowledge that. Nor did anyone want to admit that soon they wouldn't be able to live here alone. They both had failing health these days, according to Peggy's reports to Rikki.

The last big event held here had been Rikki's cousin Beatrice's wedding back in the spring. Rikki had come home for the wedding but she'd gotten here a few minutes before the ceremony and even though her mother had begged her to stay, she'd left about thirty minutes into the reception. She and Chad had been fighting. Again.

That had been the last time she'd seen her mother happy and laughing. Sonia had always loved having people in her home. Her mother had left that afternoon for a European vacation.

A few days later, Rikki had received a call that her mother had taken ill while on a Mediterranean cruise and was sent to a hospital in Italy where her brother Victor was staying at the time. Rikki had gone over to see her mother, but Victor had already left the hospital. He obviously was too busy to even sit with his mother.

Rikki had stayed there until her mother was able to make the flight home to Florida, where Franco had met her with a private ambulance and an equally private nurse.

Now Rikki took her time walking through the long, spacious kitchen with the dark cabinets and the white marble countertops. The kitchen opened to a big dining area and a spacious den, complete with a fire in the enormous fireplace and comfy leather sofas and chairs scattered all around. High, wide windows looked out over a prime spot where Millbrook Lake met up with the big bay that would take boaters all the way out to the Gulf.

Rikki glanced out at the sloping yard down to the lake where a boathouse and her father's yacht—the *Sonia*—sat moored to the big private dock. The pool glistened in the early morning light, the sun hitting the water with a brilliant clarity that Rikki could only pray she had. When she heard footsteps shuffling up the long central hallway that led to her mother and father's private suite in the back of the house, she whirled, expecting to see Peggy. The always-positive red-haired nurse had been with her mother since Sonia had come home a few months ago. But Peggy had worked for her family for as long as Rikki could remember, helping to raise children and take care of sick relatives.

Her mother adored Peggy and Peggy adored her mother.

But Peggy wasn't standing there in the archway near the stairs to the second floor. Franco Alvanetti stopped to stare at his only daughter. "Well, I see you have arrived, at last."

Rikki hated the tremble inside her heart. "Yes, Father. I got here yesterday but—"

"But you had to give the locals a report on the woman they found shot to death on your townhome patio."

His bloodshot eyes moved over her with a steady gaze that left most people quaking. Rikki had long ago learned to stop the quaking but she had to take a few calming breaths to make it work today. "So you know."

"Of course I know," he said as he moved toward her in a stooped, aged gait. "I still have friends around this town."

Her father wore a plaid robe over old silk pajamas. His slippers were Italian leather, worn in spots but still expensive-looking. Even in his night clothes with his salt-and-pepper hair scattered around his olive-skinned face, he still commanded a certain respect.

Rikki reluctantly gave him that respect. "I didn't want to upset Mother."

"She is sleeping. Peggy will be out soon to give the morning report."

He glanced toward the kitchen. "Coffee, Regina?"

"Yes, Papa, but I'll make it."

"Good." He waved a hand toward the industrial-sized coffee machine. "And then we can sit down and talk about this latest scandal in your life."

Rikki went to the cabinet and found the coffee, steeling herself against one of Franco's soft-spoken interrogations. They used to have several servants in the house but lately, it was just her parents and a maid who cleaned and cooked, along with a day nurse. Her parents didn't require much in the way of food or drink. Peggy and the day nurse made sure they both had nutritious food to eat.

When had her parents become so frail?

Feeling guilty for not checking on them more, Rikki blinked away her tears and her fatigue. "Would you like some breakfast, Papa?"

Her father glanced up from where he'd perched on a bar stool in the way he'd done on countless mornings. "You know, I miss your mother's cooking. She used to make the best omelets."

Rikki closed her eyes, the smell of breakfast wafting out as if her mother were standing at the big stove cooking and laughing and talking about her plans for the day. Sonia always had her days planned out for months, down to the pumps and jewelry she'd wear that day.

"Of course, I'll make you an omelet," Rikki said. Once she had the coffee brewing, Rikki pulled out eggs, cream, cheese and vegetables.

"Throw in some bacon," her father said.

When she nodded and glanced back at him, he had his head in his hands, his face down. His once-dark hair was salt-and-pepper now and his always-meaty hands were puffy with excess fluid. She'd noticed the deep bags underneath his eyes, too. Had he stopped taking care of himself?

Rikki turned back to her work, wishing she could

say something to him but then she'd never understood
her brooding, distant father. Only Sonia could bring
out his jovial, loving side. Her mother shone like a star
in all of their lives and Sonia's strong faith held them
all together.

"I'll pray you through it," her mother always said, no
matter what they were dealing with. "God has blessed
us in spite of it all. He'll continue to bless us."

I'll pray you through it.

Maybe it was Rikki's turn to pray them through the
latest tragedy, to pray for Blain and the local police,
to pray for Tessa's brother who didn't even know she
was dead yet. And to pray for herself and her family,
no matter what.

But right now, she'd cook for her father. For a few
minutes, she could forget about her rift with this man,
forget about her mother's illness and her own failures
in life, and maybe for just this little while, she could
forget about Tessa's vacant, lifeless eyes staring up at
her from a pool of blood.

Maybe she could even forget about the way Blain
Kent's expression had changed when he'd realized who
she really was, too. Because she knew the good-looking
detective would hound her until he figured out what
kind of trouble she'd brought back to Millbrook with
her.

Rikki intended to find out the answer to that question herself, with or without Blain's help.

Putting all of that aside, she flipped the omelet onto
a plate and brought it over to her father with a steaming
cup of black coffee. "Here you go, Papa."

Franco Alvanetti looked up at her with misty eyes.

"This is a good moment," he said. "Too bad about your friend."

Rikki couldn't decide if her father was being sincere or not, but she felt that trembling in her heart again.

Was it raw emotion? Or was it a warning to be aware?

FIVE

Blain sat at his desk in the back corner of the Millbrook Police Department, scrolling through some old news articles about the Alvanetti family. He'd read up on their philanthropic endeavors, their weddings, births, deaths and celebrations plus a few articles questioning certain tactics they used in their so-called import-export business located in a huge warehouse just outside of town.

But nothing much on their only daughter's brief marriage to Drake Allen. Nothing much about his fatal car crash but the accident report told the tale. High rate of speed and alcohol.

End of report. Could it be possible that Rikki just needed someone to blame so her grief wouldn't cut so deep?

"Kent, what've you got on the Tessa Jones case?"

Blain glanced up to find his chubby, mustached police chief, Raymond Ferrier, staring down at him like a curious bulldog. The chief trusted Blain but he was antsy about this high-profile murder, especially now that he knew it had happened at a place owned by an Alvanetti.

"Not much, sir." That was true. He hadn't found a whole lot on the Jones woman. "She lived in Tallahassee so I've got a couple of detectives there casing out friends and family. I had one of my contacts there who's tracking down the boyfriend. He's supposed to get back to me after he talks to the boyfriend and finds out where he was yesterday."

"Not good, right here at the holidays," the chief said. "I feel for Miss Alvanetti but I can't have a bunch of nervous-Nellie citizens suggesting we call off the Christmas parade or cancel the cantata at Millbrook Lake Church because they think a killer is on the loose."

"Not gonna let that happen, Chief," Blain replied, wishing the chief would quit breathing down his neck so he could get back to work. "I'm researching articles right now, trying to put things together." He shuffled through the report. "Besides, I don't think anything can get in the way of the Christmas parade."

Chief Ferrier shook his head, the red lines along his neck turning crimson. "Just keep at it. I sure don't need Old Man Alvanetti demanding justice. We all know how that'll turn out."

"I'll handle that," Blain replied. The chief had never caved underneath the Alvanetti juggernaut but he wasn't too thrilled to have to stand in the way of that juggernaut either. Up until now, things had been pretty quiet on that front. "I'm going back out to the house to question Regina Alvanetti later today."

The chief scrubbed a hand down his always-a-day-behind-beard stubble. "Be careful about that. You know how things tend to go out at that place."

"I'm always careful," Blain said. And he wasn't

afraid of the Alvanetti clan. Rikki owed him and he intended to cash in on that debt. Plus, he had one furry, demanding cat to deliver.

Chief Ferrier grunted at that confident retort. "Careful is one thing, son. But being smart is important, too."

After the chief went back to his office, Blain jotted a list of all the variables on this case. The victim resembled Regina—Rikki—Alvanetti. They'd been best friends. Rikki had a hostile ex-boyfriend named Chad Presley but he hadn't been located yet. The Tallahassee authorities called to let Blain know they had talked to Tessa Jones's boyfriend and his alibi was solid. That left Chad Presley.

Nothing of importance had been taken from the town house and there was no sign of forced entry. Blain decided this was looking more like a professional hit than a crime of passion.

Had Tessa known her murderer? What did the "K" written in blood mean? Was it an initial or had the poor woman just been grasping at the floor, trying to get up? He'd have to wait for the ballistics report and lab work to come back on the autopsy from the state lab in Tallahassee. But while he waited, Blain intended to keep plugging away, trying to find the truth.

He thought about Rikki Alvanetti. Lush and exotic, much in the same way as that imposing home and the dubious lifestyle she had tried so hard to deny. She had grown up privileged and entitled in a world that most plain folks only dreamed about.

That was about to change. Blain wouldn't let her big brown eyes or her tragic demeanor fool him. He'd ignore the tickle of awareness her spice-scented perfume caused in his system and he'd certainly ignore those black boots she wore with such an easy, classy sway.

Blain could be tenacious when he was on a case and this one was a doozy. He'd already had calls from several television stations and most of the local and regional papers, all wanting to interview him regarding the Tessa Jones murder—and how it might be connected to the mighty Alvanetti family.

"No comment."

He couldn't talk about an active case. He'd let the people in the mayor's PR department give out the talking points. He'd rather get out and beat the bushes to find out the truth.

He had to wonder if Rikki knew more than she was telling him. His trust meter on her had gone down, way down, when she'd taken him to the Alvanetti estate. Even more when he'd realized she was one of them.

He was about to head out there to confront her one more time when his cell rang.

Preacher.

"Hey," he said into the phone as he grabbed his leather jacket and walked toward the front door of the small police building right across from the county courthouse. "What's happening, Preacher?"

Rory Sanderson's laugh rolled out on a low wave. "You tell me. I'm thinking you're up to your eyeballs on this murder that happened last night."

"You got that right," Blain said. He stopped in the parking lot, near his car. "I guess I'll be the hot topic at pizza night, right?"

Blain and his three buddies always met once a week for pizza and watching sports on the popular Back Bay Pizza House.

"We're all waiting for Thursday at seven o'clock to come," Rory replied. "I just called to tell you if things get crazy—"

"You will pray for me, right?"

"Oh, I do that, anyway," the always cheerful minister replied. "I mean, if this case gets as in-depth as I think it will, you'll need someone to listen to your rants."

"I know you got my back," Blain said, thanking God for his friends.

Rory Sanderson was the popular and much-loved minister at Millbrook Lake Church now, but he'd been a chaplain in the army just a few years ago. Another member of their group was Alec Caldwell, a former marine who'd been injured and had the scars to prove it, and was now a successful businessman living in one of the old Victorian houses along the lake. Even though he'd inherited a ton of money from his late mother, he was as laid-back and unassuming as any man could be since he'd met local bakery owner Marla Hamilton. They were getting married in two weeks and Blain was the best man.

Rory would officiate and who knew what their fourth man, Hunter Lawson, would do or if he'd even show up for the wedding. The Okie came and went like a shadow but he was slowly growing on all of them and he was a solid friend if need be. Blain might have to call Hunter since Hunter had gotten his PI license recently and was now available to work cases in the state of Florida.

"So I know you can't talk about the case but...be careful out there," Rory said. "This is a bit off the reservation for Millbrook."

"Yeah, and don't I know it," Blain replied. "I'll be careful. And smart."

"I'll see you soon," Rory said.

Blain hit End and turned to unlock his car. Then he noticed he had a flat tire. "What?"

He bent to examine the tire. He'd just had the vehicle serviced, courtesy of the Millbrook Police Department since it was a departmental vehicle. The mechanics had suggested new tires so he'd had those put on, too.

Now this. Blain studied the tire and noticed something odd. A slash mark cutting deep into the still-new tread.

Suddenly, he wasn't as worried about how the department's money had gone to waste on these tires as he was about how someone had obviously slashed this tire in broad daylight.

Blain heaved an aggravated sigh and stood up to check his surroundings, thinking he'd just gotten his first hint on how things would go with an investigation involving an Alvanetti.

Or maybe, his first warning from a killer.

Rikki sat holding her mother's frail hand.

Sonia was sleeping, which was a surprise in itself. Her mother used to rise with the dawn because she had to see the sun cresting out over the water to the east. She'd make herself a strong cup of coffee and stroll down to the dock so she could be as close to the water as possible to watch the sunrise.

"Isn't that amazing?" she'd say to anyone who might want to venture down with her at the crack of dawn. "God's world is so full of joy and beauty. That same sun that shines on us each day covers the entire earth with warmth. That sun shines on all of us, Rikki. You always remember that, no matter where you are in life. Always look toward the sun, honey."

Rikki brushed at the tears in her eyes and glanced at the clock. It was midmorning but the heavy curtains in her parents' bedroom were still drawn shut.

"Hey, Mama, want me to open the curtains so you can see the sunshine?"

Sonia let out a little grunt but didn't wake up.

Franco had left for the day with the excuse that he needed to visit with Santo at the warehouse and go over some paperwork.

Rikki probably should let her mother sleep but Peggy had suggested trying to wake her in hopes that seeing Rikki would help Sonia. "She needs to get her strength back but she has a hard time staying up. Mr. A tries to get her to take a walk with him out to the water, but she just can't make it."

Rikki wanted her mother to make it. Determined and needing something positive to cling to after the last couple of days, Rikki went to the row of glass windows and opened the curtains to the big sliding doors that were usually flung open to the back garden. While the water looked inviting, the chilly temperature forced the doors to stay shut tight.

At least a cozy fire burned in the bedroom fireplace and Peggy had put up a glittering gold-and-red ornamented Christmas tree between the two high-backed brocade chairs in the corner by the doors. If she could get her mother to make it to a chair...

A knock at the bedroom door pulled Rikki out of her hopes.

The day nurse, Daphne, leaned her head in, her short

brown curls falling in her eyes. "You have a visitor, Miss Alvanetti. Blain Kent."

Rikki's heart jumped so fast she had to catch her breath. Whirling, she left the drapery gaping open. "I'll be right there. Thank you, Daphne."

The pretty young nurse nodded and went back to the kitchen where she was making soup that no one would probably eat.

"I'll be back soon, Mama," Rikki whispered. She kissed her mother's soft cheek and brushed back the spiky white-blond hair Sonia had always been so proud of.

Sonia mumbled incoherently but kept sleeping.

Rikki stopped in the wide hallway and gathered herself. Her mother used to say, "Pull yourself together and put on some color."

Rikki checked her light pink lipstick and ran a hand through her tousled hair out of habit, thinking of her mother's endearing command. Just one of many Sonia quoted often. Then she took her time making her way to the far side of the long house.

Blain was waiting in the den. He stood in front of the fire, staring at the family portrait centered over the mantel.

Daphne was still in the kitchen. She sent Rikki an inquisitive glance and then gazed back across the way at Blain.

Rikki's heart jumped again. He was an attractive man. All hard angles and dark shaggy hair, his physique muscular and solid. He wore a worn black leather jacket and jeans with battered cowboy boots.

"Detective," she said by way of a greeting. "You're out early today."

At the sound of her flats hitting the hardwood floors, he turned and swept her with a questioning gaze. And he was holding her squirming cat.

Something melted inside Rikki's bitter heart. But she poured all that softness into grabbing Pebble up in her arms and cooing to him. "You found him. Thank you."

Blain gave her an indulgent stare and wiped cat hair off his jacket. "He found me outside your town house. And now I have cat hair all over my apartment." He pointed to the bag of dry cat food on the counter. "Got this at the discount store."

"Thank you." She smiled at his obvious disapproval. "Pebble is an early riser. I'm sure he woke you to let you know he needed feeding."

"I've been up for a while," he retorted. "How'd you sleep last night?"

The question rang out more as an accusation. "Better than the night before," she replied, determined not to give him any openings.

She dropped Pebble and watched as the big cat ran to the kitchen and meowed. She moved across the room to find a bowl, and motioned toward the big leather sectional. "Have a seat. Can I get you some coffee?"

He sniffed toward the kitchen. "I thought I smelled actual real coffee. That stuff we have at the station is more like tar mixed with motor oil."

"I'll bring you a cup right away. Cream and sugar?"

He gave her a look that spoke of something besides coffee. "No. Black. Thank you."

Rikki headed toward the kitchen where Daphne was bent down petting Pebble and smiled at the curious nurse. "Daphne, would you mind sitting with my mother while I talk to the detective?"

Daphne nodded, pursed her lips, turned off the stove and then left the room. Too nosy, that one. Or maybe too interested in the brooding man sitting in the den.

"Here you go." After feeding the cat, Rikki came back to the den and handed Blain the big Christmas mug, one of many her mother had collected over the years. This one had a grinning reindeer on it.

Blain stared at the silly mug, one dark eyebrow lifting. With a smile so quick it could have been a wink, he took the coffee and drank deeply. "Good. Very good."

If she hadn't been so unsettled by seeing him, Rikki would have laughed. "I'm glad you approve."

He sat down and turned to business, his whole demeanor turning as black as the coffee. "I need to ask you a few more questions."

Rikki sank down on the other side of the sectional. "Of course." She swallowed and tried to calm herself."

She willed herself not to break down in front of him. She'd cried enough yesterday and last night, seeing her mother so frail and knowing she'd never see Tessa alive again. "Okay. Well, I'd like to help with her funerals expenses whenever that's possible. I owe her family a lot."

"Why's that?"

Did he have to distrust everything she said?

"When I first left Millbrook, they took me in and let me stay with them until Tessa and I could go to FSU together. She was my roommate all the way through college." She stared out at the water beyond the yard. "Her mother died of lung cancer when Tessa and I were in college and her father died later in a boating accident. I miss them and now I'll miss her."

"So you two were close."

"Yes. I told you she was my best friend. I don't know what I'll do without her."

Blain lowered his gaze and took a sip of coffee, but Rikki thought she'd seen a trace of compassion passing through his inky eyes. Gone in a flash but something to remember when he started grilling her.

He studied his notes then glanced back up at her. "Okay, so, your ex might have an alibi. We haven't located him yet, but several neighbors saw him at a company Christmas party the night of the murder. We checked with his coworkers and several of them vouched for his whereabouts yesterday."

Rikki nodded. "Probably at that party with his new girlfriend."

"So he still stalks you while he's dating another woman?"

She colored with humiliation. "I tend to attract real losers. He dated other people while we were together, too."

He gave her another in-depth sweeping gaze that didn't seem to have anything to do with the conversation. Almost like a silent compliment.

"So…your Charming Chad was in Tallahassee with a roomful of people at the time of the murder. We have pictures and we have statements that both support his statement. He's in the clear for now since the ME established the time of death at around 6:00 p.m."

"So you can mark him off your suspect list?"

"Yes. For now." He studied his notes. "But he didn't show up for work today. We're still trying to locate him."

A thread of apprehension curled down her spine. "That's odd. Chad never misses work."

"We'll keep checking. He might have a hangover or

maybe he took a day off." The detective didn't look too concerned. "Now on to you."

Rikki knew this man still had his doubts about her. "And what about me, Detective? What list am I on?"

SIX

Blain wasn't sure how to answer that question. He leaned forward and cupped his hands together. "I'd like to believe you're on the good list but I haven't talked to Santa yet."

Her smile wasn't as confident as she probably hoped it would be. "Don't do me any favors."

"Hadn't planned on it," he retorted, thinking he'd have to go to the extreme to make that a true statement. "But I still need to ask you a few more questions."

Rikki sat back on her side of the couch, her hands clasped. "I'll tell you anything you want to know. Just please find Tessa's killer."

Blain intended to do just that. "Tessa's boyfriend's alibi held. He had several witnesses, one who rode with him to a dinner where they were all night." Blain sipped his coffee. "From the reports, he's very upset and wants to come here, but the locals have suggested he stay away for now. He seems to be unavailable at the moment, however."

"Harry Boston." Rikki's frown said it all. "I'm surprised he hasn't come looking for me. He'd want answers."

"You don't like him?"

"He hangs out with Chad a lot and reports back with whatever he can drag out of Tessa about me. Or he did." She shrugged and played with the zipper on her jacket, a deep sadness moving through her eyes. "He always seemed a tad shady to me. But I couldn't tell Tessa that. She loved him."

"Would he murder for Chad?"

She shook her head. "He wouldn't kill Tessa. He truly loved her. I'm sure he's devastated but since you won't let me talk to him, I have no way of knowing what he's thinking."

"You don't need to call anyone connected to this case. For your own safety."

"Harry didn't approve of Tessa and I being so close."

"But you two were close before he came into the picture, right?"

"Yes, before Chad or Harry either one came into the picture. Why is it that men are so needy? Always wanting us to themselves?"

Blain did a mock frown and glanced behind him as if she were talking to someone else. "Is that a rhetorical question?"

"Of course it is," she said. "Besides, you don't strike me as the needy type. Dark and brooding and dangerous, yes. But then that sounds so cliché, doesn't it?"

She was making him forget why he came here. "Hey, I'm the one asking the questions, okay?"

"And another typical male tactic. A nonanswer."

"Let's go back to Chad and Harry," he said with a slight grin to hide his discomfort. "Do you think they could be off somewhere together, like on a fishing trip or maybe a business deal?"

"Chad and Harry liked to hang out all the time without us, so yes, that is a possibility. Long weekend or something. Chad might have taken Harry off to help him through this. They hated it when Tessa and I would go shopping or if we planned a girls' weekend."

"A weekend kind of like this weekend?"

"Yes. But Tessa assured me that Harry didn't mind her coming to meet me here. And again, he wouldn't have done this. Not to Tessa."

"Maybe he thought she was you?"

"He'd know Tessa." She shook her head. "I just can't see him doing this. He might not be on my top-ten list but I know he loved her. They were planning to get married next year." She stared at the fireplace. "He might show up here yet."

"What kind of things would the boys say to you about your girls' night and other such stuff?"

"Stay home. Let's go out. Why do you need more shoes?" She shook her head. "None of that matter now, does it?"

"It does if they're the jealous type. Domestic violence isn't pretty."

"It's never gone that far," she said. "Well, Chad's come close, which is why I got away from him."

Blain cataloged that comment for the future. "What does Chad do for a living?"

She frowned and tossed ribbons of hair off her shoulders. "He owns several restaurants in Miami and a couple in Tallahassee."

"So he's successful in his own right?"

"Yes. No, he does not hope to get his hands on any Alvanetti money if that's what you're asking."

Blain let that one slide. "And Harry?"

"Harry works in finance. He likes to take other people's money and make even more for them and himself."

Blain made a note of that. He tried to stay focused but all that hair falling around her shoulders kept distracting him. And that cute lounge outfit only added to that distraction. She was a petite little dynamo who'd withheld information—good intentions but bad judgment.

Shouldn't he hold that against her?

Yes, he reminded himself. "I need a list of any other acquaintances that might have had a grudge against you or Tessa. Anybody you'd had words with, or had a run-in with."

"Okay." She got up and found a pen and paper. "Starting now with you?"

He ignored her little joke. "Yes, and going back as far as you can remember."

"I… I don't think I have any known enemies," she said. "I work hard and I've built up a strong client base around the entire state. I've never had a client turn on me, mainly because I'm willing to redo anything that isn't right or that they don't like."

Blain put down his phone and notebook and decided to try some small talk for a few minutes. "Tell me about your work."

She shrugged. "I decorate houses. I like beach themes with a bit of understated elegance. Not too much of any one thing and not too kitschy."

"Yes, too much of any one thing can be dangerous."

She pushed at her fringe of bangs and gave him a daring stare. "Or boring."

Blain couldn't imagine anything this woman did as boring. "Could you have seen something or heard something that might put you in danger?"

"I don't think so." She hesitated and then added, "But I do deal in a lot of priceless art and antiques."

"Now we're getting some ideas," he said.

"But murder?" She looked pale and unsettled.

"Yes, murder."

"So now my career is in jeopardy?"

He nodded and refocused. "And you're comfortable financially?"

Her dark eyebrows winged up in two perfect slants. "Isn't that a bit too personal?"

"Yes. But that's the point."

She shot up off the couch. "You aren't making any sense, Detective Kent."

"None of this makes sense," Blain countered. "I have to look at every angle. Did someone have a grudge against either of you? Did someone want to steal from either of you or take you hostage in exchange for millions of dollars in ransom? Did you order a priceless antique or doodad that someone wanted? Is this some kind of vendetta against your family? Or Tessa's? Who would follow you here and kill another woman who looks almost exactly like you? And why?"

"I don't know," she said, tears forming in her dark eyes. "I've told you over and over that I don't know. I came here to visit my mother and I also planned to use the time to get my head on straight and finally get over Chad. Tessa wanted to visit with me and have some fun. I… I needed my best friend and so she came."

She shrugged, hugged herself as she stood in front of the fire. "That's all I know. I hoped to get some work done for clients who have summer homes in the area too—mainly to give me something to do that would distract me from all my problems."

Blain held firm against her misty gaze and resisted the need to tug her close and comfort her. He didn't do comfort very well. "I'll need a list of those client names."

"My clients aren't killers," she retorted.

"Anyone can become a killer for any kind of reason," Blain replied. "Anyone."

They heard a door open and then a shuffling set of footsteps coming from the hallway from the garage. Blain stood up, prepared for a guard coming to tell him he needed to leave.

But this man was not a guard.

"What's going on here?" Franco Alvanetti stopped just inside the kitchen, his hostile gaze scorching Blain with disdain.

Rikki's gaze locked with Blain's in what might have been a warning and then she turned to face her father. "The detective is following up with some more questions for me, Papa."

"Detective Kent, does my daughter need a good lawyer?" Franco asked, his hands in the pockets of his expensive trousers, his frown etched in fatigue and overindulgence.

Blain gave Rikki a questioning stare and then met her father's disapproving frown. "Not yet, sir."

Rikki wanted to drop off the face of the earth. Her father and the law—not good in one room together. And especially not good with this one. Blain had that I-won't-back-down attitude perfected. The clinched fists, the daring solid wall of an expression and the buff body braced for action.

Lots of action.

She shouldn't be attracted to a man who hated her family and had her on a suspect list. But there it was, plain and simple. Instead of wanting him to leave, Rikki just wanted to protect him from her father's wrath.

As if Blain Kent needed protecting.

"It's okay, Papa," she said to prove that point. "I can handle this."

"Can you, really?" her father asked. "You've brought danger to your sick mother's door. After refusing to associate with this family for years, you decide to come home and bring murder with you. I'll never understand you, Regina."

"That's enough," Blain said.

Rikki blinked away the raw pain that made her eyes swell with moisture and turned to find Blain standing by her side. "Your daughter is cooperating with us in every aspect of this investigation. Whoever did this also came after her last night. And regardless of how I feel, that's why she's staying here." He glanced around and pointed a finger at Franco. "You have a fortress here so even I agree this is the best place for her right now. Unless you want something terrible to happen to her, too."

Rikki expected her father to tell Blain to get out of his house. Instead, he took a deep breath and stared over at Blain with puffy eyes and a deep, puckered brow. "Do you think the killer mistook Tessa to be my daughter?"

"I do, sir," Blain said, his arm brushing against Rikki's like a warning caress. "But I can't give you a conclusive comment on that yet. Rikki is going to put together a list of everyone she's talked to or worked with over the last few weeks. And in the meantime, I'll keep in touch with the Miami and Tallahassee authorities and see what we can come up with."

Franco moved into the big den, his power practically radiating off his body. "You will keep me informed."

Blain's expression looked like jagged ice. "I don't usually keep anyone outside the department informed on an active case, sir."

"But you'll make an exception."

Blain's body went rigid again. He braced his legs apart and crossed his arms over his chest, the rustle of his leather jacket sending out "keep off" vibes. "I don't make exceptions, Mr. Alvanetti."

Her father actually looked nonplussed and confused. Rikki seriously wanted to kiss Blain Kent. Nobody ever talked back to her father.

Then she realized she wouldn't mind kissing Blain Kent, regardless of her father. Which would only make things worse for both of them.

Franco sank down in his favorite leather chair and uttered a tired sigh. "So we have a dead woman who was found at my daughter's home. Her best friend, Tessa Jones, who just happens to resemble her. Interesting, isn't it?"

Did he even care? Rikki wondered.

"Very interesting," Blain said. "The whole town is buzzing with scenarios. Which is why I don't want to release the details. Brings out a lot of wackos and wannabe-snitches."

Franco patted the cushy arms of the chair with his meaty hands. "I see." He coughed and cleared his throat. "I will make sure my daughter is safe while you do your job."

Her father nodded. A dismissal.

Rikki breathed a sigh of her own and motioned to Blain. "I'll show you out, Detective Kent."

Blain gave her a surprised glance but followed her. He stopped near her father's chair. "I want to find the person who did this so I hope you understand. And I hope you'll trust me."

"I do not trust easily," Franco replied, his gaze on the roaring fire.

Blain didn't move. "Neither do I."

"Let's go," Rikki said, almost a plea.

Blain put his hands in the pockets of his jacket and followed her toward the side door to the garage.

When they were outside, he turned to her. "I know a threat when I hear one but I'm okay with that. But you need to understand something, Rikki."

She shivered in the wind. "And what's that?"

"I'm trying to protect you, so don't do anything stupid, okay?"

"I'll try not to," Rikki retorted, anger warming her now. "I plan to stay right here and visit my mother while I try to get some work done."

"Good plan." He looked sheepish. Swiping at his hair, he glanced over at her. "At least you have a nice place to stay hidden."

"Yes, a virtual paradise," she quipped. "A comfortable prison."

"Is that what it feels like?" he asked, his gaze tearing at her with his unspoken questions.

"It's always felt that way but I try not to complain. I have everything here I could ever possibly need, except freedom."

He drew closer and touched at her hair. "Hey, I know this has been tough and I'm sorry I've had to drill you. But I have a job to do."

Before she could pull away or respond, he leaned

closer, his eyes as dark as driftwood at midnight. "But you call me anytime, you hear? Anytime."

Then he dropped his hand and walked to his car.

And left her there shivering in the wind again.

SEVEN

Blain went back over the list Rikki had emailed him late yesterday. She had several high-profile clients in the area, including one of Blain's best friends, Alec Caldwell.

Deciding to be completely transparent with Alec, Blain dialed Alec's number and waited. When Alec came on the line, Blain went right into action. "Hey, man. Listen, I'm going over a client list for Regina Alvanetti and I noticed you're on it."

Alec chuckled. "And how are you today, Detective Kent?"

"Sorry," Blain said, rubbing the throbbing nerve in his forehead. "I can't talk much about it but I guess you're familiar with this case I'm working on, right?"

"Oh, yes. Aunt Hattie and her friends are all concerned they'll be next. They read the papers and listen to the news on a constant basis. Should I be worried?"

"I don't think so. This appears to be more of a calculated hit than a random robbery. But that is not for public knowledge, especially not for Aunt-Hattie-type public knowledge. But please reassure your aunt that she and her friends certainly need to be alert and cautious but to go about their regular activities."

"Got it," Alec replied. "I'm sorry about the woman who was murdered. And to answer your question, yes, Aunt Hattie and I consulted with Rikki when we were redoing some of the rooms at Caldwell House and Marla and I asked her to help with some sketches for our wedding décor. She sent her ideas free of charge and let our wedding planner take over from there since she wasn't sure she could make it back for the wedding. She's good at her job."

"This isn't about her job but more about anyone she's worked with," Blain said. "I'm going down a list of her clients, calling people to see if anyone might be upset with her."

"I can't answer to that but I can vouch for Rikki," Alec said. "She's a good person, Blain. She tries to keep her nose clean and she only comes back here to see her mother every so often. You probably know this already but Sonia has been ill for months now." He paused and then added, "By the way, maybe Rikki will be at the wedding. If she's up to it after what she's been through."

Blain glanced at the calendar. "You're getting married in two weeks. Wow, that's soon."

Alec went silent and then asked, "Uh…you will be there, right?"

Blain had to smile at Alec being a nervous groom. "I'm your best man, so yes, I'm planning on being there."

Although if Rikki Alvanetti came to the wedding, he'd be nervous, too. For all of them.

"Just checking," Alec replied. "I know how it works with you detective types."

"I'll be there," Blain said again, making a big red reminder on his calendar. "Got measured for my fancy suit and everything. Might even get my hair trimmed. And we have your bachelor party out at the camp next week. I'll surely be there."

"Nothing fancy," Alec replied. "And no tricks."

"Don't worry. Preacher will keep us on the straight and narrow."

"Always."

Blain went over his notes. "So can you think of anyone who'd want to hurt Rikki? Did you know her friend Tessa?"

"I didn't know Tessa," Alec said. "But I do know that Rikki's family has made some enemies over the years. But most of those people tend to undercut business deals or take away clients. I can't imagine any of them killing an innocent young woman."

"But if the hit man thought that woman was Regina Alvanetti?"

That's a whole 'nother matter," Alec said. "And a hard case to crack."

"Tell me about it," Blain retorted. "Thanks, Alec. I'll talk to you soon. Tell Marla I said hello."

He hung up and called a few more of the names on the list. Most of the clients only had good things to say about her so no one stood out.

But any one of these people could put on a good act for a stranger asking questions. She'd said she had a few appointments while she was here. He'd need to go over that schedule, too. She might need to cancel those meetings. Or he could go with her to all of them and observe. And protect her while he was at it.

He'd also do background checks on as many clients as he could. Even wealthy people could turn out to be criminals. Happened all the time.

He probably needed to talk to her neighbors again. People around that complex had to have heard something or seen something. He'd send one of the uniformed officers out again since Blain liked to keep a low profile.

But this was Millbrook, after all. Everyone knew everyone else. And that could hinder this case.

Deciding to call and check on Rikki, Blain walked outside to get some fresh air. He'd had the slashed tire replaced and he'd asked a couple of the patrolmen to watch the parking lot. Could be a random thing—kids out for a dare or maybe someone else who had a beef with him.

But Blain's gut told him that tire had been slashed deliberately. Was the killer still hanging around?

He gazed around the parking lot while he waited for Rikki to pick up.

"Hello."

Her low, husky voice took away some of the December chill. "Hi. It's Blain Kent. Just checking in. How are things going today?"

"My mother is awake," she said. "A good sign but she's still disoriented. Everything else is okay."

She didn't sound okay. "Are you sure?"

When she didn't speak, he let out a breath. "Rikki, I need you to be honest with me. I can't protect you if you keep hiding things from me."

"I'm not hiding anything," she said. "Tessa's boyfriend, Harry, called me this morning. I planned on telling you but I've been fielding client calls all morning, too."

"And you took the call from Harry?"

"Yes. I thought it was one of my client's numbers.

He just needed to talk." She went silent and then said, "He sounded sincerely upset but he told me he was out with clients the night she died. I believe him. He wants to bring her body back to Tallahassee for burial."

"We can work that out later," Blain said. "Did he happen to mention dear ol' Chad?"

"No. And neither did I."

"I'm coming out there," Blain said, deciding he might need to set up a monitor on her phone calls. Someone could have a GPS tracker on her phone. "I'm at the station but I'll be there in a few minutes."

"You don't need to do that," she said. "I'm okay, really. I didn't talk to him for long."

"I'm still coming out there." He hung up and got in his car. He didn't really need to see her face-to-face but he wanted to see her. Face-to-face.

Wishing he had more willpower, Blain wondered why this particular woman had to be the one who'd finally gotten to him. He'd rather deal with a deranged junkie than an Alvanetti, but this particular Alvanetti wasn't so horrible to be around.

Who was he to question? Preacher always said things happened in God's own time. Blain hit the gas pedal once he was outside the city limits and wondered why God had chosen to test him by forcing him to protect an Alvanetti from a killer.

A lot of irony in that.

Preacher also said God had a good sense of humor at times.

He found her in the stables.

"What are you doing?"

Rikki turned from saddling a gleaming black horse

that had to be worth more than he'd made in five years. She wore tall brown leather boots and riding pants with a silvery-colored down vest over a black turtleneck.

"I needed to get some air," she said. "I have two guards with me." She motioned to the shadows where two hulking figures stood.

Blain studied the two suits. "And they'll follow you on foot? Or do they have tricycles?"

She shook her head and smiled. "They have a golf cart."

And big guns.

He stared down the stalls. "Do you have an extra horse around here?"

She glanced over at him. "Why?"

"I'm riding with you."

"I don't think—"

"I said I'm riding with you and we're staying near the corral."

She motioned again and a groom materialized from yet another shadowy corner. After asking the young man to saddle Rambo, she turned back to Blain. "I hope you know *how* to ride, Detective."

"I do."

It had been a while but it had to be like riding a bike. Only a horse named Rambo couldn't be docile.

Blain pushed away his trepidations and studied the stables. "It's too dark in here. Don't come out here at night even with your two buddies."

"I won't."

She checked her horse, cooing. "Daisy, this is Detective Blain Kent. He can be intimidating and grumpy but don't let that fool you. He's actually a nice person."

The black mare shook her mane and eyed Blain with a feminine regard.

He was getting more and more nervous by the minute. And he didn't do nervous. But she was deliberately putting herself in danger by going out into the open. Even iron gates and strong fences couldn't stop a bullet. Which is why he'd have to be on alert while she took some air.

When the young groom came around the corner with a giant red roan stallion, Blain stood back to stare. "Really?"

"Really," she said with a grin. "He's as tame as a kitten."

"Right." He wagged a finger at her. "If I get thrown—"

"We'll load you onto the golf cart."

Blain wouldn't cower. She'd like that. If getting on this giant beast meant he could watch out for her then he'd do it.

He just hoped they'd be safe. If anything happened to her on his watch, her father would have Blain shot on the spot.

Rikki glanced back at the man riding Rambo.

Maybe she shouldn't have saddled Blain on her brother's favorite stallion but she figured the detective needed a horse to match his own dominating personality. And he did look good sitting there with a certain ease that probably belied his initial concerns.

"How you doing?" she called, aware of the golf cart keeping a discreet distance behind them. Although they were circling the enclosed pasture near the stables, at least she was out getting some fresh air.

Blain nudged Rambo along beside her. "I'm fine. Never better. That wind off the water is cold and I'm sure I'll be so sore tomorrow I won't be able to walk. Plus, I'm trying to see through the trees past that elaborate fence, just in case someone might be out there waiting to shoot at you."

Rikki's heart did that little lurch. The pang of horror and fear that hit her each time she thought about Tessa settled over her like a fog. "I thought getting out of the house might help but…it's always there. The image of my friend laying there, the blood, the vacant stare in her eyes." She pulled Daisy up underneath a towering live oak and dismounted. "You sure are a buzzkill, Detective."

He followed her and tied the horses on a low hanging branch of the big tree. "I'm sorry but I have to keep reminding you that this isn't over."

Rikki turned away from him. Out here away from the shoreline, the wind whipped against the trees in a mournful wail that only reminded her of how close to that edge of hysteria she'd been over the last few days. She should have stayed inside with her mother but Franco was home and roaming around like a lost puppy. She didn't know what to say to her father.

"I understand but I'm not comfortable in this house."

"Hey." Blain turned her around, his eyes like a dark ocean. "I don't want the same thing to happen to you. I believe you don't know who killed Tessa but we don't know why someone came after you that same night. So, yes…you're still in danger."

Rikki glanced back to where the golf cart had stopped by a patch of scrub oaks near the back of the big barn. "I know and I feel guilty, trying to do normal things. I think I'm still in shock." She glanced up at Blain. He stood a foot or so away but his expression seemed so intimate and close. Too intimate. Too close.

Rikki wanted to run into his arms and let his warmth surround her. Instead, she stared out over the pasture. "I love riding. I was pretty good in the junior rodeo competition when I was younger."

Blain's dark expression softened. "You...a rodeo star?"

"Me," she said, those good memories clouding out the sad ones. "I won the barrel-racing competition three years in a row and I finaled in calf and goat roping."

"Goat roping?" His smile warmed her to her toes. "Wow, you're just full of surprises."

Rikki wondered if that had been meant as a compliment or a condemnation. "But you don't like surprises, right?"

He gave her a steady blue-eyed stare. "I like good surprises. What I don't like is duplicity and...insincerity."

"Wow, you're just full of gloom."

"I am," he said. "You know, I'm marine all the way. I was an MP toward the end of my last deployment. So call me a skeptic but I've seen the worst of people."

She should have known he was a warrior. He carried himself in that way, all gung ho and tough, never willing to back down. "Do you ever look for the best first?"

"No," he said. "Or at least, I never did before."

Rikki watched him. He didn't keep his gaze fixed on any one thing. He was always checking, always scanning the horizon as if he were still in warrior mode. But the way he'd said that gave her hope that he might be slowly coming around on things. That he might be able to look past her name and see her heart.

"So you're a hero," she said, thinking the layers beneath that dark gaze were deep. She'd love to explore those layers, maybe peel back a few barriers.

"Some might say that." He turned and glanced back at the two guards. "But not every soldier is a hero."

Rikki moved to block him and force him to look at her. "And not every Alvanetti is a criminal."

"Duly noted," he said. Then he leaned close. "You certainly don't look like a criminal to me."

Rikki could feel the heat from his body. If she moved a few inches closer, she could reach out and kiss Blain. He must have felt the same way. She saw a flare of awareness in his eyes and then—

And then the echo of a gun blast shattered the countryside and scared the horses into a frenzied dance. Blain did pull her close. He grabbed her and whirled her around behind the trunk of the big tree and held her there, his weapon trained on the woods.

EIGHT

Blain heard another shot and watched as one of the guards hit the ground. The other one managed to get behind the golf cart.

"I knew this was a bad idea," he said, his hand holding Rikki's head. "You're too exposed out here."

"The horses." She tried to turn but Blain held her tight.

"They'll be okay. You need to stay down."

Daisy decided she didn't like the situation. She broke loose and took off toward the stables.

Rambo whinnied and snorted, his hoofs kicking dirt as if ready for battle.

"They've hit one of your men," Blain said. He watched the woods past the fence line. Someone had to be up in a tree with a high-powered rifle.

Rikki gulped a breath, her gaze on the golf cart. "You're right. Bad idea. I thought I'd be safe here."

"You'd think but someone is determined."

He leaned around the tree. His Glock wouldn't do much except hold them off until he could come up with a plan.

The other guard motioned to him and pointed toward a stand of tall pines just past the fence line. Blain studied the woods and saw a glint, just a quick blink but enough that Blain got a bead on the shooter. Not enough to move in, but at least a location.

Had someone been waiting for such an opportunity?

He held Rikki and nodded. "Okay, I think I know where they're coming from but I need you to stay behind this tree for a minute."

"And what are you going to do?"

"I'm going to cover your man who has a military-grade machine gun. And I'm hoping he'll cover us until I can get you back to the stables."

She nodded, her eyes wide. "Okay."

Blain nodded to the guard and managed to sign what he needed. "Call for reinforcements," he mouthed.

The guard pulled out a walkie-talkie and spoke into it.

Blain waited until the call had gone out then pushed Rikki behind him. "If that doesn't work or no one comes soon, I'm gonna put you on Rambo and send you home."

"Not without you," she said.

"We'll argue about that later," he replied.

Then he leaned out from behind the tree and was rewarded with a sharp ping that hit the trunk and scattered bark six inches from his head. Blain returned fire and so did the guard.

The woods went silent after that.

"He's not going to give up," Blain said. "If we do get reinforcements, they could get shot, too." He pulled out his phone. "I'll have to call in the sheriff's department and give them a location of the shooter or we could be pinned down all day."

Blain had to make the call since they were outside the city limits, but his dad would hear that call on the scanner he still kept active by his recliner. Sam Kent might be retired but once a sheriff, always a sheriff.

"I'm sorry, Blain," she said, her voice low.

"For what?"

"For not listening to you. For insisting on leaving the house."

He gave her a forgiving glance. "And I'm sorry for not making you stay inside. So there, we're even."

He tried to move again and almost got hit.

"Okay, he's settling in." Blain pulled Rikki down beside him behind the three-foot tree trunk. "Which means we will, too."

She shivered. "Maybe we should send Rambo back. It's not that far. He knows the way and besides, you kept me so close to the stables, I could make a run for it, too."

"Daisy has sent out one alert, arriving without a rider," he said. "Rambo seems okay. And you are not going anywhere, understand?"

"My brother won't like that I took out his horse."

"Your brother? This horse belongs to your brother?"

"Yes."

"Great."

She shivered again and Blain tugged her into his arms to warm her. "You're determined to drive me nuts, aren't you?"

She looked down at her boots. "If you get me back home, I'll be a model citizen from here on out."

"Right." He nuzzled her hair and inhaled the spicy scent that always seemed to surround her. "We'll get you out of this, one way or another, Rikki."

* * *

An hour later, the whole thing was over.

Rikki stood near the stables and held back yet more tears. One of her father's most trusted guards was dead. The other one was shaken but he'd managed to hold off the shooter until several other bodyguards found them and got Rikki and that guard into an SUV with bullet-proof windows.

While she'd watched Blain out the window trying to cover them.

"We can't leave him," she told the driver. She could hear gunshots echoing over the woods.

"I got my orders from your father," the man shouted.

"Then stop and let me out," she screamed, her hand on the door.

The men looked at each other and then back to Rikki. "We have our orders."

"I will not go unless you help Detective Kent, too," she said. "And if I get out and get shot, you'll have to explain that."

They circled back for Blain. He managed to send Rambo home and then he hopped in beside her without a word. So much for going for a peaceful horseback ride.

By the time they arrived back at the house, her brother Santo was waiting, raging at anyone who'd listen.

"You are something, you know that?" he shouted to Rikki before she could approach Blain. "I get a call that it was like a war zone out here. What's the deal with you, Rikki?"

Blain managed to materialize beside her. "The deal is that your sister is being stalked by a killer," he said, pulling Rikki behind him. "Why won't anyone around here take that seriously?"

"Then why did she leave the house?" Santo asked, his dark eyes flashing fire. He was a younger version of their father but he had not married a woman like her mother. His own wife hated him. So he was always growling and raging at someone.

Before Rikki could speak, Blain put out his hand. "It's my fault. I... I told her I'd go with her and keep her safe."

"Well, you didn't do a very good job," Santo said, pointing a finger at Blain. "Typical of the Millbrook Police Department." He nodded toward the hired help. "This is why we have to pay people to protect us."

Rikki came around Blain. She wanted to tell her brother they had to hire guards because they might be involved in criminal activities. But she didn't say that since she didn't have any proof.

"He's doing everything in his power," she told Santo. "I wanted to go for a ride and he felt obligated to go with me."

Santo's scowl grew. "Aren't you two just all cozy?"

"Enough."

They all turned to find her father standing there with a man Rikki recognized as the former sheriff. She couldn't remember his name since she'd avoided any friend of her father's whenever she was in this house. But he looked familiar.

Blain and Santo both glanced toward her father.

"Let them alone," Franco said. "Rikki, go inside and calm down."

Santo shut up but he stood with his hands on his hips.

Blain stared at the sheriff. "Sir."

The older man looked as angry as her father and brother. "We caught the shooter. He's being held in the county jail if you want a go at him."

"I do want a go at him," Blain said, his expression grim.

Her father stepped forward. "Rikki, do you remember Sheriff Kent?"

"I believe so." Rikki looked at the sheriff and then she looked at Blain. "Kent?"

"He's my father," Blain said, his tone level and full of resentment.

"Your father." She couldn't believe this but it made sense now. "I see I'm not the only one who's been keeping secrets." Giving Blain one last glance, she turned toward the house.

She should have known she didn't need to trust a determined detective.

An hour later, Blain found Rikki in the kitchen staring at the microwave. When she heard him come in, she glanced up at him and then opened the microwave to pull out a bowl of soup.

"Rikki—"

"I have to take this to my mother," she said. "Daphne had to run some errands."

He braced his hands against the granite counter. "I'll wait for you, then."

"You don't need to do that."

"I'll be here, waiting," he said.

She ignored him and carried a tray down the long hallway toward the back of the house.

Blain stood in front of the fireplace. The afternoon had turned chilly and windy and all he wanted was a hot shower and his own bowl of soup before he went to sleep on his couch. But it would be hours before he could get any sleep.

When he heard a door slamming, Blain turned to find his father with Franco and Santo Alvanetti. The three men each gave him a pointed stare.

"I'm going to check on Mama," Santo said, his black-eyed frown clearly blaming Blain for this latest turn of events.

"Would you and your son like something to drink, maybe some coffee?" Franco asked Sam after Santo stalked away.

"I'm fine," Blain said, eyeing the hallway to the other wing of the house. He hoped Santo didn't start in on Rikki.

"And I have to go," Sam said. "I'm sure my son will want to get to the sheriff substation to question our shooter. Sorry about your man, Franco."

Franco nodded. "Comes with the territory."

Blain wanted to punch the wall. The territory? A way of life that involved illegal activities and possible killings—and blaming his only daughter for being in the wrong place at the wrong time?

Any reservations he'd had about helping Rikki dissolved right along with the ash floating up from the fire. No wonder the woman had gotten away and no wonder she couldn't trust anyone.

Especially anyone like him.

He glanced toward the hallway again then looked at his father. Sam stared at him with that smug, condescending expression he remembered so well, growing up.

"I'm going," Blain announced to the room. He'd talk

to Rikki later. "Sorry about what happened, Mr. Alvanetti. But maybe we can get the shooter to talk."

Franco's frown deepened into a craggy rock face. "If you don't make him talk, I will."

Blain shook his head and pinched his nose with two fingers. "Getting a suspect to talk is my job, Mr. Alvanetti. Not yours."

"I'll sit in, if my son will allow me," Sam said.

Blain started for the door. "Your jurisdiction, your call."

Franco chuckled at that. "I knew who you were the day you showed up here," he said to Blain. "But you're different from Sam here."

Blain looked from Franco to his father. "Yeah, I am." Then he turned and left the room.

"Mama, you need to eat some soup," Rikki said, her mind in turmoil. She wanted to get away from here, to leave and never come back but Sonia needed her. And today of all days, her mother was lucid and willing to sit up.

"I'm not that hungry," Sonia said, a skinny hand patting her bun.

"But you're sitting up today," Rikki replied, holding the tray so her mother wouldn't tip the hot soup over on herself. "That's a good sign."

Pebble ambled into the bedroom and jumped on her mother's bed. Sonia giggled and reached out a hand to pet the cat.

Santo stomped into the room. "Hey, Mama. I see you're wearing your pretty bed jacket."

Sonia's smile widened. "Santo, what are you doing here? Shouldn't you be at work?"

Santo glared at Rikki and then gave Sonia a kiss on the cheek. Pebble protested and hissed then leaped off the bed. "I'm just checking up on y'all. I worry."

Rikki heard the condemnation in that statement. She would never understand why her best friend being killed had somehow brought more shame on this family than any of her brothers' or even her father's shenanigans. Did they all know something she wasn't aware of?

"Everyone here is fine," Sonia said. She obediently took a spoonful of soup. "Rikki is home for Christmas, you know. I'm gonna get out of this bed and we'll bake and decorate and listen to Christmas music, won't we Rikki-pie?"

Rikki swallowed the lump in her throat and nodded. "We sure will, Mama. But right now, you need to take your medicine and rest. You did pretty good on the soup."

"I am a bit tired," Sonia replied. She winked at her son. "Y'all are so darlin', always fussing over me and checking on me. I'll be better tomorrow."

"Yes, you will," Rikki said, praying for that to be so.

Her sweet mother said this almost every day or at least on her good days. Today was a good day for Sonia even while it had turned out to be a bad day for everyone else.

Rikki cleaned up her mother and after moving the tray she gave Sonia a kiss. "I'm going to the kitchen. Santo is still here."

Her brother gave her another look of dismissal. "And I'll always be right here."

And another biting comment that hit Rikki right through the heart. She hoped Blain had left by now. She wasn't ready to deal with him again today.

His father was a retired sheriff. The man who used to hang around her father like a puppy, always smiling and waiting for handouts. How could she have forgotten so soon?

But she reminded herself that she'd tried to avoid her father's cronies and she'd only seen the imposing sheriff from a distance most days.

But she knew he must have taken kickbacks and bribes from her father since he hadn't made any arrests when she was growing up. It had been obvious today that Sam Kent and his son didn't see eye to eye.

Blain was so different from most of the men she knew. He was good. She could see that. So why did it hurt so much to know he hadn't told her who his father was? Especially when he'd criticized her for withholding her real identity from him?

No wonder he hated her family. His father and her father, together, doing who knew what. She and Blain had grown up in much the same way, but on different sides of the fence. It was enough to make her sick to her stomach.

But when she thought about how he'd held her there by the old oak, she had to close her eyes and take a breath. He'd told her he'd get her out of this, one way or another. Rikki didn't want Blain to get killed trying to save her.

When she got to the kitchen, that room and the big adjoining den were both empty. Blain and his father must have left. Where was Daphne? That nurse didn't do nearly the job that Peggy did.

And where was her father?

The intercom buzzed while she was giving Pebble a

treat. Thinking it might be Santo or her mother, Rikki answered. "Yes?"

"Come into my office," Franco said. "We need to talk."

Rikki took a calming breath. "I'll be right there, Papa."

She figured she was about to get a lecture.

Well, she could handle it for her mother's sake.

She would have to handle all of this and survive so she could leave again, one way or another. After all, she'd been doing that for years now.

Running away.

Always running away.

NINE

Rikki knocked on the double doors to her father's study and steeled herself against his wrath. She'd get through this and then she'd go and sit with her mother since Santo had finally left.

"Come in."

She opened the doors and saw her father standing by the mantel staring into the fireplace. This place had several fireplaces and usually they were all decorated for the holidays. But without her mother's organized supervision, no one had bothered bringing out the rest of the decorations. Maybe she could do that, to keep herself busy.

After she shut the door, Franco turned around and motioned to the sitting area by the fire. "I have coffee and hot tea if you'd like any." He pointed to the coffee table. "And some sandwiches. You need to eat."

Wondering why her father was being so solicitous, Rikki shook her head. "I'm not hungry but thank you."

Franco finally sat down and took up his cup of coffee. "I'm sorry for the things your brother said to you earlier."

"Really?" Shocked, Rikki decided maybe she did

need some hot tea, after all. "I've had the feeling since I've been home that nothing I've done has pleased any of you."

"You're wrong on that," Franco said, lowering his head. "Listen, I've been angry at you for a long time. First, you marry that boy—"

"I loved him."

"You used him to get away from me."

Rikki's heart cracked at that comment. "No, I loved Drake. We wanted to have a life together but…you had him killed."

Her father lifted his head, his eyes red-rimmed and fatigued. "What are you talking about?"

"You can tell me the truth," she said. "I know you had him killed but everyone thinks it was an accident. I had to leave after that, Papa. I… I couldn't stay here. And I'll leave again as soon as this is over."

Franco sat his coffee cup down so hard the rich liquid slapped over the sides. "I did not have Drake Allen killed." He pushed a hand down his face. "The boy was drunk that night, Regina. He liked to party when you thought he was working. He ran off the road and died in a car crash. That is the truth."

She'd heard that same story over and over. But she'd never believe it. "Why did you ask me to come in here?"

Her father stared at her, his eyes still misty. "You are so like your mother. She wanted us to make peace, you and me. I want that but I get so angry and I lash out and I hurt people."

"Atonement, Papa? Is that what this is about? You want me to forgive you in case Mama dies?"

"She will not die," Franco said. "She can't die."

And then Rikki saw it there in her father's old eyes. Fear.

Franco Alvanetti was afraid of the one thing he couldn't control. Losing his wife.

Rikki got up, her own eyes burning. "She's getting better and I'll stay to make sure she does."

Then she turned and left the room, her heart splitting as she waged anger and bitterness against acceptance and forgiveness.

Blain came out of the interrogation room located in the back of the district substation not far from the Alvanetti estate. The SWAT and K-9 teams had cornered the shooter in the woods near the state park that ran along the bay.

That meant television cameras and reporters pushing microphones in his face. People wanted answers and Blain had none to give. Yet.

Blain had gone in with a deputy to question John Darty. Fun name for a fun criminal.

"You're a piece of work, Darty," Blain said by way of a greeting. "Drug charges, stolen property, petty crimes. Seems you just got out and now you'll be going right back in."

"I want a lawyer."

The man was trained in weaponry, courtesy of the United States Army. As Blain had told Rikki, not every soldier was a hero. This soldier had gone quiet and now refused to speak. Not surprising. Whoever had sent him would probably try to kill him if he talked, in or out of a jailhouse.

"Think long and hard about telling us who hired

you," he told the fidgety man. "We can help you now but once you go back inside, it might be too late."

Sam Kent was waiting for Blain in the conference room.

"Things sure have changed since my day," his father said, glancing around. "Districts, SWAT teams, even a Major Crimes Unit. Used to be just a sheriff and several deputies."

"This county has become more populated over the last decade, Dad. Not to mention having advanced technology."

"Job never gets any easier," Sam said on a grunt. "What did our guest reveal?"

"Not much," Blain said. "Didn't you listen in?"

"Nope." Sam threw his disposable cup in the trash. "I thought I'd let you do your thing."

"My thing didn't work." Surprised at how docile his usually ornery father seemed, Blain gave Sam the once-over. "Hey, you feeling okay?"

Sam's eyebrows winged up like an eagle in flight. "Fine as a fiddle, thank you."

Blain took a good look at his dad. Sam looked tired. He'd lost weight. Not daring to ask any more questions, Blain decided his cagey father could be as tight-lipped as a career criminal at times.

So he tried another method. "What do you think?"

"About what?" Sam asked.

"This case." Blain ran a hand over his hair. "I think Regina Alvanetti is being targeted for a reason and I've got a feeling someone is after her because they think she knows something or she saw something."

"I agree," Sam said, lowering his voice. "You might consider her family. Lots of hidden agendas going on."

Surprised yet again, Blain gave his father a thoughtful stare. "Do you know something I need to know?"

Sam grinned. "I know a lot of things I've never talked about but I always knew that one day some of those things would float to the surface."

Aggravation slapped at Blain, making him snap. "I'm not sure what you're trying to say."

"Sonia," his father whispered. "Sonia knows more secrets than anyone else."

"But she's ill," Blain replied. "No way I can get to her. She's barely able to get out of bed."

"But you can get to the daughter," Sam said. "That woman trusts you and trust from an Alvanetti is a rare thing."

"She might not trust me now," Blain admitted. "I didn't tell her that I'm your son."

"I kind of gathered that," Sam said. "She'll get past that because she knows you're on her side."

Blain understood but he didn't think Rikki would appreciate him trying to get past her to her mother. "So I get to Sonia through Rikki?"

"Yep." His dad gave him a crystal-eyed stare. "You'll figure it out."

A dozen mixed emotions whirled through Blain's system. "Why are you changing your tune?"

Sam shot him a long stare and then waved his hand in the air. "Like you said, this whole county has changed over the last few years. You need to understand, the Alvanetti family has changed, too. A new guard has taken over and I've got a feeling what I saw in my day is tame compared to what could be going on now."

Blain wanted to ask his father what exactly he was trying to say but decided he'd had enough shocks for one day. This conversation was the first decent one he'd had with his father in a long time. And yet, he didn't have a clue what was being said.

"Hey, Dad," he called after his father. "What made *you* change?"

Sam stopped, one hand on the glass doors to the parking lot. "Watching you today."

Then he turned and stomped out the door.

"I've got to start back over from square one."

Blain sat back in his chair and stared out at the water. It was raining and cold but he sat with Alec and Preacher out on the screened porch of the camp house they all owned together. An electric heater buzzed nearby and the pizza boxes were now almost empty.

Alec Caldwell gave Blain a blank stare. "Sounds as if you got more information from your old man than you did from this suspect."

"Yep." Without giving away any details, Blain had told his friends what was common knowledge since it had been blasted all over the airwaves. He'd also told them about the sudden change in his father. "I can't decide where my dad fits in."

Rory Sanderson stood up, his hands in the deep pockets of his fleece jacket. "Your dad's getting on in years, Blain. Maybe he's trying to make amends before it's too late."

"I wish he'd just level with me," Blain said. "I don't need amends right now. I need cold, hard facts."

Rory shot Alec a glance. "He's a lawman like you. Maybe he can't divulge everything he's seen or heard."

"He could be trying to warn you and protect you," Alec offered. "Sure he's stubborn and hard-edged but he loves you. I'd think there was a lot he shielded you and your mother from when he was in charge."

Alec had never known his own dad and because his mother, Vivian, had mourned her military husband's death, she'd been emotionally distant toward Alec. Blain needed to take that into consideration.

"I guess so. I mean, in spite of our differences he's never once condemned me for anything I've done. Criticized my methods but he never told me I shouldn't do something. He didn't try to talk me out of joining the marines and he didn't even blink when I came home and joined the police force."

"And so he's not saying anything to condemn you now, either," Rory added. He sat back down. "I'll be praying for both of your tonight, that's for sure."

Blain lifted his soft drink in a salute. "Without ceasing."

"And what about Rikki?" Alec asked.

Blain wasn't sure how to respond. She was not taking his calls. "I don't know. I have to find out who's behind this before she gets killed. That's my job."

"We don't want her to get killed," Alec said. "I was asking more along the lines of what about how you *feel* about Rikki?"

Blain lowered his gaze and studied the plastic cup in his hand. "I don't know about that, either. She's a complicated subject."

Rory grinned. "A dangerous subject. You might need to walk away once you're done with this case."

"Worried about me, Preacher?"

"Nope." Rory found a piece of cold pizza. "Just… bemused. I haven't seen you so besotted before."

"Who says I'm besotted?"

Alec laughed. "Rikki is a beautiful woman. Mysterious and under pressure right now. You're one of the good guys."

"Your point?"

"It all adds up to trouble," Alec finished. "She'll turn to you and you'll do the right thing. Just be careful."

"I thought you had already vouched for her," Blain said.

"I did on a professional basis. And I like Rikki. But you've always avoided getting tangled in a relationship so it's different seeing you so tangled up in this one."

Blain got up and tossed his cup in the trash. "I kind of miss Hunter. The Okie doesn't badger me the way you two do." He shrugged. "He must be deep undercover. He's not returning my calls."

"Hunter *is* on assignment," Rory replied. "I guess I'd better throw in a prayer for him, too. Being a private eye is a whole new set of concerns." He chuckled. "Especially when Hunter's idea of finding answers is to inflict physical pain."

"Several concerns," Alec retorted. "But he was special ops. He does that thing—"

"Slips around without a sound?" Rory asked, grinning.

Alec glanced back over his shoulder. "Yeah, that thing."

"He'll show up, hopefully for your wedding," Rory said, glancing at Alec.

"I hope my best man shows up, too," Alec quipped, grinning at Blain.

"I'll be there, okay." Blain decided he'd had enough. "I'm beat. Think I'll head home."

Rory lifted his hand. "Hey, we didn't mean to get too personal."

Alec chimed in. "It's your business, buddy. I should know to trust you since you're good at your job."

Blain nodded. "I know you mean well. But you both need to remember something about me. I may be a bit besotted, but I'm not stupid."

Rory bobbed his head. "And stay not stupid, okay?"

"Always."

He waved to them and headed down to the open garage underneath the house on stilts. He wasn't stupid but he had to make sure Rikki was all right. Did that make him crazy?

Probably.

He got his phone out and hit her number. He didn't like the way they'd left things. They'd been through a lot together since the night he'd seen her on the boardwalk.

And she had to still be reeling from what had happened this morning. He told himself checking on her was the right thing to do.

Just in case she needed someone to talk to tonight.

Rikki wished she had someone to talk to. She'd been so tired by the day's events she'd come to her room right after dinner, taken a hot shower and was now trying to read. Pebble lay spread out in a long cat stretch by her feet. Rikki had tried telling her tale to the cat, but Pebble had become so bored he'd taken to licking his paws and grooming himself.

A sure sign of total disregard.

Her mother, always her first source and the best confidante a girl could have, was sleeping. And even if she were awake, Rikki couldn't bother her mother when she was so sick. If Sonia knew what was going on, she's worry even more.

But then, Sonia Alvanetti never seemed to worry about anything. Her faith held tight against so many things.

Rikki thought of Tessa. Her best friend. Gone. They'd never get to stay up late again, eating chocolate and watching romantic comedies. No more going shopping at cluttered boutiques and having cheesecake for dessert. No more trips to places all over the south and sometimes out of the country. No more quiet conversations about the state of their constant need to find true love.

Who do I have now?

Sonia would say Rikki had the Lord. And she knew that. Rikki had certainly done her share of praying lately. The faith her mother had instilled in her had helped her through this past week.

And you have Blain.

No, she'd thought she had Blain but after all of his bluster about her being honest, he'd withheld one important thing from her. His father's career as a county sheriff.

Why? Was he as angry at his father as she wanted to be with hers?

Her cell buzzed, causing her to toss aside the book she'd been trying to read. Pushing at the bed covers, she stared at the caller ID.

Blain.

She almost threw the phone across the room but Rikki wondered if something else had happened. It was getting late so why else would he call?

She tapped the screen. "Yes?"

"I know you're angry—"

"You don't know me at all."

"Look, Rikki, it's complicated."

"I've heard that excuse before."

"We need to talk but not over the phone."

Did he think her cell was bugged?

Just the thought scared Rikki and made her angry all over again.

"I can't leave," she reminded him. "Not even to go out and get some fresh air."

"I know. And it's better if I don't come out there."

"So we can't talk to each other. That might be for the best, don't you think?"

She ended the call, which should have brought her a certain measure of satisfaction. Instead, Rikki curled up in her bed and stared at the sliver of the moon she saw caught between the scurrying clouds high up in the winter sky.

She was still all alone.

TEN

Blain stared at the phone for a few minutes.

He guessed he deserved a hang-up or two. He hadn't trusted Rikki in the beginning and now that he did trust her, now that he wanted to help her and get to know her and see her, she'd turned on him.

Or maybe she'd never trusted him from the start.

Alvanetti. She was an Alvanetti. He needed to re-adjust his way of thinking and stick to the facts. So instead of calling her back, he headed to the police station.

He'd talk to someone else familiar with this case.

The suspect.

By the time he got to the station, a slow cold rain had set in. A winter chill covered the night. Before he could get in out of the rain, a figure stepped out of the shadows.

"Detective, got a minute?"

Blain turned to find Santo Alvanetti standing there in an expensive-looking black wool coat.

"Can I help you, Mr. Alvanetti?" Blain asked, impatient to get to the suspect. And surprised to see Rikki's hostile brother here.

Santo's dark scowl twisted around his face. "I'd like to talk to you, yes."

"Come in," Blain said. He might be able to get inside Santo's head and see if Rikki's brother could shed some light on things. But an Alvanetti being in such close proximity to the shooter they'd captured earlier today didn't set well with Blain. Santo could be here trying to warn that man to stay quiet or else.

Blain took Santo into a small conference room and shut the door. "Would you like something to drink?"

"No." Santo took off his coat and pushed his hand through his dark hair. "I'm worried about my family."

Blain sat down. "Yes, I could tell that this morning."

Santo's scowl went even blacker. "You think I was cruel to my sister?"

"You could say that. You and your father seem to like to shift blame."

Santo leaned forward and tapped a finger on the table. "My father and I have no involvement in this. We have ways of doing our own investigations, though."

"Don't interfere with this case," Blain said. "You'll regret it."

"Don't threaten me," Santo said. "You'll regret it."

Blain leaned back and stared him down. "Why are you here?"

"I don't like that someone managed to shoot at my sister and kill one of my men." He shrugged. "Our place out on the lake has always been a haven of sorts."

"Yeah, like impenetrable."

"But someone breached it today," Santo said, his dark face etched in anger and weariness.

"Nobody likes that." Blain got out his pocket notebook. "Mind if I take notes?"

"Please do," Santo replied. "I have nothing to hide."

Blain let that go on by for now. "Do you have any ideas on who might be after Rikki?"

"Here's what I know," Santo said. "We run a legitimate business. We import antiques and estate jewelry and run a vast warehouse and online site. Someone out there must want something and they think Rikki has that something."

"But she doesn't use your services, right?"

Santo stared down at the table. "Yes and no. She uses some warehouses in Miami and Tallahassee and some of the pieces she buys could have possibly been shipped through our site."

"Does she know this?"

"No and she has no reason to know this. And I'd like to keep it that way. Rikki is stubborn and smart and proud. We can't control who orders what from us or how it ships once it's out there in various establishments and venues. But if someone smuggled something into a shipment and she received it, she could be in danger. Does that make sense?"

"Yes." Blain jotted notes. "Are you willing to let me go over your shipment records? I'd have to ask her about her clients again and also about her vendors."

Santo stood. "I don't mind helping you find this criminal. But I want it clear—our family is clean now. I have children, Detective. I'm not like my father. I just need you to know that. I won't be harassed over this."

Blain didn't plan on harassing Santo but he would question him over and over if needed. "Why were you so angry at Rikki this morning?"

"Lots going on. My brother Victor's been calling,

wanting answers, too. Or at least, he called earlier today. Now I can't get him to return my calls."

"He needs to call us. We've tried to find him and he seems to be just as elusive as the victim's missing brother."

"Victor keeps to himself," Santo said. "I told him what I knew but he was fishing for information. Probably concerned about the bank accounts."

"Should he be concerned?" Blain asked.

A blank expression dropped down across Santo's olive-skinned face. "Yes, since he hasn't contributed to the family coffers a lot."

"Are *you* worried about money?"

Santo tugged on his coat. "I'd had a bad morning and as I told you, I won't be harassed over this. I've got enough to deal with right now. My wife left me." With that, he shook Blain's hand and walked to the door. "Don't disappoint me, Detective. Our family doesn't need this right now. Make it go away."

Blain stared after Santo, resenting how the entire family managed to issue orders left and right. Santo Alvanetti seemed like a hard man to deal with, a man who could be trying to cover his own secrets. Maybe his wife had had enough, too. Had Santo taken the company to a new level—a legitimate business level? Or had he somehow put everyone he loved in danger?

If so, he could be playing the locals the way his father always had. But Blain wasn't one to get played. He tried calling Hunter Lawson again. Hunter could dig into these types of things in a discreet way.

After leaving Hunter a message, he put his notebook away and started for the door.

His phone buzzed.

"What now?"

When he saw Rikki's number, he spun around and went back into the conference room. "Hello."

"Blain, my father's not home. He left a while ago and he's not home. One of the guards just let me know. He didn't take anyone with him and he hasn't checked in. I'm really worried."

"I'm on my way." He didn't stop to consider she could have called someone from the sheriff's office. He didn't stop to consider anything except that he needed to help Rikki.

His friends' warnings might be right.

He could be in way over his head.

Rikki wondered how much more she'd have to deal with. Where was Franco? Her father never left without a driver. He rarely drove himself anywhere. Why start now?

She'd left messages with her brother Santo, thinking maybe Papa had gone to the warehouse out near the river. But Santo wasn't answering his phone.

She paced the den in sweatpants and a big sweater. After checking on her mother and telling Peggy what was going on, she'd called Blain. Although some of the guards had gone to look for Franco, Rikki's heart told her to alert Blain since this was just too much of a coincidence after this morning.

Had the same people who were after her tried to take her father?

She heard the door swinging open and turned from the fire to find Blain hurrying up the hallway.

He stopped, his eyes meeting hers. "Hi."

"Hi." Rikki didn't think. She ran into his arms. "I'm

so worried. I... I shouldn't have called you but... I trust you."

There. She'd admitted it. In spite of the chasm that seemed to stretch between them, she did trust Blain. But she had to add one other thing. "And I think my father trusts you, too."

"It's okay," he said, standing back, his hands on her elbows. "Could be nothing or it could be important, considering everything that's happened so far."

She stepped back. "That's what I was thinking. So what can we do?"

"I've alerted the sheriff's department and I've got a couple of patrols searching the roads between here and town. Did your father indicate where he might be going?"

"No. I didn't even know he'd left." She shook her head. "We actually had a good talk this afternoon and then after he had dinner, he went back to his office. I sat with my mother for a while and then went to my room to read."

"Who's with her now?"

"Peggy, her night nurse."

"Trustworthy?"

"You had her vetted. What do you think?"

"I need to know what you think."

"Peggy is solid. She's one of the best people I know."

"Okay. Let's start in your father's office. Maybe he got a call or left some notes."

"I'll take you in there."

Blain followed her down the hall to her father's big study on the opposite side of the house from the bedroom wing. The curtains were open to a view of the boat dock and the water beyond. A lone security light shimmered in the rain.

Blain went to the glass doors centered between the windows. "Locked tight. No sign of forced entry."

"That rules out abduction," Rikki said, relief washing over her. "He could have gone to the warehouse but he would have let someone drive him."

"So we think he left on his own. Unless someone called him and forced him to leave alone."

Her heart hit hard again, ramping up her pulse. "I'm afraid he was involved in an accident." She started searching her father's desk. "Blain, what if...if he's hurt or worse?"

"Hey, we'll figure it out," he said, coming to help her. "I'll talk to the guards and see if they know what time he left."

"It had to have been after eight," she said, her hand going over the stack of papers near the phone. "But it's past ten now and he's usually in bed around nine thirty. I checked his room next to my mother's. His bed is still made."

"Let's keep looking," Blain said.

Rikki lifted invoices and antique magazines, a stack of opened mail and several Christmas cards.

Then she saw a scribbled note that contained one word. *Victor.*

"Your brother?"

Rikki nodded, noticing Blain's interest. "He rarely calls. He's been in Europe for years and...he and my father are not close anymore."

"Do you think he called your father?"

"Maybe. We've been trying to let him know about mother's condition." She kept glancing over the papers.

"If Victor called, he could be in trouble or he could have run out of money. He hasn't bothered to call and check on our mother very often, either." Victor wasn't the worrying type unless it involved him.

"I'll see what else I can find out about Victor's whereabouts," Blain said. "Meantime, I'll check with the guards and then I'm going out to search for your father myself."

"I'm going with you," Rikki said. At his disapproving look, she added, "I can't sit here worrying, Blain."

"This could be another bad idea," Blain said as they hurried out of the house. "Why don't you listen to me and stay here?"

"I'm too upset," Rikki said. "If you don't let me go with you I'll make one of the men take me or I'll go by myself."

"Get in the car," Blain said, his mind absorbing this latest turn of events. He'd have to watch her or she'd bolt. He'd talked to two guards and they both agreed it wasn't like Franco to just leave on his own.

"The old man's been acting strange for a few weeks now," one of the burly men told Blain. "He's always on the phone or mumbling to himself. He's a mess over Miss Sonia being so sick."

The other guard had nodded. "And now his only daughter being attacked. Something's up. Things are just weird around here."

Blain agreed with that understatement. He had to consider the Alvanetti family could be in some kind of turf war with another group. Santo had come to see him and mentioned Victor had been calling. Could their brother be involved with some sort of smuggling ring?

Blain didn't have the resources to search the entire state for competitors but he might have to do just that. He'd put in another call to Hunter Lawson but he had yet to hear from the Okie. The private detective would be an asset right about now.

Once they were on the road, he laid down some ground rules. "You have to do what I say, Rikki. If I stop this vehicle to search along the way, I need you to stay with me. Okay?"

"Okay."

"Or stay in the car."

"Okay. But… I don't want to stay in the car."

Blain let out a sigh. "You are one of the most stubborn women I've ever met."

"I'm assertive, not stubborn. Where are you going?"

"To the Alvanetti Shipping Warehouse first. You said your father might have gone there."

"Possibly." She stared out into the night. "But it's not like him to go out at night without a driver. His eyes aren't all that good from what I can tell."

Blain wanted to ask her more but she'd only been back around Franco for a week now. Did she really know anything more about her family than he did?

When they reached the warehouse, Rikki shouted and pointed. "There's his car."

Blain breathed a sigh of relief, but this wasn't over yet. "The whole place is dark," he said. "I'm calling for backup just in case."

"Good idea." She didn't wait for him but got out of the car and started toward the front office doors.

Blain barely managed to catch her. "Rikki, stop. Think, okay? We have to approach with caution."

She nodded. "I'm sorry."

He called for help and then pulled her close. "Stay behind me or I'll lock you in the back of the car, understand?"

"Yes."

Blain touched a hand to her hair. "And you should have worn a coat."

"Let's go," she said.

Blain tugged her to the car while he pulled out a flashlight. "No lights on. That can't be good."

"We might not be able to get inside," she whispered. "I can call my brother Santo."

"Let's look first." Blain had Santo's number but he'd have to explain to her why. And he couldn't do that right now.

They made it to the door and Blain checked around it. "Has to be an alarm system."

"Yes. There's a lot of valuable stuff in this warehouse." Rikki grabbed his arm. "Do you think there's something here that would cause someone to kill?" She shook her head. "I don't want my family to be involved. I couldn't handle that."

Blain didn't want to admit it, but he'd thought long and hard about her family being involved. It made sense, after all.

"Anything is plausible at this point."

He touched a hand to the glass-paneled double doors and pushed. One of the doors swung open.

"That's not good, either," Rikki said. "Blain, this is dangerous."

Blain held her behind him. "Which is why we're going to wait here for backup."

He didn't want her to see in case something bad had happened to her father. She might resent her family's reputed criminal activity and she might not be close to Franco but he could tell Rikki loved her family in spite of everything.

A good reminder that he still had to handle this case with kid gloves.

Because blood was always thicker than murder, after all.

ELEVEN

Two cruisers and a sheriff's-department SUV showed up in record time. When the Alvanetti warehouse was messed with, everyone came running.

"Whadda we got?" The sheriff's deputy asked, his gun and flashlight out.

Blain knew the young deputy. "Hey, Billy. Not sure yet," Blain said after the two Millbrook officers hurried up. "Franco Alvanetti is missing so we decided to check here, since according to his daughter, Regina, he sometimes comes here late to work." He indicated Rikki behind him. "We got here and found the door unlocked."

"He'd lock the door behind him," Rikki said. "His car is parked over there." She pointed to a big oak tree off to the side of the building.

"I'll go check the vehicle," one of the officers said, hurrying away.

"Let's get in there," Blain said. "Rikki, you stay behind me, okay?" He couldn't leave her in the car so he had to let her go in.

She nodded but her eyes held a solid apprehension. She grabbed Blain's jacket and held tight.

Soon they were moving through the dark front offices. Blain noticed opulent furnishings and several cubicles and conference rooms. They passed what looked like a kitchen and dining area.

"Where's the main office?" he asked. "Where would he go?"

She pointed to the left. "The one in the corner with the river view."

Blain saw the big windows and the glistening Millbrook River beyond the security lights and the mushrooming trees. The cloudy night didn't allow for much light to creep in so he held his flashlight over his weapon.

"There!" Rikki pointed behind the big desk. "It's him."

Blain rushed over and found Franco lying on the floor. He checked Franco's pulse. "He's alive." Then he shouted, "Call 911 and get an ambulance out here. And someone go over the rest of this place and check for any sign of intruders."

Everyone scrambled into action. Rikki fell on her knees beside Franco. "Papa? Papa, wake up." She touched his forehead and took one of his beefy hands in hers. "Daddy?"

Blain turned on the office light and pulled her away. "Let me check him out, okay?"

She nodded, her expression void of emotion. She looked as if all the blood had left her body. "I need to call Santo," she said, her voice above a whisper.

"I can do that," Blain said, his hands moving over Franco's body. When he touched the older man's head, his fingers came away with blood. "He's got a bad gash on the back of his head."

Rikki took in a shattered breath. "Someone hit him?"

"Or he fell and hit his head."

Blain grabbed Franco's overcoat from the desk chair and placed it around him. Then he checked the older man's vitals again. Weak, shaky pulse but no other obvious signs of injury. The paramedic would have to determine the rest. "Help is on the way, Rikki, okay?"

She bobbed her head. "He looks so old, Blain. When did he get so old?"

Blain held one hand to her father's erratic pulse and then took her hand. "Hang on. Both of you need to hang on."

A month ago, Franco Alvanetti had only come to mind whenever Blain thought of bringing the reputed crime boss down. That and how he resented his own father for turning a blind eye. Now his whole perspective was changing. The Alvanetti family was more complicated than he'd ever imagined.

Starting with the woman kneeling by her father with her eyes closed in prayer.

Sirens echoed out over the night. Rikki got up to run to the door. "They're here."

"And we need to stand back and let them to their jobs," Blain said.

He did a quick visual of the entire room and saw a small white statue lying by the ornate credenza. He quickly snapped a picture of the statue, sure that someone had used it to hit Franco over the head. Then he dug into his jacket pocket and found a pair of latex gloves. After putting them on, he picked up the statue. It was a goddess of some sort, heavy white porcelain. A big jagged crack indicated it had been chipped on one corner. A dark stain spread against the damaged part.

Blood?

Rikki saw his actions and gasped. "That's one of his favorite pieces. My mother bought it in Italy and teased him that the face looked like hers. He loves it." She walked to the credenza. "He kept it right here."

Blain saw bloodstains on the base of the foot-high figurine. Someone had definitely used this as a weapon.

One of the other officers hurried into the office. "Sir, we found something else." He gave Blain a pointed stare.

Rikki didn't miss a beat. "Just tell him."

Blain nodded at the officer. "Go ahead."

"We found a body," the young man said. "Out back by a Dumpster."

Rikki put a hand to her mouth. "Is it my brother?"

The man shook his head. "No, ma'am." Then he walked over to Blain and whispered, "It looks like the picture we have up at the station. The one of Chad Presley."

Blain's gaze locked with Rikki's.

"What is it?" she asked, her hand grabbing the sleeve of Blain's jacket. "Blain?"

He couldn't hide it from her. "It might be Chad, Rikki. I'm sorry."

Rikki's eyes turned a misty black. "Show me."

When he didn't move, she gripped his sleeve again. "Blain, let me see him."

Blain nodded and turned to the other officer. "Bag and tag this, Wilson."

Then he and Rikki headed out to the back of the property where a group of officers were gathered. They parted when Blain brought Rikki toward the grim scene.

She pushed past him, but he held her back, his hands on her arms. "Rikki, is this Chad Presley?"

She stood so still he was afraid he'd lost her. Finally, she bobbed her head. "Yes, that's him. That's Chad."

Blain turned her around. She was shaking. "Somebody get me a blanket for Miss Alvanetti, please."

It looked like the killer was now targeting the entire Alvanetti family and people connected with them. And it was obvious whoever was doing this wanted something very important.

Blain was more determined than ever to find out what exactly that might be.

Rikki sat at the hospital with her brother Santo, both staring at a kitschy watercolor on the waiting room wall. Caught in a grip of horror over what had happened tonight, her mind moved from finding Tessa dead to seeing her father lying so still…and then seeing a man she'd been close to for years sitting up against a Dumpster with blood all over his clothes.

And now, her brother staring off into space, his expression full of anger and what looked like his own private despair.

Santo had been furious, of course. He'd ranted at Blain and her and the police and the paramedics. Now he sat with a brooding frown, his hands in the pockets of his winter coat.

"I can get us some coffee," she offered, thinking her brothers and her had never been close. But she was rethinking that and a lot of other things these days.

Santo burrowed deeper into his coat. "I don't need any coffee."

Rikki glanced at the ER doors. They'd been in there with her father a long time. Blain had left a few minutes ago to take the bagged figurine to the station to log as evidence and to talk to the medical examiner about Chad's body. Thinking she'd never sleep again, she glanced at her brother.

"They didn't find anything missing," she said, needing to talk about this. "Nothing, even though the office was a mess. The warehouse looked intact."

"I heard that but I've got some of my staff walking it right now along with some officers to see if anything else is messed up. I intend to go over the inventory again first thing in the morning. A professional would cover his tracks."

She stood and whirled to stare at her brother. "What have I done, Santo? What is it about me that this family can't love?"

Santo pulled a hand through his thick black hair. He looked as exhausted as she felt. "What is it about this family that *you* can't love, *mia sorella*?"

That question floored Rikki. "Isn't that obvious? We live dangerous lives, lives of secrets and sins. I had to get away but our lifestyle has finally caught up with us."

Santo looked shocked and sickened. "You judge too harshly, Regina."

"I know what I see."

His dark eyes scanned her with regret. "You know what you think you see." Staring ahead, he said, "Two people you met after you left here are dead. What does that tell you?"

"You're cruel," she replied, gritting her teeth at the pain coursing through her. But he was right.

"I'm realistic," he retorted. "You always did only see what your so-called noble heart needed to see and nothing else."

"I see that someone is after me and now my family."

She tugged her sweater close. "And I'm beginning to wonder if my family isn't involved in something none of us can control."

"What do you care?" he asked, rage radiating from his eyes. "You and Victor, you both chose to leave me with this mess."

"What do you mean?"

Santo gave her a long, measuring stare. "I…"

The ER doors swung open then, causing him to stand and turn toward the doctor coming up the hallway.

Rikki watched her brother's face, sure that Santo knew something he wasn't telling her, but then that had been the pattern with her family for most of her life. But she'd have to wait to find out. The doctor didn't look as though he had good news.

Blain finished filing his report and pushed back his squeaking desk chair. He planned to head back to the hospital to check on Mr. Alvanetti and Rikki. Her brother was with her and Santo had brought his own guards with him, right along with his own uncooperative attitude.

But Blain worried, anyway. The neighborhood canvas back at the townhome hadn't brought any answers. A couple of joggers had been spotted that afternoon but the descriptions were vague and could fit anyone. Blain had been jogging there himself so he couldn't dispute the statements.

No prints anywhere. Nothing yet on the brother in Europe.

No solid evidence on any of her clients being involved. The all had alibis and clean records.

Now a shooting attempt this morning and an attack

at the warehouse and a dead ex-boyfriend. Franco was in the hospital and Chad Presley was dead. He had to wonder again what the ex-boyfriend's involvement in this could have been. Chad had somehow made his way west from Tallahassee to the panhandle, maybe looking for Rikki or maybe looking for something else. They'd never get a chance to interview Presley now. But Blain did have something to add to his notes.

He remembered Rikki telling him Chad had been at a wedding at the estate last spring. Had he scoped the place, searching for something? Maybe gone to the warehouse and confronted the old man? But then, who had killed Chad and why?

The crime scene people had determined that the slug they'd found embedded in the fence behind Chad Presley had matched the one they'd found near Tessa Jones's body. Possibly the same shooter.

His phone buzzed. Lawson. Finally.

"Hey," he said. "Thanks for calling me back."

"What you got?" Hunter asked. Not one for small talk.

"It's a long story," Blain said. He gave Hunter the particulars. "I need you to do some digging, especially in the state capital and maybe down in Miami. Are you nearby? Can you take this on?"

"Not nearby but I'll be there soon enough," Hunter replied. "Email me the facts."

"I'll get right on that," Blain said.

He hung up, relief washing over him. Now if he could just get a hit on Victor Alvanetti.

Blain didn't have a lot of resources and he had no European connections. He stared at his notes and then lifted his head.

But he knew someone who did.

Time to make this investigation a family affair.

He grabbed his coat and headed back out into the night.

When he got to the hospital, he found Rikki and Santo huddled together in a corner. Rikki glanced up and saw him and then shot out of her chair after giving her scowling brother a worried look.

"Hi," she said, meeting Blain near another hallway.

"Hi. What's the status?"

"He has a concussion," she said. "He's okay but while they were examining him his blood pressure spiked." She pushed at her tousled hair and looked over her shoulder. "They want to keep him here to rest for the night and…they want to do some more tests in the morning. The doctor said my father is suffering from exhaustion, too."

"Exhaustion?" That shocked Blain. "I thought he was retired and kind of hanging out at the house most days."

"I thought that, too," she said with a lift of her shoulders. "I think he stays up half the night, sitting with my mother even though she has a nurse."

"That's understandable," Blain said. "In spite of everything, they seem to love each other."

He looked into Rikki's chocolate eyes and wondered what that kind of love would be like. Would he ever know? Up until now, he hadn't really expected a lasting relationship with a woman. But there was something about her. Those pretty, pink lips, those exotic, slanted eyes and dark, winged eyebrows.

"Did you find anything?"

Blain tore his gaze away from Rikki to find her

brother staring him down from behind her with a dark, threatening scowl.

"Uh, no. No viable witnesses have come forward about seeing anyone entering or leaving the town house the other night and our shooter from this morning apparently has lost his will to speak. And nothing regarding tonight at the warehouse. We'll go over the security tapes and maybe that will help us identify your father's assailant since he's indicated he didn't see who attacked him." He held back and then said, "And we need to find Chad's killer."

He didn't mention the ballistics report.

"The door was open," Rikki reminded Santo. "Could you have left it unlocked?"

Her brother stepped back, his scowl widening. "No, I didn't leave it unlocked. Papa probably unlocked it and forgot to lock it back. He's been forgetful lately."

"That's a possibility," Blain said, seeing the concern flaring in Rikki's eyes. "We don't know whether it happened before or after Presley was killed, but someone entered after your dad and hit him over the head."

"And if he knew that person, that makes it all the worse that it happened," Rikki said. "I have no idea what Chad was doing there."

"Did he know your father?" Blain asked.

"No. I didn't introduce Chad to my father at the wedding that day."

Santo turned away, disgust shadowing his features. "It's bad that this happened, no matter who did it."

Blain noticed the brother's agitated state. Worry about his father, or worry about being exposed?

"I need to ask both of you a favor," he said, following Santo back to the quiet corner.

Rikki sat down by her brother. "What is it?"

Blain sank on a chair across from them. "I need to question Victor, too. But I don't have the resources or the funds to search in Europe."

"And that involves us how?" Santo asked, his frown creasing like a row of sand dunes. He started fidgeting and stared at the floor.

Blain didn't flinch. "I need your help. You know people over there, including your brother, Victor. He's been calling so now's the time to question him."

"We haven't heard from Victor in months," Rikki said. "Not since Mama got so ill while she was visiting him in Italy."

Santo looked down at the floor. "He's been calling me, KK. And Papa, too. But he's stopped since…since all of this started."

Rikki narrowed her eyes at her brother. "I found Victor's name in Papa's office. Why didn't you mention this?"

"I figured he wanted money," Santo said. "He claimed he'd heard things and that he was concerned but we both know that's not true."

Blain made a note of that. "He could help us."

"He doesn't care," Santo retorted. "Victor is all about Victor, after all."

Reminding himself that nothing was as it seemed with this family, Blain took a slow breath. "Do you think you can help me find Victor?" he asked Santo.

Rikki shot Santo an imploring glance. "Yes, we can. I don't want anyone coming after my family again. I want this over with. Two attacks and two murders in one day are more than enough for me. We lost a guard and… Chad is dead. We could have lost Papa, too."

Blain nodded and then glanced over at Santo and waited for him to speak up.

When he didn't, Rikki continued. "We'll do whatever needs to be done to end this, of course."

Santo continued to stare down at the fake wooden floor, his dark eyes as stormy as the night. "We might not be able to locate Victor."

Blain leaned forward. "You came to see me earlier tonight, Santo. You said you'd help me because you're concerned about your family. Locating and questioning your brother will go a long way toward that end."

Rikki pivoted toward her brother. "You talked to Blain?"

"I did," Santo said. "I want to keep *my* family out of this."

"Too late," Blain said. "I'm beginning to think you're all involved."

Santo shook his head. "We just need to find out what is going on so we can prove we're not."

"I agree," Rikki said. "I'm worried about Victor, too. He could be in danger, too."

"We're all in danger," Santo said on a growl. Then he got up and looked at his watch. "I have to go home and pay the babysitter and send her home. I'll check back in the morning."

Rikki looked surprised. "Where is Althea?"

Santo shook out his coat. "My wife left for Miami this morning. And I don't think she'll be returning anytime soon. We are officially separated."

TWELVE

After her brother left, Rikki sat staring out the waiting room window.

The night was dark and full of thunder and lightning. A persistent wind lifted the red bows tied around the huge posts supporting the ER portico. She shivered and felt a hand on her arm. Then a warm leather coat over her shoulders.

Blain's hand. Blain's coat.

"You don't have to stay," she said. "I have guards all around me."

He sat down beside her. "I'm taking you home. You can't see your father again until tomorrow, anyway, so you need to get some rest."

Feeling torn, she tugged the big jacket closer around her shoulders. The smell of old leather and spicy aftershave assaulted her with an overwhelming, endearing need. She was thankful for Blain at that moment, thankful that God had sent her a strong protector.

She could live right here in this warm cocoon that shouted Blain. But she needed to check on her mother. And she needed to know that no one would hurt her father. That realization left her surprised and off-kilter.

"What do I do, Blain?" she asked, surrendering to the need to let someone else help her for a change. "What do I do? My friend is dead, my ex-boyfriend is dead, and my family is at risk. My brother who never confides in me is obviously going through some sort of crisis in his marriage. I've been so out of touch and now that I'm back, everything is falling apart."

"Maybe things were already falling apart before you got here."

She hadn't considered that. Had Tessa's murder just been part of something bigger and even more sinister? "I don't know whom to believe."

He lifted her up, his hands on her elbows. "I don't have all the answers, but right now you're coming with me."

Rikki glanced at the nurses' station. "I should check—"

"He's stable," Blain said. "And we have a man at his door."

"Okay." She gave in and allowed him to guide her out the double doors and into the parking lot. A lone, fake Christmas tree in the center of a tiny park sparkled with brightly colored lights. Rikki had to keep reminding herself that this was supposed to be a season of love and peace but she expected something terrible around every corner. Too many shadows overpowered the bright lights. But she knew God was in control, no matter how she tried to fix things.

Blain held her in the crook of his arm, his gaze moving all around the nearly empty hospital parking lot. When they got to his vehicle, she noticed he was driving a big truck tonight. He opened the passenger-side door and helped her up but the truck was high and she was too short to make the step.

Blain lifted her without even a grunt and placed her on the seat. When their eyes met, a soothing warmth flooded her entire system like a warm ocean current. His midnight eyes moved over her face to settle on her lips. He held her there, his gaze washing her in a longing that only mirrored the one in her heart.

Rikki wondered why this man made her feel so different, so safe and secure, so important. She wanted to say a lot of things to him but she held back.

He's a cop, she reminded herself. If Blain found out her family was involved in Tessa's murder and everything else that had happened, he'd never forgive her.

And he'd walk away from her forever.

So she touched a hand to his face and turned on the seat, his jacket still covering her.

Blain's eyes stayed on her but he made sure she was in and then he shut the door and came around the truck and got inside.

"I'm not taking you home right away," he said.

"Why not?"

"You need a break."

"I need to check on my mother."

"Call and talk to Peggy."

"Blain…"

"Just an hour, Rikki. An hour away from all of this. I'll get you home soon enough."

What could she say? She wanted an hour away. Since she'd been home, her life had become a whirlwind of trying to stay one step ahead of a killer. She'd ignored her clients and she'd ignored her friends. She'd tried to ignore the way her heart beat a little faster each time this man came near her.

But she couldn't ignore the way Blain made her feel. Not any longer, not tonight when her world seemed to be careening out of control.

So she said a prayer, asking God to help her fight at this enemy so she could protect her family. It no longer mattered what they'd done in the past. She could forgive that and she would somehow *have to* forgive that. She asked for a blanket of protection and she prayed God would give them all the answers to save them.

And then she tugged Blain's coat around her and nodded.

"An hour would be nice."

Blain maneuvered the pickup up underneath the camp house pilings so the house would help hide the vehicle. He'd never brought a woman out to the camp house before. None of them had at first.

But he knew Alec had brought his fiancée, Marla, out here once to give her a break from her troubles so he figured it might work for Rikki, too. He accepted that bringing her here meant he had crossed the line from protector to something more personal. He wasn't quite sure what that something was but Blain knew he needed this hour away, too.

"What place is this?" Rikki asked as he helped her out of the truck.

He heard the wariness in her words. "Just an old beach cottage my friends and I bought together. We use it for fishing and hunting and downtime."

She smiled and inhaled the cold night air. "A good idea. You and your friends seem close."

Blain guided her around the truck and up the planked steps to the big screen porch on the bay side of the house. "We are. We all met after coming back here to Millbrook, over a serious dart game at the pizza house. After we compared notes, we realized we'd all been in the military. Alec Caldwell was a captain in the marines."

"I know him," she said, surprise coloring her words. "He's on the client list I gave you."

Blain nodded. "Yeah, I talked to him. He gave you a glowing report by the way."

"That's good to know."

Blain opened the door to the house and went straight to the fireplace. "I'll get it warm in here."

He motioned to a sofa in front of the fire. "Have a seat."

She settled on the old leather couch and glanced around.

Deciding small talk would calm her, Blain went about getting the fire started. "Then there's Preacher— Rory Sanderson. He was an army chaplain and now he's the pastor at Millbrook Lake Church. He'll be officiating Alec and Marla's wedding right before Christmas."

"Oh, the wedding." She shook out her hair. "I so wanted to attend but now…"

"We can make that happen if you really want to go."

"I don't want to put anyone in any danger. Especially not at a wedding."

Blain wouldn't be able to watch out for her since he had best-man duties. "Maybe you'll be safe again by then."

She leaned back on the sofa and grabbed a fleece

throw and dragged it up over her lap. "I don't know if I'll ever feel safe again."

Satisfied with the fire, Blain walked over and sat down beside her. "You can, for now at least. Sit back and relax for a few minutes."

She smiled over at him and then pointed toward the big window in the dining nook. "Nice Christmas tree."

Blain twisted around. "Preacher. He loves Christmas." He got up and plugged in the pathetic little tree. "He also sees the beauty in what most of us would deem unsalvageable."

"It is beautiful," she said, her voice soft and quiet.

Blain came back to her and looked at the tiny white twinkling lights on the scrawny little cedar tree. Then he turned to Rikki. "I guess it is, at that."

She was crying.

The real kind of crying that every man on earth dreaded.

But these silent, quiet sobs weren't about the little Christmas tree. She'd held them tight since the night she'd found her friend dead and now, the trauma of today and finding her father passed out with a gash to his head and a man she'd dated dead, had caused the letdown of emotions she'd tried so hard to hold back. And that letdown had turned into a deluge of pain and anger and grief.

Blain didn't think. He just pulled her into his arms and held her there, his hands working to pull the blanket up over her shivering body.

She turned and laid her head against his chest and then she snuggled close to him. She felt so fragile and tiny there in his embrace but she also fit perfectly. Blain had to swallow back the emotions clogging his throat. What was happening between them?

He couldn't explain it, so he held her there and watched the fire while the little Christmas tree's lights flashed off and on. Soon, Rikki's sobs turned into soft, steady breaths.

She'd fallen asleep.

Rikki's dreams changed from running in terror out in the cold to being anchored in warm and love. She could see her house, the big house where she'd grown up, off in the distance.

Then she saw her husband, Drake, waving to her from a shore that she couldn't reach. She cried out to him but he turned and walked away. Rikki looked around, searching for help. She saw a rustic square house set up on big pilings. A small Christmas tree shone inside the window.

She ran toward that house.

And then she woke up and met a solid chest.

Blain's chest.

She glanced up to find him staring at her, memories of her meltdown coming back into focus.

"Has it been an hour?" she asked, still disoriented, her eyes burning.

He checked his watch. "You have five minutes to spare."

Rikki didn't want to move. And she didn't want to tear her eyes away from Blain.

"Five minutes," he whispered. "Just enough time for this."

Then he lowered his mouth to hers and kissed her with such a sweet tenderness that she almost started crying again. Or maybe she was still dreaming. Maybe she'd kept running toward that little house and now she was with this man in that same dream.

But the pressure of his lips on hers was no dream.

It was a sweet reality that touched her and scared her and made her want to run away again.

But she was so tired of running. Turning in his arms, Rikki welcomed Blain's kiss. How had she become so thirsty? So alone and parched and wanting? Being here with Blain felt as if she'd come out of a dark wilderness. He felt like an answered prayer.

And yet they had so much between them still.

Pulling away, Rikki sat up. "I'm so sorry. I… I shouldn't have let that happen."

"*I* let it happen," he said, his eyes washed in a black regret. "I let it happen, Rikki."

She moved away, the blanket now suddenly cloying. "Did you want it to happen?"

"No. Yes. Never. Only since the minute I first saw you."

She could almost state feeling the same. "But murder is a buzzkill, right?"

"Yep." He checked his watch. "We need to go."

"After that kiss? That's all you have to say?"

Blain stood and went to stoke the fire. A symbolic move if ever there was one. "What can I say? I'd like to kiss you again but we both know how this works."

She started folding the blanket, her need to spar with him back and intact. "Why did you bring me here?"

"To give you some time to relax. Maybe to…grieve."

Embarrassed, she shook her head. "Well, I've done both and more."

He unplugged the tree's lights and walked back over

to her. "Hey, so let's not get all bent out of shape now that our hour of quiet is over." When she refused to look at him, he lifted her chin with one finger. "Rikki, we both know what we're facing here. Your family has a history—"

"I know," she said. "I know better than anyone."

"And I understand, better than anyone. My dad let things slide but I'm not my dad."

"And I'm not my father," she retorted, drained of any feelings now. "This brought us together but I won't let it tear us apart. I need you to find that killer. After that, the rest is up to you." She started for the door.

Blain grabbed her arm and tugged her around. "Hey, nothing is going to tear us apart."

"But you still have doubts about me, don't you?"

"Not about you," Blain said. "About your family, yes."

"And there it is. How can you kiss me and then tell me that?"

"I'm attracted to you," he replied. "But I have to do my job."

She nodded, the warm cocoon torn beyond repair. "Well, right now your job is to get me home to my mother."

"Let's go." He checked the house and walked with her out onto the porch. Then he said, "I know what you're doing, Rikki."

She doubted he knew anything about her. "Oh, and what is that?"

"You're deflecting what you're feeling right back onto me."

"And what exactly am I feeling?"

"You loved another man once and I don't think you're

over him yet. Or maybe you're afraid something will happen to me in the same way. Right?"

Rikki's heart did a tumble. Realization curled around her like a finger of fog over the water. She'd pushed so many men away since she'd lost Drake. But Blain? She didn't want to push him away. She wanted to be back in his arms, safe and secure.

Only she couldn't admit that yet. Not now. Not when her life was in so much chaos. And not when Blain's own life could be on the line, too.

"I'm afraid of a lot of things," she finally said. Then she turned to face him. "Thank you for bringing me here. It did help to let go and get some of this out of my system."

She saw how the implication of her words had hit him. His eyes held a trace of hurt along with that regret she'd seen earlier. So he took her down to the truck and got her inside without a word.

Rikki took one last look at the little house on the bay. And she knew she'd never forget the one hour she'd spent there with Blain. A good cry and a good kiss.

It would have to be enough for now.

THIRTEEN

They were on the bay road when Blain noticed a car tailing them. He didn't say anything to Rikki but he watched the headlights dip and sway as they moved closer. This road wasn't heavily traveled, especially this late at night.

Five miles till they reached the Alvanetti estate.

He did not need another thing to happen today but it was early morning so technically it was tomorrow. The pursuers apparently didn't want to quit anytime soon. When the car behind them edged up behind his truck, he at least was relieved they hadn't been assaulted at the beach house.

Stupid, to take her there in the first place.

But he'd never forget their time there.

When he glanced in the rearview mirror again, she turned and looked over her shoulder. "Are we being followed?"

He knew better than to try and shield her. "I believe so."

She sat straight up. "I'm really getting tired of this."

"Me, too."

"They must be watching my every move."

"Or they have someone reporting back to them."

She sent him a sharp stare at that comment but she didn't dispute his reasoning.

When the vehicle sped up and came a little too close for comfort, Blain had to decide if he should turn around and head back to town or get her inside the estate's gates as quickly as possible.

The automobile behind them was a dark sedan. The big car edged up to Blain's truck again. And this time, he felt the shudder of a bumper hitting chrome. "They're all in now."

Rikki held onto the dash and glanced back. "I know a back way onto the property," she said, a new determination sounding in her words.

"A back way?" That was a surprise. "Really now? Maybe these people know that same back way and maybe they've been coming and going whenever they please." He studied the car behind them. "They haven't shot at us yet. I'm thinking they want me to stop and hand you over to them."

She bobbed her head. "They're looking for something and they didn't find it at the warehouse."

The vehicle advanced and nudged at the truck. With the wet roads and sheer drop-offs to the bay on the right, Blain didn't want to play chicken. "Tell me about the back way."

She checked the rearview mirror on her side. "Not many people know about that road. It's practically buried in palmetto bushes and scrub oaks."

"And how do you know about it?"

"I found it when I used to go horseback riding. I used it to sneak in and out so the guards wouldn't follow me."

He could see her doing that. Reckless, rebellious and

stubborn. Good traits at times and bad ones at other times.

"How do we get there from here?"

Rikki glanced back and then at the road ahead. "They'll try to run us off the road before we reach the gate to my house," she said. "Probably on the curve since it juts out over the bay."

"You're too good at figuring this stuff out," he retorted. But she was right. "But if they want you alive, they might try to pull up and send us off into the bramble on the other side of the road. What do *you* suggest?"

"The hidden road is past the gates. If we speed up now, we can lose them on the curve and then turn off on the old road."

Blain stared into the mirror. "Okay. Hold on."

She gave him another gritty glance. "Got it."

Blain gunned it and headed toward the curve. If he lost control, they could go over the edge. If that car caught up and happened to nudge the truck just a little bit, they could crash and flip right off into the water below. But he couldn't let whoever was chasing them make it through the gates of the estate and he sure wasn't going to get himself or Rikki killed.

So he held tight and watched the upcoming curve. He knew the curve so he thought he could swing into it and make it through as long as no other cars were nearby.

The vehicle following them moved closer.

"They're speeding up again," Rikki said.

"I see that."

Blain pushed on the gas pedal and watched the dark, narrow road ahead. "Give me a hint about this private road. What should I look for?"

Rikki checked the passenger-side mirror. "A palm

tree that juts out over the road on the left side about a quarter of a mile past the gate. When you see the tree, you need to hit the brakes and turn left about ten feet past the tree."

"Sure, I can do that while I'm trying to outrun these bozos and while I'm trying to keep us out of the bay."

She narrowed her eyes at him. "I thought you could."

He watched the headlights behind them. The other driver was advancing at a reckless speed. Maybe their pursuers did want both of them dead. "Rikki, this could get ugly. Hang on."

She didn't respond but she reached up for the grab-bar over the door. Blain could see the resolve in her expression.

They might be headed around a dangerous curve but he decided Rikki had also taken up a new direction. She wasn't going to back down anymore.

And that scared him about as much as the treacherous odds they were about to face.

Rikki watched the dark rain-slick road. She'd have to make sure she had the right palm tree and that she could warn Blain to turn left once they got past the tree.

What if the terrain had changed? What if the palm tree had been cut down? A thousand terrors rushed through her system but when she saw the curve coming up, she knew Blain would handle this. He was that kind of man. He'd take them through the woods if he had to.

"Okay, we're approaching the curve," he said. "When we lose their headlights we have about ten seconds to get off this road."

"I'll keep watch while you drive."

He gunned it again and she felt the tug of the truck

as it hugged the road and hovered near the steep drop-off into the bay. This part of Florida was hilly at times and flat at other times. This road followed a long bluff where houses were built into the countryside and looked as if they were clinging to the hills over the water. Santo had a home not far from here, but her father had built on the other side of the bay, which was more leveled out down toward the water.

"Blain, I don't see them anymore. Look for the palm tree."

"Okay." He kept his foot on the gas as they headed into the sharp turn in the road.

When the truck fishtailed, Rikki took in a deep breath and stared out at the dark water about twenty or so feet below the overgrowth. Blain let off the gas and straightened the truck but not before they skidded again.

"The tree," she said as she caught the bent trunk of the ancient shaggy palm. "Now, Blain!"

They were almost there.

She glanced back just as he swerved the truck to the left and into the overgrown bushes and bramble. Headlights!

"They're coming," she shouted.

Blain held the wheel as the truck hit the dirt and bounced, the heavy tires skidding and grinding in the mud. "Are you sure this is a road?" he said over the roar of the big engine and the truck plowing into the bramble.

"It used to be. The guards probably still use it sometimes to come and go." Her head hit the top of the truck. Wincing, she held to the grab-bar.

Blain leveled the truck and slowed down. "I think

we're on some sort of lane," he called out. "Where are they?"

Rikki turned in the seat as he slowed the truck. "I don't see anything."

Blain did a one-eighty spin on the old overgrown road and turned off the truck's headlights. "Rikki, I need you to stay here while I go up to the road."

"What for?"

"I want to make sure they're not out there waiting."

"Shouldn't you call for backup?"

"Yes, but I don't have time. And if you stay with the truck you can go for help if I don't come back."

She bobbed her head and watched as he got out of the truck and hurried into the darkness. She didn't like that request. She wanted him to come back. Did she stay here or should she go after him?

Then she heard an engine roaring and what sounded like tires spinning. The other car must have tried to make the turn. Blain could be walking straight into a trap.

Rikki waited as the minutes seemed like hours and then she decided to get out and look for a weapon. She'd just put a booted foot down on a clump of dried vines when she heard a gunshot followed by running foot-steps.

Where was Blain?

She stood at the back of the truck, crouched low, her breath caught against her rib cage. Afraid to move, she wished she'd gone with him. She could make it home from here but she wasn't going anywhere without Blain.

She lifted up to search for a limb or a rock. Maybe something in the back of the truck. When she spotted a tire iron in the truck bed, she grabbed it.

But before she could make a move toward the direction Blain had gone, someone grabbed her from behind and a strong hand went over her mouth. Rikki squirmed and kicked, the tire iron still in one hand.

"Shhh. It's me."

Blain.

She relaxed against him. "You scared me!"

"I told you to stay in the truck."

She whirled to face him and watched as he put away his gun. "I was worried. I heard a car and then a gunshot."

"Yeah, they were up on the road trying to turn in here. I fired at them and they backed up and spun out."

"Did they get away?"

"Yep, but not before I got a good look at the driver and saw a partial on the license plate. There was someone in the passenger side, too."

"Did you call for help?"

"No," he said, his tone grim. "I recognized one of them, Rikki. He works for the sheriff's department."

Shock shot through her. "A police officer?"

He nodded. "A rookie deputy. He was at the warehouse earlier tonight."

"What do we do now?"

He stared out into the darkness. "We aren't going to tell anyone about this. I don't think he knows I saw his face but he has to be worried right about now. If I don't turn him in, whoever sent him will certainly read him the riot act."

"So this explains how they've been able to come after me no matter what we've tried to do."

"Yep." He did a quick glance around the woods and

then opened the truck door. "And that also means that this particular officer is probably on someone's payroll."

"Someone besides the local sheriff's office," she added.

They got back in the truck and she showed him how to get her home. But they didn't talk. What was there to say? Rikki hoped her father wasn't the one calling the shots. How could he be if he'd been assaulted, too?

Or had that been a setup? Had someone mistaken him for someone else?

When they pulled up to the house, the guards came running with drawn guns. They must have heard the gunshots. Rikki got out and waved them away. "I'm okay."

The burly men backed off but stayed nearby.

"I can see why you wanted to get away from here," Blain said. "No privacy and shady characters everywhere." He walked her to the door. "I hate to leave you."

Rikki's heart clutched at that comment but the assumption that this place was still corrupt brought her back to reality. "I'll be all right. I just want a shower and sleep."

He nodded then stared down at her, his eyes colored with a new urgency. "Do you trust all of these people who help out around here?"

She nodded. "I have to trust them, right?"

"I could move you to a safe house."

"We agreed this is for the best."

"And yet, you're still being chased and attacked and shot at."

She poked a finger against the solid wall of his chest. "And yet, you've managed to protect me in spite of that."

"I'm serious, Rikki."

"So am I," she said. "And starting tomorrow, I'm calling all of my clients and setting up the appointments I had to cancel. I'm tired of hiding."

"You can't go back to work yet," he said, shaking his head.

"I can and I will." She stared him down. "Maybe if I go on with my life, someone will slip up and we can catch them."

"Or they'll kill you."

"They want something and they think I might have it. I get that and I sure know the danger. But I can't become a prisoner here, Blain. I'd gladly give them what they want if they'd leave my family alone."

"Or they could just want *you* dead." He touched a hand to her cheek. "Rest and we'll talk about our options tomorrow."

She thought about their kiss. "Like we have any options."

"There are always options." He gave her a smile and then turned to get back in his truck.

Rikki stood there, flanked by two guards, and watched him leave. And she had to wonder, what options *were* left for her and Blain?

FOURTEEN

Blain pulled his truck onto the driveway of his parents' house and stared up and down the quiet street. It was early morning. The homes along this street were small and age-worn but the people were hardworking and good. They watched out for each other.

Now he prayed his dad would help him. He needed honesty and clarity. He needed a break in this case. Being so embedded in all the Alvanetti drama and intrigue was beginning to weigh on him.

Being near Rikki and knowing they didn't have a future together was tearing him apart, mainly because he'd never in his wildest dreams wanted a future with the daughter of an alleged criminal. He hadn't slept much last night. Instead, he'd gone over the details of this case and he still didn't have any answers. Rikki was in danger but now, he had to wonder if the killer would take out her family members, one by one, until he or she had what they needed.

The front door of the brick Florida cracker house opened and his mom came out with a cup of coffee, her smile as serene as always. She wore her old chenille robe and flannel pajamas.

He'd have to remember to buy her a new robe for Christmas.

Getting out of the truck, he smiled. "Is that for me?"

His mom brought him the big blue mug. "Of course. Saw you sitting out here and since I had to get the paper, anyway…"

Blain reached down and retrieved the paper, memories of his own early morning paper route as a teen coming to the surface, and then took the mug full of steaming coffee. "Thanks, Mom. Is Dad up yet?"

"So that's why you're here."

"Yeah. I need to talk to him."

"He's watching the morning news." She tugged her robe close. "Let's get inside and I'll make us some breakfast."

Blain took a long sip of the coffee and followed his mom past the wooden white nativity scene by the boxwood shrubs. He didn't have much of an appetite but he'd eat his mother's cooking. Because this morning, he thanked God for being blessed with good parents.

Even if his dad had the one big flaw regarding the Alvanetti clan. But now Blain could drop some of his self-righteous judgments. Because lately, Blain seem to have acquired that same flaw.

He found Sam at the kitchen table, his gaze glued on the twenty-four-hour news channel's latest updates. "Hi, Dad," Blain said before sitting down across from him.

Sam's eyes narrowed. "Morning. You're out bright and early."

"Yeah, got to see the frost on the grass and everything."

While Mom cooked eggs and bacon and browned

toast, Blain and his dad caught up on the news and sports, neither of which they agreed on.

Then they ate their breakfast and made more small talk. Finally Mom got up and cleared the table. "I'm going to get dressed. I've got an altar committee meeting at church."

She gave Blain a pat on the arm and then left with her second cup of coffee.

Sam drained his cup and then put his hands together on the poinsettia-themed plastic tablecloth. "What's up, son?"

"I need to tell you something in confidence," Blain said, hoping he'd made the right decision. "And then I need to ask for your help."

His dad cleared his throat and turned the television to mute. "I'm listening."

Blain told him about what had happened on the bay road. "I saw the driver, Dad. It was Billy Rogers."

Sam's silvery eyebrows shot up. "Billy Rogers? That hotshot rookie sheriff's deputy?"

"Yessir. It was dark but he was driving the car. He opened the door to check and see if they were bogged down. I saw him clear as day in the car's interior lights."

"Are you sure?" Sam asked. "It was rainy and dark. You said so yourself."

Blain had expected some disputes on this. "I saw him. I've known him since we were kids. It was Billy."

Sam stared out the window. Blain's mom, Catherine, had put a bird feeder out by the small patio. Two redbirds were perched on the bright stone, pecking away at their breakfast. A small yard flag swaying on an iron garden post showed a smiling Santa in a hammock and proclaimed "Christmas in Paradise."

Cute, but all Blain could think about was murder in paradise.

After a couple of moments, Sam glanced over at Blain. "If you say it's him, I'll go with that."

Blain didn't respond at first. He hadn't realized he was holding his breath until his dad continued. "So if the person you saw was Billy Rogers that means we've got a corrupt deputy in the department."

Blain bent his head, relief washing over him. "Yessir."

"What do you want me to do?" his dad asked, his dark eyes mirroring Blain's. "Just between you and me, I mean?"

"Watch," Blain said. "Listen. Observe. Ask around. You still have some pull and you can come and go without anyone wondering why you're hanging around."

"Good old-fashioned police work," Sam said. "I think I can handle that."

Blain stood up. "Do you think I'm doing the right thing here, Dad? You know how I feel about the Alvanetti family."

Sam stood, too. "You're doing your job. You're the lead detective and Regina Alvanetti seems to trust you."

"I'm the only available detective," Blain pointed out. "She has to trust me."

Sam chuckled as they walked toward the front door. "When it comes to the Alvanetti family, trust does not come easily."

One day when this was all over, Blain would ask his dad about that. He needed to hear more about what had happened with his dad and the Alvanettis. Because the more he learned about them, the more he realized he might have misjudged his father.

And maybe the Alvanettis, too. But he still needed more proof to give in to that assumption.

They made it to his truck and he showed his dad the dents and scratches the vehicle had received last night. "I've got someone running the partial on the license plates. I should have that when I get to the station."

"I'd like to know that myself," Sam said, his eyes scanning the neighborhood with a cop's habitual awareness.

Blain opened the truck door. "What do you know about Santo Alvanetti, Dad?"

Sam shook his head. "Not much. He took over the business at about the time I retired. He lives not far from his parents in a big modern house. On the bay side, I think."

Blain processed that tidbit. "I might ride out there and have a look around. He told us yesterday that his wife left him."

"You don't say? I heard he married a woman from Miami. Rumor has it she came from a very influential family."

"Just one more rabbit hole to go down," Blain said. "Somebody is after something but I can't figure out what it might be."

Sam braced one foot on the truck's bumper. "There is a lot of 'somethings' in that family. Big house, barns, the warehouse. Lots of places to hide things and keep secrets."

Surprised yet again at this change in his dad, Blain asked, "What are you saying, Dad?"

"I'm saying somebody might be after something that is valuable. Highly valuable."

"Okay, we've established that but why come after Rikki?"

"Think about it, son. She travels in circles where everything is valuable and expensive. Her clients are wealthy and some of them have questionable work ethics. She's in their homes and she orders all kinds of furniture and, you know, those artsy pieces rich people like. No telling what she might see moving through. Or what she might be hiding."

"So is that what this is about?" Blain asked. "Shift the suspicion back to Regina and take it off the rest of the clan?"

His dad shook his head. "That is not what I meant at all. If Regina, or Rikki as you like to call her, found an important artifact that could have been stolen or possibly misplaced, she might try to hide it until she could do right by reporting it."

"And yet she hasn't done that—at least not with me."

Now he was doubting Rikki again.

"I'm looking at all the angles. You know to do that," Sam said.

Blain remembered Rikki saying she was going to call some of her local clients and get back to work. "We went through a long list of people she planned to meet with. She still wants to do that but I've cautioned her against it." He shrugged. "Maybe I should let her follow through as long as I'm around to protect her."

"It might get the ball rolling," Sam said. "Especially if there is something hidden in a shipment to her or to one of the houses she's decorating."

Blain nodded. "I'll dig a little deeper in that area."

"Maybe you can tie a couple of things together."

"I hope so. We've at least ruled out the victim's boyfriend and brother." Blain left, his mind whirling with so many scenarios he felt a headache coming on.

When he passed the Millbrook Lake Church, he saw Preacher's car parked there. Maybe he needed to consult with one other person on all of this. Just for good measure.

Rikki sat by her mother's bed, her mind full of turmoil. Santo had promised to check on their father at the hospital. She hoped he'd do that soon since news of Franco Alvanetti being attacked at the warehouse had been all over the local airwaves.

Now the whole state would know what was going on.

She didn't have to be a cop to know that would put her family in even more danger.

When Sonia moaned and opened her eyes, Rikki leaned close and took her mother's hand. "Hi, Mama. How are you this morning?"

"Tired," Sonia replied. "Did Victor come home last night?"

Victor? Rikki rubbed her mother's cold hand. "Victor is in Europe, remember? He's not here, Mama."

"He knows. He knows," Sonia said, agitation in each word. "Can't help it. Can't."

"Mama, it's okay," Rikki said. "Victor's not here and everything is okay. Are you in pain?"

Sonia opened her eyes and looked up at Rikki. "For you, darlin'. I did it for you. Always."

Daphne came in with Sonia's breakfast and a medicine tray. "Good morning," she said to Rikki.

Rikki nodded at the nurse. "She's not making sense," she said under her breath. "She's worried about Victor."

Daphne's brown eyed gaze moved from Rikki to

Sonia. "The medication can make her disoriented. If we could get her outside in the sunshine, she might rally around more."

Rikki glanced out the big doors of the bedroom. "I wonder if I sat with her on the private patio. Do you think it's too chilly out today?"

Daphne stared out at the sun-dappled courtyard. "Not out there. The temperature is supposed to be in the high sixties today and with that sunshine, I'd think you'd be okay. We can bundle her."

Rikki checked her mother again. "Mama, Daphne's brought your breakfast. Time to sit up and take a few bites."

Sonia lifted her head and smiled at Daphne. "You've changed your hair."

Daphne gave Rikki a strained smile. "I got it cut."

Rikki couldn't remember anything about Daphne's hair changing recently. Maybe she'd worn it longer before Rikki arrived here. "It's cute," she said for her mother's benefit.

"I like it," Sonia replied. "Do I smell bacon?"

Rikki and Daphne both smiled. "Yes, you do," Rikki said.

Soon they had Sonia sitting up in bed, laughing and talking. When Rikki suggested they sit out in the small, enclosed courtyard by the bedroom, Sonia clapped her hands in glee. "I love my garden. Tomorrow we'll weed the rose garden and prune the camellia bushes."

"Yes, tomorrow," Rikki said.

She and Daphne helped Sonia into her wheelchair and bundled her in a robe and shawls and a heavy blanket. Then Rikki put a hat over Sonia's white-blond hair.

The sun did feel good out in the courtyard. Normally

this space was surrounded by elephant ear and banana tree plants but they'd died back so the gardener had trimmed them for the winter. But a few hearty palm trees and camellia bushes gave the space a cozy feel.

After a few minutes of small talk, Sonia turned to Rikki and smiled. "You know, that family Bible is important to me. Don't lose it."

"Which Bible, Mama?" Rikki asked. She really needed to go over her mother's medication list and consult with Sonia's doctors. Maybe Daphne was right. Maybe the medicine was contributing to her mother's incoherent mumblings.

"That big one," Sonia said. Then she looked past Rikki, back toward the open bedroom doors. "Well, hello, good-looking."

Rikki whirled to find Blain standing there, staring at them with a definite frown of disapproval.

"Hello, Mrs. Alvanetti," he said, his eyes on Rikki. "Nice day to sit in the garden, isn't it?"

Sonia nodded and smiled. "Yes, it is. Do I know you?"

"I'm Blain Kent," he said as he walked out onto the brick-covered patio. "I work for the Millbrook Police Department."

"You know Alec, don't you?"

Surprise swept over Blain's face. "Yes, ma'am, I do."

"And that adorable Preacher Rory, right?"

"He's one of my best friends. In fact, I just left seeing him."

"He prays for me," Sonia said on a chuckle. "We all need that."

"Yes, we do," Blain said. "How do you know I'm friends with Alec and Preacher, Mrs. Alvanetti?"

"Alec bragged about you when he attended your cousin Beatrice's wedding here last spring."

Rikki gave Blain a shocked stare. "You remember that, Mama?"

Sonia pulled a face. "Of course I do. I gave Alec a big check for his foundation. The Caldwell Canines Service Dog Association."

"That's right," Blain said, shrugging toward Rikki. "I'm sure he appreciated it."

"You were here that day, Rikki," Sonia said. "Remember the key, darlin'?"

Rikki shook her head. "No, Mama. I left early. I'm not sure what you're talking about."

Daphne came through the doors and brushed past Blain. "Time to rest for a while. You might get sunburn if we don't get you back inside."

Sonia shook her head. "I like it out here."

Rikki stood. "Daphne's right, Mama. We've been out here for almost an hour."

Blain helped to get Sonia back into the bedroom but Daphne waved Rikki and him away. "I've got this. I'll get her a bath and get her all tucked in. You two go ahead and visit."

Rikki took Blain back toward the den. "That was interesting. She hasn't stayed up that long in a while. And she was making some sense today."

She wanted to tell Blain everything her mother had said to her but he seemed intent on something else. "What is it?"

He pulled her down on the couch and held her hands. Then he pulled her so close, she could smell the fresh air on his skin. With a whisper in her ear and a finger to her lips for her to stay quiet, he said, "The car that tried to run us off the road the other night? Even though he wasn't driving it, it was a rental registered to your brother Victor Alvanetti."

FIFTEEN

Shock caused her to stiffen and pull away. "But he's not here."

"Or so we thought," Blain said, still whispering. "I've ID'd the man who was driving the car but we don't know who the passenger was. I know I saw two people in the car, though."

"I did, too," she said, getting up to pace in front of him. Then she hurried back and sat down close to him so she could keep her words low. "Do you think the other one could have been Victor?"

"I don't know yet. We can't locate the vehicle but we've put out a search. I have a feeling the car is long gone but we're bringing in the driver and I'm going to interrogate him later today."

"Who is he?"

"I can't say right now," he said, motioning with a finger as he pointed up and around. He mouthed, "Bugs."

Bugs? Now he thought this house was bugged, too? No wonder he'd insisted on whispers.

"Can you get away for a while?" he asked, louder now.

"I think so. Daphne's here. I wanted to go and check

on my father since I haven't heard from Santo this morning." She checked her watch. "It's midmorning. He should have called by now."

"We can do that." He stood and lifted her up and into his arms. "Go and check with the nurse and then meet me back here."

Rikki hurried to her mother's room but Sonia was already asleep. After she explained that Detective Kent was escorting her to see her father, Daphne tucked in her mother and came to stand with her near the door.

"I gave her the usual sedative for pain. She should sleep until dinnertime."

Rikki gave her mother a kiss and thanked Daphne. "I'll be back in a couple of hours."

"Take your time," Daphne said, her tone a tad impatient.

Deciding Daphne didn't like people hovering while she did her job, Rikki went to her room and grabbed her purse and a light jacket.

Blain was checking his phone but glanced up when she returned. Together, they walked outside. Rikki alerted the guards that she was leaving and sent one of them to sit inside in case Daphne and her mother needed anything.

"What's really going on?" she asked Blain when they were in his truck. "You're not in your official vehicle."

"I went by my folk's house for breakfast and came straight here," he told her. "I got the call about the car's registration right after I left there."

Then he took her hand. "And I just needed to see you and make sure you're all right."

"I am today," she said, the warmth of his touch giving her strength. "I tried not to think about last night and everything else that's happened to me lately." She stared out the window as the truck moved up the shell-encrusted land toward the iron gate. "I keep remembering Chad and how he tried to control me. What was he up to? Why was he here? He's dead now and I should feel something, but I'm so numb and in shock I honestly don't know what to feel."

"You and he were close for a while, so it's natural to mourn him. Someone murdered him and that's cause for you to be concerned for your own safety."

"Any idea who might have done this?"

"No answers on that one yet. It might take a while for the medical examiner to give us a cause of death or any other clues."

"Two people I knew just wiped away. It's not fair, Blain."

"No, it's not, but evil doesn't care about that." He gave her a solemn stare. "We have to hold out hope that God will see us through. That together, we can figure this out."

Her cell rang and Rikki jolted up in the seat. "It might be Daphne," she said. But when she saw the caller ID, her pulse shot up. "It's Santo."

"Can you come to my house?"

"Santo?" She glanced at Blain and saw the question on his face. "What's wrong?"

Her brother heaved a sigh. "I'm here with the kids and Lucia is sick with a horrible cold. I need to work and check on Papa, but my sitter didn't show up."

"And you want me to come?"

"Yes. I know you're not supposed to leave but maybe you can get someone to come with you?"

Rikki could hear children in the background. Little

Nate was just a toddler and Lucia and Adriana were eight and six. How could Althea leave her children?

After explaining to Blain, she gave him a beseeching stare. "Lucia was a toddler when I left and now she's eight. Adriana and Nate don't even know me. I have to go, Blain."

"Then I'll be the one to take you."

He turned the truck to the left instead of heading back toward the hospital. "And you can call and check on your father while we're driving."

"Okay." She told her brother they were on the way. After she ended the call, she shook her head. "I don't see how a mother could leave her little children like that. What is wrong with my family?"

"Good question," Blain said. "Hopefully, we'll soon get the answer to that question and all the others we have."

Blain took in the striking modern house sitting on a low bluff over the bay. The stark white tri-leveled home was a contrast from the Alvanetti mansion up the road. This one was more glass than wood, with calculated symmetry and shifting roof lines. He could see the sparkling blue water straight through from the massive glass doors and the wall of windows across the back of the house.

"Impressive," he said to Rikki.

"Althea's dream house." She glanced around at the oleanders and sago palms. "And now she's nowhere to be found."

Blain made a note of that. "Interesting."

"You don't think—"

He didn't answer the question since the door swung

open and Santo Alvanetti stood there looking rumpled and frazzled in jeans and a white button-up shirt. He gave Blain a hostile glare and then focused on Rikki. "Thanks for coming."

Rikki and Blain entered the big open foyer, the sounds of children coughing and calling out echoing up into the rafters of the house. Blain took in the polished wooden stairs and the high ceiling where a glass-and-wood light fixture bigger than his truck hung suspended in an artsy display. An open gallery ran around the second floor, allowing for a stunning view of the entire house. A massive Christmas tree stood on one side of the staircase, surrounded by presents all wrapped with matching paper and bows. And toys of various sizes and shapes littered the entryway and moved like a trail of colorful crumbs toward the back of the house.

When he heard more screaming and crying, he followed Santo and Rikki to the left where a large family room furnished with a white leather couch and two bright blue wing chairs seemed to be command central. The couch had splashes of a bright red goop on it and the chairs were smeared with what looked like the remains of canned spaghetti noodles.

The kitchen across the way was even worse. Dirty dishes everywhere and the distinct odor of burned toast lingering in the air. The row of windows displayed an infinity pool and a panoramic view of the water below. A big, furry dog barked to be let into the house.

And then there were the kids. The oldest, Lucia, as Rikki had called her, lay on the couch wrapped in a blue-and-white throw. Her expression exhibited dismay and fear.

Blain could identify with those feelings. He'd never

been good with kids. He'd never thought about having any children.

But then, he'd never thought about being a family man until he'd met Rikki.

Another little girl ran to Rikki and started crying.

Rikki lifted the child into her arms and patted her dark head. "Adriana, I'm your aunt Rikki." She looked over the child's head at Santo. "She was a baby when I left."

"You've missed a lot of things," her brother said with a growl.

Blain watched Rikki with the little girl and his heart seemed to grow two sizes. He pushed at the emotion roiling through his system like a giant wave. He needed to get his head back in this investigation.

"What can I do to help?" he asked Santo, hoping to take his mind off things he couldn't have.

The other man shook his head and looked around. "Do you know how to change diapers?"

"Not really," Blain said. "But I do know how to clean a kitchen and I'm pretty good at removing food stains from furniture."

Santo's look of appreciation marked yet another twist in this case. Maybe Blain's dad was right. Maybe the best way to get to the truth was to keep plugging away and earn the trust of this family. Blain could be wrong about them, but someone was definitely after the Alvanetti family for a reason.

He'd help get this situation under control and then he'd sit down with Santo and Rikki and see if he could get them to talk to him. About anything and everything.

A couple of hours later, Rikki had bathed Adriana and Nate and made sure they had a good lunch. Then she'd put them both down to rest. Adriana was reading picture books in her room and Nate was drifting off in his race car bed. Now she was sitting with Lucia. She'd checked the little girl's temperature and made her a bowl of chicken soup. Then she'd called the pediatrician and gotten advice on which over-the-counter cough syrup to use.

Now she watched as Blain cleared the kitchen and made sandwiches for the grown-ups. He'd also cleaned the floors, stacked the toys in a corner and sprayed the whole pile with disinfectant and somehow managed to get the tomato-sauce stains out of Althea's prized French blue high-back chairs.

Amazing. He'd been a real trouper. She knew he was a good man but seeing him in such a domestic situation made her dream of her own home and a man like Blain helping her with their children.

"I called the hospital," Santo said after coming downstairs. He'd had a shower and now wore a clean shirt and jeans. "Papa is awake and demanding to be released."

"That's good to hear," she said, blinking away the scene she'd just envisioned. "Can you go and pick him up, Santo?"

Her brother glanced around. "Yes, as long as you can hold down the fort here."

"We can do that," Blain said from the kitchen. "But before you leave, could I have a word with both of you?"

Santo put his hands on his hips and stared at Blain. "Is this important?"

"Yes," Blain said. "It involves my investigation."

Rikki shot her brother a warning glance. "Let me get Lucia settled in her room." She kissed the girl's head. "Is that okay, honey? Ready to take a nap now?"

The little girl bobbed her head. "Will you come up and check on me, Aunt Rikki?"

"Of course, sweetie." Rikki got up to help Lucia but Blain was there.

"Let me." He smiled at Lucia. "Wanna go for a ride up the stairs?"

Lucia's shy smile gave him his answer. He lifted her into his arms. "You can be like a little bird."

Rikki checked her brother but Santo's scowl had turned to mush as he watched his daughter laugh. His eyes went misty and he turned away.

"I'll be right back," she said, touching Santo's arm.

Then she followed Blain up the stairs and heard him ask where the princess lived. Lucia told him which room. By the time she and Blain had Lucia tucked in, Rikki's heart had told her what she'd been trying to deny. She might be falling for Blain Kent.

When they got back downstairs, Santo was sitting in a dining chair staring out at the water.

Rikki sat down beside him. "Why did Althea leave?"

He pushed at his thick black hair, his eyes filled with a faraway look. "She hasn't been happy lately. We fight a lot. She said she was just going to visit her family but I know she's not coming back."

"What about her children?"

"She's not concerned about them right now."

Blain sat down across from them and Santo clammed up and went back to staring out the window.

"So," Blain began, his notepad out on the table, "which one of you wants to go first? Somebody needs to level with me. I need the truth, and I mean all of it. I think maybe you both know who might be coming after you but you're afraid to tell me."

Surprised, Rikki shook her head. "You know that's not correct, Blain. If I knew who was doing this, I'd tell you in a heartbeat."

Blain's inky gaze moved over her. "I'd hope so." Then he nailed Santo with a hard glare. "What about you?"

Santo rubbed his eyes and looked down at the table. "I have my suspicions," he finally said. "I think our brother Victor *might* be involved."

Rikki's breath left her body. "Victor?" She turned to Blain. "Maybe he did rent that car that tried to run us off the road."

Santo's gaze moved from Blain to her. "Like I said, *mia sorella*, you've missed a lot of things."

SIXTEEN

Blain sat straight up. "We've been trying to locate your brother and you did tell me you might be able to find him. We have reason to believe he's back in this area."

Santo nodded. "I tried to talk to him but he's not taking my calls and my sources say he's evading them at every turn. I'm concerned about him and I'm worried about my wife being away during all of this. I have to protect my children."

"Do you think your children are in danger?" Blain asked.

"I pray not," Santo said. "These last few weeks have been crazy."

Rikki got up and started pacing. Then she whirled on her brother, her hands gripping the wooden chair in front of her. "What do you know, Santo?"

Santo sank back against his chair, weariness and resolve showing on his face. "The only thing I know for sure is that our company is in trouble. Between my issues with Althea and Mama's sickness, I've been preoccupied over the last few months. And of course, I have Papa on my back on a daily basis, too."

Rikki's guilt showed on her face. "And I haven't been here to help. You should have called me."

Santo expression hardened. "Why? So you could tell me how horribly we treated you and that you wish you'd never been born into this family?"

A hurt darkened her eyes. "Okay, I get that I've been deliberately distancing myself from all of this, but I'm here now. I want to find out who's trying to kill everyone I love and I want the truth. All of the truth."

Blain took notes and studied Santo. He did look haggard and tired. He also looked broken. "What kind of trouble is the company in?"

"We're losing money," Santo said. "Detective, I believe you want to find something to pin on us but once I took over the company, I tried to clean things up. I run a legitimate company now but it's not easy. My wife is angry at me because the money isn't rolling in. I can't make her understand I want something better for my children. I want honesty and integrity and dignity. Kind of hard to put a price on those things."

Rikki stared down at her brother as if she didn't even know him. "Are we going to lose the business?"

"Not if I can help it," Santo replied. "I like what I do and I'm good at it. I just need some time to bring things around."

"So…does that mean you'd do anything to save Alvanetti Imports?" Blain asked.

"No, I won't stoop to anything illegal. That was the old days before my father had a change of heart. This is now. I'm concerned someone else is possibly after the company and maybe they're going about trying to fix things in their own way. And that someone could be

Victor. He's lived off the family funds for a long time now but he's also had his own thing going on the side."

Blain scratched his head. "What kind of thing?"

"I'm afraid Victor might be into smuggling," Santo said. "And our business is the perfect cover."

"So when you mentioned possible smuggling to me last night, is this what you meant?"

"It's just a thought," Santo said. "A natural conclusion."

Rikki leaned down over her chair. "So you're saying that Victor is possibly doing illegal things and that he might be the one behind Tessa's death? And Chad's?"

"I don't know," her brother said, slapping his hand against the table. "I can't prove anything and…he's our brother. I don't want to accuse him if he's not the one."

Blain saw Rikki's pale face. "Hey, sit down. We'll find a way out of this."

"Can we?" she asked as she fell onto her chair. "What if this is Victor?"

Santo's dark eyes widened. "Our brother has done many things but he wouldn't murder an innocent woman. But he knows a lot of shady people and that bothers me."

Blain decided he should have been concentrating on the smuggling angle even more. "And what about Tessa?"

"What do you mean?" Rikki asked.

"Could she have known anybody who'd want something from you? A painting, some kind of artifact or expensive bauble?"

"I don't think so." Rikki shook her head. "Tessa was a good person."

"But can you ever really know all there is to know about a person?" he asked.

Her eyes went dark again. He'd pierced through her worst fears. "I don't know. You tell me, Detective."

Santo missed the moment and plunged ahead. "Your boyfriend could have known Victor, too." He turned to Blain. "You should check around Presley's restaurants in Miami and Tallahassee."

"He never mentioned knowing either of you," Rikki said, her tone full of anger. "And I never brought him home."

"I've got someone looking into several different possibilities." Blain saw the distress on Rikki's face and the mirrored concern on her brother's face. "Did you find anything missing after you inventoried the warehouse?"

"No," Santo said. "I wasn't able to supervise everything but last night after everyone cleared out my workers did a thorough job and found nothing missing."

"If something were missing or say, someone was searching for something, what would be most likely?" Blain asked.

Santo shrugged. "We bring in all sorts of items. Rugs, paintings, jewelry, purses, furniture. You name it."

"Jewelry. That's easy to hide." Blain was grasping at straws but he had to start somewhere.

"Or easy to hide something in if it's a locket or a jewelry box," Santo said. His phone buzzed. "It's the hospital. I'd better go and get Papa."

He got up and then turned back. "Rikki, thank you for coming to help me. I've taken a lot for granted lately. That won't happen again."

"So have I," she said. Then she walked over and

hugged Santo, taking him by surprise from what Blain could tell.

"Are you going to get Althea back?" she asked.

"I don't know," Santo responded. He checked his watch. "The babysitter should be here in about twenty minutes, if she's not late again."

Blain waited until Santo went out the front door and then he turned to Rikki. "What do you make of that?"

"I believe him," she said. "I've never seen Santo like this. Both of my brothers have always been confident to the point of being arrogant. But he looks broken, Blain. Completely broken. I never knew he truly cared about the company and that he wanted to make things right."

Blain tugged her close before he could stop himself. "Well, he seems determined and he did open up to me. This information gives us some teeth. We have a connection now between Tessa's murder and possibly your brother. We can get on this and try to find Victor. Unless both of your brothers are in cahoots."

"But I can't believe that they'd kill Tessa and Chad. This is why I had to get away but I think instead of running from trouble, I created it." She pulled back and looked into his eyes. "You might search for Victor as Victor Kenneth Alvanetti. That's his full name. We all have nicknames. Rikki, Kenny and Sandy, although Santo hated his so we quit calling him that. And we haven't called Victor Kenny for a long time either."

Blain's antenna went up. "Did you say Kenny?"

Rikki lifted her chin. "Yes, why?"

"The *K* we found by Tessa's body."

"The bloody *K*," Rikki said, a hand going to her mouth. "Do you think she was trying to write my brother's name? Kenny?"

"Another question to add to our list," Blain said. "The letter looked like a *K* but it had a slash across it. Hard to say for sure."

Rikki sat down on the couch. "Both of my brothers as possible criminals. But it all started when I returned."

Pushing at her hair, she said, "I keep telling myself to get through this for Tessa's sake. Her killer needs to be locked up. And for Chad. He was a hothead and a jerk but he was murdered, too. We need justice for both of them and the guard who was shot."

"I agree." Blain didn't know what else to say. He wanted to kiss her and take her with him to a place where they could just relax and continue to get to know each other. But he had work to do, work that meant saving her and putting someone in jail.

Dragging her back into his arms, he held her there and then he did lean down and give her a quick kiss. When they heard a car outside, Blain stepped away.

But he did so with a new promise. "When this is over, Rikki, you and I have some things to get settled between us."

Her eyes went black with longing. "I hope that's soon."

"Yeah, me, too."

They let the babysitter in and Rikki took her up to see the kids and went over what needed to be done. Then they got in the truck and headed back to the Alvanetti estate.

That moment when they would both be free and clear of this mystery couldn't come soon enough for Blain. He wanted to be with Rikki Alvanetti. And that realization floored him more than anything else.

"At least no one followed us from Santo's house,"

Rikki said after they were back at the estate. "He should be here with Papa soon."

Blain did his usual thing, checking windows and doors, calling in to the station with an update and giving her covert glances that told her he was all in.

Oh, how she wanted to believe that.

Things had been different today. No one chasing or shooting unless you counted little kids and a big dog chasing each other. Her brother had it all. A family he loved, a solid position in the company and in society, a house with a million-dollar view.

And yet, he'd looked so defeated and dejected this morning Rikki had to wonder what price he'd paid. She wanted those things, too, but she didn't have to have the big house or the view. She'd settle for a little cottage in the woods.

With a small tree and a fireplace and Blain to hold her while she slept. Knowing that might not happen hurt as much as the pain of failing her family.

"All clear," Blain said. "I have to go file my report and put out some feelers on this latest. I've got a private detective on this case, too. Hope to hear from him soon."

Rikki motioned for him to sit. "Do you ever sleep?"

"Only when my eyes shut."

"I should go check on Mama. I know you need to go but stay until I get back, okay?"

"I'll be right here."

She hurried toward her mother's room and found Daphne checking her mother's vitals. "How is she?"

"She's been restless," Daphne said, her tone sharp as usual. "She's been asking for you. I'm glad you're here. Maybe you can calm her down."

"Okay. I'll sit with her a while." Rikki pulled up a chair. "Oh, Daphne, Detective Kent is waiting for me. Would you send him back?"

Daphne gave her a curt nod and left. Rikki would be glad when Peggy arrived tonight. She and Peggy got along great but she thought Daphne judged her and condemned her at every turn.

"Mama, I'm home," she said. "It's Rikki. How are you?"

"Need to find the Bible."

"You want your Bible?" Rikki glanced around the room. It was neat and tidy but cluttered with medicine bottles and other sick-bed necessities. So was the adjoining bathroom. "I don't see it anywhere. Did Daphne put it away?"

"Library."

"It's probably not in the library, Mama. I'll check the nightstand." Her mother always kept her Bible nearby.

She was digging through the deep drawer when Blain walked in. "She's asking for her Bible and I can't find it."

"Want me to help look?"

"Check the other one," she said, indicating the matching nightstand on the other side of the bed.

Blain opened that one and looked inside. Then he rummaged around. Rikki checked and rechecked but only found some other books and papers in the one next to her mother's pillow.

Finally, she gave up and came around the bed. "Anything?"

Blain pulled out a necklace. "Nothing but this."

Rikki stared at the gold chain, confused. "That's odd. The centerpiece is missing."

Blain held up the heavy necklace. "Must have been a big gemstone, right? Was it real?"

"I don't think so," she said. The empty oval inch-wide circle looked damaged around the rim. "It's probably an old costume piece that she tossed in there and forgot. The stone must have popped out or gotten lost."

Blain handed her the damaged necklace. "Maybe you can find it around here somewhere."

Sonia moaned then and opened her eyes. "My necklace. You found it." But when she saw the necklace, she gasped, her hands going to her throat. "Where is the diamond, Rikki?"

Rikki looked from her mother to Blain. "I don't think it was a real diamond, Mama. You wouldn't keep something expensive in that nightstand."

Sonia fell back on the bed. "I need my Bible."

Rikki shook her head and motioned Blain to the hall. "I'd better try to settle her down. We have Bibles all over the house. I'll find one for her and read from it. Maybe the scriptures will calm her."

"I hope so," he said. Then he took the necklace back from her. "Have you ever seen this before?"

She shook her head. "I might have and just don't remember it. My mother is famous for her jewelry. She has several expensive pieces and a lot of costume jewelry, too. But lately, she hasn't worn much of it other than her wedding ring."

"Probably nothing," he said. "But just in case, I think I'll take this to be analyzed by the state crime lab, if you don't mind."

A jolt of fear hit at her already shattered system. "No, of course not." She moved further out into the hall.

"But, Blain, you don't think someone's been inside my mother's room, do you?"

"I don't know," he said, his inky eyes holding hers. "But at this point, anything is possible."

Then he gave her a kiss on the cheek. "I'll check back with you later."

Rikki watched him leave, her mind on the necklace. Why would someone take only part of a necklace? Did they think the fake stone was real?

But then, how had someone managed to get inside her mother's room in the first place?

SEVENTEEN

"Hey, man, I've found out some interesting things about those two brothers."

Blain sank back in his squeaky desk chair and waited for Hunter Lawson to spill it. Which might take a while. Hunter did things on Hunter time.

"I'm listening," Blain said, rubbing his grainy eyes. No sleep and barely any time to eat.

"So Victor Alvanetti got in trouble a lot growing up. Petty theft in Miami, gun violations and drug use. He hooked up with a real big-time gang down there and worked his way up to some kind of lieutenant. Got banished to Europe by his powerful daddy when he overstepped his bounds. And word has it that he's even on his brother Santo's bad side, for flirting with his wife."

"That explains a lot," Blain said. "But we can't seem to find anything to pin this on Victor."

"Give it time," Hunter said through a grunt. "Bad business, Blain. Apparently, Interpol is interested in him, too."

"For what?"

"Stolen artwork and artifacts, smuggling and reselling stolen items. But his little operation is falling on hard times."

"You've found out what I've been trying to find for days now. How'd you do that?"

"I have connections, bro. People who owe me." He laughed. "But none of this came from anybody in Europe. I kind of had to go into the belly of the beast."

Blain shook his head. He did not want to owe Hunter in a bad way or ever get on the man's bad side. But he knew he could count on Lawson to do what was needed and to stay within the law. Hunter had the same code of conduct as Alec and Preacher.

And you, he reminded himself. He couldn't step over that line, even to help a woman he was highly involved with. He'd find a way to save Rikki without losing his honor.

"Thanks," he said. After telling Hunter what Santo had told him, he urged Hunter to go on. "Okay, then, Victor is now number one on my suspect list. Whereabouts?"

"Now that's where things get interesting," Hunter said. "I've tracked him back to the good ol' USA."

Blain sat up. "Like Florida."

"That'd be my first guess."

"But how'd he get back without us knowing it?"

"That I can't answer yet. Later."

That ended the call.

Blain had never heard Hunter speak so much in one conversation. Hunter Lawson did not converse. But he did get down to business and fast.

But that revelation aside, he now had two immediate problems. One, the black sheep brother could be in the area and two, Rikki was even more vulnerable than ever. Had Victor been the one who'd possibility been rummaging around in her mother's room?

He'd question the very silent John Darty again and hopefully shake him up with this latest bit of news. If he could get Darty to spill the beans, he might be able to pin down one of them at least. And find out why they'd murdered three people to get at whatever they wanted.

"I have news, Darty," he said a few minutes later after a guard had let him in the suspect's jail cell. "I know who's been pulling your strings."

"I don't know what you mean," the greasy inmate said with a sneer. "You need to let me go, man."

"We caught you with a weapon that you'd just used to kill a man. Remember? Murder, attempted murder, use of an illegal firearm. Those charges along with your other crimes will have you sitting in a cell for a long, long time. But we will send you to a bigger, better place where you can make new friends."

Darty got a sick look on his face. "I want my lawyer."

"You'll get your day in court," Blain said. "Right now, you might want to consider helping yourself since the people who hired you are going to join you soon enough."

"I don't know what you mean," Darty said, his dirty fingernails doing a nervous dance on the old battered table top.

"I think you do," Blain retorted. "I'm working toward bringing in your boss. If you help me out, I might be able to cut you a deal."

"No dice," Darty said. "I can't help you."

"That's your choice," Blain told the man. "You'll go down with your overseer, then." He studied the man sitting across from him. "Or they'll let you take the fall if they don't have you murdered in your cell." He leaned in, his hands on the table. "That's how these people operate. If you don't do the job, they do you in."

Darty looked scared but refused to talk. "Either way, I'm going to prison," he finally said. "Not much I can do about that."

Darty's expression held a fatalistic expression that almost made Blain feel sorry for him. He'd probably hoped to make a lot of money and skip town. Now he was facing a bleak future. What did he have to lose at this point?

"Look, Darty, we need your help. If you know anything that can lead us to Victor Alvanetti, tell me now. Do it as one last gesture of goodness."

Darty glanced around as if he were afraid someone was listening. "They wanted the woman out of the way. That's all I know."

Blain waited a beat.

"I might have heard something about a piece of jewelry. Worth a lot of money. A lot, man."

Blain got up and nodded. "You just shaved maybe five years off your sentence."

Darty didn't look too happy.

Blain told the chief what he'd heard and was about to call the lab about the necklace he'd found. When his phone rang, he saw Rikki's ID and answered immediately. "Hi. Everything okay?"

"Yes. My mother is more alert today. The doctor came to visit and he thinks she's improving. So that's good news. She keeps asking for her Bible, even though I found one and read to her."

"Glad she's better," Blain said. "Listen—"

"So, remember how I said I needed to get back to work?"

"Yes, but—"

"I've called a few clients and explained but most of them are aware of what's going on. Anyway, I did a few consults over the phone and internet but a couple of them want to meet in person."

"Rikki—"

"You can go with me, Blain." She finally stopped and took a breath while Blain wondered why everyone was so chatty today. "I need to work. I love what I do and now that my mother's better and Papa's on the mend, I thought I could try to find some sort of normal. I'm getting restless."

"It's dangerous," he said. "Too dangerous."

"Have you found anything? Did the necklace show any fingerprints?"

"No word on that yet. But…my private detective traced your brother Victor." He paused and took a breath. "I don't want to tell you this over the phone. How about lunch?"

"Lunch? Out in the open?"

"Yes," he said. "We'll be careful."

"I know you'll take care of me," she said. Then she added, "And Blain, I'll watch out for you, too. I'll see you in a bit."

Blain put away his phone and ran a hand down his face. He hoped he could take care of her and while he was touched that she wanted to do the same for him, he couldn't risk that. He prayed he'd be able to end this and soon. Chief Ferrier came bumbling over, his expression full of questions. "What you got now, Kent?"

Blain filled him in and let out a sigh. "I've narrowed

it down to Rikki Alvanetti's brother Victor and I believe he's in the vicinity but I haven't told her that yet. Now she wants to get back to work, meet with clients. I don't like it."

The chief grunted. "No prints on that fake necklace, by the way. It came back clean. But her brother is after her, so we could set her up to flush him out."

"She'd do that. I think she wants to do that but I don't like that idea, either."

"Look, son, we need to end this," the chief said. "Nobody wants to deal with murder and criminals during the holidays. We got the Christmas parade tomorrow morning and I need every man on that."

Blain nodded. "My gut tells me they'll make a move of some kind when she leaves the house."

"And I can't spare you for protection detail much longer," the chief replied. "We can coordinate with the sheriff's department like we've been doing. Let me find someone else to work the Alvanetti detail for the weekend."

"I don't like that idea, sir."

He leaned on Blain's desk and pushed at his bifocals. "I've heard things, Kent. Are you and the Alvanetti woman getting too close?"

Blain stood up. "You could say that, but don't worry. It's just a matter of time before all of this is over."

"All of it?" the chief asked.

Blain pulled a blank face. "Yessir. All of it."

He grabbed his jacket and headed out the door.

Thirty minutes later, he picked up Rikki and they drove to an out-of-the-way burger joint near the lake.

"My parents are taking it easy today," she said.

"They both seem to be improving but Daphne promised to call me if anything changes."

"That's something," Blain said. "When had you planned on meeting with these clients you spoke with?"

"One later today and one tomorrow," she said. "If I'm allowed."

"I don't like this, Rikki. Your brother could be watching your every move. My PI tracked him back to the States and confirmed what we already suspected. Victor could be our man."

Her eyebrows shot up. "Are you sure?"

"Sure enough. Which is why you shouldn't meet with any clients right now."

"I'll be careful," she said. "I need to get back to work and I can't believe Victor is behind this."

"But someone is."

"You can go with me," she said after they'd ordered their food. Blain had a burger and she ordered a chicken salad.

"Can you change the appointment?"

"I'd rather not. It should only take long enough for me to measure and go over samples with my client."

The waitress brought their food and Rikki stared at her salad as if it was a bowl of bugs. "I can't believe this. If Victor wants something, why doesn't he just ask me for it?"

Blain chewed on a French fry. "I'm guessing it's the jewelry. Something that could bring a pile of money. Only, he doesn't want to ask nice. He wants to take it."

They ate in silence for a few minutes. Soft music played to soothe the lunch crowd, but Blain's nerves were all jumbled.

Finally, Rikki glanced up at him. "I don't think my

brother will try to come after me if you're with me. It's a house out on the island. A newlywed couple. Meredith and Richard are nice people."

"How'd they get your name?"

"The client called me a while back since she knew I was coming to town. She told me they were interested in a complete overhaul."

Blain thought it over. "Today would be better and I will go with you." He took a swig of his soda. "You have to understand, whoever this is, is probably watching your every move. They think you have that piece of jewelry."

"Well, then let's make them think I do. Draw them out and nab them."

"Don't play cop, okay. I'm still the point man."

She pushed her salad away after a few bites. "My own brother, possibly behind this. It doesn't make any sense."

"Do you know anything about your mother's expensive jewelry? I mean where she keeps it? Is it insured? Things such as that?"

"If she does have any valuable jewelry, it's all locked up. She's always told all of us we'd inherit her jewelry but I don't know which is which."

"I think someone thought they'd found the real deal and they took the stone from her bedside table. But now, they've realized that one was a fake and they need the real one."

"That's unbelievable. If Victor needed money, why didn't he just ask?"

"I think he did and everyone turned him down."

She pushed her food away and stared out the window. Blain put his hand over hers on the table. "This was supposed to be a nice, quiet lunch. Sorry I told you all that."

"No, don't say that, Blain. Honesty is the one thing I need right now. I've been lied to all my life, protected in the worst kind of way. But even a lie of protection is still a lie. I need to know the truth."

Blain saw the strength in her eyes. She wasn't like the rest of them. She wanted to do the right thing. She'd come home in spite of her family's sordid past, to be with her mother. And she'd even managed to get closer to her father and one of her brothers while she'd been here.

"You know, before I met you," he said, his fingers still touching hers, "I detested everyone in your family but your mother. She always stood as a symbol of good to me. But I never understood how she handled the alleged rumors that swirled around your family."

Rikki smiled and sipped her tea. "My mother has always been faithful and I don't think that will ever change. She fell in love with my father." She set down her tea glass. "I do believe she tried for years to change him. And while he's still not a churchgoer, I think he's mellowed. He let Santo take over and he seems determined to make things right."

"So you believe it's possible for a person to love another person even if that person is involved in something illegal or immoral?"

She pulled her hand away and gave him a perplexed stare. "Yes, I guess that's what I'm saying. Are you judging my mother because she fell in love with the wrong person? Or are you telling me in you're not-so-subtle way that you can't ever care about *me*, Blain?"

"No," he said, standing when she lifted out of her chair. "That's not what I'm saying."

"I love my family in spite of everything," she said, anger making her cheekbones turn pink. "I had to come to that conclusion the hard way. I lost my best friend and my ex-boyfriend."

"Yes," he said, slapping some bills on the table before he followed her to the truck. "Yes, you did. And now it looks like one of your brothers could be behind this. How will you react to him, Rikki, if that's the case?"

She whirled, one hand on the door handle of the truck. "I guess I'll visit him in jail and pray for him."

"Okay, all right." Blain reached up to touch her hair. "I'm sorry."

"No, I asked for honesty," she said. "And the truth is right here, glaring at me. No matter what happens with this investigation, one thing is for sure. You and I can never be together."

"Why not?" he asked, his heart aching in a way that he'd never felt before. "Why not, Rikki?"

She hopped up into the truck and turned to stare at him.

"Because I will always be an Alvanetti."

EIGHTEEN

Rikki waited to make sure Blain had left.

They hadn't talked on the drive back to the estate. She was still hurt that he'd ask a question that implied what he'd felt from the beginning. Her family was bad news, criminals and immoral people. That her sweet mother shouldn't have loved a man who ignored the rules and did whatever he wanted.

That Blain couldn't love a woman who had deep ties with what everyone considered to be a Mafia family.

But isn't that the reason you left?

Rikki went to her room and sat down in an armchair by the window that had a nice view of the pool and the vast lake beyond. Two seagulls flew across the water, their white wings glistening against the blue sky.

Yes, she'd left full of self-righteous indignation and a misguided determination to free herself from her father's massive shadow. But she'd also left because she was heartbroken and still grieving for her young husband who'd died too soon. He'd died and no one could explain to her why. And she'd left because she had to do things her way so she could make her *own* way in the world.

But had she done that?

She was successful and able to take care of herself but she'd paid a high price for breaking free. She'd made countless mistakes, Chad being one of those, and she'd missed years of being with her family, years she couldn't get back.

But you're here now. You can make a difference.

They all needed her. And maybe she needed to be needed. But did she need her family?

It was time she faced the fact that she *was* an Alvanetti.

So she slinked her way into her father's office and found the key to the gun cabinet. And then she picked out a pistol that she knew she could fire. Her brothers had taken her to target practice enough that she remembered the feel of a gun in her hands.

She'd protect herself. She'd always done that, emotionally. Now it was time to do it to end this horror she'd walked into.

If Victor showed up and tried to kill her, what would he gain? She didn't have any expensive jewelry. Just a few sentimental pieces that she loved and some artsy pieces that she'd bought from friends over the years. Nothing that would net a fortune. And she didn't remember her mother owning anything that would be that extremely valuable. Valuable enough to kill over, at least.

Tired of fighting, tired of running, she called her clients and asked to move their meeting up a couple of hours. Then she packed up the loaded gun along with her samples and her design ideas and started down the hallway to check on her mom.

"You can take a break, Daphne," she told the nurse.

"I need to leave in a few minutes but we'll be fine until then."

Daphne gave her a rare smile. "Okay, I'll be back in fifteen minutes."

After sitting with Sonia for a while, Rikki leaned over to kiss her mother. "I love you, Mama."

Sonia opened her eyes and smiled up at Rikki. "I love you, too, darling. I always have. I love all of my children." She took Rikki's hand. "A mother's love is the strongest on earth." Sonia clung to her. "We have to do what we need to do to protect and love our children."

Rikki saw the fear in her mother's eyes. "Are you all right, Mama?"

Sonia slowly moved her head in a nod. "I'm gonna pull out of this. I'll be back on my feet soon and everything will be better then. You'll see."

"I believe you," Rikki said. "I have some errands to run. I'll send Daphne back in and then I'll be back to check on you before dinner. If you're sure you'll be okay."

"I'm fine. Be careful out there," Sonia said, her eyes beginning to droop. Then she opened them again. "Did you ever find my Bible, honey?"

Rikki shook her head. "I'm not sure I know which one you want. I'll try again when I get back."

"And that key," Sonia said. "I need the key and the Bible."

"What key, Mama?"

"The key, darlin'." Sonia was drifting off. "The key I lost. Thought you had it."

"I only have my car keys and my house keys," Rikki replied.

"Check your purse," Sonia insisted. "Gold."

Her mother drifted off again.

More confused than ever, Rikki hurried into the kitchen area so she could grab a set of car keys. Maybe she'd find her mother's missing key there. Yet one more sign that her mother was still frail and disoriented. Rikki hoped it wasn't something worse.

"Where do you think you're going?" Franco called from his chair in the corner.

"I'm going back to work," she said, turning to walk toward him. His head was bandaged and he looked like he'd just woken up from a nap. "I'm tired of hiding."

Her father gave her one of his frowns. "Where is Detective Kent?"

"He has other things to do today."

Franco shook a finger at her. "You will not leave this property without a guard."

"Papa—"

"I mean it, Regina. Do you want to get yourself killed?"

Before she could respond, he pulled out his phone and issued an order. "Murphy will stay with you at all times."

When a giant of a man wearing a dark suit came through the door, Rikki wanted to scream her silent rage. Not that it would do her any good. Murphy didn't seem to blink at anything.

She hadn't planned for this. Rikki refused to wait for Blain to go with her, maybe because she wanted to prove to him that her own brother wouldn't kill her. But having one of her father's guards with her only made matters worse and proved Blain's point. The Alvanettis had their own code and they protected their own, no matter what it took.

Would her parents protect Victor? Was her mother trying to warn her of that possibility?

"You can leave as long as he's with you," Franco said, as if he were reading her thoughts. He pointed to Murphy. "Don't let her out of your sight."

Rikki stared at her father and then shot a frown toward the guard. "You have to stay outside while I'm conducting business."

Murphy grunted and gave her father a nod. "I'll stay in another room."

Rikki reluctantly gave in and followed the giant outside. Then she got in the back of a dark sedan and stared out the tinted window until they arrived at the beach house. They were late getting out here, due to the heavy weekend traffic but she saw another car in the narrow driveway.

At least she was doing something constructive. Something to take her mind off Blain and the memory of his dark, brooding expression when he'd left her earlier. He wouldn't like that she'd gone against his wishes, but what did it matter now?

She wasn't answering his calls.

Blain stared at his phone and wondered if Rikki would ever talk to him again. She'd seen through his efforts to get past her family dynamics but she hadn't allowed him to explain how his preconceived notions had changed over this last week.

She hadn't allowed him to explain anything. He might seem like the one with preconceived notions but she'd sure jumped to conclusions about him, too.

Now, his gut was burning with the sure knowledge that she'd go off in a tizzy and try to prove something to everyone. She was determined to either flaunt her courage to the world or to get herself into some hot water. That reckless streak *was* a true Alvanetti trait.

Blain asked God to keep her safe until he could get there, but then he figured God had this already. Still, his gut didn't want to accept that.

He was headed out of the police station when Chief Ferrier called to him. "Kent, get in here. We got some news."

Blain whirled to go into the chief's office. "What is it, sir?"

"The crime lab called. The blood on the statue is Franco Alvanetti's, but then, we figured that. But they managed to lift some partial prints, too."

Blain sat down. "And?"

"You won't believe this," the chief said. "Try Althea Alvanetti."

"What?" Blain rubbed a hand down his jaw, an alertness humming through him. "Are they sure?"

"Yes. Very sure. Apparently she had a checkered past before she married into the family. Her prints are on record for some shoplifting and other petty crimes back in the day."

"Amazing," Blain said. "So she tried to kill her father-in-law?"

"It looks that way," Chief Ferrier said. "Now we just gotta figure how to tie this to those other murders."

"Do you think she shot Chad Presley, too?"

"Don't know. We do know the slugs from both murders could have come from the same gun. Might be nice to find that gun."

Blain gave an affirmation on that. "Yep. We've got a partial on the shoe prints we found at both scenes and they seem to match, too. That could prove the same person was at Rikki's town house and out behind the warehouse."

"The murderer," the chief said, nodding.

"So the shooter could definitely be the same person."

"Yes."

Blain stood. "I have to get out to the Alvanetti estate. Regina Alavanetti is not happy with me right now. I think she might have bolted."

"As in, left the premises?"

"Yessir. She got mad at me earlier when I questioned her mother's loyalty to Franco."

"Maybe you punctured a hole in Miss Regina's loyalty, too."

"I think I did. And I believe she's just now realizing she is still loyal to her family." And so was he at the moment.

Chief Ferrier's bushy brows did their usual frowning slant. "You might want to keep digging, son. From what I hear, Sonia Alvanetti always wore the pants in that family. And I'm pretty sure she still does. I don't believe she's ever had a problem with what Franco does for a living."

Rikki and the hulking guard made their way up the wide steps to the broad porch of the stunning house out on Millbrook Island. Out here, the houses were big and spacious and pricey. The view of the Gulf of Mexico sparkled beyond the wide glass windows, the whitecaps crashing into bubbling foam against the creamy sand.

This house had been vacant for a while. What furniture the previous owners had left was sparse and covered with sheets. A blank slate for Rikki to decorate and pamper. She couldn't wait to throw herself back into work.

Murphy rang the doorbell and peered through the glass door at the empty entryway and the big room beyond. "I have to check things out," he said, indicating he would be going inside with her.

Rikki started to protest and then changed her mind. She was behaving like a spoiled brat, coming out here on her own. She didn't want to get Murphy shot, too. "Okay," she said, wishing now she hadn't been so impulsive and reckless. Wishing Blain was here with her in spite of their differences.

Blain cared about her. She knew that from his kisses.

She cared about him. She'd tried to show him that in her kisses and in all of her actions.

But it was too late to fret about Blain right now. When no one came to the door, she turned to Murphy. "They're supposed to meet us here. Maybe they're running late."

She turned to search for any other cars. A luxury sedan sat in the short drive but no other vehicles were on the property.

"Try again, Murphy," she said, her nerves wrapping around themselves.

Murphy rang the bell and then jiggled the door knob. The big door slipped open.

"Maybe they want us to go on inside," Rikki said.

Murphy blocked her from doing that. "Not yet, ma'am."

He went in ahead of her and walked like a shield in front of her through the sprawling one-level home.

"See? Nothing," Rikki said, relief washing over her after they'd checked every room. "I'm sure they're on their way. I can do some measuring and take notes while we wait." She gave Murphy what she hoped was a confident smile. "You could wait out on the terrace."

"I stay here," Murphy replied. "Where you go, I go."

"Okay, then you can hold the tape measure for me."

Soon Rikki was immersed in sketches and ideas. She typed notes on her electronic pad and got to know Big Murph—as he instructed her to call him. Murphy was soon laughing and talking and telling her about his six children.

"I never knew you had children," she said. She'd seen him through the years, always hulking around but she'd never actually talked to any of the guards much. While they went from room to room, she enjoyed their banter and promised herself she'd reach out to the people around her more.

"It's been thirty minutes," he said when they came back into the big kitchen and dining room area. "Whatta you want to do now?"

"I'll try to call again," she said, a dagger of apprehension slashing through her. She left a message with the wife and then turned to Murphy. "I think this was a bad idea."

He pulled out his revolver. "Yeah, me, too. I got a funny feeling and it ain't a good one."

They were heading for the front door when it swung open and Althea Alvanetti walked in. "Hello," she said to Rikki. "Long time, no see."

"What are you doing here?" Rikki asked, a tremble of warning moving up her backbone. Her sister-in-law looked thin, her short white-blond hair curling around her cheeks. She wore a beige wool coat over winter-white pants. Her green eyes looked a little too bright.

"I thought Meredith would be here," Althea said on a serene smile. "I did recommend you to her, after all."

Meredith. The homeowner. A friend of Althea's. Rikki's stomach roiled in tune to the waves crashing below.

"She's late and we're leaving," Rikki said, reaching a hand in her bag to locate her loaded gun. "I thought you had left town. I heard you'd gone to Miami."

"Not yet," Althea said. "Not that you'd care."

Rikki gripped the weapon, not sure if she could shoot the mother of Santo's children. "I care about my brother and my nieces and nephew."

Althea's eyes flared hot. "Yeah, and you're such a model of society. You left and never looked back until now."

"Althea, what do you want?"

"I told you, I came to see my friend."

Rikki wasn't buying that. Althea looked nervous. She kept glancing back over her shoulder. She paced back and forth, blocking the front door.

Murphy put a hand on his gun holster. "Miss Althea, don't make me have to pull out my weapon again."

"Shut up, Murphy," Althea said. "I'm not here to harm the little princess."

Rikki was about to push past her when a car pulled up. Hoping beyond hope that Blain had tracked her down, she glanced at the figure coming up the steps to the porch.

Her heart sank and she knew she'd made a fatal mistake coming here. Her brother Victor walked in, grabbed Althea in a hug and waved his gun toward Rikki and Big Murph.

"Take out your weapons," Althea said on a giggle. "Put them on the floor."

Sick to her stomach, Rikki stared at her brother. "I told them it couldn't be you. I defended you and everyone else in my family and I came out here today to prove them wrong."

"Joke's on you," Althea said. "He's with me now." She laughed up at Victor then waved her gun. "Now put your weapons on the floor."

Rikki nodded at Big Murph. They both carefully laid their guns on the hardwood. Althea shoved the guns away with her booted foot and then smiled up at Victor. "I was right that she couldn't resist showing off her decorating skills."

Victor didn't respond. Instead, he gave Rikki a thoughtful stare. "You're a hard woman to pin down, Rikki," he said. "But…at last, I've found you."

NINETEEN

Blain couldn't get Rikki to answer. He tried the estate house phone. Daphne answered.

"Listen, Daphne, this is Detective Blain Kent. I need to speak to Regina Alvanetti. It's urgent."

"She's not here," the nurse said. "She left with one of the guards. She had an outside appointment."

Blain closed his eyes and let out a breath. "Do you know where they went?"

"No. One of her clients."

He heard someone talking in the background.

"I have to go," Daphne said. Then she hung up.

He could call one of the guards but there wasn't any time. So he pulled up the client list she'd given him. Five names. One was Alec Caldwell. He'd call him if he couldn't find her at the others. He called the next one on the list.

An older gentleman answered and went on and on about how wonderful she was and how much he loved his home. But he said he'd rescheduled everything with Rikki since she was dealing with family matters.

Blain hit the steering wheel, still sitting out in the parking lot. He couldn't call and drive at the same time, but he was sorely tempted. The next call went to voice mail. He decided not to leave a message. Too dangerous.

Three more.

A maid answered the next call and explained the owners were out of town.

Number four yielded a bubbly young mother who said she totally understood that Rikki couldn't work with her right now, so they'd decided to put things off until after the holidays.

That left the last one. He checked the address after that one rang and rang. Then he remembered what Rikki had told him. Althea had given her a referral. The island. The house was out on the island.

He cranked his truck and peeled out of the station parking lot. Then he radioed in and asked for backup.

Traffic out to the island was heavy. People rented condos during the weekend of the Christmas parade. And they'd already started coming in.

Blain hit the siren that he rarely used and tried to move past a long row of cars over the causeway bridge out to the barrier island on the Gulf of Mexico, sweat beading on his brow.

Dodging the sparse oncoming traffic off the island, he finally reached the old beach road and turned toward the mansions that lined the coast. But which one?

Searching on both the Gulf side on the left and the bay side to the right, Blain blinked and tried to focus. When he reached the curve that followed the shore, he saw a big stucco house with a massive set of wooden steps with ornate banisters. And two dark sedans parked in the wide gravel and shell drive. One of the sedans looked like one he'd seen at the Alvanetti estate.

This had to be the place.

Skidding onto the drive, he barely moved off the road before he jumped out of the truck and rushed up the stairs.

The front door stood ajar.

Blain's heart beat with a burst of adrenaline. He held his weapon up and pushed through the door, a silent prayer caught against each pounding of his pulse.

He checked the big open kitchen and living area and then carefully went through the empty rooms. In the last bedroom, he found a big man lying on the floor.

Big Murph. He worked for the Alvanettis.

"Murphy? You okay?"

Blain checked his pulse and found a solid beat. He had a nasty bump on his wide forehead and but other than that, Murphy seemed to be alive at least.

Blain called it in and then rolled Murphy over. "Hey, Murphy, can you hear me?"

The big man grunted and squinted up at Blain. "Detective?"

"It's me," Blain said. "Murph, what happened? Where is Rikki?"

Murphy moaned and blinked. "That Althea. She came in and then… Victor showed up. They took… Miss Alvanetti. Took my…gun and…hit me over the head." He winced. "I'm sorry. I tried but they took her away."

Blain held a hand on the big guard and stared out at the brilliant sunshine hitting the water. And he wondered what to do now. When he heard sirens coming up the beach road, he waited.

But he called Santo Alvanetti while he was waiting.

Rikki didn't know how to pray. She was so angry at herself and the world she wanted to scream out to anyone who'd listen. She wasn't mad at God because *she* was the one who'd decided to run again. To go out on her own and do what she thought was best, rather than waiting on the Lord and the protector he'd sent to guard her.

Stupid.

Her own brother and her sister-in-law, in this together.

How could her family ever recover from this?

The sun was setting toward the west as the big SUV flew up the two-lane road. Victor drove while Althea sat in the back with a gun to Rikki's head.

"Why?" Rikki finally asked, still dazed from being dragged down the long row of steps at the house. Her whole body throbbed in protest from being forced into this vehicle.

Althea's laughter was full of a bitter bite. "Why do you think? My husband has always been too noble for his own good. He never wanted any part of the family's business but he was forced to take over when your father became too senile and disinterested to keep things going. He changed everything and became what he calls legit. Now we're struggling day in and day out. It's not right."

"Santo is a good man," Rikki said, her gaze hitting Victor's in the rearview mirror. "He wants to do what's right."

"He's weak," Althea said, her vivid green eyes widening. "Just like his father."

"And what about you, Victor?" Rikki asked. "How could you ever stoop this low?"

Victor stared at her in the mirror, a flash of warning in his eyes. "I have my reasons."

Althea pushed the gun at Rikki. "And you sit in judgment of us. You have no idea what this family's been through since you left."

"As if I'm the reason for all of your choices," Rikki shouted. "I left because of things like this. The secrets and lies, the betrayal. You all killed Drake and now you'll finish me off. And why? Over some lost piece of jewelry?"

"Rikki, Drake drank too much and had a horrible accident," Victor said. "I wish you'd accept that."

"I can't," Rikki said. "And I can't accept this."

"She knows where the necklace is," Althea said to Victor. "That's the only reason I'm here."

Victor didn't say a word.

"I don't know anything about a necklace," Rikki said. "Why would I?"

"Your mother told Victor about it the day of the wedding and then she mentioned it again when she was in Europe," Althea said. "He thought she'd give it to him eventually since he's the oldest. But then she lost her marbles and had to be shipped home. I know she must have told you what happened to it after you suddenly decided to return to the fold." Althea dug the gun into Rikki's rib cage. "You have the key to that box."

"I don't have any necklace," Rikki said. But she now understood who'd been snooping in her mother's bedroom. "And I sure don't have a key."

"She's lying," Althea said, shouting up to Victor. "Sonia let it slip that she gave the key to Regina."

"We're heading to the town house now," Victor retorted. "So relax."

The key? Her mother had mentioned a key. Her Bible and the key. Were the two connected? She almost said something but decided to bide her time. If they were taking her to her town house, she might be able to escape somehow.

A few minutes later, Victor pulled the vehicle up to her house. "We have to hurry, Althea. Find the key and get out."

"I don't have a key," Rikki said again. They ignored her.

"You have a door key," Althea said. "Open it."

Rikki did as Althea asked, praying she could find a way out of this situation. Would they kill her if she didn't find what they wanted?

The house was eerily quiet, the Christmas tree looking lonely and forlorn and the smell of a sickly sweet cinnamon scent she'd once loved making her gag.

Althea forced her up to her room. "I want you to find your gold purse," she said. "The one Sonia gave you last Christmas. You had it at the wedding."

Rikki's heart skidded. Her mother had mentioned the word *gold* to her earlier. She thought her mother meant a gold key. Now it was a gold purse?

"I can only think of one," she said as Althea shoved her into the closet while Victor stood watch. She tried to breathe, tried to put one foot in front of the other. But in her mind, Rikki was screaming for her brother to stop this and help her.

"Find it." Althea seemed to delight in holding that gun at her back.

Rikki searched until she found a square gold leather clutch that had to have cost a small fortune. The designer emblem flashed at her in a gaudy wink, making her wonder why she'd ever liked this purse in the first place. She'd left it here after the wedding, never dreaming her mother had placed a key inside.

"Look inside," Althea said, shoving at her again. "And hurry."

Rikki thought about hitting Althea over the head but Victor would just take over. Her silent prayers held her steady while she searched inside the deep pockets of the purse.

And felt a big key.

Althea pushed her against the closet door. "Give it to me now!"

Rikki pulled out the key. "Here. If it means so much to you, take it."

Althea grinned and shoved her out of the room. Rikki dropped the purse on the bed, hoping if Blain came here he'd find it out of place.

"Let's go, Victor," Althea said. "We need to get to the warehouse before dark."

Victor mumbled and gave Rikki a hard glare.

Her brother had turned into someone she didn't even know. Since when did he let Althea call the shots?

"You two deserve each other," she said as she went past Victor.

He didn't respond. Soon they were back in the SUV and zooming out toward the warehouse. The sun was beginning to set toward the west.

And with darkness, Rikki's chances of making it out alive would soon end. They had the key now. They'd kill her. They'd been trying to kill her all along, probably so they could get in her house and search it under the guise of being concerned family. She had no idea what they thought they'd find. She didn't have the necklace.

But her brother didn't seem concerned now. He kept right on driving as if they were out for a leisurely ride.

Then her sister-in-law looked out the window. "Victor, we have to get to the warehouse before they find us."

"I need to talk to Mama," Victor said. "She might be able to tell us what we need to know about the jewelry case."

"Are you crazy?" Althea asked, disbelief sounding in her tone. "That old woman won't remember a thing."

"No, Althea," Victor said. "I know exactly what I'm doing. Mother has always been on our side. If we don't find the necklace tonight, I'm going to talk to her."

Confused, Rikki stared from her brother to her sister-in-law. "What do you mean?"

Althea laughed again, all of her anger gone now. "Your mother is one smart cookie. And she's probably not happy about the way things have been going lately."

"But she's too sick to even know what's going on," Rikki replied. "Just take the key and leave her out of this."

"She's forgetful," Althea replied. "But she's still the one in charge." Althea glanced up at Victor. "Do you think she's on to us?"

"Mother always knows what's going on," Victor said. "She knew which purse she put the key in, didn't she?"

Althea giggled. "I guess so. You did manage to get that much out of her. We have it now, anyway."

Rikki thought she might be ill. Could it be possible they'd all fooled her? Could her dear, sweet mother really be involved in this, too?

TWENTY

Blain paced back and forth inside the empty beach house. Murphy had been taken away in an ambulance but not before he'd given them a complete description of both Althea and Victor Alvanetti.

"It was them. They didn't even try to hide it."

Blain couldn't believe he'd missed the Althea angle. But how did Victor play into all of this? Was he in love with Althea?

"They talked about a necklace," Murphy said. "I heard 'em right before I passed out. Some necklace that could bring them millions of dollars."

Blain stopped in his tracks. That necklace had to be either at the Alvanetti warehouse or at the estate. At least all of the clues showed that someone had been searching for it at both places and at Rikki's townhome, too.

They'd sent a patrol over there right away. A report had come back that someone had been there. An empty gold purse was lying on the bed in Rikki's room.

He wondered if she'd gone by there or if whoever had her had left that purse there.

He turned and hurried to the chief. "I have to go."

"And where are you going?"

"To the warehouse and then the estate. I think the necklace could be at either location. And that means they might have her there, too."

"But she's been at the estate for several days now," the chief pointed out.

"But they didn't know where the necklace was hidden," Blain said. "I'm beginning to think they never wanted Rikki dead. They just wanted her out of the way so they could search for this mysterious necklace."

"So they killed people all around her to scare her?"

Blain nodded. "Or they killed people all around her because they panicked. Either way, if they have what they want now, they'll be done with Rikki."

Chief Ferrier frowned and pondered. "I don't know what you're doing, Kent, but you are sure up to your eyeballs in this case. You take someone with you wherever you're going."

"I will," Blain said, turning to leave.

"I'll go with him," a deep voice called out from a hallway.

Blain turned to find his dad standing there.

"Where did you come from?" he asked, surprised. He'd been waiting to hear back from his dad about Billy Rogers and now here he was.

Sam checked the hallway and then said, "I heard chatter on the radio. So I drove out and came in the door when you were in the back." His dad moved close. "I need to talk to you. Privately."

Blain wanted to leave but he walked with his father into a bedroom. Dad wouldn't halt him unless this was important.

Sam spoke into Blain's ear. "I have Billy Rogers

handcuffed out in my car. And he's told me some very interesting things."

"Let's go," Blain said. He'd blinked and let Rikki walk right into a trap. He hoped Billy would give up the goods on the entire clan and right now, he didn't care whether they did things by the book or not.

Because the whole family was once again under suspicion.

Rikki yanked away from Althea's hold on her arm after they entered the back door to the warehouse. She'd tried to find a way to run but the night was so dark she feared she'd get lost in the thick woods near the river. That might be better than sticking around to die here, however.

She tried to get to the truth by talking. Maybe she could stall them. After they entered the warehouse, she said, "This is ridiculous. My mother has been ill for months now. She can't be in on this. She's been asking—"

She stopped and clammed up. She wouldn't give them any ammunition to use against her. The warehouse was dark and still, with large crates and boxes everywhere. She could hide here amidst the clutter until someone came for her. It was the only way.

"Asking what? What has your mother been telling you?" Althea said, whirling with the gun pressed to Rikki's chest. "You'd better tell me now."

"What are you doing?"

They all turned to find Santo staring at them from a dark corner near the hallway to the office. He flipped on a glowing yellow light that cast an eerie aura all around them.

"Santo?" Althea looked shocked. "What are you doing here?"

"I asked you first," her husband said, his tone flat, his eyes as black as coal. His gaze moved from Althea to Rikki and then back.

Althea faltered. "I...have business here. You should leave."

Santo stared at his wife. "And what business would that be since you left me and our children? Maybe I should ask Victor about that?"

Rikki tried to run to Santo, but Althea held her and pointed the gun to her head. Rikki spoke to Santo. "They claim Mama knows what's going on. They want a necklace that's worth a lot of money."

"Mama is safe at home," Santo replied, his tone as calm as the wind outside the window. "*I* have Daphne and a guard in her room. Our father is there with her."

"Daphne?" Althea's confidence was waning by the minute. "But she's—"

"In on this?" Santo asked, his dark eyes following his wife's every move. "I think you're wrong there, darling. I hired Daphne personally and she follows my orders. Not yours."

"What?"

Santo's calm, angry eyes met his wife's. "I'm not going to call in the law just yet. I'm giving both of you a chance to explain this first. So you'd better make it good."

Rikki saw the fear in Althea's cold eyes. Had she truly believed she'd get away with this? Rikki glanced from Althea to Victor. He hadn't spoken at all. But she saw a look passing between her brothers. A knowing look. What was going on around here?

"I'm waiting," Santo said. "Speak up before it's too late."

And then another man stepped around from the hallway. "It's already too late."

Blain!

"I'd suggest you two hand over that key," he said, his own gun drawn. "You're not getting the necklace and you are not getting away with anything else. But you are going to jail for murder."

Althea looked shocked. "How did he get in, Victor? You told me he'd be taken care of." Her skin turned a molten pink. "We have to end this. Go talk to your mother and get her to be reasonable."

Santo held up a hand. "No one is going to disturb our parents. You had your chance."

Victor drew a weapon and stepped up beside Althea. "Everything will work out." Holding the gun on Santo and Blain, he tugged Althea away. "Let's get out of here."

"No." Althea yanked at Rikki and tugged her back, her gun held to Rikki's head. She gave Blain a cold stare. "Put that gun down or I'll take her out of here and none of you will see her alive again."

"You won't do that," Blain said, his gun still raised. "You need Rikki to show you where the jewelry is hidden. Tell her, Santo."

Santo nodded, his hands in the air. "I know exactly where it's located. If you want that necklace so badly, well, I'll be glad to give it to you."

"I'll kill her after I find the box," Althea said, bobbing her head. "I don't need you anymore, Santo. We'll get the necklace and then Victor and I can finally leave together just as we planned."

Santo started toward them again, his dark eyes on Victor, his shaggy black hair ruffled. "My own brother, double-crossing me. Victor, you know you won't get away with this."

Victor didn't seem to care. He looked gaunt and tired, his brown eyes flashing. "Don't be stupid, brother. Your wife wants to be with me."

Rikki wondered why Victor seemed so detached and uncaring. He looked so different, too. His hair was shaved short. He'd aged into someone she didn't recognize. Had Victor truly lost his mind?

Blain tried to make a move, but Althea waved her gun again. "I said, drop the gun. I can always kill her now. I'll find the necklace on my own if I have to." She edged the gun closer to Rikki. "And if you come after us, I will kill her just like I killed Tessa and that idiot Chad."

Rikki tried to twist away but Althea held her. Rikki watched Blain, her gaze holding his. He didn't want her to try anything that could result in a shoot-out.

Blain held up one hand and then placed his gun onto the floor but shook his head. "You don't need to kill anyone else. We can work this out. Take me and I'll find the box you're looking for. I think it's hidden underneath the floor in the office."

Althea let out a cackle. "Everyone is so noble today. Take me. No, take me." She gave Santo a look of disdain and then shook her head at Blain. "I can't do that." She turned the gun toward Blain but Santo pushed Blain out of the way.

And then a shot rang out and Rikki watched as Santo stumbled to the floor.

"No," she screamed as Victor grabbed her and forced her toward the office while Althea held the gun on Blain.

"Don't do it," Blain said. "You'll regret this."

"I only regret that I married the wrong Alvanetti," Althea said. "I have the key and I'm leaving here with her. I don't care what Sonia or anyone else says. Rikki knows where that box is. She has to know. I've searched everywhere. She'll inherit the necklace but it should have been ours." She stared down at where Santo held his shoulder. "I need that necklace."

Then she shot the gun into the air and pushed Rikki up the hallway. "Don't follow us," she said to Blain.

Rikki glanced back, worried about Santo and afraid that Blain would be shot next. When her eyes met Blain's he nodded to her. "I'm going to come for you, Rikki. I promise."

But after Victor slammed the door to the hallway and locked it, she had to wonder if he'd be able to keep that promise.

Blain stooped to check on Santo.

"Go, go," Santo said. "I'll be okay."

Sam Kent came running from the back of the warehouse. "Hey, everybody okay here?"

"Check on Santo," Blain called. "He's been shot. They took Rikki."

"They won't get far," Sam shouted. "We've got people on the way."

"I'm going after them. They're headed to the office."

"Got it," Sam called. "Be careful, son."

Blain rushed outside, hoping to ambush them at the front of the big building. The dark, moonless night was draped in a heavy humidity that chilled him down to his bones. The parking area was empty now, except for the dark SUV hidden out back. His dad had parked on the road. Billy Rogers was handcuffed in the backseat.

Blain prayed their little sting wouldn't get Rikki killed.

Things had gone down fast after Billy Rogers told them the plan. Blain and his dad had decided to hurry out to the warehouse and wait for Victor and Althea, but Blain had called Santo to warn him. Good thing, too. Victor and Althea had detoured to Rikki's town house, giving Blain just enough time to get everyone situated here and warn the Alvanettis to be on the lookout. Blain should have taken them both out the minute they arrived but Santo thought he could reason with them.

Now Rikki was at the mercy of her brother and the mastermind behind this heist—Althea Alvanetti. He'd have to sort all of this out later. He had to help Rikki.

He approached the hulking building from the side, a sick kind of dread filling his heart. The door was locked tight and after checking several windows and doors, Blain decided the place was empty.

Where had they taken Rikki?

Rikki didn't know where she was.

They found the secret compartment hidden beneath a rug under the desk. Victor lifted out a heavy wooden box that looked like a true treasure chest. Then Althea insisted on hurrying toward an underground storage area.

"We need to get out of here," she kept shouting. "And we need to kill her and dump her."

Victor finally showed some emotion. "I'm not killing my sister. Do you want to spend the rest of your life in jail?"

"We can kill her and go away, Victor. To anywhere in

the world. They can't find us now. Tessa is dead. Chad is dead. We're free and clear now." Then she snorted. "Except for this one little detail—your sister." When he didn't make a move, Althea added, "Do I need to remind you that I have certain information that can ruin you forever?"

Rikki didn't dare speak up for fear that Althea would realize she'd blurted out too much information. But she now saw the truth. Althea was blackmailing Victor.

But Victor didn't seem too worried about that. "You shouldn't have shot the woman, Althea. You know what Rikki looks like. How could you have mistaken Tessa for my sister?"

Althea urged him on, her gun pressing in Rikki's back and they climbed down a set of stairs. "I haven't seen your dear sister since the wedding last year. I panicked, okay. It was an accident."

Victor let out a grunt of frustration and lifted the box onto an old table. "All because of the infamous wedding where you overheard Sonia talking to me about the necklace. Rikki stood to inherit it and you didn't like that."

"It wasn't right." Rikki heard Althea shuffling behind her. "I'd had it with Santo," Althea said. "And then your mother encouraged me to take matters into my own hands."

"Yes, she sure did." Victor sounded defeated. "But I don't think she meant for you to kill anyone or steal a priceless necklace. She wanted you to save your marriage."

They discussed and argued until all of the pieces of the puzzle fell into place. Rikki stayed quiet until they'd moved deep into the underground storage area that sat near the river. The plastic curtains to the loading dock flapped in a slow breeze. She thought she heard water lapping against a shore.

The wind surrounded her while they dragged her toward the big open doors. This part of the building smelled musty and decayed. She didn't want to think about what they planned to do to her.

"Do you think this will work?" Althea asked.

"It's the only way," Victor replied. "You're more stealthy and athletic than me. And I believe you know these particular woods. You can make it out with the necklace and I'll take care of everything else."

"I want to see it first," Althea said, her tone full of a greedy urgency. "We need to check the box."

Rikki absorbed everything. Could they be near the woods where Althea must have hidden the night she shot Tessa?

"Let's hurry," Victor said on a breath of irritation. "Detective Kent confirmed what we already knew."

Althea groaned. "Your father walked in last time and caught me. Then that stupid Chad Presley showed up."

Rikki gulped a breath. "Did you kill Chad, Althea?"

"Shut up," Althea said, yanking out an ornate key. "I had no choice. He showed up to talk to dear old dad about you, the idiot. He was worried about you after he heard about Tessa's tragic murder."

Rikki blinked back tears. Chad hadn't come here to kill her. He'd only wanted to talk to her father.

"And I guess you had no choice when you killed Tessa, either," Rikki shouted, bile rising in her throat.

"She got in the way," Althea said. "It's a shame. I planned to kill you but your friend showed up before I could find that infernal key. I had to run before you saw me. Then Victor talked me out of it but now—"

Rikki didn't care if she lived or died now that she knew the truth. "Victor, please stop this now. Stop before it's too late."

Althea cackled. "It's already too late for you. I have the key and I have everything I need now."

Rikki started to retort but Victor's hand grasped hers and squeezed tight. A warning? He must have purposely forced Althea to talk. He'd given Rikki all the information she needed. Was he going to help her, after all?

She stood silent while Althea held the ornate key that Sonia had apparently hidden in Rikki's purse on the day of the wedding. Victor didn't make a move.

Althea chuckled when the big heavy box clicked open. "Let's see what we have." She stared down and then let out a yell. "What is this?"

Victor walked over and shone a flashlight on the deep box. "It looks like trinkets."

Althea slammed her hands against the old table. "It's junk, Victor. Junk. It's like kids' toys." She turned on Rikki. "Where is the necklace?"

Rikki went on instinct after remembering something her mother had said. "I'm tired of lying. It's at the house. But you'd better hurry. Detective Kent will send out a search party."

She watched Althea pacing around, her hand pulling through her short, spiky hair, her eyes going wild and unsure.

And in that brief moment, Victor leaned close. "I'll explain later, Rikki, but… I'm not a part of this. I'm going to get you out of here."

TWENTY-ONE

Althea pulled Rikki away from Victor. "I don't like being double-crossed. I want that necklace!"

Althea was beyond reason. She lunged at Victor and knocked him against the wall. He hit his head on the corner of an iron shelf.

Rikki screamed and pushed at Althea. The other woman came at her but Althea didn't have her gun. She'd laid it on the table by the old box. Rikki kicked at Althea and pushed her toward Victor. He stumbled to his feet and grabbed Althea and held her while Rikki reached for the gun.

Althea screamed and shoved at Victor. Still disoriented, he called out to Rikki. "Get out of here. Run."

"I won't leave you," Rikki shouted.

Althea broke loose and rushed toward her. Rikki screamed and held to the gun but Althea was taller and stronger. She lifted Rikki's hand up in the air and tried to pry the gun away from her.

Victor moved toward them. "Stop it, Althea. It's over." He held his head and then he sank to the floor and passed out.

Althea screamed and bent Rikki back against the

table. "No. No. I won't let it be over. We need the money. I have to get away from this family, from this place."

Rikki stared into the eyes of a madwoman and sent up a prayer that if Althea killed her, the death would be quick. She groaned and used every ounce of her being to stop Althea.

Then she heard footsteps echoing down the stairs. "Rikki?

She took in air and tried to call out. "Blain, down here!"

But it was too late. Althea held Rikki pinned to the table and wrestled the gun closer and closer to Rikki's midsection.

Blain called out. "Let her go. Now!"

Althea didn't seem to hear him. But Rikki had a reason to fight now. Blain had given her so many reasons to live. She grunted and with one last surge of energy she kicked and lifted her body enough to force Althea up.

"Let her go," Blain shouted.

Althea turned then, the gun aimed at Blain. He lifted his gun and shot at her several times.

Althea fell to the floor and went still while Rikki stood against the table, the horror of the situation causing her to gulp and hold her hands to her face.

And then, the room went quiet and she was in Blain's arms.

Safe, warm and treasured.

Treasured.

"It's over," he said, his hands tangled in her hair. "It's all right now, Rikki."

Franco Alvanetti sat in the big chair behind his desk and stared over at Blain and Rikki. "I can't believe what you're telling me. Both of my sons in the hospital and my daughter-in-law dead. All because of a necklace."

Blain nodded. "All because of a necklace and a myth regarding some sort of ill-gained treasure."

Franco wiped at his eyes and looked over at Rikki. "We can't let your mother hear about this. It will destroy her."

Rikki swallowed and glanced at Blain. "But Althea indicated that Mama might know something more. That Mama encouraged her to…take matters into her own hands."

"Your mother was probably telling Althea to save her marriage. Althea always did love the money more than she loved your brother."

"That is so true."

They all turned to find Sonia in a wheelchair being pushed by Peggy and Daphne.

Franco got up and hurried to his wife. "What are you doing out of bed, Sonia?"

Sonia wiped at her eyes and waved the two nurses away. After they left, she said, "I know more about this than anyone. I hear things, see things, and I suppose I said things that didn't make sense but I was trying to save my family. I knew something was going on." She smiled at Rikki. "I tried to warn you but… I was all mixed up."

Rikki got up to kneel in front of her mother. "You mentioned the key and the Bible. But which key and which Bible, Mama?"

"I don't know," Sonia said. "I remember bits and pieces." She glanced around. "It started after your cousin's wedding. I went on my Mediterranean cruise and met up with Victor. He told me that Althea had tried to have an affair with him. She wanted to leave Santo and move to Europe."

"That's crazy," Franco said, sitting down on a bench next to Sonia. "Victor never liked her."

"She told him what she'd heard at the wedding. Me, telling Victor about the diamond-and-emerald necklace. I'd already told Santo that if anything happened to me, I wanted Rikki to have it." She shrugged. "He might have told Althea or he might have forgotten. He never really listens to me, anyway."

Franco went pale. "You mean the necklace I gave you when Rikki was born? Is that the necklace Althea wanted?"

Sonia nodded. "I hid it. I was afraid of it. I was afraid of the treasure you purchased all those years ago. That somehow that treasure would be the ruin of us one day."

Franco let out a sigh and explained. "I bought it from a treasure hunter and convinced him to sell it to me at a cut-rate price. But I sold off everything but the necklace. That treasure helped us to launch our business." He gave his wife a sad stare. "I'm not proud of how I forced that poor man to cut that deal but… I can't go back and change it now."

"Althea overheard Mama talking about it and she approached Victor and forced him into a plan to help her steal it," Rikki said. "I finally figured that part out when they took me inside the warehouse. Althea was blackmailing Victor. She has something on him."

"Victor wouldn't do this," Sonia said. "He's made some mistakes but he was trying to clean himself up. Both of our boys want to do what's right, Franco."

Franco patted her hand. "I know, darling. And I promised you the same." He looked at Blain. "I went legitimate years ago thanks to your dad, Detective Kent. He gave me a chance to make things right and I tried my best to do that. For my wife and for our baby daughter. And because Sonia taught me to be faithful in God's plan, not my own." He stared out at the water. "I've failed miserably."

Rikki wiped at her eyes. "Victor was trying to protect me. But why didn't he come forward sooner?"

Both of her brothers walked into the room. Santo had his right arm in a sling, his upper arm bandaged. Victor followed, looking pale, his head bandaged.

"We broke out of the hospital," Santo said. "I want to see my children."

"They're fine," Franco said. "Peggy is with them. You can see them after we get to the bottom of this mess."

Santo kissed his mother. "I'm so sorry, Mama."

Victor glanced at Rikki. "I had to pretend to help her. I sent Mama home after she became ill but I worried that Althea would do Mama harm so I kept trying to distract her by pretending to go along with her crazy plan. I told Santo what was going on but—"

"I didn't want to listen," Santo said. "I couldn't believe my wife could be so conniving and callous."

"We fought about it for months," Victor said, "but when she killed your friend, I had to follow through. She found out about some items I smuggled and she held it over my head. I had to come back home and try to stop her."

"But I got shot at," Rikki said, trying to fathom his reasoning. "Someone killed one of the guards."

"Althea's doings," Victor said. "She hired John Darty. But Althea shot Tessa, thinking she was you. Your friend tried to leave a clue. That wasn't my initial. It was probably an A."

"For Althea," Rikki said. "We couldn't figure it out."

"And the night we got chased on the bay road?" Blain asked.

"Billy Rogers was working undercover," Victor said. "And so was I. I had to pretend to keep her calm so we tried to scare you. We never intended to send you over the bluffs.

"When Althea left Santo, I was afraid she'd gone off the deep end. But we met in Miami and then I came back here with her. I agreed to help bring her in, in exchange for…a lighter sentence. We had to make it look like we'd tried to scare you, Rikki."

"You did," Rikki said. "A dangerous game, Victor."

"I'm sorry I let it go so far," Victor replied. "So sorry."

Santo nodded, his eyes full of fatigue. "I feel the same. Now I have to tell my children that their mother is dead."

"She was unstable," Sonia said. "I knew it, too. I tried to encourage her but she misunderstood my intentions."

"She said you were in charge of this family," Rikki replied.

"I am," Sonia said on a smile. "But in a good way."

"I can vouch for that," Franco said. Then he turned to Rikki. "I need to clarify one more thing, however. Drake's accident—"

"Was just that," Rikki said. "I have to believe that or all of this has been in vain." She glanced around. "And I have to accept that sometimes, things just aren't what they seem."

"Not what they seem." Sonia glanced around the room and then let out a gasp. "I remembered. I just remembered." She pointed to the bookshelf behind Franco's desk. "The big Bible up there. Would someone please get it down for me?"

Blain hurried to lift the ornate Bible off the shelf.

He placed it on the desk. "Do we need the key?"

Rikki pulled out the key Althea had used back at the warehouse. "Will this one work?"

Victor nodded. "The fake box was never locked. It had a latch that easily opened. Althea never even noticed when she used the key."

"I found it on the floor," Rikki explained. "It should be evidence, right, Blain?"

He smiled at that. "You've learned a lot, hanging with me."

"Open it," Sonia said, a bittersweet smile on her face.

Blain turned the key in the big lock that held the Bible closed. When he opened the Bible, he found a secret compartment inside. Rikki reached in and pulled out the necklace.

She looked at Blain and then held the intricate necklace up. A diamond-encrusted chain held an inch-wide emerald-and-diamond teardrop necklace that shimmered in the early morning light.

"This has to be worth millions," she said.

"It is," Franco replied. "Sonia hid it because she was afraid it would only bring her heartache." He touched a hand to his wife's shoulder. "And I never even knew it was here."

"You should read your Bible more often," Sonia said to her husband, her old brilliant smile lighting up the room. "I always told all of you that."

Franco kissed her. "Don't get sick again, darling. I'll read the scriptures to you every night, I promise."

"I'm better now," Sonia promised. "But I wanted you to have the necklace, Rikki. Your father changed after you were born."

"We've all changed," Santo said. "But we've paid a heavy price. I don't want any part of that necklace."

"I hope you all can forgive me," Victor said. He stared at Blain. "I know I gave a statement the other night and I understand I can only hope for a short prison sentence or at the least, probation. But I've kept records and I have taped conversations to prove that Althea planned most of this." He looked at Rikki. "I only wish I'd stopped it sooner."

Blain rubbed his forehead. "We'll have to sort it all out, but I think we can safely say that this case is closed. We've matched the partial shoe prints to Althea's sneakers and along with Billy Rogers's statement and Althea's jumbled confession to Rikki, I think we're okay."

Sonia cried and hugged everyone. Blain bagged the necklace as evidence. Then Sonia said, "I have a splendid idea. Why don't we donate this to Alec Caldwell's next fund-raiser for the Alexander and Vivian Caldwell Canines Service Dog Training Facility? I can't think of a better way to make this completely right."

Blain leaned close to Rikki. "I can think of a few other ways to make this right."

"Such as?" she asked, her heart hopeful for the first time in weeks.

"Attend Alec and Marla's wedding with me and then we'll celebrate Christmas together."

"I like that idea," she said. They waited until her

brothers and her parents had left for breakfast. Finally, they were alone in the office.

Blain pulled her in his arms. "I don't know where we're going from here, but I want you in my life, Rikki. Do you think we can make it?"

Rikki tugged him close. "I think we have a good chance. We've survived the worst and we were both wrong about so many things."

"Let's make a new start," he said. "After all, this is a special time of year."

She stared down at the sparkling necklace. "Yes, and we both know what the real treasure is, don't we?"

"Yes, we do," he said.

Blain leaned close and kissed her. "Merry Christmas, Rikki."

"Merry Christmas," Rikki said. She kissed Blain and held him close, a sweet peace settling over her. She had so much to be thankful for.

Together they went into the big den where her family had gathered by the Christmas tree.

And she thanked God for a chance to start over again.

One week later
Christmas Eve

"This was such a lovely wedding," Sonia said, all bundled up in her big evening coat. "Thank you, Hattie, for inviting our family."

Alec's jovial aunt Hattie held her hand against her baby-blue cape and patted Sonia on the hand. "It was our pleasure. I understand you need to get home, but I'll come out and visit soon."

Sonia nodded and reached up from her wheelchair

to take Rikki's hand. "Bring Blain back to the house for cookies and punch tonight, darling."

Rikki kissed her mother and watched her parents leave through the open garden gate. "Well, at least we didn't manage to distract attention from the bride. Marla looks so pretty."

The bride wore a white lacy dress with a white long-sleeved lacy bolero over it and the groom wore a tuxedo. The big outdoor fireplace, along with smaller fire pits and heaters set in discreet locations around the yard, kept everyone warm but the evening had turned out to be mild, anyway.

Rikki looked over to where Marla and Alec were dancing on the makeshift floor that had been set up underneath twinkling lights in the big garden of Caldwell House. The white Victorian mansion had been decorated to the hilt with red and white bows, white and red flowers of all kinds, several different decorated Christmas trees, and more white lights. "This place looks like a big wedding cake."

"Yes, and I hear Marla baked her own cake," Blain said. "Let's go try a piece."

"It does look good." Five white tiers covered with creamy eatable magnolias and bright red ganache poinsettias. "And they look happy."

"I'm happy myself." She loved Blain in a tuxedo, loved watching him stand as Alec's best man.

He smiled over at her and took her hand. "Before we have cake, let's dance. You know, we've never danced together."

"We have a lot of firsts to get through," Rikki said.

"And a lifetime to try them all over and over again."

Rikki looked into his eyes. "So do you want that?"

He pulled her into his arms and they started waltzing to the soft music. "A lifetime with you? Yes, I do. I love you in this amazing green dress and I love that little black furry muff around your shoulders and... I love your eyes, your pretty lips." He stopped. "I love you, Rikki."

"I love you, too," she said. "But my family—"

"Will now have a police officer hanging around."

"I think we can all live with that," she said. "I know we still have a lot to work through but I think we're on the right path now."

Then she kissed him and smiled up at him. "I'm coming home, Blain. To you."

* * * * *

HOLIDAY ON THE RUN

Laura Scott

This book is dedicated to all the sisters of my heart, Renee, Marianne, Lisa and Sarah Iding. Love you all and thanks for the great Christmas memories!

For the Lord is good and his love endures forever;
his faithfulness continues through all generations.
—*Psalm* 100:5

ONE

SWAT team member Nathan Freemont ducked his head against the swirling snow as he jogged across the megamall parking lot to reach the entrance of the building. The place was jam-packed with people, and he knew it was his own fault for waiting until the week before Christmas to do his shopping.

He had only a couple of gifts to buy, one for his dad and another for his dad's new wife, Amelia, so with any luck he could be in and out within thirty minutes. At least, that was his plan. As he was still wearing his uniform, he had no intention of lingering.

Of course, it would help if he had a clue what to buy. He was hoping something in the mall might inspire him.

Nate headed toward the escalator leading up to the second floor, where he could see a shop that specialized in scented lotions. Amelia would probably like something like that, wouldn't she? Didn't all women like that stuff?

He eased through the crowd to step onto the escalator, scanning the sea of faces intensely. He was first and foremost a cop, and he instinctively made sure there wasn't anyone looking suspicious enough to cause trouble.

But he didn't see anyone suspicious. Instead, on the other side of the escalator, a pretty woman caught his attention. She held the hand of a small girl who he estimated to be about five years old. The woman's features looked familiar, and as they grew closer, his eyes widened in surprise.

"Meredith? Meredith Dupont?" he called above the din.

The woman's head jerked up, her gaze clashing with his, and he noticed her pupils flared in recognition before she deliberately turned her head away, ignoring him.

Was he losing his mind? Hadn't Meredith died years ago? He clearly remembered the devastation he'd felt at the news. He'd even attended her memorial service.

But no matter what his old reality might be, he couldn't seem to tear his gaze away from the woman. As they passed each other, he was convinced he was right. Despite her dark hair, rather than the honey blond he remembered, he knew that the woman was Meredith Dupont. He'd know her anywhere, since he'd fallen in love with her during their senior year of high school.

"Meredith!" he shouted again, louder. She continued to ignore him, and since the escalators were taking them in opposite directions, he made a split-second decision.

He planted his hands on the center area between the set of mechanical stairs and jumped over, prying his way into the crowd. People around him muttered and moved away with annoyance, but he didn't care.

"Meredith!" He dodged around people in an attempt to reach her. "Meredith, wait!"

Meredith swiftly moved farther down the escalator, urging the child along with her. When they reached the ground level, she headed straight into the crowd of adults and children who were waiting in line to see the mall Santa.

Nate followed her, wondering if he was crazy to think the woman was really Meredith, after all. He hadn't seen her in twelve years, since she'd broken his heart by disappearing right after graduation. He'd practically staked out her father's house, begging for information. Her father had claimed she was in rehab and wouldn't provide any details. But her dad had agreed to give Meredith his address.

He'd never heard from her again. And a mere four years later, he'd been told she'd died in a terrible car crash—a result of driving under the influence.

Was it possible he was wrong? No, she'd jerked her head up to look at him when he'd called her name earlier. And her dainty facial features and her wide hazel eyes were exactly as he remembered.

The woman was Meredith. He was sure of it. He zigzagged his way around the display of Santa's elves decorating the North Pole. As he scanned the area again, he noticed two men wearing black leather jackets were also weaving a determined path through the crowd of shoppers toward the area of the mall where Santa was being photographed with children. The tiny hairs on the back of his neck tingled in warning.

Were these two guys actually following Meredith and the little girl? And if so, why?

Nate quickened his pace, dodging around people in an effort to catch up with Meredith. He thought for sure he'd lost her, but then he caught a glimpse of her dark hair above the navy blue parka she'd been wearing. He could see her moving rapidly through the mall, only this time, there was no sign of the little girl.

Surely she hadn't left the child behind?

As much as he wanted to keep an eye out for the two leather-clad guys, he didn't dare take his gaze from Meredith. As he gained ground, she turned back to see if she was being followed and he caught a glimpse of the bulge beneath her jacket.

A flash of admiration made him smile grimly as he realized she was holding the child against her, hiding the girl beneath the bulky winter coat. Smart move, especially since she could dart around shoppers more easily this way.

Meredith was headed toward one of the side exits, and he followed, risking a glance behind him. The two guys in black leather were farther back but still making headway directly toward them.

Nate picked up speed, determined to catch up to her. He no longer needed to confirm she was Meredith. Now it seemed he had to help keep her and the child safe. Her head was averted as he came up alongside.

"This way. We need to ditch the two guys following you," he urged in a low voice.

For a second he thought she would resist, but then she glanced over at him, giving a terse nod.

He tugged at her arm, taking her down a hallway that led to the public restrooms on one side and a staff break room and lockers on the other. He remembered the area all too well from working a mall shooting eighteen months ago.

"Mommy, I'm scared."

"Shh, Hailey, it's okay," Meredith whispered. He could see the very top of the little girl's head poking out from beneath Meredith's parka. "We're fine. Just hang in there a little longer, okay?"

"Through here," he said, pushing open a door that led to the break room.

Meredith had barely got through the doorway when he heard the distinctive poofing sounds of a gun being fired through a silencer.

"Get down," he shouted, ducking his head and slamming the door behind them, blocking Meredith and her daughter with his body as much as possible.

He pulled his .38 and then dragged Meredith farther back into the locker room. "There's a bathroom up ahead. Get inside and stay low on the floor next to the toilet if you can. Don't come out until I tell you."

Meredith nodded again. Her eyes were frightened, but she was calmer than most women would be under the circumstances. Maybe she didn't realize the extent of the danger, but somehow he didn't think so. No time to consider the implication of that fact now.

Once Meredith and Hailey were safely in the bathroom, he pulled out his cell phone and called for backup, even though he knew it was probably a useless effort. If these guys kept coming, he'd have no choice but to defend himself.

Nate had no idea what he'd stumbled into, but right now, he didn't have time to think about the various possibilities. He grabbed the break room table across from the lockers and flipped it over on its side so that he could use the wide metal slab as a shield.

It wasn't foolproof, but since he wasn't wearing body armor beneath his uniform, it was the best he could do. He hoped that the guys would come in aiming high so he could shoot from his lower position.

He crouched down behind the table, waiting patiently for the gunmen to approach. He couldn't hear a peep from either Meredith or Hailey, which was good.

The doorknob of the break room slowly turned, and he held his pistol steady on the top edge of the table. Nate held his breath, knowing he couldn't shoot until he knew for sure who was on the other side of the door. He didn't dare fire at some innocent mall staff member.

The door swung open, and several long seconds passed before one of the guys in black leather edged around the corner to peer into the room. When he caught a glimpse of the guy's gun, Nate knew the waiting time was over.

"Police! Drop your weapons!" he yelled. When the guy didn't comply, Nate fired off two rounds, one of them lodging in the wooden door frame a fraction of an inch from where the guy's face had been. Instantly, the face disappeared.

Nate swallowed hard and kept his gaze trained on the doorway, knowing his situation was grim. The gunmen had the advantage, not only because there were two of them against one but also because they knew exactly where he was located. Plus, it wasn't exactly as if the metal tabletop was a bulletproof barrier.

But he refused to give up. If he died today, that was fine, but he'd make sure to take these two gunmen with him. He had no idea why these guys were following Meredith and Hailey, but no way would he allow either of them to be hurt.

Nate adjusted his aim, trying to anticipate the gunmen's next move. Seconds passed by with impossible slowness, but he knew the value of patience.

The two men came in with a one-two punch, guns

blazing. Nate fired in return, taking the first guy down even as one bullet whistled past his own head, while another plowed through the tabletop, mere inches from Nate's right shoulder. He fired at the second guy, catching him in the upper arm. The gunman cried out in pain and dropped his gun, sliding to the floor with a surprised expression in his eyes.

Nate didn't hesitate, leaping over the table and kicking both of the gunmen's weapons well out of the way before checking to see if they were still alive.

They both were.

The first guy was bleeding from his abdomen, so Nate grabbed some towels and pressed them over the wound. He pulled a chair over, tipping it on its side to add pressure and slow down the bleeding.

The other guy was still conscious, holding his own hand over the wound in his biceps. "You're not going to get away with this," he said in a harsh tone.

"You're the one who fired at a cop," Nate said grimly, even though he had no idea what he'd stumbled into. He quickly cuffed the man to a metal bar beneath the table and then spun on his heel to head back to the bathroom where Meredith was hiding with Hailey. He was stunned to hear singing, catching the phrase "Jesus loves me." The choice surprised him since Meredith hadn't ever been particularly religious in high school.

Obviously things had changed. She not only was alive and had a daughter but also believed in God.

"Meredith? It's me, Nate. Are you and Hailey all right?"

The singing stopped, and he could hear movement inside before the door opened a crack, revealing Meredith's face. "We're fine, but what happened?"

"The guys who followed you are both—taken care of." Nate amended what he was going to say in deference to the little girl. He pushed the bathroom door open wider, giving Hailey a reassuring smile. "The bad guys are going to be arrested so they can't hurt you anymore. I have backup and an ambulance on the way. Meredith, I need to know what's going on."

She shook her head. "My name isn't Meredith. It's Melissa. Melissa Harris. And we can't stay. We need to get out of here, now. Before anyone else sees us."

Nate knew the woman was Meredith, and the name Melissa wasn't that much different. She'd obviously changed it, but for the life of him he didn't know why. "Meredith—Melissa, your name doesn't matter to me. I remember you from high school, and I know very well you remember me, too." He crossed his arms over his chest and planted himself in front of the bathroom doorway. "You're not leaving. Not until you tell me what's going on."

Her gaze implored him to listen to reason. "Please let us go. Making me talk to the police will only put us in more danger."

Nate stared at her, trying to understand what was going on. "I've wounded two men," he said bluntly. "I'm a sheriff's deputy sworn to uphold the law. I can't just leave."

Melissa actually winced. "I know, and I'm sorry. Of course you can't leave. We'll go on our own. You have to trust me on this, Nate. I refuse to put my daughter's life in jeopardy."

Nate glanced down at Hailey. Her tear-streaked face and the fear reflected in her hazel gaze ripped a hole in his heart.

He closed his eyes and sighed, knowing he was likely going to regret this. "Okay, let's get out of here. I'm coming with you."

Melissa's eyes widened in surprise. "Where?"

"If you think I'm letting you go off on your own, you're nuts. You have two choices. Stay here and wait for my backup or allow me to take you someplace safe."

She hesitated and then reluctantly nodded. "Okay. We'll go with you, for now."

He planned to stick with her longer than *for now*, but there wasn't time to argue. His team would be here at any second.

His boss, Griff, would likely fire him for leaving the scene of a police shooting, but there wasn't anything he could do about that now. Not when the fear he saw in Melissa was too real. No way was he going to put a woman and her child in danger.

And he was determined to get to the bottom of whatever Melissa was involved in.

Melissa couldn't believe that out of all the people to stumble across in Milwaukee, Wisconsin, it would be Nate Freemont.

Her old high school sweetheart.

The man she'd been forced to leave behind.

She wasn't totally surprised to find out he was a cop, since law enforcement was all he'd talked about back when they were in school. Twelve years later, fate, or maybe God, had brought them back together. Being with a cop was dangerous, and she told herself that after he'd helped her get away, she'd ditch Nate as soon as she could.

Deep down, she was relieved not to be alone. Hailey

didn't deserve to be in danger like this. Melissa knew coming home to see her father in the hospital before he passed away had been a mistake. She'd thought for sure everyone around here believed her dead and buried.

Apparently not. Something she should have been prepared for, since after all, there was no statute of limitations on murder. Despite the fact that she'd changed her identity and faked her death, they'd found her. She'd noticed a tail on her as soon as she'd left the hospital, so she'd come to the busy megamall, trying to disappear into the crowd of people. Her intent had been to hop a bus, but Nate had shown up before she'd been able to make her way back outside.

And then he'd solved the problem by taking down the two men who'd followed her.

She picked up Hailey and followed Nate out of the break room, glancing at the two men who lay wounded. She shivered, feeling sick at the thought of what might have happened if Nate hadn't seen her and recognized her. Granted, hearing him call her by her birth name had been a shock. But she might not have escaped the gunmen if not for Nate's help. She'd prayed for him while she and Hailey had hidden in the bathroom singing church songs.

"This way," Nate said, gesturing over to the right. There was a long hallway that ended with a door marked Exit. She took Hailey's hand and headed down the hall.

"Mommy, I'm hungry," Hailey whined.

"I know, sweetheart. We'll get something to eat soon," she said, trying to soothe her daughter.

Nate nodded, and when he smiled, he reminded her so much of the young man she'd fallen for all those years ago. "We'll get something to eat, but first we need to get to my car, okay?"

Hailey gazed up at Nate with big solemn hazel eyes, and Melissa's heart squeezed in her chest at the hero worship she saw reflected there. Hailey was too young to remember her own father, who'd died before she was even born. It was only logical that she'd latch on to Nate as a father figure, especially after he'd saved their lives.

"We're going to have to walk in the snow," Nate said, his tone apologetic as he gestured to the heavy metal door leading outside. "I'm parked way on the other side of the mall."

"No problem," Melissa said. She didn't want to go anywhere near her rusty old sedan, even though it had cost her dearly—five hundred in cash. The gunmen had followed her from the hospital, which meant her license plate number was compromised. For all she knew, they'd already reported the information to whoever was paying them.

She tried not to give in to the wave of hopelessness. She would not only have to escape from Nate but also need to find a new vehicle. She didn't have enough money to buy another car, so she'd be forced to take a series of buses to their next destination. Wherever that might be.

Nate pushed open the door and gestured for her and Hailey to go out first. A blast of cold air hit her in the face, stealing her breath. Melissa bent over to tie Hailey's scarf over her daughter's nose and mouth.

"It might be better if I carry her," Nate said in a low voice. "We'll get to my car faster that way."

She nodded, knowing he was right. "Hailey? This

is my friend, Nate. He's going to carry you to the car, okay?"

"Okay," Hailey agreed.

Under normal circumstances, Melissa wouldn't have been at all happy to know her daughter was willing to let a stranger carry her. But nothing about this trip back to Milwaukee was normal. She wished she'd made a different decision, but it was too late to go back and change the past. After all this time, it should have been safe enough to fulfill her father's dying wish to see his only grandchild.

But it wasn't. The only thing she could do now was to disappear again, creating new identities for herself and Hailey.

Melissa quickened her pace to keep up with Nate's long strides as they made their way through the snow-covered parking lot. She hadn't seen snow like this in years, although Hailey had been thrilled with the idea of having a white Christmas. Thankfully the snow had stopped, but the ground was still slippery.

A half dozen police cars were parked around the entrance to the mall where she'd come into the building, and her heart leaped into her throat. Was the dirty cop there right now? Pretending to be one of the good guys?

Nate didn't glance over at the police cars, leading the way to the furthest part of the parking lot.

When they reached the vehicle, she remembered Hailey's booster seat.

"Hailey will have to ride in the back," she said as Nate opened the passenger-side door. "Her car seat is still in my car, along with our suitcase."

"We'll pick them up," Nate assured her.

"Thanks." Melissa scooted into the backseat beside

Hailey, while Nate slid behind the wheel. He started the car and then went back outside to brush off the light covering of snow.

She shivered, trying to remember where she'd left her car. Not far from here, she recalled, but near the area where the police cars were gathered. The thought of going any closer filled her with dread.

Should she forget about the child safety seat and their meager belongings? She'd rather not, since the lack of a booster chair could get them pulled over. Either way, it would bring her too close to the police for comfort.

"All set?" Nate asked as he came back into the car.

"Yes." She forced herself to sound more confident than she felt. "I parked three rows over, closer to the building."

"Okay." Nate backed out of the parking space and followed her directions. She huddled beside Hailey as the red-and-blue lights flashed around them.

"There—the tan sedan parked beside the white pickup truck." She pulled the keys out of her purse, which was slung across her chest beneath her coat, and handed them to Nate.

Within five minutes, Nate had their suitcase stored in his trunk and the booster seat secured in the backseat with Hailey belted in. Melissa chose to stay in the back with her daughter, but Nate didn't object.

It wasn't until they left the mall parking lot that she was able to breathe easier. It was a huge relief to know that she and Hailey were safe, from both the gunmen and the police.

Well, except for Nate.

The sick feeling in her stomach returned with a vengeance. Nate was a good guy, and she knew that he'd put his career on the line to help them.

Yet he was the last person she could trust with her secret. He couldn't know the reason she'd run away from Milwaukee days after their high school graduation twelve years ago.

The same reason she remained a target all these years later. All because she'd witnessed something she shouldn't have seen. Corruption of local politics as well as local law enforcement.

Dragging Nate into this mess would only hurt him and damage his reputation beyond repair in the long run. The best thing she could do for him was to disappear once and for all.

Never to be heard from again.

TWO

Nate kept an eye on Melissa using the rearview mirror. Her face was pale, her expression strained. He squelched a flash of empathy. Granted, she and Hailey had been through a lot, but he wasn't about to let her off the hook, not by a long shot. The minute Melissa and Hailey were safe, he was going to get the answers he needed about what was going on.

Leaving the scene of the crime after he'd shot and wounded two men, even in self-defense, was the hardest thing he'd ever done. Doubt battered his conscience as he drove through the darkness of night.

What did he really know about Melissa after all these years? Obviously she wasn't the same girl he'd fallen for in high school. For all he knew, Melissa could be mixed up in all sorts of things now, even something criminal.

Yet he'd risked everything by leaving with her. What on earth had he been thinking?

"Mommy, I'm hungry," Hailey said, her tone plaintive.

He'd almost forgotten his promise to feed the little girl. He gestured through the windshield. "There's a fast-food restaurant up ahead. Do you want me to go into the drive-through?"

"Yes, please," Melissa said, reaching over to put her hand on her daughter's arm. "Would you like some chicken bites?"

Hailey's head bobbed up and down. "Yay! Chicken bites!"

Despite the seriousness of the situation, Nate found himself smiling at the child's enthusiasm. And the truth hit him like a fist to the solar plexus. The real reason he'd left the scene of the crime was for Hailey's safety. The little girl didn't deserve to be dragged into danger, to be chased by men with guns.

Hailey was the true innocent in all of this. And he was determined to do whatever was necessary to keep the child safe from harm.

He pulled into the drive-through lane and waited in line for their turn. "Chicken bites for Hailey. What do you want, Mer—uh, Melissa? And what would you like to drink?"

"I'll have a cheeseburger and water. Milk for Hailey, please." She dug in her pocket for money, but he frowned and shook his head, waving it away.

Nate ordered a cheeseburger for himself, too, before pulling up to the next window to pay. When they were given their food, he handed the bag back to Melissa.

"Thank you," she said softly. "Here's your sandwich," she added, handing up his wrapped burger.

"No problem." He pulled over to park so he could eat. He listened while Melissa assisted Hailey with her chicken bites, encouraging the little girl to drink her milk.

He couldn't deny Melissa was an attentive mother.

Was she putting on an act for his benefit? He didn't think so. But just caring about her daughter didn't necessarily mean she was completely innocent in whatever had caused the two men to follow her through the mall. As much as he wanted to believe she wasn't a criminal, he knew better than most that power and greed could turn the most innocent to a life of crime.

And he was determined to get to the bottom of whatever she'd got herself involved in.

"Why did you disappear after graduation?" he asked.

Melissa didn't say anything for a long moment. "I'd rather not talk about this right now, Nate," she murmured in a low voice, tipping her head toward Hailey.

He drew in a ragged breath, fighting his frustration. He understood that she wanted to protect her daughter from whatever had happened back then. Or from whatever caused her to run away now. Still, he couldn't help feeling as if she had no intention of cooperating with him, despite the fact that he'd risked his career for her.

Shot two men to keep them safe.

Nate forced himself to finish his burger, which tasted like sawdust on his tongue. He'd find a motel room for Melissa and Hailey to stay in for tonight, but he wasn't about to let them out of his sight.

Not until he found out who she was running from and why.

Melissa wasn't hungry but knew she needed to eat to keep up her strength. The grief of her father's impending death, which she'd pushed into the background when faced with the threat of danger, returned full force, making her throat swell with repressed tears.

A wave of fury filled her chest, and she had to make

herself let go of her anger at the unfairness of it all. Since when was life fair? Right from the beginning, she'd been an innocent bystander. In the wrong place at the wrong time.

Hadn't she suffered enough? She'd lost her home and her life, not to mention Nate. She'd started over in a new place with a new identity, not just once but twice. Thankfully she'd been able to find enough work to support herself—work she could do primarily at home with a computer. But still, it wasn't as if designing websites and doing freelance graphic art work would have been her first career choice.

And surely her daughter deserved a better life?

The very idea of going back on the run, starting over and changing their identities again, filled her with despair. Her father had helped finance her new life twelve years ago.

But this time she was on her own.

Melissa closed her eyes, silently praying for strength and for safety. When she opened them, she was disconcerted to find Nate turned in his seat, staring at her.

For a moment her mind flashed back to the last time she'd seen Nate. The night of their graduation, when he'd kissed her beneath the oak tree in her backyard.

The night before her world had turned upside down.

If only she could go back to change the sequence of events. But those kinds of thoughts were useless. Better to concentrate on moving forward. She needed to stay focused on sheltering Hailey by doing what needed to be done.

"Are you ready to go?" Nate asked, breaking the silence.

"Sure. Finish your milk, Hailey," she said, turning toward her daughter.

"Okay, Mommy." Hailey drained the last of her milk with a loud slurp through her straw, making Melissa smile. "All done."

She bagged up the trash and passed it up to Nate. Would he go outside to dispose of their trash? And if so, did she have the guts to steal his car, drive off and leave him behind?

Thankfully, he took the decision out of her hands by simply setting the bag aside and pulling out of the restaurant parking lot.

Melissa didn't want to steal a car, anyway, especially not Nate's, but what else could she do? Asking Nate to take her to the bus stop would be futile. He'd already insisted on taking her to a motel, and once Hailey was settled for the night, she wouldn't be able to continue avoiding his questions.

Nate had had a strong stubborn streak even back when they were dating in high school, and she doubted that trait would have faded over time. Especially now that he was a cop.

She needed to find some way to convince him to let her go without him knowing the details that had the power to hurt him.

Far more than she'd hurt him already.

"Wait. Where are you going?" she asked in alarm when she realized he'd made a U-turn to head back toward the shopping mall. Even from this distance, she could still see the red-and-blue flashing lights from the police cars gathered outside the mall entrance.

No doubt there were officers searching for her. And she didn't want to think about what would happen if they found her. Hadn't they already tarnished her reputation? If they used the same tactics again, she could lose custody of her daughter.

Hailey would be the one to suffer, another innocent bystander in a political web of deceit and lies.

"Relax. There's a motel not far from here called the Forty Winks Motel," Nate assured her. "We'll stay there tonight. They have several adjoining rooms."

Adjoining rooms? She tried to hide her dismay. Did that mean Nate was planning to stay all night, too? If that was his intent, it would be difficult for her and Hailey to sneak away.

Difficult, but hopefully not impossible.

She refused to consider failure an option.

Melissa held her breath as Nate drove past the mall and turned left onto a side street. Her chest was tight with tension, and even after he pulled into the motel parking lot, she couldn't seem to relax.

They weren't far enough away from the mall—or the hospital, for that matter—for her peace of mind.

Then again, Melissa was certain she wouldn't find peace until she left the Milwaukee area forever. And this time, once she left, she wouldn't look back.

"This doesn't appear to be the type of place to take cash," she said, digging into her jeans pocket as he parked near the lobby entrance. "We'd be better off driving out a ways. The smaller motels aren't as picky about payment."

Nate turned around in his seat. "One of the reasons I wanted to come here is that they're cop-friendly. All I need to do is to show them my badge and they'll take cash."

She smiled through her trepidation and dug in her

pocket for the small wad of bills she'd tucked there. "All right. I have my share." Now that they were here at the motel, she wondered about his personal life. "So, uh, are you sure your girlfriend won't mind?"

He lifted a brow. "No wife, no girlfriend," he said lightly.

The news shouldn't have been reassuring, yet she couldn't squash the brief flash of relief.

When she held out the cash, Nate scowled and shook his head. "Keep your money. I'll take care of this."

Before she could argue, he pushed open the driver's side door, letting in a blast of cold air. When he shut the door behind him, she couldn't help watching him as he walked into the building. Not that she was interested in picking up where they'd left off twelve years ago, but it was surprising to realize just how much taller and broader across the shoulders Nate had become.

Melissa tore her gaze away, glancing over to make sure Hailey was all right. Her daughter's eyelids were drooping. No doubt she would fall asleep as soon as they were inside their motel room.

Melissa told herself that it was a good thing, since Hailey needed her rest. They'd been on the move for the past two days, making the trip from South Carolina up to Wisconsin. The moment they'd arrived in Milwaukee, Melissa had called the hospital, only to discover her father had taken a turn for the worse. She'd headed straight over, despite the fact that Hailey had been travel-weary from the long car ride.

She'd been happy to see that her father was still conscious, that he'd smiled at her and seemed so happy at meeting his granddaughter in person for the first time.

Oh, sure, they'd been using Skype to keep in touch, but it wasn't the same.

Within five minutes of leaving the hospital, she'd noticed the tail. Two men in a dark car, keeping pace behind her. She'd tried to lose them, taking a turn into the mall parking lot and quickly parking the car to dart into the building.

Where Nate had recognized her, despite the fact that it had been twelve years and she'd changed her hair color. Unable to master the art of wearing tinted contacts, she hadn't been able to do much more to change her appearance.

She was so completely lost in her thoughts that she didn't hear Nate return until he slammed the trunk, the noise making her startle.

He opened the passenger-side door closest to Hailey. "I have your suitcase. Can you carry Hailey?"

"Of course," she said, pasting a smile on her face.

"I wanna walk," Hailey said in an abrupt flash of independence.

"Okay, that's fine," Melissa assured her. She disconnected the lap strap, allowing Hailey to climb down from the seat onto the slush-covered parking lot. She edged around the seat to follow Hailey, disconcerted when her daughter skipped alongside Nate.

"We stayed in lotsa hotels on the way here, right, Mommy?" Hailey said, her previous sleepiness seeming to have vanished. "Do they have the kids' channel here?"

"I'm sure they do," Nate assured her, holding the door open for them so they could precede him into the building. "Our rooms are on the second floor," he said, leading the way up the stairs. "We're in 210 and 212."

Melissa nodded, moving slowly enough to match Hailey's small steps climbing the stairs. As they made their way down the hall, she watched the numbers outside the doors until they arrived at the correct ones. Nate didn't hand her a key, though. He simply unlocked a door and held it open for her.

"Thanks," she murmured, glancing around the room to locate the connecting door.

Nate set her suitcase down on the bed and then placed the key card on the dresser. "I'd appreciate it if you'd keep the connecting door between our rooms unlocked," he said as he crossed over to it and opened it.

"I understand," she said evasively, unwilling to make a promise she might not be able to keep.

"Movie, Mommy! Check and see if there's a children's movie that I can watch."

Since Hailey didn't look sleepy anymore, Melissa obliged by picking up the remote and flipping through the channels until she found the one Hailey wanted.

Nate left, presumably to go to his own room. A few minutes later, he opened his side of the connecting door.

"It's time we talked," he said in a low voice. "Hailey will be fine here, watching her show. We'll leave the connecting doors open in case she needs something."

Melissa wanted to protest, but of course there wasn't a rationale for putting this discussion off any longer.

As she followed him into his room, she tried to figure out how much she could safely tell him. He needed just enough information to understand the level of danger.

Including a good reason to let her go.

Full of apprehension, she dropped into a seat next to the small round table tucked in the corner of his room.

Her heart was beating too fast, and she took several deep breaths in order to bring her pulse down.

"Who were those men following you?" Nate asked, his tone soft but firm.

"I don't know," she answered honestly. "I've never seen either of them before in my life."

Nate's mouth thinned as if he wasn't sure he believed her. "Okay, then why were they following you?"

"I don't know that, either," she said. When his face tightened in anger, she knew she'd have to tell him something. "Listen, Nate, you need to understand, all of this started a long time ago."

He folded his arms over his chest. "I'm listening."

She licked her suddenly dry lips. "You remember how I waitressed at the restaurant back in high school, right?"

Nate nodded. "At El Matador, which is still there, believe it or not."

Still in Brookmont, the elite suburb of Milwaukee that she and Nate had once called home.

The thought of the upscale restaurant being there all these years later was not reassuring. Did it continue to be a meeting point for the upper echelon of Brookmont? Or had they moved their little clique somewhere different after that fateful night?

"Melissa, what happened back then? What caused you to move away and change your name?" Nate asked.

"Something terrible occurred the night after graduation," she said.

Nate nodded slowly. "Go on," he encouraged her.

She couldn't for the life of her find the words to explain in a way that didn't give away the entire truth. The silence stretched painfully long between them.

"I heard about the drugs that were found in your room," Nate finally said. "I didn't want to believe that you were an addict, but your father admitted that he sent you to rehab."

She snapped her head up to stare at Nate. "You believed that?" she asked in an agonized whisper. "Even though we spent every free moment we could together, you still believed that?"

"You weren't here to tell me otherwise," Nate said, accusation lacing his tone. "What was I supposed to think? You disappeared and I never heard from you again, not one letter in response to all the ones I sent you."

She blinked in surprise. "What letters?"

Nate's gaze narrowed. "The letters I gave your father to send to you. He wouldn't give me your address, but he agreed to send you my letters. I kept waiting and waiting to hear back from you, but I never did."

Melissa's entire body went numb, as if someone had dumped a bucket of ice water over her head. "I'm sorry," she murmured. "I'm so sorry."

"For what?" Nate challenged her. "For leaving without saying goodbye? For not even trying to get in touch with me? I commuted to college my first year because I was afraid you wouldn't find me when you came back. But you never did."

The anguish in Nate's voice lashed at her like a whip. It wasn't her fault that she'd been forced to leave, but he'd been deeply hurt by her actions nonetheless. And why hadn't her father passed along his letters? Had her father been afraid that Nate would come after her?

Looking at Nate now, she knew that was exactly what he would have done.

"Well?" he demanded in a harsh tone.

She glanced over her shoulder at the open connecting door between their rooms. "Not so loud, or Hailey will hear."

Nate's jaw tightened with anger, and she knew that there was no way of getting around the fact that he needed to hear a portion of her story.

"I was working at the restaurant the night after graduation. In fact, I was scheduled to close. It was pretty busy. The place was packed, but as the hour grew later, there were only a few tables left. A group at one table in particular lingered, so I was trying to get as much of the cleanup work done as possible." She paused, shivering at the memory of what transpired that night.

"Go on," Nate urged.

"I cleaned out the large coffeepots in the back room, and then I hauled some garbage out to the dumpsters. Usually the dishwasher does that, but he was busy, and I was anxious to leave."

"To meet me," Nate said in a quiet voice.

She bit her lip and nodded, remembering the plans they'd made long ago. "Yes, to meet you."

"So what stopped you from coming?"

"I couldn't lift the garbage bag, so I set it against the Dumpster and was about to go back inside when I heard raised voices. The Dumpster was located not far from the alley, so I went over to investigate. The yelling grew louder, and I should have left. To this day, I wish I had followed my instinct to run away."

Nate's expression grew grim. "What did you see?"

"Five men arguing. I recognized them from the restaurant. They were the ones who had been lingering at the table in my section. In fact, I'd waited on them. I was trying to figure out why they were hanging around when one of the men pulled out a knife and stabbed the guy across from him in the stomach. I was so surprised, I didn't move. Even after he fell to the ground, blood pooling beneath him, I still didn't really understand what had happened. Not until the man with the knife happened to glance in my direction." Melissa drew in a harsh breath and forced herself to meet Nate's gaze. "That's when I knew that he'd recognized me."

Nate stared at her in horror. "Are you saying you witnessed a murder?"

She nodded slowly. "Yes, that's exactly what I'm saying. And I think it's obvious that the man responsible is determined to silence me once and for all."

THREE

Unbelievable. Nate stared at Melissa, stunned by her revelation. He'd imagined dozens of scenarios in the long months after she'd disappeared, but never anything remotely like what she'd just described.

Yet even knowing that she'd witnessed a murder didn't explain everything. Why had she decided simply to disappear? Why hadn't she called the police for help? Or talked to him about what she'd seen?

"And the drugs that were found in your bedroom?" he forced himself to ask.

"Planted, as a way to discredit me." Melissa's expression was full of hurt. "A ploy that worked, since you fell for it just like everyone else probably did."

Nate couldn't ignore the flash of guilt. Twelve years ago, he hadn't wanted to believe the girl he'd loved had been a secret addict, but what else was he to think when her father had looked him straight in the eye and explained that she'd been sent to rehab? It wasn't as if he'd had any other theory to explain what had happened.

"You really wrote me letters?" she asked, her tone hesitant.

He nodded slowly. "At least a dozen of them," he admitted. "I didn't realize your father hated me so much that he wouldn't pass them along to you."

Melissa frowned and shook her head. "It wasn't like that, Nate. My father didn't hate you. He was determined to keep me safe, that's all. I'm sure he was afraid that if he gave me your letters, we'd find a way to get back together."

Since that was true, at least on his part, he couldn't argue. Besides, all of that was in the past. He needed to keep focused on the present. Although wrapping his mind around the idea that the men who'd followed Melissa had, in fact, intended to kill her wasn't easy.

"Okay, tell me about these five men," Nate said. "You mentioned at the mall that you couldn't go to the police without risking your and Hailey's lives, which makes me think one of them must be a cop."

Melissa didn't meet his gaze, and the way she twisted her fingers in her lap made him wonder if she was trying to find a way to avoid the truth.

"Listen, you have to tell me what you know," Nate urged. "Otherwise I won't have any choice but to call my boss and have you taken in for questioning."

Her head jerked up, her stormy gaze clashing with his. "Don't," she said sharply. "Hailey will be the one to suffer if you do that."

Nate wanted to yank out his hair in frustration. "Then cooperate with me. What do you know about the five men you saw twelve years ago?"

She hesitated and then let out a heavy sigh. "You were right. One of them was a cop," she confirmed. "I saw him come in several times in uniform, although he wasn't wearing it the night of the murder."

"Do you know his name?" Nate demanded. "Can you

describe him?" He didn't like believing a cop had gone bad, but unfortunately it wasn't the first time that one had succumbed to temptation. And probably wouldn't be the last, either.

"I don't know his name," Melissa said. "I wish I did. And he wasn't the one who actually committed murder, but he was there watching the whole thing."

"Party to the crime," Nate muttered. "And could easily be arrested as an accomplice."

"Yes, I'm sure he could. And I think he must have other cops who are willing to bend the rules, too. Otherwise, how would they have got away with stashing drugs in my bedroom?"

Nate could see her point. "Did you find them? Is that why you left?"

Melissa bit her lower lip, another sign of nervousness. "No, I didn't find the drugs. I was too afraid to go home. I ran away and hid until morning, catching a bus when the early route started."

"I don't understand why you didn't come to me for help." Nate knew it was ridiculous to be wounded by actions she'd taken twelve years ago, but he couldn't seem to help himself. "Especially when you knew I was planning to major in criminal justice."

"I didn't want to drag you down with me," she murmured. "I found out from my father that the police showed up on our doorstep first thing in the morning, demanding to speak with me about a stabbing victim found outside the restaurant. My dad thought I was in my room, so he let them in."

"Without a warrant?" Nate asked in dismay.

She nodded. "My dad was shocked to realize I wasn't home. And when the police searched my room and found the drugs, he wasn't sure what was going on. Don't you see? They would have tried to discredit you, too."

"Maybe, or maybe I would have been a credible witness on your behalf," he said grimly.

"I wasn't going to take that chance," she said firmly.

Nate didn't agree with her decision, but there was nothing he could do now to change the past. If he'd paid more attention back then he might have connected the stabbing victim with Melissa's disappearance. But he hadn't. For now, he needed to stay focused on the present. "You must know at least one of the men's names," he said. "You told me you waited on their table. Surely you noticed a name on a credit or debit card?"

"No credit cards. They always paid in cash."

Nate couldn't believe Melissa didn't have a clue to the identity of at least one of the men. "There must be something you remember about these guys. Did they have any scars? Tattoos? Any distinguishing features at all?"

Melissa shook her head, spreading her hands in a gesture of surrender. "I'm sorry, but there's nothing that stands out in my memory."

Nate stared up at the ceiling for a moment, trying to push back the wave of helplessness. "Okay, so you've told me what happened all those years ago, but what about today? How was it that these two guys found you?"

"I noticed the tail as soon as I left the hospital," Melissa said in a low tone.

"Hospital? What were you doing there?"

She blinked rapidly, and Nate was disconcerted to realize she was on the verge of tears. "Visiting my father. His dying wish was to see his granddaughter in person."

The anger he'd felt toward Melissa's father for keeping them apart instantly evaporated. "I'm so sorry," he said huskily.

Melissa sniffed and wiped at her eyes. "Me, too. I honestly didn't think coming home after all this time was that much of a risk. Especially since my father and I faked my death."

"Why did you wait four years to do that?" Nate asked.

"Because they found me in California. So I conveniently died and moved all the way across the country to a new location, with another new name."

Nate couldn't help sympathizing with her. He'd hated the idea that she'd been forced to go on the run, not just once but twice. "Go on. So, you left the hospital and noticed what?"

"I was being followed, so I headed into the mall, hoping to lose them in the crowd."

"Carrying Hailey beneath your winter coat was a smart move," Nate told her.

A slight smile tipped the corner of her mouth. "Thanks. Anyway, from there you know the rest."

Yeah, he knew the rest. The men with guns had shot at him, and he'd shot at them in self-defense. Then he'd left the scene of the crime.

Too bad he didn't have a clue what their next steps should be. He wanted to keep Melissa and Hailey out of harm's way, but right now, he didn't even know who the bad guys were.

"Excuse me. I need to check on Hailey." Melissa rose to her feet and quickly made her way into the other room.

Nate hovered in the doorway between their connecting rooms, listening as she coaxed Hailey into brushing her teeth and putting on her pajamas.

Then the little girl insisted on saying her nighttime prayers.

"God bless Daddy up in Heaven, and Mommy, and Mr. Nate, who saved us today. Amen."

"Amen," Melissa echoed. "Sleep tight, Hailey. I'll be right here if you need anything."

"Okay, Mommy," the little girl murmured sleepily.

Nate was touched by the fact that Hailey had included him in her nighttime prayers.

There were so many things that were different about the woman Melissa was today compared with the girl he'd loved years ago. Yes, she was a mother now, but that wasn't the only thing that had changed.

She was raising her daughter as a Christian. Because of Hailey's father? Did she love him still, even though he'd passed away?

Not that Melissa's feelings were any of his business. He wouldn't risk getting emotionally involved. And not just because he sensed she was still holding something back from him.

She'd left him without a word, breaking his young heart.

No way was he willing to risk another heartbreak.

Melissa took her time getting ready for bed, admittedly as a way to avoid spending more time with Nate.

She'd already told him far more than she'd intended. Anything else would only hurt him.

Closing her eyes for a moment, she mourned what they'd lost. Their young love, so pure, so sweet. They'd never done anything more than kiss, but even twelve years later, she could still remember the sweetness they'd shared. For several weeks after she'd left, she'd find herself looking for him, wishing he was still there for her to lean on.

Why hadn't her father mentioned the letters Nate had written? Surely he hadn't thrown them away. Why not pass them along, especially after she'd been forced to fake her death? They'd both thought she was relatively safe from that point forward.

And where were Nate's letters now? Hidden somewhere in her father's house?

For a moment, she actually considered going back to the house where she grew up to search for them. But of course, she couldn't take the risk. For one thing, she was pretty sure her dad's house was being watched, the same way the hospital had been. How else had they found her? Besides, heading there was probably exactly what they'd expect her to do.

No, going to her childhood home wasn't an option. Besides, whatever Nate had written hardly mattered now. She'd been married all too briefly before losing her husband to a rare infection that had settled in his lungs. Jeremy had helped her find God and had given her Hailey, the two greatest gifts of all. No reason to go back and attempt to recapture the past.

Far more important to plan the next steps of her mission to keep Hailey safe.

By the time Melissa emerged from the bathroom, Nate's room was dark except for the blue glow of the television. Relieved that she didn't have to talk to him anymore, she slid into the bed next to Hailey. Wearing her jeans and sweater wasn't exactly comfortable, but she didn't plan on sleeping.

Once Nate fell asleep, she'd take Hailey and slip away. Hopefully he wouldn't notice they were gone until morning.

Yet, in spite of herself, Melissa dozed, jerking awake a few hours later. She took a moment to orient herself before sliding out of bed.

Moving silently, she eased toward the doorway between their connecting rooms. The television was off now, and she stood for what seemed like endless moments listening to Nate's deep, rhythmic breathing.

It was tempting to venture into his room to search for his car keys, but she didn't want to risk waking him. No, her best chance to escape was to slip away without making any noise.

She gently closed the door on her side of the room, hoping to muffle any errant sounds. She packed the few meager belongings they had back into the suitcase and then took out her mobile phone.

Only twenty percent of battery left, but enough juice to enable her to call for a taxi once she was far enough away from the motel.

After setting the suitcase near the door, she went over to the bed to wake Hailey. This would be the most difficult part of sneaking away. If Hailey cried or made any noise at all, she knew Nate would be up in a flash to see what was wrong.

Thankfully, the little girl was so sleepy, she simply curled up against Melissa's chest, snuggling into the hollow of her shoulder.

Since the hallway outside their rooms was heated, she decided to wait until they were safely away before putting Hailey's coat, hat and boots on. Carrying everything with her wasn't easy, but she managed to open the door, wincing when it creaked a bit.

Moving as quickly and silently as possible, she stepped out and then closed the door behind her. The hallway was brightly lit, making it easy to navigate as she headed toward the stairs on the far side of the building, opposite from the lobby.

Inside the stairwell, she paused to get Hailey into her winter gear. She was still half-asleep, so Melissa couldn't exactly make her stand to get dressed. Somehow she slipped her daughter's arms into the coat sleeves. Getting her hat on was no problem, although the boots were difficult. She hoped they wouldn't fall off.

She carried Hailey and the suitcase down the stairs, and when she reached the bottom, she paused to catch her breath.

Melissa hated the thought of leaving Nate for a second time without saying goodbye, but she forced herself to go anyway. The cold winter air stole her breath as she went outside, and Hailey instantly started crying.

"Shh, it's okay. We're going to be fine."

"It's cold," her daughter sobbed.

"I know, sweetie. We'll get someplace warm soon." Hailey wasn't used to northern winters, having spent her entire life in South Carolina. And the idea of snow was more fun than the cold reality of it.

Melissa stayed alongside the shelter of the building as long as possible before making her way toward the sidewalk. There was a gas station on the other side of the street, but the windows were dark, indicating the place was closed.

Headlights cut through the darkness, heading in her

direction. For a moment she froze, fearing she'd been found. But she sighed in relief as the vehicle kept going.

She carefully walked across the slippery surface of the gas station parking lot, wondering if venturing out like this was such a good idea. Would she manage to find a taxi this late? She fumbled for her phone, intending to search for a local car service.

Another pair of headlights approached, only this time, they abruptly turned into the gas station rather than driving past. Melissa froze in the center of the bright lights, her heart lodging in her throat as the car came to an abrupt stop. The driver's side door opened, and a tall figure stepped out.

Survival instincts kicked in, and she dropped the suitcase and turned to run. But she quickly lost her footing on the slippery, snow-covered pavement. She felt herself falling and twisted as much as possible, landing on her shoulder in an attempt to avoid landing on her daughter.

She tried to scramble to her feet, but the driver of the car was on her too quickly, preventing her escape. In the dim recesses of her mind she realized Hailey was crying, but her gaze was focused on the man looming over her.

"Now I've got you," he said with savage satisfaction. He reached down and roughly grabbed her arm as if to yank her to her feet.

No! Melissa kicked at the stranger, screaming for help. She tried to jerk from his grasp, but he held on tight. She let go of Hailey. "Run, Hailey! Run!"

Something hard hit her in the face and she bit back a cry of pain, tears springing to her eyes. At the moment all she cared about was giving Hailey time to get away.

Desperate, she kicked at her captor again.

Out of nowhere, a second figure came out of the darkness, grabbing the man around the throat and dragging him off her. At first she didn't understand what was happening, but then she recognized Nate.

She pushed herself to her feet, taking off after Hailey, scooping her daughter into her arms. Still slipping and sliding, she made her way behind the shelter of the gas station building. As much as she wanted to help Nate take down the guy who'd grabbed her, she knew her priority had to be keeping Hailey away from harm.

Resting against the building, breathing heavily, she closed her eyes and thanked God for sparing them.

"Melissa?" Nate's deep voice cut through the darkness.

"Here," she managed in a low tone.

"Are you all right?" he asked, coming over to where she was huddled with Hailey.

Her cheek throbbed with pain, but she nodded. "We're fine," she whispered.

"Come on. We need to get out of here," Nate said grimly.

She shifted Hailey in her arms and made her way toward Nate. He put his hand on the small of her back, guiding her back toward the motel. He paused just long enough to pick up the suitcase she'd dropped and brought it along with them.

She didn't want to go anywhere near the man who'd hit her, but forced herself to trust Nate. They passed the black car, and she couldn't help glancing over in that direction.

All she could see was the vehicle listing to one side.

It took a minute for her to realize the driver's side tires were flat.

Had Nate done that to prevent the man from following them? And where was the driver?

She shivered, her stomach clenching with dread. She hadn't heard the sound of gunfire, but she had to believe Nate had neutralized him somehow. She was deeply thankful he'd noticed she was gone and had come after her.

But how had the driver of the black car found her in the first place?

They must have known she was with Nate. What had he said back at the mall? He'd called for backup? Anyone with a scanner could have heard that information.

Including the dirty cop who'd tried to frame her as a drug addict.

Nate opened the back passenger door of his car and she quickly put Hailey into her booster seat. When Melissa was about to crawl in beside her daughter, Nate stopped her with a firm hand on her arm.

"In front, with me."

She swallowed hard and nodded, shutting the door and then climbing into the passenger seat. Nate slid in behind the wheel, and soon they were back on the road, heading west, leaving the lights of the city behind.

Silence hung heavy between them.

"What happened to the driver?" she finally asked.

"He's unconscious, but he'll be fine," Nate said in a cold, clipped tone. "Do you mind telling me what you were thinking when you left like that in the middle of the night?"

Protecting you, she thought, but she held her tongue.

"What? No snappy comeback? Do you realize how

cold it is outside? What about your daughter?" He was starting to raise his volume, and Hailey whimpered, making him lower his voice. "Where were you going to go without a car?"

She swallowed hard. "I planned to call for a taxi."

"And go where?" he pressed.

"The bus station." She looked away from him, staring out at the darkness through the passenger-side window. Several houses were decorated with brightly colored Christmas lights, reminding her of home.

Not her apartment in South Carolina, but the home where she'd grown up. Where she'd lived with her father. Gone to school. Dated Nate. She closed her eyes and pressed her forehead against the cool glass. She'd been so happy back then. How had everything gone so wrong?

"I shouldn't be surprised you tried to leave without telling me. After all, that's your usual response."

The bitter note to his voice made her feel terrible. She forced herself to turn and look at him. "I'm sorry, Nate. I'm sorry I hurt you all those years ago, and I'm sorry I hurt you now. Obviously I've put you in danger, too. They must know you're with me. Otherwise they never would have found us."

"Yeah, and frankly that's what's bothering me the most," Nate said. "Maybe you should try being honest with me for once. Before we all end up dead."

She sucked in a harsh breath as the reality of what he was saying struck home. He was absolutely right. Her attempt to protect him had backfired in a big way.

If there had been two men instead of one, this situation could have ended much differently.

They all might have been killed. Murdered in cold blood.

"You know the identity of the five men you saw that night, don't you?" Nate asked.

"Not all of them, but yes, I knew one of them besides the cop," she admitted.

"Who?"

She licked her dry lips. "A man with an important job."

"Yeah? Like what?"

She forced the words past her constricted throat. "Like the mayor of Brookmont, Tom McAllister."

"Uncle Tom?" Nate repeated hoarsely. "My uncle Tom?"

"Yes. I'm sorry, Nate." Melissa knew she should have felt better now that the secret was out, but she didn't.

Because she wasn't at all sure Nate would believe her. Why would he take her side over his uncle's? This was exactly the reason she'd left without saying anything to him all those years ago.

She shivered again with fear that chilled her to the bone. These were men who'd tried to discredit her as a drug addict. When that hadn't worked, they'd set out to kill her. If Nate decided to haul her in to be questioned, there was no telling what might happen. They'd lied before, why not try to frame her again?

Or worse, set up some sort of scheme to have her killed in jail?

A sense of desperate hopelessness pierced her heart. She absolutely needed to find a way to make Nate believe her.

Or risk losing Hailey, forever.

FOUR

Nate didn't want to believe Melissa's claim. Ridiculous to think his uncle Tom was part of some big cover-up. Especially something as serious as murder. Tom McAllister was the mayor of Brookmont. Why on earth would he get involved in something criminal?

But there was no denying Melissa was in trouble. He'd been livid when he'd seen the guy slap her across the face. It was clear the guy's intent was to take Melissa with him, and there was no telling what might have happened if Nate hadn't got there in time. Thank goodness he'd heard her door shutting behind her when she'd left the motel. It had taken him a few minutes to verify that she was gone.

A few minutes that could have cost her life.

But was it really possible that his uncle Tom was involved?

Nate shook his head helplessly. He tightened his grip on the steering wheel and considered his options. Taking Melissa and Hailey straight to his boss was top on his list. Griff was a good, honest cop, and Nate could trust his boss to get to the bottom of whatever was going on.

Or he could take Melissa somewhere safe and begin investigating this on his own.

As much as he'd rather do the latter, he knew that it was a better option to take her to his boss. But it was one o'clock in the morning. There wouldn't be anyone at the sheriff's department headquarters other than the single dispatcher who manned the graveyard shift.

He reached for his phone and handed it over to Melissa. "Do me a favor and take the battery out of the back so I can't be traced. And you need to ditch your phone, too."

She grimaced but did as he asked, dropping both the device and the battery back into the cup holders located in the center console. Then she opened her window and tossed the disposable phone she'd been using.

"Nate, please, you have to believe me," Melissa said in a low, desperate tone, as if reading his turbulent thoughts. "You asked me why I didn't come to you after I witnessed the murder. Well, this is the reason. I was afraid your uncle would turn you against me."

He clenched his jaw so tight his temple ached. "Why would my uncle be involved in covering up a murder?"

"I don't know," Melissa insisted, frustration edging her voice. "I wish I had answers for you, but I don't."

"Yeah, and isn't that convenient?" He felt his anger rising and did his best to lower his tone so he wouldn't disturb Hailey. "You've been keeping secrets from me since I saw you on the escalator. Give me one good reason why I should believe you now."

"Because unfortunately, you were right," she whispered. "Now that you've helped me, I'm afraid you're in as much danger as I am."

"Maybe, but I think it's time I listen to my instincts,

which are telling me to hand you over to my boss right now."

Her eyes widened with fear. "If you do that, they'll find a way to kill me." The grim certainty in her tone nagged at him. "Tell me one thing, Nate. How did they find us at that hotel? You said yourself it's a cop-friendly place. How many cops would know to look for your vehicle there?"

Good question—one that had bothered him from the moment the guy in the black car had grabbed and hit Melissa. It couldn't be a coincidence that they'd been found so quickly. "I don't know," he admitted.

"Please don't take me in. Not when there are dirty policemen involved who obviously won't stop until I'm dead."

He couldn't deny the fact that she was in danger. And if corrupt cops were in on this, keeping her safe would be even more difficult. He let out a heavy sigh and continued driving through the night.

Melissa was right. He couldn't take her in. Not yet. Not until he knew what they were dealing with.

"Okay, fine," he agreed in a resigned tone. "But no more lies, Melissa. No more escape attempts, either. We work together from this point forward. Understand?"

"Yes," she whispered. "I'm sorry I dragged you into this mess. I know this wasn't at all what you bargained for."

"It's not your fault," he said. In all fairness, she hadn't dragged him into anything. He was the one who'd recognized her on the escalator. And he was the one who'd followed her through the mall. Shooting and wounding two men hadn't been part of the initial plan, but he knew that given the same set of circumstances, he'd do it all again without hesitation.

"Maybe not entirely my fault, but I'm concerned that your reputation will suffer if you continue to help me," she said in a resigned tone.

He didn't bother pointing out that his reputation had already taken a hit the moment he'd decided to leave the crime scene at the mall.

The way she truly seemed to care about his fate helped ease his anger and frustration at waking up and discovering she'd sneaked away during the night.

"I can't worry about my reputation," he said, even though being a cop was important to him. "Hopefully I'll be able to salvage it once we get to the bottom of this mess."

"I hope so," she whispered, resting her head back against the seat. "I truly hope so."

Nate reached over to give her hand a reassuring squeeze, a bit surprised when she responded by tightening her fingers around his and flashing a tentative smile.

They would uncover the truth of the murder Melissa had witnessed twelve years ago.

Because the alternative was too painful to contemplate.

Melissa stared down at their joined hands for a long moment, humbled by Nate's forgiveness. He had every right to be angry, but at least he wasn't taking her to his boss.

She was sorry that she'd inadvertently involved Nate, but she was relieved that she and Hailey weren't alone. If Nate truly believed her, then maybe they could get to the bottom of this by working together.

The warmth of the car caused her eyelids to droop heavily, but she forced them open. She was going to be Nate's partner in this, and she needed to stay awake and alert.

Glancing into the backseat, she was glad to see Hailey had fallen asleep.

"Where are we going?" she asked when Nate turned onto a remote country road.

"Another motel. We need somewhere to crash for what's left of the night," he said. "But I'm not about to use anyplace I've been before."

She was relieved to hear that, although that meant they might be forced to use a credit card.

She racked her brain for an alternate plan but couldn't come up with anything better. "I'd offer my father's house, but I'm sure they have the place staked out, since they found me at the hospital."

"Yeah, I was thinking of using one of my buddies' places," he admitted. "But if they know who I am, it won't be too hard to find out the names of my friends, and I don't want to expose any of them or their families to danger."

She didn't blame him. She thought about the church friends she'd left back in South Carolina and knew she wouldn't be willing to put any of them in harm's way, either.

"There's a place up ahead," Nate said, breaking into her thoughts. "It's small and well off the highway. Should work for our needs."

"Sounds good." She hoped and prayed his uniform would convince the motel clerk to let them pay cash rather than leaving an electronic trail.

Nate pulled into a parking space near the lobby, then

turned to face her. "It will be easier to request one room, pretending we're a family. I'll make sure there are two double beds. You and Hailey can share one, and I'll crash on the other."

"All right," she agreed.

Nate slid out from behind the wheel and then disappeared inside. He returned about fifteen minutes later, a satisfied expression on his face.

"I convinced the clerk to take cash, so we should be safe for now."

"Great," she murmured. "I'm exhausted. And sore."

"You need some ice for your face," Nate added with a frown.

She was touched by his concern, although a bruise was the least of her concerns. She was just glad they'd escaped anything worse.

He drove up to the door of their room, pulling the suitcase he'd rescued out of the backseat. "We're in room 5," he told her.

She unbuckled Hailey from the booster seat and carried her daughter inside. It took her a few minutes to get Hailey out of her winter clothes, but thankfully the little girl didn't put up a fight. Soon she had her tucked into the bed closest to the wall.

She turned to face Nate and frowned when she noticed he'd brought in Hailey's child safety seat. "It's probably better to keep that in the backseat in case we have to leave in a hurry."

"I'm planning to find someplace to stash my car," he said. "You and Hailey get some sleep. Don't wait up for me. I don't know how long I'll be gone."

After everything she'd been through, she wasn't looking forward to staying in the tiny motel room alone.

But of course, hiking through the snow carrying her daughter wasn't an option, either. "Try not to go too far," she said.

"I won't," Nate promised. The smile that tugged at his mouth reminded her of the way he had looked as a hunky teenager. Too handsome for his own good.

As he let himself out the door, back into the cold winter night, she crossed over to the window, moving the heavy curtain enough to watch him drive away.

Biting back the urge to rush outside and beg him to stay.

Nate drove around the area, looking for a place to hide his vehicle. The trees were bare of leaves, and anything dark showed up all too easily against the snow-covered ground. Too bad he didn't have a white car.

After a couple of miles, he found an abandoned farmhouse, complete with a barn that unfortunately looked as if a strong wind would cause it to come tumbling down.

Since it was better than anything else he'd passed, he drove up through the snow to the crooked doors. He got out of the car and pulled them open, then drove inside.

After locking up his vehicle, he closed the barn doors and then broke off a branch from an evergreen tree and used it to obliterate his tire tracks and footprints. Maybe he was being paranoid, but better safe than sorry.

By the time he reached the road, he was sweating beneath his winter jacket. The result of his attempt to hide the location of his car wasn't perfect, but it should work.

Especially since he was absolutely positive he hadn't been followed. The road was isolated and empty, which suited him just fine.

Shrugging out of his jacket, he tied it securely around his waist so he could jog the mile back to the motel. Thankfully it was late enough that he could use the center of the highway, where there wasn't any snow or ice.

Running through the night gave him a strange sense of peace. As he ran he tried to formulate their next steps. Get some rest, obviously, but after that, they needed to figure out where to start their investigation.

He considered confronting his uncle but didn't want to do that without some kind of proof. Something other than Melissa's word. Not because he didn't believe her, but because he did.

No, the proof they needed was something indisputable. Something that couldn't be discredited as a lie from an unreliable source. Eyewitness testimony was good, but twelve years had passed since the original crime had been committed. They needed to prove that Melissa witnessed a murder.

Which meant they needed the identity of the man who'd died that night.

Nate knew his way around computers and technology, although he didn't have anything with him. First thing in the morning, they needed to find a laptop so he could get decent access to the internet. Having his personal laptop would be even better so that he could use his work search engines.

Satisfied that he had some semblance of a plan, he increased his pace until he could see the lights of the motel. As he came closer, he slowed his pace in an effort to cool down.

He quietly let himself inside the room, hoping not to disturb Hailey or Melissa.

But the moment he crossed the threshold, Melissa raised her head and glanced over at him.

"Sorry to wake you," he whispered, closing the door softly behind him.

"You didn't," she assured him. "I couldn't sleep."

"Get some rest," he advised. "We have work to do in the morning."

It wasn't easy to see in the darkness, but he thought she nodded. "Good night, Nate."

"Good night." He made his way to the bathroom so he could take a shower. Nothing he could do to salvage his uniform, which was damp with sweat. By the time he emerged twenty minutes later, he could hear Melissa's deep, even breaths.

She was asleep at last. He crawled into the empty bed and did his best to shut down his brain.

It seemed like barely an hour later when he woke up to Hailey's plaintive whining. "Mommy, I'm hungry."

"Shh, we have to be quiet and wait until Mr. Nate wakes up, okay? Look, I found a kids' movie for you."

Nate pried his eyelids open, trying to read the time on his watch. Five minutes past six in the morning. He swallowed a groan. It wasn't the first time he'd been forced to work on less than four hours of sleep.

Man, he was getting too old for this.

"I'm awake," he managed, propping himself up on one elbow. "Give me a few minutes and I'll run back and get the car."

"The motel offers a free continental breakfast," Melissa informed him. "I'll take Hailey over there while you rest for a few more hours."

He pushed himself upright and scrubbed his hands over his face, wishing for a razor. "You were up as late as I was," he said. "Just give me a few minutes to get ready and we'll all go to breakfast together."

"Okay," she agreed.

He headed into the bathroom to wash up and use the facilities. Just as he opened the bathroom door, he heard Melissa talking.

He frowned, realizing she must be on the motel phone, since she'd tossed hers out the window.

He strode into the room to find her sitting on the end of the bed, holding the receiver to her ear. "When did he die?" she asked.

He realized that she must be talking with the hospital. He crossed over and sat down beside her.

"Okay, thanks for letting me know," she said. She disconnected from the call and glanced up at him, her eyes filling with tears.

"I just wanted to check on my dad's condition. He passed away about an hour ago," she said in a low voice.

"I'm so sorry for your loss," he said, wrapping his arm around her slim shoulders.

She nodded and buried her face in her hands, her shoulders shaking with suppressed sobs.

He gathered her into his arms, feeling helpless to do anything but hold her in an attempt to offer comfort. Nate knew that even though Melissa and her father hadn't seen each other in person for the past twelve years, they'd remained close. After all, she'd mentioned that her father's dying wish was to see his granddaughter.

"He was a good man," she whispered.

"I know," he agreed.

Melissa surprised him by wrapping her arms around his waist and pressing her face into the hollow of his shoulder. Thankfully Hailey seemed to be preoccupied with her television show, despite her earlier complaints about being hungry.

Nate ran his hand down Melissa's back, trying to think of something to say. "Is there anything I can do to help? What about funeral arrangements?"

He felt her draw in a deep breath and then let it out slowly. She lifted her head. "Thanks, but he's already taken care of everything. I'm just upset at knowing that I won't be able to attend his funeral."

He brushed her damp hair away from her cheeks. "We could try to find a way," he offered, even though he had no idea how they'd manage that.

She sniffled loudly and swiped at her tears. "It's too dangerous for Hailey," she said. "I can't risk putting her at risk, not when I've already had a chance to say goodbye."

Nate had to tamp down a flash of anger. It wasn't fair that Melissa had to forgo her father's funeral.

"We can try to sneak in before the funeral home is open to the public," he offered.

"No, that's not necessary," she murmured. "In my heart, I know that my father is in a much better place with God. That will be enough to see me through the next few days."

He was touched by her faith and couldn't think of anything to say in reply. She stared up at him with her wide hazel eyes, and for a moment it seemed as if time had stood still. The old feelings he'd buried long ago came rushing to the surface.

Reacting instinctively, he bent his head intending to capture her mouth in a poignant kiss.

FIVE

Melissa froze for a split second before melting against Nate, and responding to his kiss. The twelve year gap in their relationship faded away, and it was as if they were young and in love once again, excited about the future possibilities stretching ahead of them.

And if she was honest with herself, she'd admit Nate's kiss filled a tiny void in her heart that she'd done her best to ignore ever since.

"Mommy? Why are you kissing Mr. Nate?"

Hailey's voice jerked her roughly back to the present, and she quickly pulled away from Nate, her cheeks flaming with embarrassment. She jumped up from the foot of the bed and gave herself a mental shake.

What on earth had she been thinking? She couldn't allow herself to forget about Hailey. She was the most important person in her life.

Her future didn't include Nate. They were different people now. Her life was about providing a safe and secure future for her daughter, not rekindling an old high school romance.

"Um, well, I guess I was just sad for a minute, Hailey. But now it's time for breakfast. Isn't that right, Nate?" she said, forcing a smile on her face.

"Sure," Nate responded in a low, gravelly tone. She reached for Hailey's coat, avoiding his gaze, because she didn't want to know if he had been as affected by their kiss as she'd been.

When she managed to get Hailey's winter gear on, she glanced around for her coat, only to realize belatedly that Nate was holding it out for her.

She swallowed hard and slipped her arms into the sleeves, murmuring her thanks as he pulled her parka up over her shoulders. Her pulse beat frantically in her chest, and she couldn't remember the last time a man had knocked her off balance like this.

As much as she'd loved Jeremy, they'd been friends long before they'd married. They'd met at her church group and having finally felt safe, she'd allowed herself to date him. But even then, there hadn't been this strange frisson of adrenaline that raced through her bloodstream at his slightest touch. Jeremy had been sweet, kind and gentle. Everything she'd wanted in a husband. In a father for her children.

So why was she suddenly acutely aware of Nate?

Stress. She was under an incredible amount of stress. Not just because of her father's death, but in the daunting task of attempting to figure out who'd murdered the man she'd seen get stabbed, while trying to stay alive and out of harm's way.

With her feet back on steady ground, Melissa took Hailey's hand as they walked outside into the frigid air. The sunny sky was an extreme contrast to the wind chill. She shivered and quickened her pace in an effort to reach the lobby faster.

"Brr, it's cold, Mommy," Hailey said, echoing her thoughts.

"I know, sweetie. But look at all the snow. Isn't it pretty?" She forced herself to sound happy, even though her heart mourned the passing of her dad.

Hailey nodded eagerly. "Very pretty."

Nate stepped ahead and opened the door for them. Melissa ushered Hailey inside in front of her, grateful for the warmth.

There was a pair of truckers inside the lobby enjoying breakfast, and instantly Hailey cringed and clung to her hand.

"No!" Hailey cried.

"Shh, it's okay, sweetie. You don't have to be afraid of all strangers," she hastened to reassure her daughter. Apparently all the discussions at the preschool about staying away from strangers, along with their mad dash through the mall, had really frightened her daughter. "We're okay here with Mr. Nate. Remember how he's been keeping us safe? There's no need to be afraid."

Hailey didn't respond, her gaze full of doubt, and she stuck to Melissa like a burr as they approached the breakfast bar.

"What would you like to eat, Hailey?" Nate asked in a cheerful tone. "Cereal? Toast?"

Melissa hated seeing her daughter so afraid, although she shouldn't have been caught off guard by Hailey's response to the strangers. After all Hailey had been through since they arrived in Milwaukee, she was surprised the little girl was coping as well as she was.

"Look, they have your favorite fruity cereal," she said, injecting enthusiasm into her tone. "How about that?"

"Okay," she said in a quiet, subdued voice.

"We can sit at this table here," Nate said, choosing

the table farthest from the door and from the two truckers, who hadn't paid them any attention.

"Great. Hailey, why don't you sit with Mr. Nate while
I get you some breakfast?" she suggested as they made
their way over to where Nate stood. "Do you want anything besides cereal?"

"I want toast, too, with strawberry jelly." Hailey
nodded her head for emphasis. Melissa was relieved to
see that the stark moment of fear had faded from her
daughter's eyes.

"All right. Just wait here and I'll be right back." Melissa went to the buffet counter to get Hailey's breakfast,
ignoring the way her stomach rumbled with hunger at
the rich scent of freshly brewed coffee.

She returned to the table, only to stop short when
she caught a glimpse of Nate's and Hailey's heads bent
close as they worked on coloring a picture together. Her
chest tightened, making it difficult to breathe. For a moment she wished for something she couldn't have, but
then she shook off the useless emotion with an effort.

Hailey was Jeremy's daughter, not Nate's. And she'd
loved her husband. Nate was just being nice. Enough
with confusing the past with the present. They had work
to do.

"Here you go," she said loudly as she approached
the table.

"Goody," Hailey said, quickly abandoning her picture and turning her attention to her food.

Melissa pulled out a chair to sit down, but Nate
stopped her with a hand on her arm. "Why don't you
get yourself something, too?" he suggested. "I'll stay
here with Hailey."

Had Nate always been so gallant? So considerate?

She couldn't help thinking that he'd grown up to be quite an amazing guy.

"All right." She returned to the buffet, not just because she was hungry but also because she needed a bit of distance from Nate.

She was grateful for his determination to protect her and Hailey, but remaining in proximity and working with him would be more difficult than she'd anticipated. At least, on a personal level.

Grimly she realized she'd need every ounce of strength and willpower she possessed to get through the next few days.

Because allowing herself to become emotionally involved with Nate again was not part of her plan.

Nate couldn't seem to tear his gaze from Melissa as she filled a mug of coffee and helped herself to a toasted English muffin.

Not just because she was beautiful. There was something about her that tugged at his senses.

He scrubbed his hands over his face, willing the feelings away. Obviously he shouldn't have kissed her—still had no idea why he had. He'd only intended to offer comfort, but that plan had backfired in a big way.

Watching Hailey as she dug into her fruity cereal only reminded him that there was no going back to the past. Melissa was vulnerable. She'd just lost her father and her life was in danger. Plus he suspected she still had feelings for her dead husband, and even if she was willing to consider getting involved in another relationship, it was clear that she'd made a life for herself and Hailey down in South Carolina.

Now that her father had passed away, there would be

nothing to keep her here once they figured out who'd murdered a man and why.

Still, Hailey was a cutie, and for a moment he found himself wanting what so many of his fellow teammates had. A wife and family to come home to. Not that he knew much about growing up in a happy household.

"Your turn," Melissa said as she returned to sit beside Hailey.

He nodded and rose to his feet. What he desperately needed was a megadose of caffeine to wipe away the cobwebs from his brain. A clear head to figure out their next steps.

For one thing, he had to jog back to the old barn where he'd hidden his car. From there, he needed to get his hands on a computer. Maybe he could risk going to his place to pick up his state-of-the-art laptop.

Alone, he wouldn't think twice about doing what needed to be done, but he had Melissa and Hailey to consider. No way would he expose them to danger.

"I'll be back in about twenty minutes or so," he said once he'd finished his breakfast and gulped two cups of coffee. "I should get here before checkout time."

"All right," Melissa agreed. "I'll keep Hailey occupied with the kids' channel while we wait."

He nodded but then hesitated, turning back to face her. "Now, remember, you gave me your word, Melissa," he warned in a low voice. "Don't go off on your own."

She lifted her chin and met his gaze square-on. "I don't break my promises," she assured him. "I know I took off before, but we will be here when you return."

It was on the tip of his tongue to refresh her memory on what had happened when she'd run away the night before, but he managed to bite back the scathing comment. There was nothing they could do but move forward from here.

Nate walked outside in time to see the two truck drivers heading to their respective rigs. "Either of you heading south?" he asked. "I could use a lift to the next intersection, just a few miles up the road."

Maybe it was his uniform, because the two men looked at each other and shrugged. "Yeah, I'm heading that way," the shorter of the two said. "Hop in."

"Thanks. I really appreciate your help."

The trucker didn't say much, and Nate didn't either. The mile he'd jogged last night seemed like nothing while riding in the truck. "Here you go," the guy said, pulling up to a stop sign.

"Thanks again," Nate said before jumping down. He waited until the driver pulled away and was out of sight before he walked back to the old barn.

The area around the outside of the structure didn't look as if it had been disturbed since he'd left last night. Maybe he'd been foolish to go to such extreme measures.

He hauled open the barn doors and quickly backed his car onto the driveway. He climbed out to close the doors behind him and then made a left turn toward the motel.

He made it back so quickly, he could see that Melissa and Hailey were still sitting inside the restaurant. Nate parked his vehicle outside their room and then replaced the battery in his phone. He took a deep breath and called Jenna Reed, the only female cop on their SWAT team.

She answered on the second ring. "Nate? Where are you?"

"I—uh—need a favor."

"Griff is looking for your head to be served up on a platter after the stunt you pulled at the mall."

He winced at Jenna's bluntness. "Yeah, well, things are complicated. A woman and her five-year-old child are in danger, so I took them someplace safe."

"Listen, Nate, you seriously have to call Griff as soon as possible."

"I will, but I'm calling you because I need help."

Jenna didn't speak for a long moment. And honestly, he couldn't blame her. Helping him would only put her on Griff's bad side.

"Never mind," he said hastily. "I don't want to drag you down with me."

"What do you need?" Jenna asked. "I don't have a lot of time. We're shorthanded with you AWOL and Simms handing in his resignation."

"Simms resigned?" he echoed in surprise. "What's that about?"

"No clue," Jenna said shortly. "But you're burning daylight, Freemont. Tell me what you need and I'll be happy to help."

As much as he hated involving anyone else, he figured this favor wouldn't put Jenna in too much danger. "Okay, here's the deal. I need my computer, and I have reason to believe that someone might be watching my house. I was hoping you could slip in, grab it for me and slip out without anyone noticing. Once I have computer access, I should be fine working this thing alone."

"Piece of cake," Jenna said, obviously willing to assist in any way possible. "I should have time to get your computer as long as we don't get a SWAT call."

"Great. If you could meet me someplace, I'd appreciate it. Maybe out at the strip mall on Highway 24?"

"Sure thing. Anything else you need as long as I'm going to your place?"

The thought of Jenna going through his closet to pick out clothes didn't sit well with him. He'd be better off buying new items. "No, but thanks. I'll buy what I need at the mall."

"I'll bring some cash, too," Jenna said. "That way you'll avoid leaving an electronic trail."

Taking money from Jenna wasn't much better, but then again, he was good for the loan. "Okay, thanks again. I really appreciate your help."

"No problem," Jenna responded lightly. Despite the fact that they'd worked together for over a year, she kept her distance from the rest of the team when it came to anything outside of work-related concerns. Nate suspected she did that on purpose to avoid appearing weak. Or to avoid getting too personally involved with anyone she worked with. Either way, he totally understood her logic. "I'll be in touch later."

He disconnected from the call, then removed his battery from the phone once again. No reason to stop being paranoid now. He slid out of the driver's seat in time to see Melissa and Hailey making their way back to their motel room.

"You're back already?" Melissa asked.

"One of the truckers gave me a lift," he acknowledged, reaching over to unlock the motel door for her.

"Okay, I'll pack our things so we can leave," she murmured.

"No rush. We may as well wait until checkout time." He didn't want to get to the meet point too early. And it wouldn't take more than fifteen minutes to pick up some jeans and a sweatshirt to have something to wear other than his uniform.

He glanced at his watch, trying to estimate how much time Jenna would need to sneak in and out of his house with his computer. Difficult to know, since she'd have to figure out if anyone was watching the place or not.

Nate let out a heavy sigh. Allowing someone else to do something potentially dangerous on his behalf wasn't easy. Not that he didn't trust Jenna's skills, but sitting here and waiting while others exposed themselves to danger didn't sit well with him.

And he felt even more guilty knowing that Aaron Simms had resigned. Staffing was always dicey around the holidays, anyway, but with Simms gone, things would be tighter than usual.

He needed to find some evidence of the murder Melissa had witnessed, the sooner the better. Once he had some leads to go on, he might be able to approach Griff for help and support.

And hey, maybe Griff would be less likely to fire him now that Simms had resigned.

Melissa's tentative voice interrupted his thoughts. "We're ready to leave whenever you are."

"Okay. Did you grab the toiletries from the bathroom, too?" he asked. "There's no sense in leaving them behind."

"I tossed them in our suitcase," Melissa said.

He nodded and crossed over to pick up the bag. Its light weight only reminded him that they hadn't planned on staying here in Milwaukee for very long.

He stored the luggage in the trunk of his car while Melissa tucked Hailey into her booster seat. Once they were all settled in, he drove back out onto the highway.

"I'm planning to stop at a mall that's about twenty minutes from here," he told her. "Might be a good time to pick up anything else you and Hailey need."

Melissa's smile was a bit strained. "We're okay. I can't think of anything in particular."

Nate found himself wondering about Melissa's life down in South Carolina. He didn't know what she or her husband had done for work or who her friends were. He was bothered by the fact that she'd been willing to give up her life in Wisconsin to start over using a new name. Although she'd said herself that she didn't feel as if she'd had a choice.

They rode in silence for a good ten minutes before Melissa reached out to put her hand on his arm. "Nate? Do you think it's possible that dark green van is following us?"

He frowned, checking in his rearview mirror. The van wasn't hugging his bumper but seemed to be keeping pace. He tried speeding up and then slowing down, and still it stayed about two car lengths behind.

Nate wished he'd taken the interstate. This particular stretch of highway was fairly deserted. He scanned the area, trying to think of a good way to lose the possible tail.

"Hang on," he warned as he put on his left turn signal. He slowed to a stop but then gunned the engine, making a hard right at the last minute.

The other vehicle swerved sharply but recovered quickly, and this time, it was clear the driver was following them. Nate pushed the speed limit, aware that he couldn't afford to take too many chances with Melissa and Hailey in the car.

"Should I call for help?" Melissa asked, her voice trembling with fear. "Where's your phone?"

He had to admire her courage, considering she was just as afraid of the police as she was of the driver behind them. He dug out his cell. "Yes, here—call 911. We're in Washington County, so we should be able to trust them."

Melissa dialed the emergency number, and he could hear the ringing on the other end of the phone as she waited for the dispatcher to answer.

Abruptly the van came up alongside him, driving in the wrong lane on the highway. Nate glanced over and then gaped in shock as the guy in the passenger seat lowered his window and aimed a gun at him.

"Look out!" he shouted, hitting the brakes hard enough that the car shot past them, even as he heard the sound of a bullet hitting the side of his car.

"I dropped your phone!" Melissa cried.

"Mommy!" Hailey screamed.

Nate wrestled with the steering wheel, trying to keep them from crashing. He managed to yank it to the side enough to make an illegal U-turn. When he was facing the opposite direction, he punched the gas, anxious to get as far away as possible.

"I think they're still behind us!" Melissa whispered hoarsely as she frantically searched for the phone she'd dropped.

Nate gripped the steering wheel tightly, his foot to

the floor, as Melissa finally connected with the 911 operator. She gave their approximate location, and the dispatcher promised to send help to the scene.

But as Nate watched the green van gaining on them in the rearview mirror, he was afraid the police response would arrive too late.

SIX

Clenching her teeth together, Melissa tried to remain calm, despite the overwhelming sense of dread. She wanted to crawl into the backseat and throw her body over Hailey's. But the seat belts had locked up tight when the car braked, and Nate was now driving like a maniac in his effort to stay ahead of the van.

She whispered, "Please, Lord, keep us safe in Your care. Guide us away from the threat behind us. We place our lives in Your hands. Amen."

"Sing 'Jesus Loves Me,' Mommy," Hailey begged.

She sang the church lullaby while Nate continued to speed down the country highway. From what she could tell, the other vehicle seemed to be gradually closing in on them.

When Hailey joined in singing, tears pricked Melissa's eyes, and her heart squeezed in her chest. She knew God had a master plan, but she sincerely hoped that He would spare her daughter's life.

The high-pitched scream of a siren pierced the air. Melissa faltered in her singing, glancing wildly for the source of the siren. Would the police get there in time?

There was a loud crack as a bullet penetrated the

back window of the car. Hailey screamed again and Melissa twisted in her seat, trying to figure out if she'd been hit.

"Hailey, are you okay? Where do you hurt? Tell Mommy where you hurt!"

"I'm scared," she cried between heartbreaking sobs.

Melissa couldn't see any blood. The bullet hole was on the opposite side of the glass from where Hailey's booster seat was.

She grabbed Nate's arm. "Are you okay? Did the bullet hit you?"

"I'm fine," he said curtly.

Melissa was relieved and panicked at the same time. "Nate, we have to do something. They're shooting at us!"

"I know, but hear those sirens? We have to hang on long enough for the police to get here."

She knew Nate was right, but listening to Hailey crying was too much to bear. She wrestled with the seat belt, finally managing to get the clasp to release. She hastily scrambled between the front seats to get to Hailey.

"What are you doing?" Nate asked harshly. "You're exposing yourself to more danger."

She ignored him, hovering over her daughter. "Shh, it's okay, we're okay," she said, rubbing her hand over her daughter's hair. She felt along the child's body, making sure that there wasn't any sign of injury. "The police are going to be here any second."

"No bad guys," Hailey sobbed.

"Let's sing, okay? Come on, Hailey. 'Yes, Jesus loves me! The Bible tells me so,'" she sang in a soft tone. Soon

Hailey joined in, and together they continued the entire first verse and the chorus.

The sirens grew louder, so Melissa paused and glanced at Nate. "Is the van still behind us?"

"I don't see it anymore. It dropped back as soon as the sirens grew louder. I think we're okay for now."

Melissa dropped her chin to her chest in a wave of relief. "Thank You, Lord," she whispered.

She could feel the car slowing to a stop as Nate pulled over to the side of the road. The sheriff's deputy vehicle came up right alongside them, the lights on the top of the squad car flashing blue and red.

"Is everyone okay in there?" the deputy asked with obvious concern.

"We're fine. They shot through the rear window, but no one was hit," Nate said.

"You're a deputy?" the officer asked in surprise.

"Yeah, Deputy Freemont from the Milwaukee County Sheriff's Department."

"I'm Deputy Holmes. Deputy Shaker is searching for the other vehicle. Did you happen to get a plate number?" Holmes asked.

"No, things happened too fast," Nate admitted. "They shot at me twice. I'm fairly certain there's a bullet hole somewhere in the side of the car."

The deputy glanced into the backseat where she was sitting with Hailey. Melissa froze, fear lodging in the back of her throat. Logically she understood it wasn't likely that this deputy would know the cop involved in the murder she'd witnessed, but her distrust toward the police was deeply ingrained in her blood.

"Ma'am, are you sure you and the child are all right?" he asked.

She did her best to smile. "Yes, we're fine. Thank you." The words came out in a hoarse whisper, but it was the best she could do.

"I'm going to need statements from each of you," Deputy Holmes said. The radio on his collar squawked, and he straightened and turned away, speaking in low tones.

Melissa reached forward to tap Nate's shoulder. He turned in his seat to look at her. "How long is he going to keep us?" she asked. "I don't want him to run a background check on me."

Nate grimaced. "I'm not sure, but I'll see if I can convince him to let us go once we give our statements."

She nodded but couldn't relax. The very real physical threat was over, but that didn't mean she and Hailey were completely in the clear.

Not when there was no way of knowing if her fake ID would stand up to this officer's scrutiny. If it didn't, she couldn't bear to think about the possible consequences.

Nate could feel the tension radiating off Melissa but wasn't sure what he could do to make her feel better. He was grateful he was still in uniform, so the officer who'd come to their rescue easily realized he was one of them.

There was a brotherhood among police officers—at least, most of the time. Nate hoped that this guy would be willing to give him the courtesy of taking him at his word.

Although it was just as likely that the officer would want to conduct a full investigation, which meant doing background checks on both of them. How would Deputy Holmes react if he learned Nate wasn't currently on duty, despite being in uniform? He'd violated a lot of rules in the past twenty-four hours, and being off duty in uniform was just one of them.

Nate didn't want to think about the fact that Griff had so many reasons to fire him.

"I'm afraid my partner lost sight of the van," Deputy Holmes said, breaking into his depressing thoughts.

Nate turned back to face him. "That's not good news," he said. "But maybe we can find the bullet."

"Good point. Let's take a look."

They both searched in the backseat area, estimating by the trajectory the bullet might have taken. When Nate found the bullet lodged in the back of his headrest, he couldn't suppress a shiver.

Way too close.

He pried it out of the wood frame and then handed it to Deputy Holmes.

"Let's go to my squad car so I can take your statements separately," Holmes said.

"No problem." Nate glanced back at Melissa and Hailey. "If you get too cold, start the engine. I won't be long."

Melissa gave a tiny nod, although the pinched expression on her face didn't lessen at all. He knew that she was worried about giving her statement and racked his brain for some way to get Deputy Holmes to expedite the process.

Since Nate had interviewed many people himself, he knew exactly what the deputy wanted to hear. He gave a concise yet thorough account of what happened.

"Is there a reason you were being followed?" Deputy Holmes asked.

Nate didn't want to lie, so he nodded. "Yes, I'm actively involved in a case. Melissa Harris and her daughter Hailey are in danger, and I believe they're the real targets."

Deputy Holmes frowned. "You have a suspect?"

"Not yet, but this is the third attempt I've personally witnessed of someone trying to get to them. I'm meeting one of my colleagues as soon as we're finished here. Together we're going to see if we can come up with a list of suspects." Nate paused and then added, "I'm happy to keep you up to date as our investigation unfolds."

"I'd appreciate that," the deputy said. "You must have some theory of why the woman and her kid are in danger?"

Nate shrugged. "Lots of theories. Nothing I can prove." He hoped Deputy Holmes wouldn't push the issue, because he didn't want to give any additional details. "You know how it is with active investigations."

"Yeah. We'll get the bullet analyzed for you. Why don't you have your lieutenant give mine a call? Our districts can work together to get this guy before he strikes again."

Nate nodded. "Sure. My Lieutenant is Griffin Vaughn."

Deputy Holmes scribbled on the back of a business card and handed it to Nate. "Have him call Lieutenant Max Cooper. I'll give Max a heads-up to expect the call."

"Thanks." Nate slid the card into his breast pocket, hoping Holmes didn't speak to Cooper too soon. "Do you want to interview Melissa Harris now? I'd like to get back on the road soon, to get her and the child stashed in a safe place."

"Understood."

Nate solemnly shook Deputy Holmes's hand. "Thanks again for the quick response. Even though you didn't find the van, at least we're all right."

"Do you need me to escort you to the meeting you've set up with your colleague?" Holmes asked.

Nate considered his options before slowly nodding in agreement. "Actually, that would be great. We're just meeting up at the strip mall off Highway 24."

"No problem."

Nate walked back to his vehicle and slid into the driver's seat. "Your turn," he said, meeting Melissa's gaze in the rearview mirror. "I explained that I'm working a case and that you and Hailey are the real targets."

Her lips thinned, but she nodded and slipped out of the passenger-side door. She hunched her shoulders in her parka as she walked over to the deputy's vehicle.

Nate glanced back at Hailey, hoping to put the child at ease. "Your mom will be right back, okay?"

"Okay," Hailey whispered.

"Why don't you teach me the song you and your mom were singing?" Nate asked. "I've never heard it before."

"You don't know the words to 'Jesus Loves Me'?" Hailey asked, clearly surprised.

"I know the first line," Nate said. He sang it, imitating the lyrics he'd heard coming from the backseat, and then paused, waiting for Hailey to sing the rest. He remembered hearing Melissa praying while he was doing a good imitation of a race car driver.

Oddly enough, listening to her prayer had helped keep him calm and focused. Which was strange, since he hadn't embraced church and faith the way so many of his buddies had.

But maybe he should? After all, it seemed to work for Melissa and Hailey. Could be that he was missing out on something important.

And he liked the idea of Melissa showing him the way.

Melissa twisted her cold white fingers together, hoping Deputy Holmes wouldn't notice. She gave her account of how the green van had followed them and then came up alongside to shoot at Nate.

"So you think Deputy Freemont was the intended target?" Holmes asked.

She swallowed hard. "Yes, for the moment. But I suspect that's because he was driving. I believe the van intended for us to crash."

"Surely you have some idea who's after you?" he asked.

Melissa had no idea how much Nate had told him. "Actually, I don't know. If I did, I would give Deputy Freemont a name and have him arrested."

"What about your daughter's father?" Holmes pressed. "Is he the one after you? Are you in some sort of custody dispute?"

She forced herself to look straight into the deputy's eyes, hoping that he would believe her. "No. My husband, Jeremy Harris, died before Hailey was born."

"I'm sorry for your loss," he said, looking embarrassed.

"Thank you. Is there anything else you need? I'm sorry to say this, but I don't feel safe staying in this area, considering it wasn't that long ago that someone tried to kill us."

"That's all for now."

She nearly buckled with relief, but forced herself to smile and hold out her hand. "Thank you for coming as soon as you did," she murmured. "I'm very grateful."

"You're welcome. I just wish we'd captured the ones responsible."

"Me, too. Have a merry Christmas, Deputy." Melissa pushed open the car door and climbed out of the vehicle, quickly making her way back to Nate. She slid into the passenger seat, grateful that he'd left the motor idling to keep the interior warm.

"Are you okay?" Nate asked as he pulled out onto the highway.

"Yes. It wasn't as bad as I anticipated." She rubbed her hands together, trying to get the feeling back into her numb fingers.

"I let him know this situation was part of an active investigation," Nate said. "He wants Griff to call his boss so they can work together to find the guys who chased us."

Her stomach knotted with fear. "Are you going to call your boss?" she asked.

"Not until I talk to Jenna."

A spear of jealousy hit her out of nowhere. Nate had said he wasn't married and didn't have a girlfriend, so who was Jenna? She reminded herself that since Nate didn't belong to her, it didn't matter who the other woman was. "Oh, are you planning to call her?"

"Jenna is a friend and I arranged for her to meet us at the strip mall. She's bringing my computer so we can start researching the murder you witnessed."

"I see. Are you sure we can trust her?" As soon as the words left her mouth, she wanted to call them back. Why was she questioning Nate's friendship with this woman? If he didn't trust her, he wouldn't have asked her for help.

"I'm sure. She won't go to Griff unless I tell her it's okay."

Melissa blinked. "You mean, you work with her? Jenna is a deputy on the SWAT team?"

"Yes, she's one of our best sharpshooters." Nate smiled. "I told you I'm not seeing anyone. Jenna is a friend and a colleague, nothing more."

Her cheeks grew warm, and she wished she could roll down her window so the arctic air would cool her off. "Your love life is none of my business, Nate."

He was silent for a moment. "Maybe not, but you should know that I wouldn't have kissed you if I was seeing someone else."

She swallowed a groan. Did he have to remind her about that idiotic kiss? The one she never should have indulged in?

The one she wanted to repeat far more than she should?

Melissa twisted in her seat to look at Hailey. "Are you okay back there?" she asked. "Are you cold?"

"I'm not cold," Hailey said, swinging her feet so that they hit the back of Melissa's seat. "Are we almost there, Mommy?"

"Less than ten minutes," Nate spoke up.

"We haven't been driving that long, Hailey," Melissa reminded her. "And will you please stop kicking my seat?"

"Sorry, Mommy," Hailey said, lowering her legs. "I teached Mr. Nate how to sing 'Jesus Loves Me.' Can we sing it again?"

She was surprised to discover they'd been singing

songs while she was busy talking to the deputy. "Did you teach him all three verses?" Melissa asked with a smile.

"No, just the first one. Right, Mr. Nate?"

"That's right," Nate agreed. "But, look, Hailey, there's the strip mall up ahead. Why don't we sing later?"

"What's the matter? Did you forget the words already?" Melissa teased him.

Nate grinned. "No, but I doubt I have the best singing voice compared with how amazing you and Hailey sound together."

She was touched by his compliment, which was ridiculous, since he'd only heard them singing in the heat of danger. Melissa shifted in her seat to better pay attention as Nate pulled up next to a rusty and dented sedan. He waved, indicating the deputy who'd followed them could leave now.

"That's Jenna's car?" she asked with a frown. Truthfully, she didn't think it would last very long.

"Her old one. She recently bought a brand-new truck." He rolled down his window as Jenna approached. "I didn't realize you were still driving that thing," he said by way of greeting.

"Actually, I figured we'd swap," Jenna said, bending over to lean her forearms on the edge of the open window. The female cop gave Melissa a curious look. "Hi, I'm Deputy Jenna Reed."

"Melissa Harris, and my daughter, Hailey," she replied. The young, willowy blonde wasn't anything like Melissa expected. She looked tough yet fragile at the same time.

"Thanks for bringing the computer," Nate said. "Did you run into any trouble at my place?"

Jenna hesitated and shrugged. "I managed to get in and out without anyone seeing me, but there was definitely someone staking it out. I wrote down the license plate number and tucked it into your computer case along with some cash."

"Thanks, although I'm surprised you didn't run the plates yourself," Nate said with a grin.

"I will when I get home. I didn't want to be late." Jenna held out her car keys. "But as soon as I realized your house was being watched, I decided to bring my old car with me."

"Thanks, but I hate the thought of putting you in danger," Nate said with a scowl. "We were ambushed while driving here. Luckily no one was injured, but the bullets easily could have hit any of us."

Melissa knew that if Hailey had been on the other side of the car, her daughter would have been hit.

Possibly killed. She shivered and tried not to think about it.

Jenna grimaced. "You were lucky, that's for sure. But I'll be fine. I'll drive your car to our headquarters and leave it there."

Melissa could tell Nate wasn't convinced.

"What's the matter, Freemont?" Jenna demanded. "Haven't you figured out by now I can take care of myself? Admit it. You'd swap in an instant if I was Declan or Isaac."

"Okay, fine, we'll swap rides." Nate pushed open his door, and they quickly exchanged car keys.

It didn't take long to get Hailey's booster seat and Melissa's small suitcase moved over to Jenna's old sedan.

"I threw a duffel of your clothing in there, too, Nate,

so no need to shop," Jenna said. "Oh, and here. Bought a couple of disposable phones for you."

Nate took the phones, obviously grateful. "You've thought of everything, haven't you? Thanks."

Jenna shrugged off his gratitude. "Where are you headed?"

"An old fishing cabin. Belongs to the brother of my dad's new wife. I'll give you a call once we get there."

"All right. Stay safe." Jenna lifted her hand and slid into the driver's seat of Nate's dinged-up car.

Surprisingly, Melissa was sad to see the female deputy leave. Was she doing the right thing by going along with Nate? He'd already risked his life multiple times.

And she knew she'd never be able to forgive herself if something terrible happened to him. They had to find out who was behind these recent attempts.

There had been too many close calls already.

SEVEN

With a frown, Nate tried to remember the directions to Amelia's brother's cabin. He'd been there only once and didn't have an address to punch into a GPS device. He knew the name of the town, though. New Haven. And the cabin was on Lake Haven.

Should he call his father to get the address? At the very least, he should warn his dad to be careful now that he was involved.

The idea of his father being in danger continued to nag at him as he drove. But Melissa's father had never been targeted, so he wanted to believe the same would hold true for his dad. If anything, he'd be watched to see if Nate came home.

"I'm thirsty," Hailey complained.

Nate shot a guilty glance at the clock. The hour was well past noon. "Sorry. I should have thought of stopping earlier," he said to Melissa. "Keep an eye out for something Hailey would like."

"Any fast-food place is fine," she assured him. "Take the next exit."

Nate did as she asked. When he was about to enter the drive-through lane, Melissa put her hand on his arm. "Might be best to go inside so Hailey can use the bathroom."

He nodded, realizing he didn't know much about what kids needed. "Sorry," he mumbled, swinging Jenna's rust bucket into a parking space.

"It's okay," Melissa said. "It would be good to stretch our legs for a bit, too."

He opened the door to the restaurant and then followed them in. While Melissa took Hailey to the restroom, he quickly called his dad using his personal cell phone, since the disposable ones Jenna had given him weren't charged up and ready to go.

"Hi, Nate, you caught me on my way out. How are you?" His father's cheerful tone made him smile. Ever since his dad had met Amelia, he'd been like a new person.

"Good, Dad. How are things at home? Notice anything out of the ordinary?"

"No, why?" His father's tone immediately turned serious. He was a firefighter, which was just as dangerous as being a cop, and he understood all too well the types of situations Nate faced on a daily basis.

"I'm working a case and discovered that someone is watching my house. I don't want to alarm you, but you and Amelia really need to be on alert. If you notice anything out of the ordinary, I want you to call it in. In fact, it might be a good time for you two to take a vacation."

"Six days before Christmas? No way. Amelia will never agree to that. Don't worry, son. We'll be fine."

Nate closed his eyes for a moment, tightening his grip on his phone. "Please be careful, Dad," he said again. "They've already taken shots at me twice now."

"Twice?" his dad echoed in horror. "Where's your boss? Why aren't you in protective custody?"

Nate winced, realizing too late that he shouldn't have mentioned that fact. "I'm fine, Dad. Trust me. Just be on the lookout for any problems, okay? I'll check in on you as often as I can."

"All right," his dad reluctantly agreed. "But I hope you're able to wind this case up before Christmas. We're looking forward to spending some time with you."

"I hope so, too. Take care, Dad." Nate let out a heavy sigh as he disconnected from the call.

"Something wrong?" Melissa asked as she and Hailey approached.

"Not at all," he said, forcing a smile. "What do you want to eat?"

Once they placed their order and received their food, he carried the tray to a small table that afforded him the ability to keep an eye on the front door.

Before he could open his sandwich, Melissa closed her eyes and bowed her head. "Dear Lord, we thank You for keeping us safe today, for guiding us on Your path and for this food we're about to eat. Amen."

"Amen," he and Hailey said at the same time, causing Hailey to giggle.

"How long until we get to the hunting cabin?" Melissa asked as she nibbled a french fry.

He grimaced, realizing he hadn't asked his dad for the address. He called again, but this time his father didn't pick up, no doubt because he was driving.

"It should be no more than fifteen to twenty minutes, providing I can avoid getting lost," he admitted. "I haven't been there in two years."

To his surprise, Melissa didn't seem too upset. "I'm

sure you'll find it," she assured him. "You always had an excellent sense of direction, at least compared with me."

He was reminded of the time they'd taken a drive down to the beach on the shores of Lake Michigan. It wasn't difficult to find the lake as long as you headed east, but she'd kept insisting that they were headed the wrong way.

"Just because I could find my way around here doesn't mean I'll find Amelia's brother's cabin," he said drily. "Everyone else could find the lakefront, too."

"I don't know how I managed to get so turned around," she murmured. "We were late to the senior skip beach party, all because of me."

"We had a lot of fun back then," he said, momentarily lost in high school memories.

Melissa's expression softened and she glanced over as if to be sure that Hailey wasn't listening to their conversation. Fortunately she was busy coloring a picture. "We did. But we also didn't have any responsibilities."

She was right. They were both different people now than they were twelve years ago. "True. But I still missed you after you left."

Melissa's gaze darkened, and she set her chicken sandwich down as if she'd lost her appetite. "Leaving you, my home, everything I knew, was the hardest thing for me to do, Nate. You have no idea what it's like to start over in a new city without knowing anyone."

"I wish you had trusted in the system. In me," he added, knowing that was the part bothering him the most.

She shook her head. "I was young. I truly thought no one would believe me. Not even you. Not when your uncle was there that night."

Maybe she was right. It was easy to say now that he would have believed her, but would he have gone against his uncle back when he was barely eighteen? His mother had been gone for eight years by then, and he'd grown closer to his mother's brother after she'd left him and his dad.

"Mommy, can I go play?" Hailey asked, gesturing to the play set just a few yards away.

"For a few minutes, until Mr. Nate and I are finished eating."

"Goody," Hailey shouted, jumping down from the table and running over to where a couple of other kids were already playing. Nate was impressed that Hailey wasn't overly shy about joining the others.

"I hope you don't mind giving her some time to run around," Melissa said softly. "Hailey sometimes gets lonely, being an only child. Besides, we've done nothing but drive for what seems like days."

"Of course not," Nate said. He took another bite of his sandwich. "In fact, I can bring the computer in here and use the free Wi-Fi for an hour or so if you think that would help."

"Really? That would be great." Melissa's eyes brightened at his suggestion. "I want to give Hailey at least some semblance of normalcy after everything that's happened. When I think about how close that bullet came to hitting you…" Her voice trailed off.

"Hey, try not to worry about that," he urged her, reaching over to cover her hand with his. "We're going to get through this, Melissa. I'll do everything in my power to keep you and Hailey out of harm's way."

Her smile was tremulous. "I know. I have faith in you, Nate. And I have faith in God's plan. I hate feeling so helpless, though, not knowing how we're going to find the actual murderer."

"I know." He gave her fingers a gentle squeeze before releasing her. He didn't understand why he was so drawn to this more mature version of Melissa, the conscientious mother and the believer in faith and God. She was the exact opposite from the type of woman he generally dated.

From the type of woman she'd been when they'd dated so many years ago.

Was it possible he'd been subconsciously searching for a replacement for the young, carefree girl she'd once been? Instead of moving on with his life?

It occurred to him that it might be better to stop living in the past. Watching the mother-and-daughter duo, he realized that he was tired of his usual dating scene.

Ironically he wanted something more. A home, a family.

Not with Melissa, since she'd be leaving as soon as they'd figured out who was trying to kill her and why.

But maybe with a different type of woman than he normally went out with.

Surely the right person was out there, somewhere.

Melissa's hand continued to tingle with awareness even after Nate let her go. "That was good," she said, balling up her empty wrapper and tossing it on the tray.

"Agreed. I'll be right back with the computer," Nate said, avoiding her gaze as he piled the garbage on the plastic tray.

"Sounds good." She watched as he took care of their trash on his way outside to the car. She couldn't seem to tear her gaze away. Although she normally stayed far away from cops, there was something about a guy in uniform that oozed strength, confidence and protectiveness.

All traits Nate possessed in full force.

She forced herself to look away. Turning in her seat, she swept her gaze over the area, searching for Hailey. When Melissa spotted her daughter, the little girl looked as if she was having a great time.

Suddenly she noticed something else. A dark van pulling into the parking lot.

She froze, her heart pounding with fear. Had the gunmen found them?

No, this car was blue, not green, and there was a young couple sitting in the front seat, not two menacing men. She let out a heavy sigh of relief.

When Nate returned with the computer, she shook off the feeling of doom.

She wanted to help him research the murder she'd witnessed. The sooner they discovered the identity of the man who'd been stabbed to death, the better.

Nate sat down, opened the computer and booted up the hard drive.

She scooted closer so she could see the screen. "Where on earth are you going to start looking for the victim of a twelve-year-old murder?" she asked in a whisper.

"It won't be easy, although we can start with the police database," Nate admitted. "I'm hoping that they didn't take time to bury the body and that it was found not far after the incident." He opened a document and then glanced at her questioningly. "You're sure the victim is male, correct?"

"Absolutely," she said with conviction.

"Do you remember what he looked like?"

Melissa braced her head in her hands and closed her eyes, putting herself back in the restaurant as she'd served their table. She'd waited on them often enough that the image was fairly clear. "He was roughly six feet tall with blond hair that was long, almost to his shoulders, giving him a bit of a surfer look."

Nate took notes. "Do you have an approximate age? And what he was wearing?"

She shrugged helplessly. "Age is going to be difficult. You know everyone looked old to us back then. But in comparison with your uncle Tom? I'd say roughly the same age, maybe a little younger."

Nate pursed his lips. "My uncle is the same age as my dad, fifty-five, and my mom was two years younger. So twelve years ago, Tom would have been forty-three."

"That sounds about right," Melissa agreed. "The man who died was dressed more casually than the others, as if he didn't quite belong."

"What do you mean, casually?" Nate asked.

"He wore dress slacks and polo shirts, compared with your uncle, who always wore very expensive suits and shirts with his initials embroidered on the cuffs."

"I'd almost forgotten that detail," Nate murmured with a frown. "Okay, anything else stand out in your memory?"

Melissa had relived the night of the stabbing about a hundred times in her mind. "I remember that the blond surfer guy wasn't always included in the conversations. Sometimes he just sat there, listening."

"What kind of conversations?"

"Politics, mostly. To be honest, I never paid that much attention to what they discussed, since that topic didn't interest me. Although they did talk about money a lot, too."

Nate lifted a brow. "Money? Anything more specific?"

"Campaign contributions," she said slowly. Bits and pieces of the conversations were coming back to her. "Something about how to protect the income from campaign contributions."

"That seems strange, if the only elected official there was my uncle Tom," he said thoughtfully.

"Not just your uncle. I seem to remember that the blond surfer guy also talked about his campaign contributions on occasion."

"Bingo," Nate muttered under his breath as he opened a search engine. "Knowing the dead guy was an elected official should help narrow our search."

Melissa knew how to use graphics to create designs, but watching Nate's fingers fly over the keyboard made her realize he was no slouch when it came to computers, either.

A high-pitched cry made her leap to her feet. "Hailey?" she called, rushing over to the play center.

"I bumped my head," her daughter whimpered, rubbing a spot on the side of her temple.

"Let me see," she said, gently probing the area. There was a slight bump, but the skin wasn't broken. "Come sit at the table. I'll get you some ice."

"I'll grab some ice for you," one of the other mothers offered helpfully.

"Thanks." She carried Hailey back to the table where Nate was waiting, a concerned expression in his brown eyes.

"Is she okay?"

Melissa nodded. "Just a bump on her head. Nothing serious." She took the ice from the mother of the little girl Hailey had been playing with. "Thanks."

She pressed the cold napkin against Hailey's temple for a few minutes, which was as long as her daughter would sit still.

"It's too cold, Mommy," Hailey said, pushing her hand away.

"But the ice will make it feel better," she pointed out. "Just a little while longer, okay?"

Hailey tolerated the ice for another three minutes before wiggling off her lap. "Can I play some more?"

Melissa hesitated, glancing over at Nate. "How much longer do you need?"

"Thirty minutes would be great, but if you want to leave now, that's okay, too."

"Thirty more minutes, please?" Hailey asked, the bump on her head clearly forgotten.

"All right, but be careful, okay?" Melissa watched with exasperation as her daughter ran back to the play set, knowing that it was better for Hailey to burn off a little more energy before they had to get back in the car again.

She wasn't sure what to expect at the cabin. Did it even have electricity and running water? She sincerely hoped so. Not that she could afford to be picky.

"Melissa, come here and take a look at these photographs," Nate said, drawing her attention back to the issue at hand. "Tell me if you recognize any of these men."

She went over to sit beside him so she could see the computer screen. "That's your uncle Tom," she said, pointing to the man standing in the center of the group.

"Yeah, I know. What about the others?"

She stared at the screen for a long moment. "I'm sorry, but none of the others look familiar."

Nate grimaced. "I was wondering if this blond guy here might be the same one you saw that night. He has short hair in this picture, but it was taken a year before we graduated from high school."

She leaned closer, trying to imagine the guy with longer hair. "I'm sorry, but I just can't say for sure."

"Okay, I'll keep looking."

Melissa caught a glimpse of the titles listed in the caption beneath the picture. "Wait a minute. These are all city aldermen?"

"Yes, why?"

The memory clicked into place. "I remember your uncle referring to the blond guy as an alderman. Oh, if only I could remember his last name."

"If he's an alderman, I can narrow the search even further," Nate said with satisfaction.

She waited patiently as he typed commands into the search engine and watched as Hailey and the other girl took turns going down the slide.

"Here we go," Nate muttered. He turned the computer so that she could see the screen without any glare from the sunlight. "Scroll through these. See if anyone looks familiar."

She did as he asked, taking her time with each photograph. Three pages down, she gasped at the familiar face on the screen.

"That's him," she whispered. "That's the man who was stabbed that night."

"Alderman Kevin Turner," Nate said in a low voice. "He was the alderman of our district, the one where I

grew up. In fact, my dad still lives in the area, although
he moved into a smaller house once I moved away. Back
when I was younger, Kevin Turner lived directly across
the street from us."

Melissa shivered, thinking about the irony of the situation. The interpersonal relationships back then were
too close for comfort. "I guess now that we have a name,
we can verify when and how he died."

"Absolutely. Just give me another couple of minutes
here." Nate turned the computer back toward himself
and went to work. For several long moments, there was
nothing but the tapping of his fingers to break the silence.

"Here it is," Nate said. "Alderman Kevin Turner,
died on June 16 from a stab wound in a brutal mugging in Milwaukee."

"Milwaukee?" Melissa scowled. "That's not true. He
died in Brookmont."

"Unfortunately, it won't be very easy to prove otherwise," Nate murmured.

She read the article twice, the old, familiar sense of
dread seeping into her stomach.

These men had covered their tracks exceedingly
well. Finding the victim hadn't helped reveal the truth
about what happened that night and why.

In fact, she was beginning to believe that the men
involved had the money and power to do whatever they
wanted.

Including the ability to get away with murder.

EIGHT

Nate battled a wave of helplessness. In his heart he knew that Kevin Turner was the victim Melissa had watched die twelve years ago, but proving that fact was something else entirely.

Yeah, sure, they had Melissa as an eyewitness, but they needed forensic evidence to support their theory. Something more than the word of a girl who'd had drugs found in her room and who'd disappeared, then faked her death.

The biggest issue was motive. Why on earth had Kevin Turner been murdered?

"This doesn't help us one bit, does it?" Melissa said in a dull, flat tone.

The listlessness in her voice bothered him, spurring a sense of determination. "It's the first step in uncovering the truth," he said firmly. "We know that money was involved, be it campaign funds or otherwise. We'll just need to find out more about this Kevin Turner. And to understand why he was murdered that night. From what you described, it doesn't seem as if he was killed in a fit of anger."

"I'm really not sure," Melissa said with sigh. "It

looked like they were just talking when suddenly the guy next to your uncle pulled out a knife and stabbed him."

"So it could have been a crime of opportunity," Nate mused half to himself.

"Maybe we're kidding ourselves, Nate. We could dig into this for days and still not know exactly what happened."

"Hey, you're not giving up on me, are you?" he asked gently. He hated seeing the dull, resigned expression in her hazel eyes. "Aren't you the one who told me to have faith?"

"Yes," she acknowledged with a self-deprecating smile. "You're right. Sometimes I still struggle with it. Especially now. I feel like every time we try to take a step forward, we're given a massive shove backward."

"But we're still on our feet," Nate said encouragingly. "And that means we're still fighting."

Her smile widened. "Okay, yes, we're still fighting. And since someone is trying to silence us once and for all, there just might be something they're afraid we'll find out. Something that will lead us to the truth."

"That's my girl," he said, enjoying the way she blushed. "I hate to leave, but we should probably get back on the road. I'd prefer to reach the cabin before it gets too dark."

"Sounds good," Melissa agreed. "I'll get Hailey."

Nate nodded as he quickly shut down the computer and glanced at his watch. From what he remembered, Amelia's brother's cabin had the basics—water, non-perishable food and electricity—but he couldn't be sure there was any computer access.

Too late to consider stopping at a store to purchase

a satellite modem, even if he was willing to use up a good chunk of his cash, which wouldn't be smart. No, he'd have to make do with going to public places that offered free services as needed.

"Goodbye, Sally," Hailey said, waving to her new-found friend.

"'Bye, Hailey."

"That was so fun," the little girl declared as they walked outside to the car. "Can I see Sally again, Mommy?"

Melissa's smile was strained. "We'll see."

"'We'll see' means no," Hailey muttered, obviously disappointed.

Nate felt bad for her. It couldn't be easy to be so far away from her friends, especially less than a week before Christmas. Obviously keeping her safe was more important, but that didn't make him feel any better.

If things were normal, he could take Melissa and Hailey to visit his teammate Caleb, his wife, Noelle, and their daughter, Kaitlin. He was sure the girls would get along great.

Caleb and Noelle had recently been blessed with a son they'd christened Anthony. Seeing the expression on Caleb's face when he stared down at his son had filled Nate with an odd sense of longing.

Having a family seemed a distant dream. Especially considering his own upbringing. His mother had left when he was ten years old, never once talking to him or even sending a letter. She certainly hadn't missed him.

He remembered overhearing his parents arguing but had never thought too much about it. All parents fought sometimes, didn't they?

But one day he came home from school to find there

was no one home. He'd called his dad in a panic, and for a short time, they'd feared his mother had been taken against her will.

Until they realized all her clothes were gone.

For months after, he'd wondered if his parents had been fighting over him. If he'd done something that had caused his mother to leave.

"Nate? Are you okay?"

He realized he'd been sitting and staring blankly through the windshield, lost in the memories. "Uh, yeah, I'm fine," he said gruffly. "I'm just trying to remember the route to the cabin."

That much was partially true. Nate drove out of the parking lot and headed north. "Are there any landmarks that I can help look for?" Melissa asked.

"First we have to find Highway 44," he said. "The town the cabin is located in is called New Haven, and it's not far off the highway. Unfortunately, I can't think of the street name."

"I'm sure you'll recognize it when you see it," she said.

He sure hoped so.

Neither of them said much for the next few miles. He was thinking about turning around when Melissa leaned forward excitedly. "Hey, there's a highway sign up ahead."

"Junction 44," Nate read out loud, relieved he'd been on the right track. He slowed down and then turned left so they were headed west.

"I'll read the street names out loud," Melissa offered.

He listened as they passed one intersection and then another. So far, neither street sounded familiar. Nate grew tense as he concentrated on navigating in the deepening dusk. And found himself silently praying for God's help in remembering the way. How did Melissa phrase it?

Dear Lord, please guide me on Your path. Amen.

Instantly he felt more calm and relaxed. Maybe it was all in his head, but since he'd met her, he'd begun to realize that leaning on the power of prayer could help a person get through difficult times.

"Turkey Hollow," Melissa said, breaking into his thoughts.

"That's it!" Nate exclaimed. "That's the road that will take us to Lake Point Drive."

"That means we're almost there, right Mommy?" Hailey asked from the backseat.

"That's right." Melissa reached over to touch his hand, and he glanced at her questioningly. "What sort of cabin is this?" she asked in a low tone. "I'd like to prepare Hailey if we're going to be camping out."

He grinned and shook his head. "No need to worry. The cabin has running water and electricity. I just can't remember if there was computer access or not. The last time I was here, I spent most of the time fishing on the lake with my dad."

"You and your father were always very close," Melissa murmured. "Just like me and my dad were."

"Yeah, we were. After my mother left, we learned to lean on each other a lot. I was angry with him at first, but then one night I found him crying, and that really shook me. I'd always thought of my dad as a tough firefighter, and I'd never, ever seen him cry."

"Oh, Nate, that must have been so hard."

He shifted in his seat, uncomfortable with her sympathy. "That's all in the past now. It's no big deal. My dad and I have only got closer over the years. He finally remarried after I graduated from college, to a very nice lady who makes him happy."

"And you've never heard from your mother since the day she left?" Melissa asked.

"No." He didn't want to talk about that now. He gestured toward the windshield. "Help me look for Lake Point Drive. I'm pretty sure that will take us to the cabin."

"All right," she agreed.

Nate was glad she'd dropped the subject of his mother. Why was he wasting his time now thinking about the woman who'd left him? There was no point. He needed to stay focused on investigating a twelve-year-old murder.

And if watching Melissa interact with her daughter reminded him of the mother he'd missed, that was nobody's problem but his own.

Melissa sensed she'd struck a nerve asking about Nate's mother. Even back when they were dating their senior year of high school, he'd refused to talk about her.

She hadn't appreciated what Nate had really gone through until she'd given birth to Hailey. How any mother could willingly give up her child was beyond her realm of comprehension.

"There's Lake Point Drive," she said in case Nate hadn't noticed. "Right or left?"

"We'll head left, although I think the road completely encircles the lake," he said. "So we should be able to find the cabin."

"Is it right off this road?" Melissa frowned when

they passed a cross street. "There seem to be a couple of cul-de-sacs along the way."

"No, it's not on a cul-de-sac," he said. "I remember it seemed to be surrounded completely by trees, giving it a sense of isolation, with a nice view of the lake. So it has to be off to the right side of the road."

Melissa nodded and stayed alert for possibilities. She estimated they'd gone halfway around the lake before Nate slowed down.

"Found it," he said as he turned onto a snow-covered driveway. Thankfully the snow wasn't too deep, so the car was able to make it all the way up to the structure.

Although it looked more like a cottage than a cabin. The wood siding was gold in color, blending nicely with the trees, with green trim and green shutters. There was no garage, and she could see a glimpse of the lake, which appeared to be frozen solid.

"Why don't you wait here for a minute?" Nate suggested. "I'll get the door open and turn on the lights so you can see."

"All right." She waited patiently with Hailey as he dug around for the key and let himself inside. Less than ten minutes later, there was a welcoming glow illuminating from the windows, and Nate returned to the car.

He grabbed the computer case, his duffel and her suitcase, leaving her to walk with Hailey.

"Look, Mommy, lots and lots of pretty white snow!" There was a good two feet here, double what had been on the ground in Milwaukee. Her daughter ran over to scoop up a handful and tossed it in the air. "Can we build a snowman? Can we?"

"Yes, but not now. It's too dark. We'll make one in the morning, okay?"

For a moment Hailey wavered, as if she wanted to press the issue, but then she nodded and joined Melissa at the door.

"Wow, this is nice," she said as she stepped inside. The interior was warm and cozy, nothing at all like she'd expected. A comfortable leather sofa and love seat were set up in front of a fireplace, and the kitchen had several decent amenities, including a stove, refrigerator and microwave. "Not as rustic as I imagined."

"Best of all, I see there's wireless internet access," Nate said as he set the computer case on the oak kitchen table. "Unfortunately, there's not much food, but if you give me a list of things you'd like, I'll run to the general store."

"Okay," Melissa agreed. She wrote down some basic food items that Hailey preferred and handed it to Nate.

"Make yourself at home," Nate said as he headed toward the door. "You and Hailey will want to share the master bedroom. I'll use the guest room."

She nodded and busied herself with unpacking their small suitcase. The so-called cabin was larger than her two-bedroom apartment, yet cozy at the same time.

Nate returned twenty minutes later and they worked at throwing together a quick beef stew for dinner.

Melissa felt a little off balance with Nate so close, but she needn't have worried. As soon as they'd finished their meal and cleaned up the dirty dishes, he sat down and retreated behind his computer.

She searched around for something for Hailey to do, and when she found an old game of Chutes and Ladders, her daughter was delighted to take her on.

They played until Hailey's eyelids began to droop. "Come on. Time to brush your teeth and get into bed."

She didn't argue the way she normally did, and Melissa was even more surprised when she didn't have to remind her daughter to say her prayers.

"God bless Daddy, Mommy, my new friend Sally and Mr. Nate. Amen."

"Amen," Melissa murmured.

"Amen," Nate said from the doorway behind her, making her jump.

She glanced around in surprise, but then leaned down to give Hailey a hug and a kiss. "Good night, sweetie."

"Good night, Mommy. Good night, Mr. Nate."

Melissa walked toward Nate, trying not to be annoyed that her daughter kept including him in her prayers. It wasn't as if Nate could ever replace Hailey's real father.

She gave herself a mental shake. What was wrong with her? She should be glad that Hailey had someone like Nate to protect her.

"Find anything more about Kevin Turner?" she asked, anxious to veer her thoughts elsewhere.

"No, but I was wondering if you could take a few minutes to look at more photos, see if you can identify any of the other men who were at the scene of the crime that night."

"Sure." She brushed past Nate to return to the kitchen, the woodsy scent of his aftershave filling her head.

It took several minutes for her to scroll through the images. When she got to a group shot, she increased the size of the picture so she could study their faces.

"This guy here," she said, tapping her finger on the screen. "He's the cop who was there that night."

"Randall Joseph?" Nate asked in a shocked tone. "Are you absolutely sure?"

She looked again and nodded. "I'm sure. That's him. Why are you so surprised? Because he's still a cop?"

"Not just that," Nate said slowly, a grim expression in his eyes. "Randall Joseph is the Brookmont chief of police."

"The chief of police? Are you serious?" She stared at Nate in horror and then abruptly jumped up from the chair, knocking it over in her haste to get away. "That's just perfect. He's in charge of all the police officers. There's no way in the world anyone will believe my story now."

Nate righted the chair, eyeing her warily. "Calm down, Melissa."

"Calm down?" Frustration welled in her chest to the point that she felt as if she might explode. "How can I calm down? As if having the mayor involved wasn't bad enough, now we have the chief of police, too? What's next? A judge? The state governor?"

She knew her voice was rising and she was losing control, but she couldn't seem to get a grip. The odds were overwhelmingly stacked against them. She and Hailey might never be safe.

Ever!

"Shh, it's okay." Nate was there, gathering her into his arms and pulling her tightly against him. For a moment she wanted to pummel him with her fists, but then she buried her face in his shoulder, breathing in his familiar scent. She squeezed her eyes shut, trying to keep the tears that threatened at bay.

"Oh, Nate, what are we going to do?" she whispered, her voice muffled against his shirt.

"We're going to get to get to the bottom of this crime," Nate said grimly. "No one is infallible. And you said it earlier. They're coming after us because they're afraid we'll succeed in uncovering their dirty little secrets."

She desperately wanted to believe that. It wasn't like her to lose faith like this. But losing her father and being in danger were wearing her down. She relaxed against Nate, soaking up some of his strength. It felt good to be in his arms.

Too good.

Reluctantly, she pulled herself together and eased away from him, swiping at her damp eyes. "Sorry about that," she said. "I'm okay now."

"You don't have to apologize to me," he said, lifting a hand to brush a strand of her hair off her cheek. His touch was feather-light, yet she felt the ripples down to the soles of her feet. "I believe the truth will prevail. These guys are probably right now trying to find a way to find us, determined to keep their crime hidden in the past."

Melissa nodded, imagining these men sitting at the restaurant the way they used to, talking in low tones among themselves. "Wait a minute. That's it!"

"What?" Nate asked, clearly confused.

"The restaurant, El Matador. You said it's still there, right?" When Nate nodded, she rushed on. "What are the chances that these guys still eat dinner there?"

Realization dawned in Nate's eyes. "I'd say pretty good."

"Exactly." Melissa couldn't believe she hadn't thought of this before. "Why couldn't we go there and see if we can overhear what they're saying? I could disguise myself, dye my hair red or wear a pair of thick-framed glasses. I could even dress up like a server, although I'm sure their uniforms have changed."

"Not an option," Nate said in a flat tone. "They'll probably still recognize you. But you might be onto something. We could use cameras and hidden microphones to find out what they're talking about."

"Really? You can do that?" she asked in amazement.

"Yeah, although we'll need some help getting the equipment," Nate said thoughtfully. "I'll give Jenna a call tomorrow, see what we can come up with."

"Good." Melissa longed to move back into Nate's arms, so she forced herself to take a step away from the temptation and to focus on their next steps.

Maybe the task of bringing down a chief of police and the Brookmont mayor wasn't as ridiculous as it sounded.

She was beginning to believe that with Nate at her side, anything was possible.

NINE

Sleep eluded him, causing Nate to toss and turn, his thoughts spinning in circles as he ruminated over the mystery of Alderman Turner's murder. Eventually he gave up, dragging himself out of bed early in the morning. The cabin was quiet, and he found himself glad that Melissa and Hailey were still asleep.

He needed some quiet time to come to grips with the fact that his uncle Tom was involved in something criminal. More than just covering up a murder, as if that wasn't bad enough. The motive for killing Turner had to have been big enough to take the risk of getting caught. And for all he knew, his uncle was still involved in whatever illegal activities had led to the murder in the first place.

After getting dressed in the comfortable jeans and sweatshirt that he'd found packed in his duffel and securing his weapon in deference to Hailey, he padded into the kitchen to make some coffee. Waiting for the pot to brew, he stared out the window, squinting at how the sun reflected blindingly off the snow.

Another beautiful day out, but all he could think of was that this was just another day closer to Christmas.

It didn't seem fair that Hailey should have to be here, hiding in a remote lakeside cabin over the holiday. He needed to step up the investigation, to get the proof he needed to convince Griff to take a chance on continuing the case as soon as possible.

Nate filled up a large mug with steaming black coffee and headed over to the table where he'd left his computer. He created a new email address and then wrote a note to Jenna, asking her to bring him the electronic supplies he needed from his house.

Too bad he hadn't thought about this before now. He hated the idea of Jenna having to sneak past whoever was staked outside his place once again. And unfortunately his gadgets were stored all over the living space, so she'd have to search around to find everything he needed.

If he didn't hear from her in a couple of hours, he could finally charge up one of the new disposable cell phones and call her.

Sipping his coffee, he began to search further back in time in order to figure out what Alderman Turner might have been involved in. Not an easy task, but Nate knew how to make the most of the technology he had at his fingertips.

"Good morning." Melissa's soft, husky voice startled him so badly he spilled coffee on his jeans.

"Uh, hi," he said awkwardly, turning in his seat to face her. How was it possible that she looked so beautiful first thing in the morning, even with sleep-tousled hair and no makeup?

"Thanks for making coffee," she murmured, heading straight over to the pot. "I'll get breakfast started. Anything you're craving in particular?"

He didn't want her to feel as if she needed to cook for him, and he was about to offer to do it himself when Hailey bounded into the room.

"Can we build a snowman, Mommy? Can we?"

"After breakfast," Melissa said with an indulgent smile. "What would you like? Oatmeal or eggs?"

"Oatmeal," Hailey said, jumping up and down with excitement. "I want oatmeal."

"Works for me," Nate said, pushing the computer off to the side and then rising to his feet. "I'll make it."

"No, no, I'll do it," Melissa said hastily. "Just sit down. You're working, and I don't know how to search the internet the way you do."

He sank back down, making a mental note to do the dishes afterward. Even as he continued to search, he was distracted by Hailey's chatter.

Melissa was patient and kind, allowing Hailey to stand on a chair to help stir the oatmeal. He couldn't help comparing her to his own absent mother.

Nate vaguely remembered making Christmas cookies with his mom one time. In fact, she'd scolded him for eating too many and making himself sick. He couldn't recall what she'd looked like that day, but surely there must have been other tender moments they'd shared.

Too bad he couldn't think of anything specific.

No sense in dwelling on that now. He went back to the case at hand, but so far he hadn't found out much about Kevin Turner. He was tempted to ask his dad what he remembered since they'd lived just across the street, but he doubted that old neighborhood memories would be much help.

"Thanks," he said when Melissa set a steaming bowl

of oatmeal down on the table. She and Hailey sat and then bowed their heads to pray.

"Dear Lord," Melissa said, "we thank You for this food and shelter. We also ask for Your continued protection and guidance as we continue to seek the truth. Amen."

"Amen," he said, appreciating the content of her prayer.

"Dig in," Hailey said with enthusiasm as she added brown sugar and raisins to her bowl. It was weird being together like this, as if they were a family.

But they weren't. A fact he needed to remember.

"Have you thought about our plan to go back to the restaurant?" Melissa asked.

"Yeah, I sent Jenna an email with a list of supplies that we'll need. I don't like making her go back to my place again, but it's better than trying to buy everything new. I haven't heard from her yet, though."

"You have cameras and listening devices at your house?" she asked in surprise.

He could feel the tips of his ears burning with embarrassment. Could he sound like a bigger nerd? Probably not. "I happen to like electronics," he mumbled. "Mmm, this oatmeal is really good."

She didn't ask anything more, and as soon as they were finished eating, he jumped up to do the dishes. "You cooked. My turn to clean up," he insisted.

"Let's go outside, Mommy!" Hailey pleaded with wide hazel eyes. "Please?"

"Take her outside. I'll wash the dishes and continue working," Nate said firmly.

Melissa hesitated, and when her gaze met his, he was struck by the fact that she'd expected him to come outside with them. And while the thought was tempting, he had work to do.

At least, that's what he told himself. But as he finished drying the plates, watching as Hailey and Melissa laughed and played, building a snowman in the front yard, Nate knew that he'd insisted on staying inside to prevent himself from getting too close.

He settled down behind the computer, determined to find something that would help. After some more digging he discovered that both Kevin Turner and his uncle, Tom McAllister, ran for office at the same time, roughly six years before the murder. Then they were also re-elected four years later.

Had they made some sort of pact back then? Obviously they'd both received campaign contributions, but were some of them illegal? Or worse, did they use the campaign funds as a way to hide dirty money? Like from drugs?

The idea of his uncle Tom being involved in something illegal was deeply disturbing, but he also couldn't deny the fact there were drugs planted in Melissa's room to discredit her story. Were those narcotics part of their scheme? Unfortunately, the connection seemed to make sense.

Nate had no idea how much time had passed, but just as Melissa and Hailey came back in, he found a bunch of campaign celebration photographs from the second election.

He scrolled through the pictures and then stopped abruptly as a large group photo bloomed on the screen. He stared at it in shock.

"Nate?" Melissa's voice was faint, as if she were

speaking through a thick blanket. "Nate! Are you all right?"

No, he wasn't all right. His chest hurt as he struggled to breathe.

"What did you find?" Melissa crossed over and leaned against his shoulder. "That's Alderman Kevin Turner," she said, pointing at the man standing off to the side. "Who's the woman he's talking to?"

The band around his chest finally loosened enough for Nate to respond. "That's my mother, Rosalie Freemont."

Melissa caught her breath at Nate's terse admission. His mother? The woman who'd abandoned him and his father? She found herself leaning closer, trying to get a good look at her.

Rosalie was stunningly beautiful. Her hair was darker than Nate's sandy color, but they shared many of the same facial features, and it was easy to see where Nate had inherited his good looks. But she couldn't help thinking that the closeness between Nate's mother and Alderman Turner was far too cozy for comfort, especially since there was no mention of Nate's father.

"I wonder if she knew that this picture was taken," Nate said in a low tone.

"I'm sorry," she said, putting a soothing arm around his shoulders. It couldn't be easy to come face-to-face with a painful part of his past.

"No need to apologize," he said gruffly, pushing away from the computer and breaking away from her embrace. He stood and began to pace. "Fact is, I barely even remembered what she looked like until I saw the photograph."

"I lost my mother to a brain aneurysm," Melissa said. "It was a total shock. One minute she's alive and talking. The next she was gone. Not like my father, who knew he had cancer and that he only had a few months to live."

"I'm sure that was terrible for you, but at least your mother didn't leave voluntarily," Nate said.

"Do you know that for sure?" she pressed. "Isn't it possible something awful happened to her?"

"No. In fact, my uncle Tom told me and my dad that she was living out in Arizona. Even with that news, my dad didn't initiate divorce proceedings until I was in college. He asked Tom to get them to my mother, and they were returned with her signature on them."

"That's awful, Nate," Melissa said, her heart breaking for him. No little boy should have to go through something like that. Why couldn't his mother have tried to stay in touch?

"Never mind that now," Nate said with an impatient wave of his hand. "I still haven't heard from Jenna about getting the technology we need to bug the restaurant. I'll try calling her with one of the disposable phones."

"I just looked at mine, and there's only one bar, so I'm not sure we'll get service up here," Melissa said with a sigh.

Nate looked at his phone and scowled. She watched as he tried to call Jenna, only to receive an error message. Tossing his device aside, he crossed back over to the computer. "I'll try one more email, but if that doesn't work, my regular cell gets better service so I'll have no choice but to use it."

She followed him and was relieved to see that Jenna had responded. "What did she say?"

Nate read Jenna's message out loud. "'Happy to help,

but have no clue what any of this stuff looks like. I'll distract the guys watching the place so you can go in and get what you need.'"

Melissa straightened and glanced at him. "Are you sure that's a good idea?" She hated the thought of Nate putting himself in danger.

She read over his shoulder as he typed a response.

Sounds like a plan. What time can we meet?

Jenna quickly replied back.

I swapped for a day shift today, so how about when I'm off work, maybe around 4:30? I'll meet you at my place.

Sounds good. See you then.

Nate sent off his reply, and once again, Melissa squashed a flash of jealousy. He'd made a point of explaining that he and Jenna were friends and colleagues, nothing more. So why did the familiarity between them bother her?

Quite honestly, it shouldn't.

"So, what should we do in the meantime?" Melissa asked.

Nate glanced at his watch. "I'm sure Hailey needs to eat lunch soon, right?" When she nodded in agreement, he continued, "We're almost two hours from Brookmont, so we'll head in as soon as we finish eating."

"All right," she agreed. "It wouldn't hurt to drive past the restaurant to see if anyone is there who we recognize."

"I think that's a good idea. I really don't like dragging you and Hailey with me, but I'm not sure that leaving you here alone is a good option."

"I'd rather go with you," she said hastily. "Between the two of us, I'm sure we can protect Hailey."

Nate nodded, but there was a troubled expression in his eyes as if he had doubts about the plan.

Too bad. No way was she letting him go off on his own, leaving her and Hailey here to wonder what was going on.

Melissa draped Hailey's hat, scarf and mittens around the heat vent near the floor so they would be dry by the time they needed to leave. Then they played another game of Chutes and Ladders before heading back into the kitchen to make soup and sandwiches for lunch. She'd been touched by the fact that Nate had insisted on cleaning up the breakfast dishes. She hadn't had anyone helping her with the chores since Jeremy died.

Although if she were honest, Jeremy hadn't really helped out in the kitchen much. He was a good man, and she believed he'd have been a great father, even though he hadn't been given that chance.

She remembered praying in church those first few months after his death as she'd grown large with his child, trying to make sense of God's plan. Her pastor had helped a lot, but it wasn't until now that she realized maybe this was all happening just the way God intended.

Had He brought her and Nate together for a reason? Something other than finding out about the murder she'd witnessed?

She'd been disappointed that Nate hadn't joined them outside, assuming that it was more than just working on the investigation that had kept him away.

Despite how great he was with Hailey, she didn't get the sense that he relished the idea of being a role model for her daughter. Which was a little odd, considering that he had a great relationship with his dad.

"I'll clean up," Nate said when they'd finished their meal.

"We'll finish faster if we do it together," she pointed out. "Hailey, why don't you get your handheld computer game for the car ride?"

"Okay," Hailey agreed. The little girl disappeared into the bedroom to fetch what she needed.

Nate didn't say much as he washed the dishes. She placed the leftover soup in the fridge before picking up the dish towel to begin drying.

"Do you really think using the cameras and microphones will work?" she asked in an effort to break the strained silence.

"I hope so," Nate said in a grim tone. "We need something more to go on. Finding the man who'd been murdered didn't help as much as I'd hoped."

"I know," she agreed with a sigh. "I wonder if the interior of the restaurant has changed over time."

Nate shrugged. "They renovated the kitchen a few years back, but I think the layout of the dining room is basically the same."

"That will help," she murmured. She could already envision the best places to plant the cameras and listening devices.

But first they needed to get the equipment out of Nate's house.

The time was close to one thirty before they were on the road, heading back toward civilization. The two-hour drive seemed to fly by as their car ate up the miles.

Nate exited the interstate and took side streets until they reached the restaurant.

Melissa twisted her fingers together as he first drove past the restaurant and then circled around to pull into the parking lot.

He sat there for a moment, staring out through the windshield.

She put her hand on his arm. "What's wrong?"

"That's my uncle's car," Nate said, gesturing to an expensive SUV parked near the front door. "I assume some of the others are here, too. Unfortunately, I don't know what the chief of police drives these days. You were right. They must still meet here on a regular basis."

She wasn't sure what to say to make him feel better. And she thought it was creepy that these men were still holding meetings here. Did that mean whatever criminal activities they were involved in had continued over the years? The thought made her feel sick.

After several long minutes, Nate put the vehicle in Reverse and backed out of the parking lot. "Looks like we'll get there early," she said, attempting to lighten things up.

"Yeah, I know." He drove toward the meeting point, showing her his place along the way. Melissa was dismayed to realize just how close to his female coworker he lived.

Jenna joined them about twenty minutes later, earlier than they'd originally planned. Nate got out of the car and went over to talk to her, while Melissa tried to be patient.

She was glad to see that they seemed to be all business, speaking only for a few minutes before Nate came jogging back to the car.

"I need you to drive," he said, opening the passenger-side door and holding out the keys. "Jenna will give us a few minutes to get in position before confronting the vehicle that's parked a few doors down from my place."

"Okay." Melissa took the keys and slid out to go around to the driver's side. She adjusted the seat for her shorter legs and then followed Nate's directions to the street behind his place.

"I want you to drive around for about five minutes," Nate said as he slid out of the seat. "My house is right behind this white one. It won't take me long to get what I need. I'll meet you back here, okay?"

"Got it." She forced a smile, glad that thanks to the winter solstice, darkness was already starting to fall. Within moments Nate disappeared into the shadows.

Melissa gripped the steering wheel tightly as she drove, committing the street names to memory. The five-minute drive seemed to drag on forever, but soon she pulled up to the curb where she'd dropped Nate off.

Her heart pounded with nervousness as she peered out, searching for Nate. It was probably a good thing that the windows in the white house that butted up against Nate's were dark, indicating no one was home. But where was he? Had Jenna's diversion worked? What if he'd been caught?

Melissa belatedly realized that there was no way for Nate—or Jenna, for that matter—to get in touch with her if something bad had happened. She had her disposable phone, but neither one of them had the number.

One minute ticked by and then another. Her stomach tightened with concern.

Where in the world was Nate?

TEN

Moving quickly and silently, Nate grabbed a duffel bag and then gathered all the cameras, listening devices and receivers he needed. He didn't have his gadgets well organized, but fortunately he knew exactly where everything was located.

When he walked past the front window, he caught a glimpse of Jenna standing beside a parked car along the curb. She stood right in front of the driver's side window, effectively blocking the occupant's view of the house.

Relieved that her diversion tactic appeared to be working, he made one last sweep of the place, trying to think of what else he might need. Since he was here, he tossed more clothing in the bag, along with the spare cash he had stored in his father's watch case.

Satisfied that he wouldn't need to return anytime soon, Nate turned to leave his bedroom, the jam-packed duffel slung over his shoulder, when he heard a loud banging on the front door.

His heart jumped into his throat, and he melted back into the shadows of the bedroom, trying to understand what had happened.

"Police! Come out with your hands up!"

What? Had they seen him moving around inside? Nate quickly considered his options. He could stay and face the police since this was, after all, his house, but he didn't trust this situation. The cops outside his door were more likely to arrest him for attempted murder for shooting those guys at the mall, or for harboring a fugitive, than to help him.

No, a better option was to make a break out the back door, but what if they'd managed to have his house surrounded?

He'd have to take his chances. While he listened to their attempts to break in his door, Nate held his weapon ready as he darted through the kitchen and opened the back door.

He barely noticed the cold air as he rushed outside into the darkness of his backyard. He'd taken only a couple of steps when the dark figure of a man emerged from the shadows to his left. "Freeze!"

His heart thudded in his chest as he imagined the weapon that was trained on him. But he refused to go down without a fight. Nate swung the duffel at the guy, hitting him square in the chest and knocking him off balance.

He managed to hang on to the bag, and then ran, darting between the trees, mentally braced for the sound of gunfire.

He covered the area between the houses in seconds, hating the fact that he was leaving footprints in the snow behind him. Just as he hit the driveway belonging to the white house, mere yards from the car where Melissa was waiting, he heard loud shouting behind him. "Back here! He's getting away!"

He yanked open the passenger door. "Go, go!"

Melissa floored the gas pedal, tires squealing as she pulled away from the curb. He managed to get the passenger door closed and fumbled with the seat belt, impressed by the way she took a quick right and then another left, zigzagging her way through the neighborhood in an effort to make sure no one was following them. Thankfully, the crazy driving didn't wake Hailey up from her deep slumber.

Several long minutes passed before he broke the silence. "Head out onto the interstate. There's plenty of traffic, so we should be able to blend in."

"Okay, but tell me what happened." Melissa's gaze was glued to the road, her fingers gripping the steering wheel tightly, making him realize that she'd been afraid on his behalf. "How did they find you?"

"I'm not sure," he said honestly. "I could see Jenna standing next to a car parked on the road, but a few minutes later there was banging on the door, and the police were demanding that I come out. One of them was waiting for me in the backyard, too."

Melissa glanced briefly at him, shock evident on her features. "They saw you inside the house?"

"Either that, or they just assumed Jenna showed up for a reason and decided to take the chance on confronting me." The more he thought about it, the more likely that scenario seemed. They must have considered Jenna's confrontation suspicious.

"How did you get away?"

He glanced down at his duffel bag with a grimace. "I hit the guy with my bag. Hope I didn't break anything."

"That was too close," Melissa muttered.

Nate couldn't help but agree. "I guess this means

we're both officially fugitives from the law," he said, trying to lighten the somber mood.

"That's not funny," she said in a low voice. "Maybe we should change our names and disappear, never to be heard from again. I hate knowing I dragged you into this."

He shook his head and reached over to take her hand. "Melissa, I was the one who followed you through the mall, remember? You don't really want to live in hiding, do you?"

"No," she admitted. "But I would continue to do so to keep you safe."

"We're not beaten yet. I promised to keep you and Hailey safe, and that means getting to the bottom of this mess."

She squeezed his hand, holding on for a long moment before letting go. "Maybe you should check the equipment in case we have to stop and buy replacements."

He grimaced and pulled the duffel bag onto his lap. "I can look for obvious signs of damage, but I won't know for sure until I have a chance to hook everything up."

"Does that mean I should head back to the cabin?" she asked.

"Yeah, for now. We can't plant anything inside the restaurant until after it closes, anyway." Nate poked through the bag, disappointed to see that one of the cameras was clearly broken. But as he peered at the rest of the equipment, everything else appeared intact. He'd brought several cameras, so there was a good chance the others might still function well enough to get the information they needed.

The receivers were the most important part, though,

because they really needed the audio feed to understand what they were dealing with.

"Maybe we should find a place closer," Melissa said as she took an exit that advertised cheap gas. "We'll end up spending a lot of money on fuel driving back and forth."

He knew she was right, but he wasn't willing to move locations yet. Tracing the cabin to him would be difficult, so as far as he was concerned, it was their best chance at survival.

He thought back to Melissa's idea of changing their names and disappearing without a trace. It shouldn't have been appealing—after all, being on the run, constantly looking over your shoulder for the threat of danger was no way to live.

But being with Melissa and Hailey once this was over? That sounded way too good to imagine.

Melissa waited inside the car while Nate filled up the gas tank and then went inside to pay with cash. The darkness outside made the hour seem much later than the six o'clock reading on the dashboard.

"Where do you want to eat?" she asked when Nate returned. "I'm sure Hailey will be hungry soon."

"I'm hungry now, Mommy," her daughter piped up.

"Why don't we go inside the pizza joint up the street?" Nate suggested. "I'd like to try and call Jenna to see what happened with those cops outside my house."

"All right," she agreed, pulling back onto the street and heading toward the pizza place Nate had indicated. "Do you think she's in trouble?"

"I hope not," Nate muttered. "Otherwise we're completely on our own."

Melissa swallowed hard and tried not to think the worst. When would this madness stop? Things were spiraling out of control, and now Jenna had risked her career to help them, too.

When she put the car in Park, Nate inserted the battery in his personal cell and powered it up. So much for having those disposable phones. She waited as he made the call, but the phone went to voice mail.

"Jenna, it's Nate. Please let me know you're okay. Thanks." He disconnected from the call and then went through the process of popping the battery back out of his phone.

"What if she tries to call you?" Melissa asked as they slid from the car.

"I'll try again when we're finished eating," he said, opening the back passenger door and unbuckling Hailey from her seat. His actions were rote, leaving her to wonder if he was getting used to traveling with a five-year-old after all.

"Carry me, Mr. Nate," Hailey said when he was about to set her down on her feet.

"All right." He hiked the little girl higher and took her inside. Watching the two of them together caused a funny feeling in Melissa's chest.

"Hailey only likes cheese and pepperoni," she said in an apologetic tone as they approached the counter. "So we'll need to order one half with the works, the way you like it. I'll share with Hailey."

"What if we order everything except onions and anchovies? How about that?" he offered, listing the two items he knew she didn't care for. "We can share whatever's left once Hailey is finished."

"Uh, sure. Thanks," she murmured, placing their

order for a large pizza. Once again, she was struck by Nate's easygoing nature. Not that he'd been super demanding back when they'd been together in high school, but she didn't remember him being quite this chivalrous.

She glanced over as he walked Hailey so she could touch the sign hanging from the ceiling outside a mini-arcade. "Look how tall I am, Mommy!"

"Pretty cool," Melissa said, unable to hold back a smile as she watched them together. Whatever had caused him to distance himself earlier seemed to have vanished now.

They took seats at a booth in the corner, and she knew it wasn't by chance that Nate sat so he was facing the door. He dug some quarters out of his pocket and gave them to Hailey so she could play a video game.

When they were alone, Nate spread a napkin out on the table. "Can you draw the interior of the restaurant for me?" he asked. "I need to know the best places to hide the cameras and microphones."

She shook her head. "Nate, I think it's better if I go in and place the devices."

"No way," he said with a frown. "It's too dangerous."

"Give me a chance to explain," she said calmly. "We need to get this right on the first try. I don't know how to use this equipment. You do. I think it's best if you stay outside to make sure the camera and microphones are in a good spot or tell me if they need to be moved. You can test them right away so we'll know they're working."

Nate's scowl deepened, but he seemed to be considering her theory.

"We have one chance to get this right," she added. "We can't afford to mess this up. I worked in that res-

taurant for two years. I know the nooks and crannies
better than you would."

"I don't like it," Nate muttered. "But you have a
point. We can't afford to blow this."

Their pizza arrived, so Melissa slid out of the booth
to find Hailey. When she returned, she was surprised
to find that Nate hadn't started eating yet, as if he was
waiting to pray with them.

She urged her daughter in first and then slid in beside her. Melissa bowed her head, but before she could
say anything, Nate began the prayer.

"Dear Lord, we thank You for this food we're about
to eat and for keeping us safe today. I hope You continue to watch over us as we search for truth and justice. Amen."

Her eyes were a bit misty as she echoed, "Amen."

"Dig in," Hailey chimed in.

"Here, let me help you." Melissa put a slice of pepperoni pizza on Hailey's plate and cut it into small
pieces. "Be careful. It's hot."

Nate had piled two slices of pizza on her plate while
she was helping Hailey, and she flashed him a grateful smile.

"When did you start attending church?" Nate asked
as they enjoyed their meal. Hailey had finished early
so they gave her more quarters to play in the arcade.

It wasn't easy to remember the dark days before she'd
found her faith. "When I first arrived in California I was
scared. Being all alone in a strange city wasn't easy. I
worked in a pub serving food, and the only friends I
had were other servers. They all liked to party a bit too
much, but it wasn't until I woke up in a strange place
with a strange man next to me that I realized I needed

to pull myself together. While I was walking home, I came across a church."

"Go on," Nate urged, and she was relieved not to see any condemnation in his eyes.

"The bells were ringing, and the sound was so pretty that I stood for several long moments just listening to them. People walked past me, several of them greeting me nicely even though I'm sure I looked terrible." She glanced at him and shrugged. "I can't explain why, but I ended up following a group of people inside. I slipped into a pew in the back and listened to the service. It was as if the pastor was speaking to me directly, although he couldn't have known who I was or anything about me. But when the service was over, I felt as if I'd been given a second chance to do things right."

"I'm glad," Nate said in a low voice. "I hate thinking of how lost and alone you must have felt."

"I was at first, but the church soon became my family."

"Is that where you met your husband?" Nate asked.

"Not then, because I soon realized the bad guys had found me. I packed up and left that very night. But when I arrived in South Carolina, the first thing I did was to join the local congregation, and that's where I met Jeremy."

"I'm happy you found someone, at least for a little while," Nate said. "You deserved to be happy."

"I was happy. Having Hailey was a true blessing." She paused, then continued, "But as much as I cared about Jeremy, he wasn't you."

Nate stared at her for a long moment, a mixture of surprise and attraction reflected in his dark gaze. "I've thought about you often over the years, but I have to be honest. My thoughts weren't always kind."

"I understand." She knew leaving so abruptly, without so much as a word or note, must have hurt him. Especially considering his mother had done the same thing eight years earlier.

"I'm sorry, Nate," she said, reaching out to touch his hand. He surprised her by quickly turning and capturing her fingers in his. "I'm sorry I left the way I did. At the time, I didn't see another way out. But I was young and foolish. I should have trusted in you."

"I would like to think that I would have stood by you no matter what," Nate said. "But we were both young. Maybe things happened this way for a reason."

She nodded. "God always has a plan. Besides, I can't regret my decisions. If I hadn't left and met Jeremy, I wouldn't have my daughter."

"She's a cutie, that's for sure," Nate agreed. He released her hand and finished his slice of pizza. "I'm going to try Jenna once more, and then we should probably head back to the cabin."

"All right," she said. Hailey came running back and helped herself to more pizza. After eating a second slice, her daughter declared herself full. Using napkins, Melissa cleaned up the girl's hands and face and had boxed up the leftovers by the time Nate returned.

"Still no answer, and no emails, either," he said grimly. "I changed my mind. Let's find a motel room nearby to use while I check out the equipment. No sense in driving another hour out of our way, only to head back into town later tonight. And maybe now our new phones will work."

"Sounds good."

They made their way across the street, where a motel stood opposite from the pizza place. Nate wasn't wearing his uniform any longer, but he still had his badge, which helped them gain rooms without using a credit card.

Soon they were situated in a small but clean room. Melissa kept Hailey occupied with the children's channel while Nate worked, muttering under his breath as he linked items of equipment together. She couldn't help being impressed, especially when he showed her just how it all worked.

"The clarity on these cameras is amazing," she said in awe.

"The listening devices are just as good," Nate said with a smile. "Looks like we only lost the one camera. Everything else is working fine."

Her gut clenched as she realized this was it. Tonight she'd have to sneak into the restaurant to plant the equipment. "I'm assuming the restaurant still closes at midnight, so what do you think? Should we go at one in the morning? And how will we get in?"

"Yeah, that sounds good. And don't worry, I have my lock-picks. We'll get in." The tone of his voice left no room for uncertainty.

And true to Nate's word, hours later they were back in front of the El Matador restaurant.

She stayed in the car with Hailey who was sleeping, while Nate went over to unlock the back door. Thankfully, someone had shoveled back there so there was no need to worry about leaving footprints in the snow.

It seemed like forever but was really less than five minutes when he returned. "The door is unlocked. Are you ready?"

"Of course," she said, ignoring the way her fingers trembled as she packed the cameras and bugs into the pocket of her hoodie sweatshirt.

"I'll be here, watching everything," Nate said, tapping the laptop computer screen. "Once you get inside, make sure your earpiece works before you do anything, okay?"

"Okay." She opened the door, chanting "I can do this, I can do this" under her breath as she slithered past the putrid dumpster toward the back door of the restaurant.

The years slipped away, everything looking and smelling the way it had when she worked here. The door was ajar, so she pushed it open and stepped over the threshold into the kitchen.

Here things looked different, and she remembered Nate saying they'd updated the appliances and functionality a few years ago. There weren't any lights on inside, but she easily found her way past the counters and into the main dining area.

"Melissa? Are you in there?"

"I'm in," she said softly. "Can you hear me?"

"Yes. Good job."

She didn't feel as alone with Nate's low, husky voice in her ear.

One glance revealed the layout hadn't changed much, except maybe a few more tables added, no doubt as a way to increase revenue. The round table in the far corner was there, and she imagined the mayor and his entourage still used it as their meeting point. There were Christmas decorations, including a garland that framed a picture on the wall behind it.

A perfect spot for one of the cameras.

After she had the first one placed and the listening device nearby, she waited for Nate's approval.

"Looks good. Now get another angle if you can."

Sure, easy for him to say. She managed to find another crevice in the coffee station that faced the table, so she put the second camera there, along with the listening device. She hid the third one near the front door, but decided to put the listening device beneath the round table, for optimal coverage.

"I'm finished," she whispered.

"Nicely done," Nate murmured.

Melissa smiled and nodded as she headed back toward the kitchen. A thud and a crash stopped her in her tracks.

She dropped to the floor, crouching near the coffee station, her heart hammering so loudly she could barely think.

Someone was here!

ELEVEN

One minute Nate was watching Melissa plant the last listening device on the underside of the table, and in the next he saw her drop like a stone behind the coffee station, glancing around in fear as if something was wrong.

"Melissa? Everything okay?" he asked, feeling his pulse kick up a notch.

She shook her head and pointed behind her, toward the kitchen. What was wrong? Did she hear a noise? The listening devices were designed to pick up local sound, not something from another room.

He'd parked down the road behind the restaurant for two reasons: to stay far away in case there were cops patrolling the area and to make sure the equipment Melissa had planted would work from a distance.

Unfortunately, he was too far away to see the back door. Was it possible someone had slipped inside?

"Did you hear something?" Nate asked in a whisper.

Melissa nodded her head in an exaggerated motion making sure she was in direct view of the camera she'd hidden in the garland around the picture.

"Stay where you are. I'm going to get closer." He glanced back to make sure Hailey was still asleep. She was, but that didn't mean he was comfortable leaving the little girl alone in the car while he went in to investigate.

"Any chance you can get past without being seen?" he whispered. He put the car in gear and made a Y-turn to drive back to the restaurant.

It wasn't easy watching the computer screen and at the same time scanning the area to see if there were other vehicles or people lurking around. But he saw Melissa shrug and then peer around the corner of the coffee station.

Nate pulled into the back of the parking lot, tightening his grip on the steering wheel and hating the fact that she was in danger.

He never should have agreed to let her plant the equipment. How had they been discovered? Were there other cameras inside that he hadn't known about? Nothing else made sense. There was no other way for anyone to know Melissa was inside.

And if that was the case, their cameras and listening devices would be quickly disposed of.

But that didn't matter now. He wanted her safely out of the restaurant. He closed his eyes for a moment, opening his heart to prayer.

Dear Lord, please keep Melissa safe in Your care. Amen.

When he finished, he felt calm. "Never mind trying to slip past whoever is in the kitchen. Maybe it's better to get out through the front door," he said in a low tone.

Melissa shook her head again but didn't say anything, so he wasn't sure what she was thinking.

Then she eased around the corner of the coffee station, disappearing from view.

He gently tapped the accelerator, bringing the vehicle closer to the back door without using the headlights, peering through the darkness to see if there was anyone around.

But he didn't see anything out of place. No movement. Nothing.

Was it possible Melissa had imagined the noise?

As the thought formed in his head, the back door edged open, and a short dark figure eased out and ran toward the car. Nate made sure the locks were disengaged so that she could get into the passenger seat.

"Go," she whispered, pulling the earpiece out and dropping it into the console between them.

He was already backing up, just as anxious as she was to get out of Dodge. Neither of them spoke until they were far away from the restaurant.

"What happened?" Nate finally asked, breaking the strained silence.

Melissa let out a heavy sigh. "I heard someone in the kitchen. You didn't see anyone go inside?"

"No, I moved farther down the street," he admitted. "I didn't have a view of the back door. How did you get away?"

"You asked if I could get past them without being seen, so I crept into the kitchen in time to see a tall, dark figure go into the freezer. I took advantage of the moment to slip out."

Nate was impressed with her bravery. "I'm so glad you're okay." He reached over to take her hand in his. "But why would there be someone in the kitchen, anyway? Especially in the freezer?"

"I don't know," she said, holding on to him. "But I'm glad I closed and locked the door behind me when

I went inside. At least there was no reason for him to be suspicious."

"Excellent," he said with admiration. "I'm not sure I would have thought of that."

She smiled at him, and his heart squeezed in his chest. Melissa was different from the girl he remembered from high school.

How was it possible to be even more attracted to her now than he'd been back then? Had to be the adrenaline rush of facing danger, nothing more.

"I wonder if they're using the restaurant for something else," Melissa mused, interrupting his thoughts. "Like drugs?"

He lifted a brow, turning her idea over in his mind. "It could be that one of the workers just came back to pick up something they forgot."

"Except most employees don't have keys," Melissa said in a grim tone. "Maybe I'm prejudiced against this place, but I think there's something more going on here."

"I guess it's possible the person you saw was hiding drugs in the freezer."

She grimaced. "Sounds pretty silly, huh?"

"Not silly at all," he said, pressing on the brakes and executing a U-turn. "Maybe that's the evidence we need."

"We're going back there?" Melissa asked incredulously. "Seriously?"

"I'm going in this time, to check out the freezer," Nate said. "Don't you see? Having hard evidence of a crime can only help us."

"And if you don't find anything illegal in there?" she asked.

He shrugged. "Then we're right back where we started, right? We can listen in on their conversations and monitor them through the cameras, but you said yourself that they were always careful not to say too much in front of the servers. This is a chance we have to take."

"I guess," she said with a sigh. "But be careful, Nate."

"I will." Fifteen minutes later, he pulled onto the street where he'd parked while waiting for Melissa. "Stay here. I'll be back shortly."

"But I can't see the back door from here," she protested.

"I know, but since we don't know for sure if the person in the freezer is still hanging around, it's better that you and Hailey stay out of sight." He paused, pulling out his lock-picking tools. "And if for some reason I'm not back within ten minutes, get out of here."

"I'm not leaving you," she said firmly.

He appreciated her support, but he caught her gaze in the moonlight. "I mean it, Melissa. If I don't come back, get in touch with Jenna and Griff. They're your best shot at being safe if something happens to me."

Her lips thinned, but she didn't say anything more as he slid out of the driver's seat.

"Just remember you promised to be careful," she said just before he closed the door.

He gave her a thumbs-up and moved into the shadows, making his way to the back door of the restaurant. Nate estimated that they'd been gone at least thirty minutes, certainly long enough for the intruder to have left.

The lock wasn't too difficult to get open, and he silently opened the back door, straining to listen. But he didn't hear a sound.

Still, he stepped carefully over the threshold, using a small penlight to show him the way. He wasn't as familiar with the layout of the restaurant, and besides, he'd need light to see what was inside.

The kitchen appeared to be empty. He couldn't be sure that the dining room wasn't occupied, but if Melissa's theory about drugs was correct, there'd be no reason for the guy to stick around.

He silently walked across the kitchen to the giant walk-in freezer, grateful that the overhead light came on automatically as he pried the door open. And just to be sure it didn't close on him, he propped it open with a large box labeled Steaks.

Thankfully, the freezer wasn't too full, but it would still take him time to go through the various containers.

Minutes later, having searched through several boxes of various food items, Nate came across a box labeled Shrimp. But when he looked, there wasn't any seafood inside. Instead, the box was full of bags of white powder.

Cocaine? He pulled out his phone and snapped a picture of the box, then took one of the bags out before closing the box back up.

He wished there was a way to replace the bag with something like flour, but he'd already been in the freezer longer than he'd planned. Nate set the box labeled Shrimp back on the shelf, then left, hiding the bag of what he assumed was cocaine under his sweatshirt.

He held his breath until he was back outside, crossing the parking lot. Headlights pierced the darkness, and he ducked behind the Dumpster, plastering himself against its hard metal side.

Just then, a car pulled into the parking lot, and his

instincts screamed at him to stay hidden. Granted, there was a possibility that Melissa was behind the wheel, but somehow he didn't think so.

The vehicle rolled silently across the lot, and when it turned around, Nate could see by the rack with the lights on top that it was a police car.

Sent by the Brookmont chief of police? To protect their drug investment?

Nate went still, all too aware of the fact that he had what was very possibly a kilo of cocaine beneath his sweatshirt. If he was caught, he'd be arrested before he could blink.

He hunkered down, praying that Melissa had caught sight of the police car and had moved along before they had a chance to see her. The last thing they needed was for the officers to get the license plate number, tracing the car back to Jenna. After what had gone down at his house, his colleague was no doubt in enough trouble already.

The vehicle eventually moved on, rolling out of sight, but Nate stayed where he was for several long minutes. For all he knew, the cruiser was parked nearby. Cops working graveyard didn't have nearly the level of activity as other shifts did, and it was entirely feasible that the officers were involved in whatever was going on.

The Dumpster sheltered him from the wind, but the air was still cold, settling deep into his bones. He forced himself to wait a full twenty minutes before edging out from behind the Dumpster.

He swept his gaze over the area, taking his time to make sure that the cruiser wasn't anywhere in sight. He lightly ran to the road, but didn't see Melissa. He was grateful she'd listened to his instructions to stay safe and left.

Although being stranded here alone wasn't exactly a great option either. He tried to figure out which way to start walking, in hopes that Melissa would return to pick him up, when he noticed a car backing out of a driveway.

He held his breath but then relaxed. It wasn't the police cruiser.

It was Jenna's car with Melissa behind the wheel.

He couldn't help but grin at her ingenuity for managing to hide in plain sight. He jogged out to meet her.

Once Nate was settled in the passenger seat, she drove off, heading in the direction of the interstate. "I take it you saw the police car?" he asked, breaking the silence.

"Yes, just in the nick of time, too," she said, glancing over at him. "I was more worried about you, though. I was afraid they'd catch you leaving the restaurant."

"I was forced to hide behind the Dumpster," Nate admitted. He pulled out the bag of white powder from beneath his sweatshirt. "And I found this in a box labeled Shrimp."

Melissa gasped. "Is that cocaine?"

"I believe so, but we'll need to get it tested for sure. I also took a picture of the other bags in the box." He stuck the bag beneath his sweatshirt again, just because having drugs out in the open wasn't smart on the off chance that they were pulled over.

"So we have evidence that the restaurant is a hub for drug trafficking," Melissa murmured. "Do you think that's enough for your boss to believe us?"

Good question. "Maybe, but I think we should check

to see if there is any way to directly implicate the people we suspect are involved."

"And what if they don't go to the restaurant tomorrow?" Melissa asked. "How long do we wait?"

Nate wasn't sure how to answer that. He knew that having the drug evidence along with Melissa's eyewitness testimony should be enough to convince Griff to give Melissa the benefit of doubt. "I'd like to wait until I talk to Jenna, to see what happened at my house after I managed to escape."

"All right, but if we don't hear from her soon, and if we don't pick up anything useful from the listening devices, then we go to your boss, agreed?"

"Agreed." Nate found it difficult to tear his gaze away from her profile. She deserved so much better than this, slinking through the night, hiding from the police. Deep down he trusted Griff, would be willing to put his life, his career on the line to turn himself in to his boss.

But putting Melissa's life in jeopardy was an entirely different matter. He couldn't bring himself to do that.

Not without finding a way to protect her and her daughter if the situation went south.

Their lives were far more important than his.

An hour and a half later, Melissa pulled into the driveway of the lake cabin with an overwhelming sense of relief. It was almost four in the morning, but she was still wide awake.

They'd made it!

There had been so many times when she'd thought for sure they'd be caught, like when that police car arrived. She'd been so afraid, especially for Nate.

"I can carry Hailey inside for you," he offered when she pushed open her driver's side door.

It was crazy, but she absolutely didn't want to touch that bag of white powder. "I'll get her. You have the computer and other stuff to bring in."

He must have understood her apprehension because he didn't argue. He held the door for her, and within minutes she had her daughter tucked into bed.

Nate was in the kitchen, staring down at the bag of cocaine. "I'm not sure where to put this," he said grimly. "I don't really want it in here, yet we need to keep it as evidence."

"What about putting it in a bag and hiding it in a snowbank?" she suggested. "I'd really rather not have that in the house, either."

"All right."

Melissa huddled near the doorway while Nate wrapped the package up in a couple of plastic grocery bags and took it outside. She noticed he'd buried it to the left of the doorway. Then he returned, closing the door behind him. "We should probably get some sleep. I suspect Hailey will be up bright and early."

"Yeah, that's true." Melissa went over and dropped into a kitchen chair. Despite the exhaustion that weighed her down, the night's adventure would no doubt keep her awake for hours yet. "I know I suggested it, but I never really expected to find drugs," she said in a low voice.

Nate dropped into the chair beside her. "It was a shock to me, too."

"I can't help thinking that the person in the freezer must be an employee at the restaurant," she continued.

"Otherwise it's odd that he or she would have a key to get in."

"That's a good point. I wonder who owns it?" Nate asked as he booted up the computer.

Melissa frowned and tried to think back to the time she worked there. She must have known who the owner was, but in her teenage ignorance, she probably hadn't paid much attention.

She leaned over Nate's shoulder, inhaling the woodsy scent of his aftershave, as he searched Brookmont city records for the proprietor. She'd had no idea these types of websites existed, but then again, her job was all about designing them, not searching for data. In her opinion, Nate was trying to find a needle in a haystack.

"Come on, come on," Nate muttered under his breath. He was scrolling through the various screens so fast she began to get dizzy.

Leaving him to his search, she rose to her feet and helped herself to a bottle of water, bringing one over for Nate, as well. All that nervous energy made her feel as if she'd run a marathon.

"Here we go," Nate said with satisfaction. He took the bottle of water from her, his expression full of gratitude, before he gestured to the name on the screen. "Ralph G. Carter is the owner."

"The name doesn't sound familiar," she said with a frown. "But I wonder what he looks like?"

Nate was already one step ahead of her. He'd typed the guy's name into the search engine, and soon there was a photograph of Ralph George Carter on the screen.

Melissa gasped. "That's him!"

"Who?" Nate demanded.

"One of the men who was at the restaurant that

night." She stared at the picture as realization dawned. "They're all in this together."

"So it would appear," Nate agreed grimly. "The pieces of the puzzle are sliding into place."

Melissa hoped Nate was right. The sooner they had the big picture, the sooner she and Hailey could get on with their lives.

Although she couldn't deny that leaving Nate would be difficult. Despite her best efforts, she was becoming emotionally attached to him.

The big question was, did he feel the same way?

TWELVE

Nate woke up several hours later, groggy and sleep-deprived, as he listened to mom and daughter in the kitchen. He dragged himself upright, feeling guilty for sleeping in when Melissa had been up just as late.

He quickly finished up in the bathroom, then followed his nose to the enticing scent of French toast in the kitchen.

"Good morning," Melissa greeted him. She had her dark hair pulled back in a ponytail, which somehow made her hazel eyes look bigger than usual. "You're just in time for breakfast."

"How long have you been up?" he asked, taking a seat beside Hailey at the table.

"About an hour," she said as she served a platter stacked high with French toast.

"You should have woken me up." She'd got only three hours of sleep, while he'd slept for four hours. "It was my turn to cook."

"It's not a problem. Besides, Hailey was hungry, so I needed to get something going."

Bowing his head, he listened to Melissa's quick

prayer and Hailey's inevitable "Dig in" before getting up to grab some coffee.

Caffeine helped blow some of the cobwebs out of his brain. He sat back down and helped himself to a couple of pieces of French toast.

"Can we play outside in the snow again, Mommy?" Hailey asked as she poured a liberal portion of maple syrup over her breakfast. "This time let's make a snow fort!"

"I'm sure we can go out for a while," Melissa agreed.

Nate dug into his meal with gusto, surprised at how hungry he was. Maybe it was because of the events of last night.

Or maybe it was Melissa's cooking. He honestly wasn't used to anyone cooking for him. Not that he could afford to become accustomed to the luxury. He knew that she was making meals for her daughter, not for him personally.

"Have you thought about what our next steps should be?" Melissa asked, interrupting his thoughts.

"I really need to get in touch with Jenna, make sure she's doing okay," he said between bites. "Then I'd like to see if we can pick anything up through the cameras and audio feeds."

Melissa nodded. "Christmas is just four days away," she said in a low voice. "I need to know if we'll be spending the holiday here."

He understood she wanted some sort of celebration for Hailey. "I'll figure out something within the next twenty-four hours," he promised.

Nate knew that they were getting close to having enough evidence to go to Griff. But he wanted as iron-clad a case as possible, especially considering they intended to leverage some very serious allegations against several high-profile community leaders.

A daunting thought.

When he finished eating, he began clearing the table and stacking the dirty dishes in the sink to be washed. Melissa helped, once again adding a strange sort of intimacy as they performed the mundane task together.

He told himself that this wasn't what it would be like to be married with a family. For one thing, he'd be going to work, sometimes on odd shifts.

Which made him wonder what she did to support herself. She must have left a job behind in South Carolina. Was it waiting for her? Or would she have to start over someplace new?

"Do you need my help for anything?" Melissa asked as they finished the dishes.

He flashed her a grin. "Looking to get out of building a snow fort?"

She grimaced. "Maybe. I'm not used to such cold weather."

"Give me a few minutes to check my email and set up the computer cameras. If there's nothing going on, I can play outside with Hailey for a while."

"No need for you to do that," she said, obviously backpedaling. "She's my responsibility, and it's probably better you stay inside to work since I can't search the internet the way you can."

He glanced over at her curiously. "I truly don't mind. I'm sure we can spare an hour or so."

She hesitated, then nodded. "All right."

Nate went over to the kitchen table and opened up his laptop. The cameras were good, but he couldn't validate the listening devices as the hour was still too early for any activity at the restaurant. He logged into his new email account, happy to see a message from Jenna.

I'm okay. The officers were suspicious, but I think I managed to convince them I was on their side. Hope you got everything you needed out of the house.

Nate was relieved she was all right. He quickly typed a response:

We have cameras and bugs planted inside the restaurant. Also found some interesting evidence. Let me know if you have time to meet today.

He sent the email, feeling better about being on the right track. Although he was sure Jenna wouldn't be thrilled to find out that he'd taken potential evidence from the restaurant.

Deciding to cross that bridge later, he closed the laptop and headed over to put on his winter coat, hat and gloves. Hailey and Melissa were already outside, hard at work clearing an area in the snow for the fort.

Hailey was wearing snow pants and boots, but the adults didn't have that luxury. When Melissa's teeth started chattering, he sent her inside.

"I'll hang with Hailey for a while," he said, ignoring the cold dampness of his jeans.

"Thanks. But don't stay out here too much longer," she cautioned him.

"We won't."

Melissa disappeared inside the cabin, and he continued helping the little girl build her fort.

"Are you going to be my new daddy?" she asked.

He felt his jaw drop in shock, and struggled to come up with a good answer. "I think that's something your mom needs to decide," he finally said. "She has to find a man to fall in love with, and once she gets married again, then you'll have a new dad."

Hailey scrunched up her face. "Don't you love my mommy?"

His heart lurched in his chest. "I care about your mom very much, Hailey. We're good friends."

The flash of disappointment in the little girl's eyes stabbed deep. He wanted to make her feel better, but what could he say? Even if he voiced his true feelings for Melissa, he couldn't give the child false hope that they'd all be one big happy family someday.

No matter how much he was beginning to like that idea.

Melissa hung her wet clothes near the heat vents in an effort to help them dry out. When she crossed back over to the window overlooking the front yard, she noticed that Hailey and Nate were deep in conversation.

This was what she was afraid of. Hailey was already bonding with Nate more than Melissa was comfortable with. What would happen when she and Hailey left to go back home? Sure, she could convince herself that her daughter would forget about Nate eventually, but in the meantime, Hailey would miss him.

And so would she.

Melissa gave herself a mental shake and told herself to stop thinking about Nate on a personal level. She was feeling close to him only because he was risking his life and his career to protect her. She'd probably feel the same sense of closeness and gratitude no matter who she was here with.

No, that wasn't true either. For one thing, no one else would have done what Nate had for her and for Hailey. Plus, Nate had kissed her, rekindling the old feelings that she'd buried a long time ago.

She sank onto the sofa, her knees feeling weak. Was she crazy to fall for Nate? Hadn't she done that already with disastrous results? Not that her leaving twelve years ago was his fault. But she'd meant what she'd said about not regretting the past. Her daughter was a precious gift.

Yet if Melissa were honest, she'd admit that she'd married Jeremy because he was a good, God-fearing man. Not because she was hopelessly in love with him. At the time, she'd believed the feelings she'd experienced with Nate were nothing but silly romantic fantasies.

Being here with him like this made her realize that her feelings for him weren't childish at all.

Although they were definitely romantic.

Melissa leaped to her feet, uncomfortable with the direction of her thoughts. She didn't have time to dwell on her feelings, romantic or otherwise. She strode into the kitchen and put on the teakettle to make hot chocolate for Hailey.

As the kettle warmed on the stovetop, she crossed over to open Nate's laptop computer. There would be a lunch crowd trickling into the restaurant soon. And that meant the staff would be getting ready for their patrons.

She peered at the screen, knowing it wasn't at all likely that she'd recognize anyone from when she'd worked there. But she was soon surprised to see Gayle Flannery, one of her fellow waitresses, making coffee in the large urns. The uniforms had changed over the years, and when Gayle turned around, Melissa could clearly see the silver manager pin on the older woman's lapel.

Melissa sat back in her chair with a frown, wondering just how much Gayle knew about what was really going on at the restaurant now that she was in a manager role. Was the owner, Ralph Carter, keeping her in the dark? Or was she an active participant in the potential drug ring?

Thinking back, she remembered Gayle being a young woman who was attending college in the evening while working the day shift as a waitress. Had Gayle finished her degree? Or had she given up on school?

The front door opened, letting in a blast of cold air as Nate carried Hailey inside. A few seconds later, the tea kettle whistled loudly.

"Ready for some hot chocolate?" Melissa asked, rising to her feet and hurrying into the kitchen to take the kettle off the stove. "Nate, I can make more coffee if you'd prefer."

"Hot chocolate with mini-marshmallows!" Hailey said, waving her arms eagerly.

"That sounds good to me, too," Nate agreed.

"Let's get you out of these wet things," Melissa said, going over to her daughter.

Nate bent over to help at the same time she did, and their heads lightly bumped together.

"Oh, sorry," he muttered, moving out of the way. He followed her example by taking off his damp clothes and spreading them around the heat vents that she hadn't used.

He disappeared in the bedroom while she finished getting Hailey out of her winter clothes. After hanging

Hailey's wet things up, too, she poured her daughter a
steaming mug of chocolate.

"Be careful," she warned, setting the cup down on
the table. "Let it cool off a minute."

Nate returned a few minutes later wearing dry jeans
and a navy blue sweatshirt that had SWAT emblazoned
across his chest in white. He walked over and helped
himself to a mug of hot chocolate, pouring one for her,
too.

"Thanks." Why did things suddenly feel so awkward
between them?

He nodded and then took a seat behind the computer.
"I see you're already watching."

She shrugged. "I recognized one of the employees.
Gayle Flannery used to be a waitress on the day shift
while I was there. Now she's the manager."

"Interesting." Nate blew on his chocolate and then
took a sip. "I wonder how many other employees are
still there."

"Probably not many," she said, taking a seat next to
him. She looked at the computer screen. Nate fiddled
with the controls until they could see both cameras in
a split screen format. She leaned forward with curios-
ity as customers entered the dining area. "Why can't
we hear anything?"

"I don't have the volume on yet," Nate said. "I'd
rather wait until we have something in particular to
listen in on."

"Worried about invading people's privacy?" she
asked.

"Yeah, a bit. After all, this isn't exactly an approved
undercover operation."

It took a minute for his words to sink in. "So you're

saying we can't really use any of this information against them?"

"That's correct. We can't. All we can do is hope to get intel we can act upon."

She tried to hide the sharp stab of disappointment. But then a familiar face caught her eye. "Look! Isn't that your uncle?"

Nate's expression hardened. "Yeah, that's Tom. Seems like he's at that restaurant quite a bit. After all, we saw his car there last evening, too."

She felt bad for Nate. It couldn't be easy suspecting your own flesh and blood of being a criminal. "Maybe they're meeting so often because of me."

He lifted a brow, the corner of his mouth kicking up in a crooked smile. "Yeah, because of both of us. It just occurred to me that Tom must realize by now we're together."

"Probably, although I guess we don't know for sure what the Brookmont chief of police has told him."

"We're going to find out," Nate said, gesturing to the computer screen. "Randall Joseph, aka Brookmont chief of police, just walked in."

Melissa's stomach knotted when she watched the two men greet each other with terse nods, neither one of them looking very happy. They walked over to their usual table, the one where she'd planted the listening device.

Nate enabled the microphone, but as the men began talking, Hailey interrupted. "Mommy, can we play a game?"

"How about you play your handheld computer game for a while instead?" she suggested, knowing it would be best to get Hailey out of Nate's way. "Come on. Let's sit in the living room."

"Okay," she agreed, scrambling down from her seat at the table.

Melissa couldn't hear what was going on in the restaurant, but once she had Hailey settled on the corner of the sofa, she went back to glance over Nate's shoulder. "Are you getting anything?"

"Not yet," he said with a sigh. "They're being very careful with what they're saying."

Melissa nodded, leaning forward so she could listen in, too.

"Why haven't you found them yet?" the mayor asked in a low voice.

"We're working on it," the police chief replied. "We came close yesterday."

"Close doesn't count," Tom muttered in a harsh tone. "We need to find them today. Top priority. Use more men if you need to."

"That's not as easy as it sounds," the police chief argued. "Sooner or later someone's going to start asking questions."

The two men fell silent as their server approached, asking if they were ready to place their orders.

Melissa looked at Nate. "They're obviously talking about us."

"I know." He scrubbed his hands over his face in a weary gesture. "It's hard listening to them talk about hunting us down."

She couldn't stop from reaching over to put her hand on his. "I'm sorry," she said helplessly. "I wish I'd been wrong about your uncle."

Nate summoned a grim smile. "It's not your fault.

So we know they're still looking for us, and we know that they're using the restaurant as a drug drop. But we don't know why they killed Alderman Keith Turner."

"Don't you think it's probably because he found out about the drugs?" she asked. "It only seems logical."

"Yeah, maybe," Nate said, although he didn't sound at all convinced. "But I still feel like there's a piece of the puzzle missing. It's possible Alderman Turner would have gone along with their drug trafficking."

Nate opened a search engine and did more research on Alderman Kevin Turner. She listened to the conversation in the restaurant, but the men were simply ordering food.

A third man joined them. She recognized him as Ralph Carter, the restaurant owner, but still the conversation remained social.

"That's three, so where's the fourth guy?" Nate asked.

"I'm not sure," Melissa said, unable to tear her gaze from the screen. It was so strange seeing these men sitting at the same table. They all looked a little older, but not terribly so. The police chief had put on about thirty pounds, but the other two men looked very much the same as they had twelve years ago.

"There's a problem with our package," Ralph Carter said. "We're a little short on shrimp."

The three men looked at each other for a long moment. "How is that possible?" Nate's uncle asked.

"I think we have to assume the worst," Ralph Carter said.

Melissa tugged on Nate's arm. "They're talking about the drugs you took from the freezer," she whispered.

He nodded, his gaze focused on the scene at the restaurant.

"I wouldn't have expected him to skim off the top. We pay well enough," Nate's uncle said with a dark scowl. "Are you absolutely sure?"

Ralph's face got red. "Think I can't count? Of course I'm sure. I just checked."

"I'll send a message," the police chief said with an evil grin. "A message our deliveryman won't forget."

Her mouth dropped open in horror. "Oh, no! They're going to do something to that man who placed the drugs in the freezer."

Nate momentarily closed his eyes. "I didn't expect them to discover the missing bag so soon."

Melissa knew they needed the evidence, and she knew that anyone involved in dealing drugs had to be punished, but she wasn't prepared for something like this. The leer on the chief of police's face made her think he enjoyed teaching lessons.

A little too much.

These men had to be stopped and soon. Before more people died.

THIRTEEN

Melissa's face went pale, and Nate clenched his jaw, hating to see how upset she was.

"We have to do something," she urged him. "If they kill that man, it will be our fault."

Although he understood exactly where she was coming from, there wasn't much he could do. "Melissa, if we knew who the deliveryman was, I'd ask Jenna to arrest him, convince him to talk so that we could place him in protective custody. But we don't." He spread his hands helplessly. "I don't know the name of this guy, and you don't, either."

She sat there for several long seconds, despair shadowing her hazel eyes. "I can't stand the thought that this man will die because we took the evidence from the restaurant."

Nate reached over and held both her hands in his. "Keep in mind that this guy chose to be involved in drug dealing."

Melissa shook her head. "We don't know that. It could be that he stumbled into something and wasn't given much of a choice."

Nate wanted to believe there was always a choice,

but thinking back to what had happened to her all those years ago, he could see why she might think that way. Certainly she'd been an innocent bystander whose life had been turned upside down. "You're right," he acknowledged. "Maybe we should try praying for him?"

She lifted her incredibly long lashes to look him straight in the eye, and the hope reflected there made his heart squeeze in his chest. "I'd like that."

It wasn't easy to swallow past the lump in his throat. He took a deep breath to steady himself. Praying didn't come naturally, so he had to concentrate on what he needed to say. "Dear Lord, we ask that You show mercy toward the deliveryman who is currently in danger. Please continue to guide us on Your chosen path. Amen."

"Amen," Melissa echoed.

He couldn't seem to bring himself to release his grip on her hands, as he fought the urge to sweep her into his arms and kiss her. "Mommy, I won! I won the game," Hailey shouted excitedly, breaking into his thoughts.

"That's great, sweetie," Melissa said, subtly tugging at her hands. Nate let her go, instantly missing her warmth.

"Let's play a different game." Hailey tossed aside her computer game and jumped off the sofa.

"How about you draw pictures for us first?" Melissa asked in an obvious attempt to keep her energetic little girl entertained for a while longer. "Mr. Nate and I still have some work to do here."

"Okay," she said before running into the bedroom to get her coloring book and crayons.

There was a small flash in the lower right corner of the computer screen, indicating he had a new message.

He quickly checked his email, relieved to see that Jenna had responded.

Evidence? I'm curious. Can't meet tonight, working, but could meet sometime tomorrow. Let me know when and where, J.

Nate was disappointed in the delay, but obviously he couldn't ask Jenna to sacrifice her career for him. He was doing a good enough job destroying his own reputation, and he hated to consider what Griff would think if his boss knew he'd dragged her into this mess. He racked his brain for a moment, trying to figure out where they should meet.

Email me tomorrow when you get up. We'll meet at Caroline's Corner Diner, a halfway point between us, off Highway 83.

Okay.

Nate minimized the email program and returned to watching the screen displaying the restaurant. The three men around the table wore grim expressions on their faces.

It occurred to him that this would be a good opportunity to check out his uncle's house. The way Tom was dressed, in a nice suit and tie, it was clear he was working. Was it worth the risk? Would he really find anything of value to their investigation?

"What's wrong?" Melissa asked, her brow puckered with her frown. "You look upset."

He glanced at her. "Not upset, but I was thinking that this would be a perfect time to search Tom's house."

She sucked in a harsh breath. "Are you sure that's a good idea?"

"Not really, but we need to do something." Nate stared at the men seated around the table again. "It's only a few days till Christmas, but he's clearly working today. This is my best shot at getting in and out without being noticed."

"What if the chief of police has someone watching his home?"

She had a good point. "Jenna's working, but she could still swing by the neighborhood while she's patrolling the streets, to make sure it's safe."

He typed a quick message to Jenna. "And once we know the area is clear, we'll use the same approach we did to get my equipment out of my place. You'll drop me off and then come back later to pick me up."

Melissa didn't look thrilled, but she did nod in agreement.

"We need to get going since it's a long drive to the city." Nate couldn't hide his deep sense of urgency. "I'll have Jenna contact me via our throwaway phones if there's any sign of trouble."

He was glad Jenna responded quickly to his message, agreeing to drive past his uncle's place to make sure there weren't any cops stationed nearby.

When he heard Melissa telling Hailey they were going for a ride, he briefly considered going alone. After all, there was no reason to expose them to further danger.

But before he could voice his idea, Melissa shook her head as if reading his mind. "Don't even think of leaving me here alone without a car and with that…

you-know-what hiding in the snowbank. We're coming with you."

There wasn't time to argue. They needed to get back to Brookmont as soon as possible.

But if Nate were honest with himself, he'd admit that he didn't really want to leave Melissa and Hailey behind.

They were a team. Not exactly the same way he and his SWAT teammates were.

But close. Very close. There was a different sort of bond growing between them. And for the life of him, he couldn't bear to do anything that might break it.

Melissa tried not to squirm under Nate's intense gaze, but it wasn't easy. She helped her daughter on with her hat, coat and mittens before drawing on her own winter things.

Nate was standing near the door, with the laptop tucked under his arm, waiting for her. She made sure to grab Hailey's handheld computer game before they headed outside.

Within minutes they were on the road, leaving the cabin behind.

"Are you okay?" Nate asked, breaking the silence that hovered between them.

"Sure." She glanced back to make sure her daughter was preoccupied. "If we're going to be in the cabin over Christmas, I'd like to pick up a couple of gifts for Hailey."

"Okay, we'll do that on the way home," he said. "And we'll decorate the cabin a bit, too."

She was glad he seemed to understand. "Thank you. I'd also like to find a church so we can attend services.

I want Hailey to grow up knowing the true meaning of Christmas."

"Shouldn't be too hard to find one where no one will recognize us, although we'll have to stay in the back. I'll search out a couple of options for you when we're finished."

"I appreciate that. Do you attend church on a regular basis?"

Nate didn't answer right away. "A couple of the guys on my team attend one just outside of town, but I haven't been." He paused and glanced at her, a wry expression on his face. "To be honest, I always resisted their efforts to include me in church services."

"Why?"

He shrugged and turned his attention to the highway stretching out in front of them. "Not really sure. Caleb, Declan and Isaac all fell in love with women who believed in God, and I figured they were just going along to keep peace."

She tried not to roll her eyes. "You honestly thought they'd go to church just to make their wives or girlfriends happy?"

"Yeah, pretty much." A defensive note crept into his tone.

"So there isn't a single guy you work with who believes in God and faith?"

"Well, yeah, Hawk—er, Shane Hawkins does. And actually, now that I think about it, Jenna's been going, too." He sent her a sheepish grin. "Guess I've been in denial, huh?"

"Maybe a little," she said with a smile. "But Nate, believing in God and faith doesn't make you weak. It gives you strength."

He nodded, his expression thoughtful. "I don't know that I would have believed that before, but I do now."

Melissa was secretly thrilled he'd admitted it. Out loud. Just like when he suggested they pray for the deliveryman who'd stored the drugs in the restaurant freezer.

"I'm glad," she said. "Because we need all the support we can get."

"That's for sure," he muttered.

The sound of a ringing phone echoed through the car, and Nate quickly pulled it out and handed it over to her. "Put the call on speaker."

Melissa did as he requested.

"Hello? Nate?" Jenna's voice came over the line.

"Hi, Jenna. I'm here with Melissa. We're on our way to the city."

"Everything looks good. Nothing to worry about at your uncle's house."

"Great. Thanks for letting us know."

"Wait, don't hang up," Jenna said urgently. "You need to know that Griff called me this morning. He told me to report to his office before roll call."

"That doesn't sound good," Melissa said.

"No, it doesn't," Nate agreed. "Jenna, I don't want you to get into trouble over me."

"Yeah, I think it's a little late for that," Jenna said in a dry tone. "You mentioned evidence in your last email."

Melissa found herself holding her breath, waiting for Nate's response.

"Yeah, but I don't think it's enough," he admitted.

"Listen, I think it's time you talked to Griff. The sooner the better. MPD wants your head on a platter, and Griff can't hold them off forever."

Melissa caught the look of surprise that flashed into Nate's eyes.

"He's holding them off?" he repeated, as if he hadn't heard correctly.

"Yeah, but I suspect that's why he wants to talk to me prior to my shift. I think he's already grilled the other guys on the team about where you might be."

A knot formed in the pit of Melissa's stomach. She knew he'd eventually planned to bring what they'd uncovered to his supervisor, but not yet.

Please, not yet!

She wasn't ready and sensed Nate would insist on taking her along. The more she thought about going in, the more worried she became. What if Griff didn't believe her? What if she was arrested? They'd put Hailey into foster care since she didn't have anyone else to take care of her daughter.

"I'll think about it," Nate answered evasively. "I'd like to get more evidence."

"If you wait much longer, you'll be arrested first and questioned later," Jenna said.

"I understand. Thanks."

Melissa pressed the button to end the call, not exactly happy with the reprieve. She sensed Nate truly wanted to go to his boss. And she couldn't blame him for wanting a chance to salvage his career. But she didn't say anything, and they drove the rest of the way without broaching the subject.

When Nate turned down a neighborhood street, she tried to keep her attention focused on the houses they were passing by.

"That one there, the tan brick house with the green trim, belongs to my uncle," Nate said as they rolled past.

She nodded. He drove around the corner, pulling over to the curb directly behind his uncle's place. "Give me twenty minutes," he said as he pushed open the driver's side door. "Maybe head to a fast-food restaurant to get Hailey something to eat."

"Okay. Be careful," she added, hating the thought of leaving him here alone. She awkwardly climbed over the console into the driver's seat and quickly adjusted things for her smaller stature. When she looked outside, Nate was already gone.

She glanced at the dashboard clock, marking the time, before she pulled onto the street.

For a split second, she considered driving away, leaving Nate and the Brookmont murder far behind.

Could she do it? Did he need her anymore? He had the drugs and the cameras. Would her eyewitness testimony really be helpful?

She didn't realize how tightly she was gripping the steering wheel until her fingers cramped painfully. She drew in a deep breath and forced herself to relax.

She drove down the street, turning right at the corner, and then headed toward the chain restaurant they'd passed along the way.

But the idea of taking Hailey someplace safe continued to nag at her.

Unsure of what to do, she tried to open her heart and her mind to prayer.

Creeping into the back door of his uncle's house without being seen wasn't easy. Picking the lock took longer than it should have, but he finally heard the satisfying click as the door opened. Good thing his uncle had never installed the security system he used to talk about.

Nate slipped into the kitchen and paused, making sure no one was home. After a long minute, he proceeded to make his way through the kitchen into the large living room.

The place was immaculate, hardly a speck of dust or anything out of place. He'd been there before, but not in the past few years. For some reason, after his mother deserted them, he and his father had kept their distance from Tom McAllister.

Was he nuts to think he'd find anything to tie his uncle to the drug trafficking here? Probably. Yet he couldn't ignore the urge to poke around a bit.

Nate headed over to his uncle's home office, which wasn't nearly as tidy as the rest of the house. After sifting through the papers that were on top of the desk, he moved on to the drawers.

There was a file labeled Laredo. Wasn't that a city in Texas? He frowned and pulled it out, noticing that there were receipts from a car rental company located there. Thinking quickly, he used his uncle's printer to make copies of them, wincing at how loud the machine sounded in the silent house.

He folded the copies and stuffed them into the front pocket of his jeans. Nate suspected there was probably more to be found, but since he was running out of time, he headed into his uncle's bedroom.

The master suite was just as neat as the rest of the house, and Nate stopped short when he noticed the photograph sitting on the bedside table. He recognized the laughing woman standing beside his uncle as his mother, Rosalie.

Helpless to resist, he crossed over and picked it up to examine it more closely. The picture had obviously been taken a long time ago, based on how young his uncle looked.

Nate turned the frame over to open the back. People didn't use film as much in this day and age, but they did twenty years ago.

Sure enough, he could see the date printed on the back corner, which coincided with the year of his eighth birthday. The same year his mother left, abandoning him and his father.

For a moment he stood frozen, trying not to relive his painful past.

The photograph on his uncle's dresser shouldn't have been shocking. His uncle claimed to have kept in touch with his mother long after she'd left. Hadn't Tom got the divorce papers signed just a few years ago?

He did wonder though, why didn't his uncle have more recent images of his mother? Or did he have them locked away? If so, why?

Letting his imagination get the better of him wasn't helping. Nate put the picture frame back together, trying to ignore the slight trembling of his fingers. Then he quickly wiped it beneath his sweatshirt to remove any fingerprints before returning it to the bedside table.

A loud thud, sounding very much like the slamming of a car door, roused him from his trip down memory lane. Nate left his uncle's bedroom, his heart thumping loudly in his chest. Through the front window, he could see an older model car in the driveway. A woman dressed casually in jeans and a sweatshirt pulled a large bucket and a pile of rags out of the passenger seat.

It took a minute for Nate to realize his uncle must have a cleaning lady. Without wasting another second, he ducked through the living room into the kitchen, and let himself out the back door. He headed out to the street, glancing up and down for any sign of Melissa. Granted, he was a couple of minutes early, but somehow he'd still expected her to be there waiting.

Nate told himself she'd probably made a trip around the block rather than simply parking there with the car idling. But when one minute ticked by, and then another, he began to get nervous.

He turned and started walking, realizing he was only drawing unwanted attention to himself by standing on the street, obviously waiting for a ride. But with each step he took, dread seeped deeper and deeper into his bones.

Where was she? Had something bad happened? Surely their vehicle hadn't been compromised.

A shiver snaked down his spine. Melissa had listened to Jenna's plea to turn themselves in to Griff. Was that it? Had she decided to drive away, leaving him behind?

She'd agreed they were in this together, but maybe that promise didn't mean much to her. After all, he'd learned the hard way that some women just couldn't be trusted.

His mother's wedding vows hadn't meant anything. She'd had no trouble leaving him and his father behind.

Nate swallowed hard and tried not to think the worst. He desperately wanted to believe Melissa would be here any minute.

Because if she didn't show, he honestly wasn't sure what he'd do next. No matter how angry he would be, he didn't think he'd be able to bring himself to turn her in.

FOURTEEN

"Hailey, it's time to go," Melissa said for the third time, exasperation lacing her tone. She understood her daughter was tired of being in the car, but they needed to leave.

Now.

"I'm coming," her daughter said in a muffled voice from deep within the fast-food restaurant's play area.

She was contemplating crawling in there herself to drag Hailey out when a cold draft washed over her. She glanced at the door and froze. A Brookmont police officer had walked in.

Run! Hide!

Melissa automatically ducked behind the slide, her pulse leaping into triple digits. Was the officer looking for her? Had the police somehow figured out what car they'd been driving?

And what about Nate? Had they found him inside his uncle's house?

She stayed where she was, hoping, praying that the officer would get some food and leave. And when she finally mustered the courage to step out of her hiding spot, she saw him standing at the counter, obviously placing an order.

She took a deep, calming breath. Okay, he was probably just getting a burger, so that meant he wasn't here looking for her. But the very thought of walking past him with Hailey made her knees weak. It was entirely possible that he had a photograph of her with instructions to arrest her on sight.

Or worse.

"Boo!" Hailey yelled, jumping out at her with a mischievous grin on her face.

Melissa yelped, badly startled, which only made Hailey laugh harder.

"I scared you, Mommy!" Hailey crowed between giggles.

"Yes, you sure did." She put a hand to her heart and took a deep breath in a vain attempt to calm her frayed nerves. When Hailey turned to head back into the play area, she quickly caught her daughter's hand. "Oh, no you don't. Playtime is over. We need to go. Where's your coat?"

"Over there," Hailey said, pointing to the far corner, where the garment had been carelessly tossed in a crumpled heap.

Melissa walked over to pick it up, dismayed to realize the police officer had taken a seat right near the door. Did she dare attempt to walk past him with Hailey? Or should she let her daughter play longer?

Nate would be waiting for her to come, so lingering wasn't an option. She'd just have to do her best to act casual.

She helped Hailey put on her coat, zipping it up to her chin. Then she carried her daughter up into her arms, holding the little girl at an angle so that Melissa could cover her own face as they walked past the police officer.

"So, Hailey, what did you ask Santa to bring you for Christmas?" she asked as they walked past, hoping that the normal conversation would distract her daughter. The last thing she needed was for the little girl to ask where *Mr. Nate* was.

"I want a Cuddle-Me Carrie doll and a new computer game," Hailey said. "Are we going to be home for Christmas, Mommy?"

Melissa almost tripped over her feet in her haste to get outside. "Sure, sweetie, of course," she said as they walked past the police officer. She pushed the door open with her hip but didn't breathe normally until they were safely inside the car and backing out of the parking space.

She cast a quick glance over her shoulder at the cop as they drove out of the lot. Was it her imagination, or was he talking into his radio? No, surely he'd come after her if he was suspicious.

Melissa forced herself to concentrate on the traffic around her rather than worrying about the fact that the officer might be calling for reinforcements. She retraced the route back to where she'd dropped Nate off, driving right past him before realizing it.

Her hands were still shaking from the adrenaline rush, so she simply pulled over and threw the gearshift into Park. Nate jogged over, his expression full of relief.

"I was worried something had happened," he said as he opened the driver's side door.

She managed to get out of the car, but her legs didn't work properly, causing her to stumble against him.

Nate caught her up against his chest, concern darkening his eyes.

"What happened, Melissa? Are you all right?"

She tried to nod, unable to speak. She knew she was overreacting, but the rush of fear overwhelmed basic logic.

Nate simply held her close, waiting for her to calm down. When she tipped her head up to look at him, his mouth was close enough to kiss.

As if he'd sensed the direction of her thoughts, he narrowed the space between them, gently covering her lips with his. His kiss was sweet and gentle.

When he lifted his head, she knew that he'd been just as affected by their kiss as she'd been. But obviously this wasn't the time or the place to relax their guard. They weren't that far from his uncle's house.

"Sorry I'm late," she said, breaking the silence. "It wasn't easy to get Hailey off the play set, and then a Brookmont police officer came in. I wasn't sure what to do."

Nate scowled and quickly glanced around the area. "We need to get out of here."

She was in full agreement with that plan. She pulled away from his embrace and then hurried around to the passenger door. Less than thirty seconds later, they were on the road, putting as many miles as possible between them and the city of Brookmont.

"For a few minutes there, I thought you'd decided to disappear again," Nate said.

She licked her lips and glanced over at him. "I'd be lying if I didn't say that the thought briefly crossed my mind," she admitted. "But I gave you my word that we'd stick together."

"Yeah, I know." Nate's grimace reminded her that he still didn't completely trust her. Because she'd left all those years ago? Or because his own mother had also walked away?

Most likely a combination of both.

But if he had believed she'd broken her promise, why kiss her?

"Mommy, I dropped my game," Hailey said.

Melissa unlatched her seat belt and twisted around to sweep the floor of the car with her hand. She found the game and handed it back to her daughter.

"Now it's my turn to apologize," Nate said once she was settled in her seat. "Obviously trust is something I need to continue working on."

"For me, too," she said. "I know that we have to take everything to your boss, but it's difficult to trust he'll believe in me."

"I'm on your side." Nate reached over and took her hand in his. "And I'll do everything in my power to convince Griff he should be, too."

Melissa nodded, clinging to Nate's hand as if it were a lifeline.

Nate pulled into the parking lot of a crowded shopping mall, belatedly remembering how Melissa wanted to purchase a couple of gifts for Hailey. "I'll hang out with Hailey for a while. You get what you need."

"Thanks. I won't be long."

He caught a glimpse of a coffee shop adjacent to a bookstore that boasted free Wi-Fi. "We'll wait for you over here," he said, gesturing toward the coffee shop.

"Sounds good."

He walked into the building with his laptop under

one arm and holding Hailey's hand. She skipped along, obviously full of energy.

"I want to look at the books," she said, tugging impatiently on his hand. "This way, Mr. Nate."

"Okay." How could he resist when her wide hazel eyes reminded him so much of Melissa's? As much as he wanted to begin investigating the new Texas connection, he allowed Hailey to drag him over to the tall shelves of children's books.

When he caught a glimpse of a children's Bible, he paused and reached for it, thinking that it would be a good gift for him to give to Hailey for Christmas. "Stay here for a few minutes, okay?"

She nodded, her attention already on the picture book she'd found on one of the lower shelves. He listened to her talking, maybe even reading, while he took the Bible over to the closest desk to make the purchase.

It wasn't until he turned back toward the little girl with his new purchase that he realized he didn't have a gift for Melissa. Ridiculous, considering they weren't dating or anything. No reason to think she'd get him a gift. Their holiday celebration was all for Hailey's benefit, nothing more.

The image of the small diamond heart pendant he'd purchased for her back in high school flashed in his mind. Since she hadn't come to meet him that night, he had the necklace buried somewhere in the top drawer of his dresser.

Didn't matter now, he told himself. They were not teenagers anymore. He took a seat at a small table close enough to keep an eye on Hailey and opened the laptop computer. When he activated the cameras, he was disappointed to realize the round table in the corner was occupied by a large family, two parents and three kids. Tom, the police chief and the restaurant owner were gone, most likely back at their respective jobs.

Did they have someone tracking down the delivery-man? Nate hated knowing the guy was in danger all be-cause he'd taken one of the cocaine bags. If only they had a clue as to who he was.

He let his breath out in a heavy sigh, wondering how much longer he'd be able to delay before meeting Griff. The urge to reach out to his boss was strong, but he'd promised Melissa he'd make sure they had a good case with plenty of evidence first.

Nate scrubbed his hands over his face, then turned his attention back to his computer. He searched a bit on Laredo, Texas, located near the Rio Grande, the river that just happened to be the natural separation between Texas and Mexico. A possible drug-trafficking site? Maybe. Drugs were known to come into the US from Mexico. He pulled the rental car information out of his pocket, noticing for the first time that the car hadn't been rented under his uncle's name.

The name on the receipt was Enrique Gomez. Nate knew it to be a common enough Hispanic name that searching for a connection wouldn't be easy.

He was deep in thought when Hailey tugged on his sleeve. "I'm thirsty," she announced.

"Ah, okay. What would you like to drink?"

"I want a cola."

He nodded, reaching for her hand, when Melissa walked up holding a small bag. "No cola," she said firmly, obviously having overheard her daughter's re-quest. "How about we find some chocolate milk in-stead?"

"Yay, chocolate milk!"

Nate was glad he hadn't already purchased the soft drink. Of course chocolate milk was a better option, but the obvious choice hadn't crossed his mind. More proof that he knew next to nothing about raising kids.

"Find anything?" Melissa asked while they waited in line for their turn.

He shook his head. "A few things. I'll fill you in later."

She lifted her brow and nodded in agreement. Hailey insisted on carrying her milk as they all walked back out to the car, looking very much like a happy family finishing a Christmas shopping trip.

Since meeting Melissa and her daughter, he'd been thinking a lot more about having a family of his own.

His chest tightened as he realized just how empty his life would be once they'd got out of this mess.

Nate cleared his throat and unlocked the car, stowing his purchase beneath his seat. If Melissa noticed his package, she didn't say anything. As they headed out to the cabin, he filled her in on the little bit he'd found at Tom's house.

"Texas, right across the river from Mexico," she echoed with a frown. "Seems odd. I can't imagine why he'd draw attention to himself going down there so often."

"That's just it. The receipts aren't in his name. The driver is listed as Enrique Gomez." He glanced over at her. "Does that name sound familiar?"

Her lips thinned and she shook her head. "Afraid not. No one named Enrique was working at the restaurant while I was there."

He shrugged, knowing it had been a long shot anyway. "The more I think about it, the more I think they must have been in the early stages of their illegal business back then. The fact that my uncle is still in office and the cop you remembered is now the chief of police makes me believe they've been moving up in the world since then. Getting richer and more powerful each year."

Melissa wrinkled her nose. "You're probably right, but I'm bothered by the fact that they found me after all this time. I find it hard to believe that they've had my father's house staked out since then, too."

"True," Nate said. "Twelve years is a long time. I can't imagine they would have someone watching your dad's house for that long." Then another thought hit him. "Wait a minute. You said you kept in touch with your father over the years, right? That's how you knew he was sick."

"Yes, we kept in touch using Skype. Why?"

"They didn't need someone staking out your dad's house. They only needed a way to hack into his computer."

Melissa gasped. "You really think that's what they did?"

"Yeah, I'm afraid so. It's the only thing that makes sense. Although honestly, if they had done that, I'm not sure why they wouldn't have just gone to South Carolina to find you."

"Maybe they only hacked in recently," she murmured, the corners of her mouth dipping into a frown. "Everyone in town knew my dad was sick, so they may have suspected I'd communicate with him and come home to see him. So much for trying to use a different name and IP address, huh?"

"Don't beat yourself up about this, there's nothing you can do to change it now. We'll just have to be smarter than them moving forward."

She nodded but didn't look entirely convinced. He couldn't blame her. She'd been through a lot since that fateful night.

They made good time getting back to the cabin. Once they were settled inside, he booted up the computer once again, determined to find something to tie his uncle into the drug running.

Not just his uncle, but all three of the men who were there the night Alderman Kevin Turner died. It would be nice to have the identity of the fourth man, but nailing the other three would have to suffice.

With any luck, one of them would turn in the fourth guy for a chance at a lighter sentence.

Searching for Enrique Gomez was like looking for a penny in Lake Michigan. After several attempts, Nate gave up and decided to try another tactic.

Maybe he could use the cameras in the restaurant to make a list of the some of the employee's names who worked there. He wished now that he'd asked Melissa to place one in the kitchen. Then again, he doubted they would be wearing name tags anyway. Still, it was worth a shot.

"Is spaghetti for dinner okay with you?" Melissa asked.

"Absolutely, love it." Once again, a tiny twinge in the area of his heart made him realize how empty his life had been until she'd returned.

"What are you doing?" she leaned over his shoulder, her enticing scent reminding him of her kiss.

"Recording employees, hoping to find one named Enrique."

"I hate to say this, but what if the guy who placed the drugs in the freezer was Enrique?" she asked in a low voice. "He might be the one in danger."

"I know, but I can't very well ask Jenna to track him down when I don't know where to look."

She sighed and straightened. "I'll just keep praying that he survives."

Once he'd recorded as many names as he could, Nate returned to his search efforts. But instead of looking for Enrique Gomez, he typed in his mother's name.

Going back in the newspaper archives, he found several articles and photographs mentioning her name—all of which stopped the year she'd run off on him and his father.

He turned his attention to the Arizona newspapers, looking for any sign of her, without luck. Though that might not mean much, since the average everyday person didn't end up in the newspaper very often.

Nate couldn't get the image of that photograph in his uncle's house out of his mind. A moment frozen in time. He couldn't help feeling as if his mother had disappeared right off the face of the earth.

Or had she died?

No, why would his uncle lie about something like that? Especially about his own sister. For what purpose? To punish him and his father for some egregious action?

With the scent of oregano and tomato sauce simmering in the air, he returned to the Milwaukee area newspapers, searching for information on any Jane Doe investigations.

And hit pay dirt fifteen minutes later.

A young Caucasian woman, in her late twenties or early thirties, with dark hair and a small strawberry birthmark on her shoulder was pulled out of Lake Michigan just south of Gary, Indiana. Unfortunately there isn't enough of her face left to identify the remains. Please call Indiana's Missing Persons Bureau for additional questions.

Nate stared at the date listed at the top. It was three weeks and two days after his mother's disappearance. And she had a strawberry birthmark on her shoulder, too.

A coincidence? Doubtful. A surge of anger mixed with horror washed over him.

Was it possible his mother hadn't voluntarily left him and his father? That she had, in fact, been murdered?

FIFTEEN

Concentrating on making dinner wasn't easy, every sense Melissa possessed seemed to be aware of Nate. His brief kiss had left her feeling off-kilter, especially because she wanted him to do it again.

Soon.

She glanced over at him, noticing that he seemed to be sitting frozen, staring blindly at the computer screen. Instantly she dropped the spoon she was using to stir the sauce and headed over.

"What's wrong?" she asked, leaning over his shoulder. The woodsy scent of his aftershave was a momentary distraction. She blinked and focused on the computer. She'd expected him to be staring at the cameras located in the restaurant, but instead there was a newspaper article on the screen.

The phrases "Jane Doe" and "dark hair" captured her attention. She bent closer, scanning the short article.

"Gary, Indiana?" she asked.

It took Nate several seconds to answer, and when he did, his voice was rough, as if he could barely get the words out of his throat. "Several hundred miles southeast from Milwaukee."

The realization hit her like a brick to the forehead. "You think this woman might be your mother?"

Nate shrugged, continuing to stare at the computer. "I don't know what to think. All these years, Uncle Tom led us to believe she was alive and well, living in Arizona with some new guy. He'd even got her signature on my dad's divorce papers. Why would he go to all that trouble to lie to us?"

The raw pain in his voice made her heart squeeze in her chest, and she put her arm around his broad shoulders. "If this Jane Doe is your mom, and he did something to her and didn't want you or your dad to investigate it, a lie like this would make sense."

"I can't seem to wrap my brain around it," Nate admitted. He let out a heavy breath and finally turned to look at her, pain and frustration shadowing his eyes. "But you're right. That's the only possible explanation."

"I'm sorry, Nate," she murmured. "After seeing those photographs of your mother with Kevin Turner, I can't help but think Turner was involved in the drug running, and while spending time with him, your mother stumbled upon the truth."

Nate rose to his feet, breaking away from her embrace and pacing the length of the small kitchen. "I can't believe my uncle killed his own sister," he said harshly. "They were so close."

Melissa pressed her lips together, unwilling to point out that Nate didn't really know firsthand that his mother and his uncle were close. For all they knew, that was yet another story Tom McAllister had fabricated to keep Nate or his father from uncovering the truth.

"I'm sorry," she repeated. "We're probably way off

base. There's no concrete evidence to prove the Jane Doe found in Gary, Indiana, was actually your mother."

Nate sighed. "Except for the birthmark, my mother had one just like it. It's crazy. I hate knowing my mother might be dead, but at the same time, it's a little comforting to know she didn't leave me and my dad voluntarily. How senseless is that?"

The hint of wistfulness in his tone made her want to comfort him all over again. She curled her fingers over the back of his vacated chair to prevent herself from reaching out to him. "Not crazy at all."

"I'm losing it," he said, scrubbing his hands over his face. "The timing of my mother's disappearance and the discovery of the Jane Doe could be coincidental. Besides, that all happened almost eight years before you witnessed Kevin Turner's murder. Not likely the two events are related."

"Mommy, the food!" Hailey's voice drew her attention from Nate.

Her dinner! Melissa hurried over to stir the sauce, thankful to realize she hadn't scorched it. "Almost ready," she said.

It took another fifteen minutes to make the noodles. Nate had returned to his seat in front of the computer, closing the lid once she announced dinner was ready.

Melissa led a quick prayer, thanking God once again for the meal they were about to eat and for keeping them safe.

"Dig in," Hailey crowed, reaching for her fork.

A hint of a smile tugged at Nate's mouth at her daughter's antics. She couldn't help feeling relieved that he appeared to be getting over the shock of finding the article on the Indiana Jane Doe. For several long minutes, they were all silent as they concentrated on their food.

When they finished the meal, Nate stood up and carried his dirty dishes over to the sink.

"I'll take care of the dishes," she said, jumping up to join him. "You need to keep an eye on the cameras in the restaurant."

"You cooked," he stated in protest.

She shook her head. "Doesn't matter," she said firmly. "You're making headway on the investigation, more so than I ever could."

He looked as if he wanted to argue, but instead he gave her a hug, so quick that she almost thought she'd imagined it.

"Thanks," he said gruffly. "I owe you one."

No, he didn't. After all, he'd been keeping her and Hailey safe for days now. He'd more than upheld his end of their bargain.

"Mommy, can I watch a movie?" Hailey asked.

She quickly finished washing the dishes, leaving them to air-dry. She wiped her damp hands on the dish towel before turning to her daughter. "Sure, let's see what we can find."

After heading into the living room, she flipped through channels and the cartoon version of *Dr. Seuss' How the Grinch Stole Christmas* flashed on the screen.

"Grinch! I wanna watch the Grinch!" Hailey said, jumping up and down excitedly.

"Okay," Melissa agreed, grateful that the show had just started. She tucked Hailey into the bed, hoping that the little girl might fall asleep afterward.

She left her in the bedroom and headed back into the kitchen. Nate glanced up when she walked in and gestured for her to come over. "I caught a glimpse of a guy named Carlos," he said, showing her the frozen image on one of the split screens.

Melissa sucked in a harsh breath. "I know Carlos," she said. "He was one of the dishwashers back when I was working as a server. Wow, I can't believe he still works there."

"Do you remember his last name?" Nate pressed.

Her heart thudded in her chest. "I can't believe it," she whispered. How could she have forgotten it? "Gomez," she said in a hoarse voice. "His name is Carlos Gomez."

"Is it possible he has a brother named Enrique?" Nate asked with barely repressed excitement.

She cast her memory back to that time in her life. "It's possible," she finally said. "There was an older kid who used to pick him up after work. Could be a brother, or maybe a cousin."

Nate typed in the two names in the computer search engine. "I doubt they lived in Brookmont," he said, half under his breath. "It's too expensive for a restaurant worker. More likely to be commuting from Milwaukee."

"Carlos was a year younger than me," she said. "I remember asking him once because he seemed so young."

Nate nodded without taking his attention from the computer screen. The second stretched into a full minute before he sat back in his seat. "Found him. Enrique Gomez, age thirty. Was caught dealing drugs in Brookmont twelve years ago but copped a plea for a lighter sentence." His grim gaze met hers. "I have to believe these two are related."

She nodded. "Me, too. But which one do you think is the deliveryman? Enrique?"

"Possibly. I'll give Jenna a call, see if she can pull him in for questioning as a person of interest."

"What about Carlos? Maybe you should have her pick them both up, just in case?"

"Not a bad idea," Nate agreed, reaching for his throwaway phone. He tried again, hoping for better luck with the cell service, but then had to switch back to his personal one. "For all we know, they're working this thing together."

She nodded, listening as Nate left a terse voice message for Jenna about the two suspected drug dealers. When he disconnected from the call, he swung back to the computer, typing an email to Jenna, as well. Finally he turned to face her, taking her hands in his.

"Melissa, I think we have enough circumstantial evidence to convince Griff," he said in a low voice. "We should return to the city."

She blanched, wishing she could find the courage to believe in Nate's boss. "You might be right," she said, forcing herself to remain calm. "We can go tomorrow."

Nate's grip on her hands tightened. "Tonight. I think we need to go in tonight."

"No," she protested, yanking her hands from his and jumping to her feet so fast she knocked over the kitchen chair, wincing when it landed with a crash. "It's too late to drive back into the city tonight. Hailey needs a decent night's sleep."

"Melissa," he said again, but she continued walking away, unwilling to listen to any more.

In the bedroom, she glanced at her daughter, who looked as if she were already half-asleep. The Grinch movie was still on, but she suspected Hailey wouldn't stay awake long enough to see Cindy Lou Who save the Grinch from himself.

Her eyes burned with unshed tears at the knowledge that this could very well be their last night together. Anything could happen once Nate turned her in to his boss. If Griff didn't believe her, she could be arrested and thrown in jail, leaving Hailey in the clutches of the foster care system.

The need to run was strong. Her mind spun with possibilities. Once Nate fell asleep, she could escape in his car, leaving all this behind. Granted, the last thing she wanted to do was to start over again in a new place with a new name. Hailey deserved roots. A home. But at what cost? Not her life.

Melissa never should have promised to stay with Nate. Although really, would it matter if she changed her mind? What difference would it make if he didn't forgive her?

If she gave in to her impulse to leave in the middle of the night, she'd never see him again.

Nate let out a heavy sigh as Melissa stalked away, obviously upset with him. On the one hand, he didn't blame her for wanting her daughter to get a good night's sleep—if that was the real reason for wanting to wait until morning.

But he couldn't shake the feeling that they were running out of time. Ridiculous, because they'd been safe enough here at the cabin. Even if his uncle Tom did a search on his father's new wife, she'd been married before, so her last name didn't match her brother's.

Nate turned his attention back to the cameras planted within the restaurant. The round table in the corner remained unoccupied for the moment. He swallowed a flash of disappointment. Oddly enough, he'd fully expected his uncle and his cronies to gather there again to talk about the crisis of the missing drugs and the fate of the deliveryman.

He went back to his search on Enrique and Carlos Gomez. He discovered Carlos had experienced a run-in with the law, also for possession of drugs. Carlos must not have had enough on him to qualify as a dealer, unlike Enrique, and had been given nothing more than a slap on the wrist for his crime.

Yet being arrested hadn't caused him to lose his job. Most likely because the drugs had something to do with Ralph, his boss at the restaurant.

The two brothers, or cousins, had to be in this thing together. Enrique was obviously the one traveling to Laredo, Texas. Carlos likely had the key to get into the restaurant's kitchen to stash the drugs.

Nate wished he had a concrete way of connecting his uncle Tom to the drug running. Something more than a couple of invoices with Enrique's name on them. They needed something more before they could hand everything off to Griff, his boss. No way could they get a search warrant yet. There had to be more evidence somewhere.

Nate checked his email, but there was no reply from Jenna. No call or text to his cell, either. He told himself that she was busy at work, but the same impending sense of doom wouldn't leave him alone. He kept the battery in his personal phone, just in case she did decide to return his call.

He rose and stretched, fighting exhaustion. He'd had very little sleep since this mess started, so maybe Me-

lissa was right to want to wait until morning to talk to
Griff.

Glancing toward the sofa, he decided to stay in the
living room for the night. The sofa was too short for
him, but that really didn't matter since he couldn't relax
enough to get any shut-eye.

He passed the main bedroom, glancing in to verify
that Hailey was all right. When he saw that Melissa
was packing their small suitcase, he froze, his pulse
jumping erratically.

"What are you doing?" he asked in a harsh whisper.

Melissa gasped and jumped around to face him, her
cheeks red with embarrassment. And suddenly he understood she was planning to leave.

Tonight.

Sneaking away while he was asleep.

Just as she'd done that first night.

"Packing," she whispered back, regaining her com-
posure.

Gritting his teeth, he walked in, grabbed her hand
and tugged, his intention clear.

With a helpless glance at her sleeping daughter, Melissa accompanied him outside the room.

"I can't believe it," Nate said, battling a wave of fury.
"So much for your promise not to leave on your own."

Melissa yanked her hand away and crossed her arms
over her chest defensively. "What is wrong with packing
our things tonight so that we're ready in the morning?"
she asked, fire sparking from her hazel eyes.

"Don't lie to me." Nate practically spat the words
at her, the sense of betrayal stabbing deep. Logically
he knew he shouldn't be surprised. She probably figured that the drugs combined with the truth about his

mother's death were enough so that her eyewitness testimony wouldn't be needed. She was wrong, but that wasn't the worst part.

He was hurt, emotionally.

Because he cared about Melissa and her daughter far too much.

"I'm not lying," Melissa argued calmly. "You want to know the truth, Nate? Yes, I was upset. The thought of facing your boss, knowing he could arrest me the moment we meet, scares me to death. Do you think it's easy for me to accept the possibility of Hailey being stuck into the foster care system? Even if we do eventually straighten things out enough to clear my name, my daughter would be alone over Christmas, with strangers who won't love her or care about her the way I do."

Nate could tell she was fighting with her conscience, and the layer of ice around his heart cracked a bit. "Look, I know you don't know Griff, but—"

"You're right, I don't," she interrupted. "And the thought of spending one night away from my daughter fills me with fear."

"Okay, I get it," Nate said, knowing he couldn't quite relate to her parent-child relationship.

Although the idea of never seeing Hailey again once this mess was over caused a flutter of panic.

"No, you don't," Melissa said with a tired sigh. Her shoulders slumped in defeat, and he had to force himself to stay where he was, when all he wanted to do was to pull her into his arms and hold her close.

He struggled to find some sort of compromise. Something that would make her feel better. "What if you dropped me off so I can talk to Griff first, alone?"

he asked slowly. "I'll text you to let you know if it's safe to come in or if you should leave."

Hope flashed in her eyes. "Really?" she asked in a choked tone. "You'd really do that for me?"

He didn't want to, but how was that any different from how she felt about presenting herself to Griff? "Yes. I would."

She stared at him for several long moments, as if trying to see into his head. *Good luck with that*, he thought wryly. Even he couldn't make sense out of his thoughts.

"Why?" she asked, breaking the silence. "Why would you do that for me?"

Because I'm falling in love with you. Again.

He opened his mouth, closed it and then tried once more. "I couldn't live with myself if you ended up getting arrested," he said, keeping the depth of his feelings to himself. When her eyes widened in alarm, he mentally smacked himself.

"Not that I think it would happen," he added hastily. "I told you before that the sheriff's department has a broader jurisdiction than the Brookmont police do. My boss doesn't answer to them."

"Okay," she said with a tiny nod.

He lifted his brow. "Okay, what?" For some reason, he wanted to hear her say the words.

"I'll drop you off and stay somewhere nearby until you text me one way or the other."

"Good. Then we have a plan," he said, his gaze moving over her as if he could commit her face to memory. As much as he trusted his boss, he couldn't help thinking that there was a slim possibility Griff would demand Melissa be taken into custody. Although he'd already checked to make sure there wasn't an outstanding warrant for her arrest. But that could be only because she'd faked her death. The minute they knew she was alive, things could change.

Facing Griff wouldn't be easy, especially after everything that had happened. Yeah, he had gathered evidence to help prove a full investigation was necessary, but his boss was a stickler about rules, and no way would Nate escape unscathed.

He could only hope that his boss wouldn't suspend him or, worse, fire him. He could survive having a formal reprimand on file, but anything more could seriously impact his position on the SWAT team.

And that was a consequence he couldn't bear to think about.

"Have you heard from Jenna?" Melissa asked, changing the subject.

He grimaced and shook his head. "Not yet." He crossed over to the kitchen table and double checked his email, disconcerted when Melissa followed him.

"No sign of the foursome, huh?" she asked, glancing at the computer screen with a frown. "I'm surprised."

"Me, too," he admitted. "But they were there over the lunch hour, and I'm sure they're trying not to attract too much attention."

"Yeah, right," Melissa said, wrinkling her nose with distaste. "That never stopped them before."

He paused, thinking about that statement. Was the fact that the men weren't hanging out in their usual spot something to be concerned about? Surely they didn't go to the restaurant twice a day, every day?

"Nate?" Melissa's urgent tone jerked him from his thoughts. "Look, headlights."

He leaped over to shut off the nearest light switch,

plunging the room into darkness. "Get Hailey and hide," he commanded.

She nodded and disappeared into the bedroom. He pulled his weapon and made his way over to the window overlooking the driveway.

And froze when he realized a dark car had pulled up, blocking them in.

Nate took out his personal cell phone and dialed Jenna's number, nearly falling over in relief when she answered. "The cabin has been compromised," he said in a harsh whisper. "I need backup, now!"

"I'm already on the highway heading west, so I'll take care of it," Jenna promised, disconnecting from the call.

He stuck his phone back into his pocket, peering once more out the window. Two figures emerged from the car. Even in the darkness of the night, Nate could easily recognize his uncle Tom.

Nate swept a frustrated glance over the yard, knowing that they'd easily see the snowman and the snow fort Hailey had worked on over the past two days. And even inside, signs of her presence were everywhere. Hailey's drawings were scattered about, and the board game she had played with her mom was lying on the table in front of the sofa.

He swallowed hard, knowing he'd have to stall at least long enough for Melissa to escape out the back with Hailey. If they were armed, it would be difficult to hold them off long enough for Jenna and the rest of his SWAT team to arrive. Maybe Jenna would call in the local police, but would they believe him, over his uncle?

He had no idea.

Which meant he was on his own.

SIXTEEN

There wasn't a second to spare. Melissa scooped up their winter gear from the floor near the heating vents on her way into the bedroom. Getting Hailey dressed while the little girl was still half-asleep was no easy task, and she remembered a similar struggle the night she'd sneaked out of the motel room.

"No, Mommy, sleepy," Hailey protested.

"I know, but we have to leave, Hailey." Melissa didn't want to frighten her daughter. The poor child had already been through too much, but they needed to get out of here, now. Before it was too late. "The bad men are here, sweetie. We have to hurry."

Hailey's eyelids opened wide, and Melissa hated seeing the stark fear reflected there. But at least her daughter didn't fight any more, helping to put her arms into the sleeves of her winter coat.

Moments later, she picked Hailey up in her arms and carried her out to the main room. Her heart squeezed painfully in her chest when she saw Nate standing by the window, holding his gun.

"Go out the back. Hurry," he said in a low tone. "I'll hold them off for as long as I can."

Her stomach clenched at the dire expression on his

face. She didn't want to leave Nate here alone, but she couldn't deny the desperate need to keep her daughter safe. What could she do to help? Maybe find a neighbor? It was better than nothing.

With renewed hope, Melissa opened the back door of the cabin, gasping when a cold blast of air hit her in the face. The wind was howling, but she didn't have a choice but to go outside. She ducked her head against the frigid air and quickly waded through the snow, closing the door behind her.

It took a few minutes for her eyes to adjust to the darkness. There wasn't any moonlight, but at least the brightness of the snow provided a nice contrast to the dark cabin and surrounding trees. She hugged the wall of the cabin, inching farther and farther from the back door, trying to decide which way to go.

There were several large pines to the right of the cabin. If she could make it that far without being seen, she'd be in good shape. Of course, there was absolutely no place to hide between the corner of the cabin and the trees.

"Mommy, I'm cold," Hailey whined.

"Shh, I know. Don't talk, okay?" Melissa didn't think her daughter's voice would carry to the front of the cabin, but she wasn't about to take any chances. She hiked Hailey higher into her arms and took a deep breath, preparing to make a run for it toward the safety of the trees.

The idea of running was a joke. Her feet sank deep into the snow, making it difficult to walk, much less move at a fast pace. She didn't even want to think about the fact that she was leaving footprints in the snow behind her. As long as Nate kept the bad guys occupied, the footprints wouldn't matter.

She hoped.

Abruptly a large shadow loomed to her right, and she gasped when strong fingers clamped on her arm. "Gotcha," a deep voice said in her ear.

No! She tried to wrench away from him, but he hauled her more firmly against him and then poked something hard against her ribs.

A gun? She wasn't sure but couldn't take the risk. Not with Hailey.

"Come on. We're going back inside." The stranger tugged forcefully on her arm, leaving her little choice but to obey. It took a minute for her to realize the guy was the same man she'd seen twelve years ago. The man who'd stabbed Alderman Turner outside the restaurant.

A murderer.

Hailey started crying, and Melissa didn't blame her. She wanted to cry, too. But somehow she needed to keep her wits about her.

They weren't beaten yet. Jenna would come to their rescue, right? All they needed to do was to hang on long enough for Nate's teammates to arrive.

As she stumbled toward the cabin, she silently prayed.

Dear Lord, please keep us safe in Your care!

Nate waited until the door closed behind Melissa before looking for a place to hunker down. The sofa was the best choice, and he quickly dove behind it just seconds before the sound of a muffled gunshot hit the front door. He could hear his uncle Tom and Ralph Carter, the owner of the restaurant, tramping inside.

Nate sat with his back against the wooden frame of the sofa, holding his weapon ready, thankful that Melissa and Hailey had made it out in time. He needed to stay focused, and having two innocent bystanders nearby would only be a distraction.

"Drop your weapons," Nate shouted. "Don't force me to shoot."

"Come on, Nate, you're not going to be able to take out both of us," his uncle said in a calmly detached voice. Nate remained hidden, knowing that his uncle was right. He was trapped behind the sofa, and there were at least two of them. He hadn't seen any sign of Randall Joseph, the chief of police, or the mysterious fourth man, and Nate wasn't sure if that was good news or bad.

He could only pray the other two weren't outside watching the back door. He shook his head against that possibility.

There had to be some way out of this mess.

"I know everything," Nate said, stalling for time. "I know you were part of the group who murdered Alderman Keith Turner. I know you've sent men after Melissa, also known as Meredith, to silence her because she witnessed the crime."

"Listen, Nate, I don't want to hurt you," Tom said in a cajoling tone. "It's obvious you believed that woman's lies, but there's a lot you don't know. She's the dangerous one. She's a drug addict, Nate, and we know that she actually killed the alderman because she needed money for drugs. Trust me, you shouldn't believe anything she says. All we want is to arrest her. The judge can take it from here."

Nate shook his head at his uncle's audacity to try to

turn this against Melissa. He knew from the newspaper article that the alderman's body was found in Milwaukee. She'd been right to fear being turned over to the police. No doubt they'd have an eyewitness of their own who would blame the murder on her rather than on the true culprit.

The man they had yet to identify.

"How did you find the cabin?"

"Took a while, but I have resources. Although using your stepmother's family was smart. I'm just glad we got here in time to prevent you from making a big mistake."

His error had been in staying at the cabin for too long. But it was time to switch tactics. "I know my mother is dead," Nate said. "You've been lying to us for years, Tom. She's dead, and I know her death is directly related to the alderman's murder."

There was a long pause, as if he'd shocked his uncle with the depth of his knowledge. Was Tom right now trying to come up with another explanation? Did he really think he and his cronies could simply walk away from this?

There was a loud noise as a door banged open, letting in a cold breeze. Nate's heart sank to the bottom of his stomach long before he heard the words.

"We have the woman and her kid, Nate," Tom said in a harsh tone. "Come out with your hands up where we can see them."

The odds were overwhelmingly stacked against them. He tucked his gun in the small of his back, knowing that it wouldn't take long for the men in the cabin to find it once they frisked him. But since it didn't sound as if they knew for certain he was armed, he figured it wouldn't hurt to bluff.

"Okay, I'm unarmed and coming out," he said in a loud voice, raising his hands over his head. Moving slowly, he rose to his feet and swept his gaze over the room. He could see that Melissa was being held at gunpoint by a tall stranger who he could only assume was the man who'd killed Alderman Turner. Melissa's face was pale, her eyes wide with fear, as she held a sobbing Hailey in her arms.

He hated seeing her being held captive but tried not to let his expression show how helpless he felt. He switched his gaze to his uncle, pondering a way to get to him.

"I know all about the drug running scheme," Nate said in a matter-of-fact tone. "I know you're using Laredo as your point of entry for the drugs and that you're funneling the cash through your respective campaign funds."

The flicker of surprise in his uncle's gaze gave him a small sense of satisfaction.

"Where do you think that kilo of cocaine went?" Nate continued. "I found your stash and turned it over to my boss. In fact, my boss is aware of every bit of evidence I've collected over the past few days. He's probably working on a search warrant for both your house and the restaurant as we speak."

Bluffing his way through this was his only option. Maybe, just maybe, he could keep them alive long enough for Jenna to get here. Or maybe Jenna had already called local law enforcement for help. Either way, he hoped they'd hurry.

"I guess there's no reason to keep him alive, then, is

there?" Ralph asked with a menacing scowl. "You were wrong, McAllister. The hotshot cop knows too much."

Nate swallowed hard, knowing that this was the risk he'd taken by being so forthcoming.

"That is regrettable," Tom agreed. "I was hoping to avoid it, but obviously my nephew is too smart for his own good."

"Wait. Before you start shooting, I need you to answer one question for me," Nate said, glaring at his uncle. "I need to know what really happened to my mother. You owe me that much, at least."

His uncle stared at him for several long seconds. "I guess it can't hurt to tell you the truth now." Tom's eyes darkened with grief. "Rosalie was murdered by that no-good jerk she'd decided to sleep with."

Hearing the truth out loud caused Nate to take a shaky step backward. "You mean Keith Turner, don't you? She was having an affair with Alderman Turner."

"Yes, I'm afraid so," his uncle admitted. "She was young and foolish, falling for his pretty-boy surfer looks. I convinced her to break it off before she ruined her future. She agreed and promised to tell Turner that their illicit relationship was over."

"What happened?" Nate pressed, determined to hear every detail.

"I'm not entirely sure. She went missing," Tom said. "I was afraid she'd decided to just walk away rather than confront Turner. So I told your father that she ran off with another man. But then, a few weeks later, a woman was found in Lake Michigan. The minute I heard about the birthmark, I knew the truth. I knew the body was that of my little sister."

"So why keep lying?" Nate asked, truly bewildered. "Why not tell me and my dad that she was dead?"

Tom's expression turned angry. "Because we were searching for her killer, that's why. I suspected Turner but couldn't prove it. Not until years later."

Years? Like eight years? "The night he was stabbed outside the restaurant," Nate said.

His uncle shrugged. "Yes. Apparently your mother found out about our plan to make extra money on the side. Between that knowledge and her determination to break things off and return to you and your father, Turner lost it. He snapped and killed her."

"An eye for an eye," Ralph said with an evil laugh.

And suddenly it all made sense. "You didn't tell my father the truth because you were trying to protect your secret drug business," Nate accused him. "You were afraid the drug running would come out if the authorities dug into the motive for her murder."

Tom lifted his shoulder in an insolent shrug. "It worked, didn't it?"

A haze of fury flashed before Nate's eyes. "You lied to us for years, letting us think she was alive and well and wanting nothing to do with either of us. You didn't even give us a chance to bury her properly. And for what?"

"Enough," Tom said harshly. "Carter is right. You obviously know too much."

Nate ground his teeth together in frustration. "So, what? You're going to kill all of us now? And what's your cover story going to be this time? Lake Michigan is frozen for a good thirty feet along the shoreline. How on earth are you going to explain this away?"

"Murder-suicide, what else?" Carter leered at Melissa, who looked exhausted from holding her daughter for so long. "We'll kill the woman and the kid first, and then you'll conveniently shoot yourself. No one will ever suspect us of any wrongdoing."

"And the evidence that I've turned over to my boss?" Nate asked, trying not to look at the clock on the wall. What was taking Jenna so long? Granted, even going at top speed, Jenna wouldn't get here for a good hour. Was it possible she hadn't called the local authorities for help? "Do you really think the sheriff's department is going to believe a murder-suicide theory when they have the kilo of cocaine and the rest of the evidence we've collected? Not a chance."

Ray's face flushed red and he took a threatening step forward, lifting his gun and pointing it directly at Nate. "You're lying," he said. "If your boss has the evidence he needs, why are you hiding out here?"

"Griff's team is on their way right now," Nate said, maintaining his bluff. He'd been lowering his arms inch by inch, hoping to get a chance to pull his weapon in a last-ditch effort to save Melissa and Hailey. "I just turned over the rest of the evidence a few hours ago."

"I don't believe you," Carter sneered.

"He's telling the truth," Melissa said. "And if you shoot us, the neighbors will hear and call the police."

"Nice try, sweet thing. The houses on either side of you are dark. Nobody home." The stranger holding her spoke up for the first time since dragging them back inside. "We checked the place out. Besides, we'll be long gone before you know it."

"Danny's right," Carter said. "Now, let's set the scene." The restaurant owner glanced between Nate and Melissa. "I like the fact that she's wearing her coat. Looks like she's leaving him, providing a good reason for him to go crazy and shoot her."

Danny? Nate had no idea who he was or his role in all of this, but it didn't matter. He lowered his hands another inch, feeling sick to his stomach. Even if he managed to take out Carter, Danny was still holding Melissa hostage.

There was no way he could put her in more danger. "Tell you what. Let the lady and the kid go, and I'll back your drug scheme. I'm sure you could use another cop on the payroll. Especially one with a wider jurisdiction than the Brookmont area."

"We don't need you," Danny said in a snide tone. "The Brookmont police department has been handling our needs just fine. Come on. Let's get this done already."

"Now, wait a minute," his uncle said. "Nate has something there. We've been looking for a way to expand our enterprise. We could use someone inside the sheriff's department."

"You're getting soft, old man," Danny accused, waving his gun toward Nate. In these precious seconds, the gun wasn't trained on Melissa. Nate could see that she wanted desperately to move, and he tried to signal her not to do anything foolish with a tiny shake of his head.

"Enough already. We've been here long enough," Carter said. "We'll shoot the woman in the back, as if he'd stopped her from leaving. Then you can shoot him in the temple to make it look as if he killed himself."

Nate was barely listening, knowing he needed to make his move. Now.

He reached behind to grab his weapon at the same time Melissa threw herself to the ground, covering Hailey with her body. He shot at Danny seconds before the sound of another gunshot filled the air.

Nate ignored the searing pain in his shoulder and blood running down his left arm and turned to shoot at Carter, too. Within moments, the two armed men were lying on the cabin floor, while Tom stared at him in horror.

For the first time, he realized his uncle wasn't armed. Foolish mistake on his part. "Get on the ground, now!" Nate shouted at him.

Melissa staggered to her feet and picked up Hailey, running over to Nate's side for safety. "I need you to get the handcuffs from my duty belt. It's in my bedroom, near my uniform," he said to her.

She gave a jerky nod and carried Hailey with her into the spare bedroom, as if she couldn't bear to be apart from her daughter. Not that he blamed her.

Turning back, Nate watched as his uncle slowly lowered himself down and stretched out, giving wide berth to Ralph Carter, who was lying on the floor in a pool of blood. From what Nate could tell, Danny was also severely injured.

He took a cautious step closer, prepared in case Tom tried to make a run for it, when the front door to the cabin burst open. Nate assumed that Jenna's backup had finally arrived, but when he swung his gaze over to the door, he was stunned to realize the man standing in the doorway was none other than Randall Joseph, the Brookmont chief of police.

Nate instinctively fired at the man and then hit the ground, tucking and rolling across the floor to make himself a smaller target. But another gunshot echoed through the room almost simultaneously.

He felt the punch of the bullet hitting his left side, but this time didn't feel the corresponding pain, maybe because he was numb. Nate fired again, catching the police chief high in the shoulder. The man let out a howl as his gun hit the floor. He saw Randall drop to his knees, holding pressure over his shoulder wound.

Seconds later, Jenna barreled through the door, pushing the police chief down onto his abdomen and planting her knee in the middle of his back. "Don't move," she warned, yanking his arms around to the back. "You're under arrest for the attempted murder of a deputy."

Nate wanted to sag with relief. But the room spun wildly around him, and he realized he was losing blood. Too much blood.

"Get an ambulance here, now," Jenna shouted, slapping handcuffs on the police chief. When she finished there, she quickly came over to where Nate was slowly sinking to his haunches.

Melissa hurried out with the second pair of cuffs. She handed them to Jenna, who didn't waste any time in securing his uncle's wrists behind his back.

"Check the other two," Nate ground out, fighting against a wave of dizziness. "Secure their weapons."

"We will," Jenna assured him. Once she finished cuffing his uncle, she headed over to kick the other weapons far out of reach.

Melissa crouched beside him, her eyes wide with fear. "You're bleeding," she whispered.

"It's not too bad," Nate said, even though his vision was getting fuzzy around the edges. There was a fire in his left side, and he suspected he was losing blood at a rapid rate. "Don't leave, Melissa," he begged. "Stay. Make sure they get all the evidence."

Her eyes were full of tears, but she nodded, shrugging out of her coat and pressing it firmly against the oozing wound in his side. "Where's the ambulance?" she cried. "Nate's bleeding badly."

"Don't leave," he repeated, fighting to stay conscious. He wanted to memorize her features just in case she wasn't there when he woke up.

He opened his mouth, trying to tell her he loved her, but he couldn't seem to make his throat work.

Darkness surrounded him.

SEVENTEEN

Melissa wanted to scream in frustration as she watched Nate lose consciousness. "Hold on," she whispered to him despite knowing he couldn't hear her. She swept her gaze around the interior of the cabin. "Jenna! Hurry!"

Nate's teammate was busy explaining to the local authorities why she needed the two less injured suspects, Randall Joseph, the police chief, and Tom McAllister, the mayor, taken into custody. It was clear the locals weren't sure if they should believe her.

"Contact my boss, Lieutenant Griff Vaughn," Jenna snapped, losing her temper. "We need you to cooperate with us on this."

"Okay, okay," one of the local deputies said. "We'll haul them out of here."

"Thanks." Jenna crossed over to kneel beside Melissa, her blue eyes full of compassion. "Don't worry. Nate's tough. He'll make it."

She knew Jenna was only trying to help, but the blood-soaked ball of fabric beneath her hands told a different story. When the paramedic crew crossed over to the more seriously injured patients first, the two men Nate had shot, she couldn't bear it.

"Nate's a deputy. Shouldn't they be prioritizing his needs first?" she asked Jenna.

Jenna felt along the side of Nate's neck, obviously searching for a pulse. "There's more than one ambulance crew on the way," she said, skirting Melissa's question.

She knew she wasn't being fair, but Nate's life was on the line, too. She glanced helplessly up at Jenna. "There must be something we can do."

Jenna gave a curt nod. "I'll be right back."

Melissa continued to use all her strength to hold pressure on Nate's wound. When she felt Hailey come up beside her, she glanced at her daughter.

"Is Mr. Nate going to be okay, Mommy?"

Tears pricked at her eyes, but she forced a confident smile. "Of course he is, Hailey. Another ambulance will be here any minute."

"I'll help," Hailey offered, placing her small hands over Melissa's. Her daughter's effort to assist only made her want to cry.

Clearly her daughter had grown attached to Nate. And Melissa couldn't blame her.

She'd grown far too attached, too.

She loved him. Not the teenager she'd dated back in high school, but the man he was now.

Her rock. Her partner. Her protector.

"We'll take it from here, ma'am," a male voice said.

She glanced up, surprised to see another ambulance team had arrived. She forced herself to nod, letting go of the pressure she'd been holding over Nate's wound. Moving away from him wasn't easy, but she lifted Hailey, drawing comfort from the way her daughter wrapped her arms around Melissa's neck, hugging her.

She closed her eyes for a moment, sending up a silent prayer that God would heal Nate's wounds. When she opened them, she could see the paramedics had worked quickly, establishing IV access and running in fluids. It didn't take them long to apply a pressure dressing to Nate's left side and bandage up the wound on his left shoulder.

"Wait. Where are you taking him?" she asked when they bundled Nate onto the gurney.

"To the closest trauma center, University Hospital in Madison," one of them told her.

Jenna stepped up beside her. "I'll take you there," she offered.

"You're not going anywhere, not until I hear exactly what went down." A tall, broad-shouldered man with close-cropped blond hair scowled at them. Melissa could see by his nametag that this was Nate and Jenna's boss, the infamous Griff Vaughn.

A shiver of apprehension skittered down her spine. What if Griff didn't believe her? Although certainly he'd listen to Jenna, his own deputy. Wouldn't he?

"Well?" Griff demanded, crossing his arms over his massive chest. "Start talking."

Melissa darted a glance at Jenna, who didn't seem the least bit intimidated by her boss. "I'm happy to report what I saw," Jenna said calmly. "But most of the action was over by then. It might be better for Melissa to start at the beginning."

Melissa swallowed hard. "Okay, but can we go over to the kitchen? I'd like to give Hailey something to do to keep her busy."

Griff grimaced as he looked at the little girl but nodded in agreement. "Fine."

She needed to believe Nate was getting the best care possible, especially since sitting in the blood-spattered cabin was the last thing she wanted to do. But she understood that the faster she gave the lieutenant her statement, the sooner she could get to the hospital in Madison.

She plopped Hailey in the seat beside her and gave her daughter a coloring book and crayons. "Why don't you draw Mr. Nate a get well soon picture?" she suggested. "We'll take it with us to the hospital."

"Okay," the little girl eagerly agreed.

She noticed the pained expression on Griff's face but wasn't sure what was going through his mind. Did he resent the fact that Nate had got close to her daughter? Melissa took a moment to gather her scattered thoughts. Jenna had told her to start at the beginning, but that meant going all the way back to that fateful summer night.

"Twelve years ago, I witnessed a murder outside the restaurant where I worked, called El Matador." Griff's eyes widened at her blunt statement. "And I've been on the run ever since."

Griff and Jenna exchanged curious glances. "Keep talking," Jenna encouraged her.

Melissa told them about the drugs found in her room, her escape to California, and after she was found there, her move to South Carolina. To his credit, Griff appeared to be listening intently, while Jenna scrawled copious notes on a sheet of paper.

Reliving the past wasn't easy, but Melissa pushed herself to be as calm and factual as possible. When she described the incident at the mall, Griff leaned forward, capturing her gaze with his.

"Deputy Freemont should have come straight to me

after shooting the two suspects," he said in a curt tone. "He'll be lucky to have a job when this is over."

Melissa tried not to be intimidated by his gruff approach. "That's my fault," she freely admitted. "I knew there was a cop present the night of the murder, and it turns out he's now the Brookmont chief of police." She narrowed her gaze. "So you'll have to forgive me for not trusting the authorities. After all, they planted drugs in my room to discredit me."

"Go on," Jenna urged her. "Tell us what happened next."

Melissa described their discovery at the Forty Winks Motel and the green van opening fire on them.

"Yeah, I heard from Lieutenant Max Cooper," Griff said, anger etched on his features. "Wasn't happy to hear about it from some stranger rather than directly from my own deputy."

She didn't have a good response to that, so she continued her story, explaining how they'd planted the cameras and bugs at the restaurant. "Oh, that reminds me," she said, leaping to her feet. "I forgot about the evidence."

"What evidence?" Griff demanded.

She went over to the back door and pulled on a pair of Nate's gloves since hers were stained with blood. She darted outside and pawed through the snowbank to the left of the doorway where Nate had buried the cocaine. It took her a while, but she finally found it. She carried it inside, dropping it on the kitchen table in front of Griff. "Nate found this in a box labeled Shrimp in the restaurant freezer."

Griff looked poleaxed. "Is that...?"

"I think so, yes." Melissa explained how Nate had

confronted his uncle Tom about the drug running. "Nate discovered receipts that indicate the mayor might be paying Enrique Gomez to fly down to Laredo several times a year. We believe that's the source of the drugs coming into the US."

"Wow," Jenna murmured. "I wonder which cartel they've got themselves involved with."

Melissa was losing patience with this. She wanted— no, needed—to get to the hospital. "Listen, Nate planned to give you this evidence along with the rest of the information he'd uncovered. But before we could head into town, the men showed up here. I tried to sneak out the back door with Hailey, but some guy named Danny caught me and dragged me back in here. Nate risked his life to save ours. He shot Danny and then Carter, the owner of the restaurant. We thought it was over, but then Randall stormed inside and shot Nate." She paused to take a deep breath. "That's it. That's the whole story. Now can we please go? I need to find out how he's doing."

Griff looked as if he wanted to argue, but Jenna rose to her feet. "Sure, I'll take you right there."

Melissa saw the lieutenant sigh heavily, but surprisingly, he didn't argue. She couldn't wear her coat but saw Nate's jacket flung over the edge of the sofa, so she pulled it on, burying her nose in the fabric and inhaling his woodsy scent.

She couldn't bear to think that he might not make it. Not when they'd just found each other again. Granted, she didn't really know how Nate felt about her. The way he'd begged her not to leave hurt her. It was evidence that he still didn't completely trust her.

And if that was the case, what chance did they have at a future?

* * *

Nate blinked, squinting against the brightness shining in through the window. His mouth was Sahara dry, and throbbing pain kept time with his heart.

It took a minute for him to realize he was lying in a hospital bed. His gaze swept over the room, and he became starkly disappointed to find it empty.

He tried to tell himself that Melissa was likely giving her statement or taking care of Hailey, but he couldn't help but acknowledge their time together was over. She and Hailey were no longer in danger. She had a life of her own down in South Carolina. Yeah, maybe she'd stay through the holiday, if it hadn't passed already.

He started at the clock and then at the calendar on the wall with the dates crossed off, realizing that he'd lost a day. It was already the day before Christmas Eve. How long before Hailey would have to return to school?

Nate shifted in the bed, grimacing as pain stabbed deep. He considered calling the nurse for medication, but the idea of being in a fuzzy haze wasn't appealing. He reached for the plastic cup of water with his right hand, spilling several drops onto his chest as he took a sip.

Gingerly he moved his hand along his left side, feeling the bulky dressing that folded over his torso, covering the gunshot wound. The area was tender, no doubt about it, but he hoped that maybe he'd escaped any damage to his vital organs.

He found himself closing his eyes and thanking God for sparing his life. A sense of peace washed over him, making him realize that while Melissa wasn't here, she'd given him a precious gift.

Faith.

His life would never be the same from this moment on. Somehow he needed to find a way to convince Melissa to give him a chance. And if that meant giving up his job with the SWAT team, then fine.

He'd relocate to South Carolina if he had to.

But first he needed to talk to her. His last memory was seeing her beautiful face hovering over him right before he blacked out. He needed to find out what happened after he'd been taken to the hospital.

Nate used the bed controls to lift himself. Then he gathered his strength and swung his legs over the edge of the bed while pulling himself upright with his good arm. White-hot pain slashed through him, and beads of sweat popped out on his forehead. Still, he forced himself to sit there for a few minutes, fighting the urge to pass out.

A pretty nurse who looked to be about his age walked into his room, her eyebrows shooting up in shocked surprise when she saw him sitting on the edge of his bed. "Mr. Freemont, what are you doing?"

"Deputy," he ground out between clenched teeth. "Deputy Freemont. And I need to get out of this bed."

"Why? Do you need to use the bathroom?" She crossed over to put a hand on his arm, as if that would prevent him from rising. He suspected that she didn't have the strength to prevent him from doing a face-plant on the floor, so he tightened his grip on the bed rail.

"No," he responded, although now that she'd said it, he discovered it might not be a bad idea to make the trip across the room. "Maybe, yeah. Then I need you to find me a wheelchair. I have to talk to my boss."

He wasn't amused at the way she rolled her eyes. "I hate to tell you, *deputy*, but you're not going to be able to report to work in this condition." She pushed a button on some sort of device around her neck. "Lifting assistance needed in room 18."

Lifting…what? "I can walk there on my own," he said stubbornly. "I just need you to help with that IV machine."

"The macho ones fall the hardest," she said with a sigh, but she obliged him by unplugging the IV pump and rolling it closer. "Ready?"

He wasn't but nodded anyway. He grabbed the IV pole and staggered to his feet. For a moment his knees wobbled like jelly, but then he managed to find his bearings. Walking across the room to the bathroom actually felt good.

He emerged a few minutes later, surprised to find a wheelchair waiting for him. "Uh, thanks," he said, sinking down into the seat.

"Don't go too far," the nurse told him.

Nate nodded, realizing that using his left arm in an effort to propel him forward hurt. He wondered how long it would take Griff to come talk to him. Was his boss still with Melissa? He hoped for her sake that she'd been able to clear her name.

There was a soft rap on his door, and when he saw Melissa hovering there, his heart leaped in his chest. "Hey," he greeted her with a smile. "How are you?"

"That's my line," she said dryly, stepping into his room. There was no sign of Hailey, and he couldn't help wondering where the little girl was.

"You look better than you did yesterday. And earlier this morning," she commented.

She'd been there? His smile widened. "Yeah, well, that's not saying a whole lot, now, is it?"

Melissa's laugh brightened the whole room. "Are you sure you should be up out of bed?"

"I'm sure." His fingers itched to reach out to her, but he forced himself to let her take the lead. "I'm so glad you stayed," he said in a husky voice. "I hope Griff didn't give you too much trouble."

She shrugged and flashed a wry grin. "Jenna protected me in your absence. By the way, one of your buddies picked up Enrique Gomez, and you were right. He spilled the beans about the drug operation for a chance at a lighter sentence."

He nodded, relieved to know the young man hadn't died because he'd stolen the evidence. "Did we find out who Danny was?"

"Jenna did. She discovered his real name was Daniel Mendez and he's connected to the Mendez-Guadalupe cartel. Unfortunately, Mendez died, but your uncle, the police chief and Ralph are fine. They're not talking, but I think that's just a matter of time."

"Wow, so that's that. Mystery solved," Nate said with relief. "I'm glad that Griff didn't arrest you. I was worried he'd take his anger toward me out on you."

"Has he come to talk to you yet?"

"No, but I'm sure he'll be here soon." Nate wasn't looking forward to that conversation, although oddly enough, he wasn't as uptight about the prospect of losing his job as he had been when this mess started.

"I took the blame for everything," Melissa said, stepping closer.

He was touched by her attempt to shelter him, although in Griff's mind, Nate would still be the one at fault. "Thanks. I appreciate that. But in the end, I own my actions."

Melissa stood there for a moment. Then she reached into her purse to pull out a stack of faded letters. His heart jolted as he recognized them. "I went back to my father's house and found these in a shoe box under his bed," she said softly.

He remembered pouring his heart out to her in those letters and shifted uncomfortably in the wheelchair, hating the way the tips of his ears burned with embarrassment. "Did you read them?"

She nodded, her eyes glistening with tears. "Every single one. You claimed you loved me and would help me through whatever I'd got mixed up in if I'd just come back home."

He nodded, realizing now just how much trouble she'd been in through no fault of her own. "I missed you a lot."

"I missed you, too." Melissa set the letters on the bedside table. "But, Nate, I'm not that same girl anymore. And you're not the same eighteen-year-old boy, either."

Where was she going with this? "Trust me, I'm well aware of how much we've both changed over the years."

She licked her lips nervously. "Hailey was pretty upset when you got hurt."

"I'm sorry she had to see that," Nate said. "Speaking of...where is she?"

"Jenna's keeping an eye on her in the cafeteria."

Nate couldn't imagine Jenna, with her tough-girl attitude, spending time with a five-year-old. For a moment he almost smiled, but then it hit him.

Melissa hadn't brought Hailey into his room, because she was leaving.

She was saying goodbye.

He gripped the armrests of his wheelchair, searching desperately for something to say that might make her change her mind. But then again, he didn't want her to stay out of pity, either.

"Melissa, I want to thank you for showing me the way to God," he said in a low voice. "I know I have a lot to learn, but you've certainly opened my eyes to what is truly important."

Her face filled with joy, making her more beautiful than he'd thought possible. "Oh, Nate! I'm so glad to hear you say that. And I want you to know how much I appreciate everything you did for me and Hailey, too. You risked your life for us."

He couldn't stand it a moment longer. "I love you," he blurted with all the finesse of an elephant charging through a garden. "I know it's probably too soon for you, considering everything you've been through, but I'm begging you to give us a chance."

Melissa's mouth dropped open in shock. "You love me?" she echoed. "I thought you didn't trust me?"

"Of course I trust you. And yes, I love the woman you've become. Your strength. Your faith. The way you interact with your daughter. I love you, Melissa. And I understand Hailey is in school, so if I have to move down to South Carolina, then that's what I'll do." He was willing to promise whatever she wanted in order to keep her.

"What?" Griff's deep baritone rang from the doorway. "You're quitting the team? Since when?"

Nate wished his boss would go away, but instead he bulldozed his way into the room.

"Listen, Lieutenant, I'll give you my statement in a little while, okay? Just leave us alone for a few minutes."

Griff looked taken aback, but Melissa stepped forward and dropped to her knees beside his wheelchair. "Oh, Nate. I love you, too. And I'd never make you choose between me and your career."

Nate let out his breath in a heavy sigh and pulled Melissa up so that he could wrap his uninjured arm around her. "We'll work everything out later," he murmured, completely ignoring Griff, who was pacing restlessly behind her. "Nothing else matters as long as we love each other."

"I know," she whispered back.

He lowered his mouth and kissed her, then buried his face in her hair.

Griff cleared his throat loudly, making Nate groan under his breath. Sometimes his boss could be a royal pain.

"Go away, Griff," Melissa repeated Nate's earlier sentiment. "We need a few minutes alone."

Nate chuckled, then winced as the movement caused some discomfort around his incision. Griff let out a loud harrumph and walked out of the room.

"That's my girl," Nate said with a smile.

She gazed up at him. "He'll be back, I'm sure, so let's not waste a second. Kiss me again, Nate."

"Always," he promised, his heart swelling with love and a renewed hope for their future.

EPILOGUE

Melissa couldn't believe Nate was being discharged on Christmas morning, but she wasn't going to complain, either. With help from his teammates, his father and Amelia, Melissa and Hailey decorated Nate's house for the holiday, using everything he had stored in the basement.

She'd purchased a gift for him and was nervous about whether or not he'd like the gold watch she'd picked out.

Waiting for Jenna to pick up Nate and drive him home was nerve-racking. Christmas music wafted through the house, and one of Nate's teammates, Isaac had built a fire in the fireplace for them. She'd cooked a hearty chicken soup from scratch in deference to Nate's recent injury. Hailey had been thrilled to find video games stored in the basement, too, and Melissa knew she should feel guilty for using them to keep her daughter distracted.

When Jenna's SUV pulled into the driveway, she took a deep breath and let it out slowly. She opened the door, watching as Nate insisted on walking into the house under his own power.

"Stubborn man," Jenna muttered loudly enough for Melissa to hear.

She couldn't help but smile. Nate's face brightened when he saw her standing there, and he pulled her in for a quick hug. "You're an amazing sight to come home to," he said. Then he swept his gaze over his fully decorated house, including a bright Christmas tree in the corner. "Wow, you've been busy."

"Santa's elves helped," she teased, taking his hand in hers.

Jenna rolled her eyes and crossed over to place a few gifts beneath the tree. Melissa assumed they were gifts from Nate's teammates and was glad they'd remembered him. Jenna moved toward the front door. "I'm heading out since I'm on duty tonight. Call if you need anything."

"Thanks, Jenna." Melissa closed the door behind her, appreciating the female deputy's wry humor.

Nate made his way to the sofa, sitting gingerly in the corner. "My house has never looked this wonderful," he said. "I'm in awe of how you transformed it."

"I wanted you to have a merry Christmas," she said, coming to sit beside him. "Are you hungry? I have soup simmering on the stove."

"Food can wait," Nate said, reaching over to take her hand in his. "Where's Hailey? I think it's time we opened presents, don't you?"

Melissa was surprised but nodded in agreement. "Sure, I'll get her. She found your old video games in the basement. Hope you don't mind."

"Of course not," Nate said, sitting back against the sofa cushion with a sigh. "Man, it's great to be home."

It didn't take long to convince Hailey that opening presents would be more fun than playing video games. The little girl ran into the living room and headed straight for Nate. "You're home!" she said, crawling up beside him and easing herself into his arms, mindful of the injuries Melissa had warned her daughter about.

Melissa's eyes misted as Nate hugged Hailey close, pressing a kiss to the top of her head. "I sure am. It's good to see you, Hailey."

"Mommy said we're opening presents," Hailey announced. "I have one for you."

"I have one for you, too," he said. "It's the one with the snowman wrapping paper."

Hailey didn't waste any time scooting down from the sofa and running to the tree. She picked up her gift and quickly pulled off the gift wrap. "Look, Mommy, a Bible!"

"That's wonderful, Hailey. We'll read the story of Christmas after lunch, okay?"

"Okay."

"Hailey, bring the other present over here, the one with the Christmas tree paper," Nate said. "That one's for your mom."

Melissa glanced at him in surprise. "When on earth did you get that?" she asked, taking the gift from Hailey.

"Open it and I'll explain," he said with a smile.

She opened the small box. Her breath caught at the sight of the small diamond heart necklace nestled inside. "Oh, Nate, it's beautiful."

"That was my high school graduation gift for you," he said. "I'm hoping you'll let me use those diamonds as accents in your engagement ring."

"Engagement ring?" she echoed, wondering if she'd heard him right. "Oh, Nate, are you sure?"

"Come here," he encouraged her, reaching out for her. She scooted over and took his hand in hers. "Melissa, will you do me the honor of being my wife? I promise to love you and to be a good father for Hailey."

"Yes," she whispered, her heart lifting with joy. "Oh, yes, Nate. Of course I'll marry you."

As he kissed her, Melissa knew with a sigh that she was home at last.

* * * * *

Robyn thrashed helplessly in the river current, her body
numb from the twin assaults of shock and the ice-cold
water.

Gasping for air, she managed to keep her head above
the water for several minutes and strained to listen. She'd
heard two gunshots moments before Slade had gently
pushed her over the ridge, but now there was only the
rushing sound of water.

Did that mean they were safe? She had no idea.

And where was Slade? She tried to turn in a circle, but
the river was moving too fast for her to take more than a
quick sweeping glance around to look for him.

She knew she couldn't stay in the water for much
longer. With renewed determination, Robyn angled
toward the shore.

Up ahead was a large tree branch hanging over the
water. With herculean effort, she reached up and snagged
the branch. She used every last bit of strength she
possessed to pull herself up and out of the water.

Her feet found the ground, and she emerged from the river to sprawl on the grassy embankment.

"Slade!" Panic clawed up her throat, threatening to strangle her.

She didn't know who she was or who was after her. She couldn't do this alone.

"Robyn!" The sound of her name made her want to weep with relief.

A splash caught her eye, and she saw a dark shadow getting out of the water about twenty yards from where she lay.

"Robyn, I'm so glad I found you. Let's get into the cover of some brush, okay?" Slade's voice was near her ear. "We want to stay hidden from view."

Because of the gunshots.

With Slade's help, she stood, and together they moved away from the river into the wooded area.

"Are you going to start a fire?"

"Not yet. I don't want to draw undue attention if someone is out there looking for us."

"For us? Or me?"

He hesitated, then said, "I'm not leaving you alone, Robyn. We're going to stick together from here on out."

Until when? Her memory had returned? And what if it didn't?

Don't miss
Hiding His Holiday Witness *by Laura Scott,*
available November 2021 wherever
Love Inspired Suspense books and ebooks are sold.

LoveInspired.com

LOVE INSPIRED

Stories to uplift and inspire

Fall in love with Love Inspired—
inspirational and uplifting stories of faith
and hope. Find strength and comfort in
the bonds of friendship and community.
Revel in the warmth of possibility and the
promise of new beginnings.

Sign up for the Love Inspired newsletter
at **LoveInspired.com** to be the first
to find out about upcoming titles,
special promotions and exclusive content.

CONNECT WITH US AT:

 Facebook.com/LoveInspiredBooks

Twitter.com/LoveInspiredBks